KAKULOA: A RISING TIDE

a novel of T-Space

Alastair Mayer

Mabash Books

KAKULOA: A RISING TIDE

This is a work of fiction. Names, characters, places, and incidents are either the product of the author's imagination or are used fictitiously, and any resemblance to real people or incidents is purely coincidental.

Cover © 2018 by Mabash Books
Cover image credits:
  Beautiful view of exotic islands from aircraft © d.travnikov, Depositphotos.com
  V-Class Starship Entering Atmosphere © Alastair Mayer
Interior map © Alastair Mayer
Images used by permission.

T-Space is a trademark of Alastair Mayer

For announcements about other T-Space books and special offers, sign up for Alastair Mayer's mailing list at http://www.alastairmayer.net/

A Mabash Books original.

First printing, January 2019, minor corrections April 2020

Mabash Books, Centennial, Colorado

Trade Paperback Edition: ISBN-13: 978-1-948188-07-4

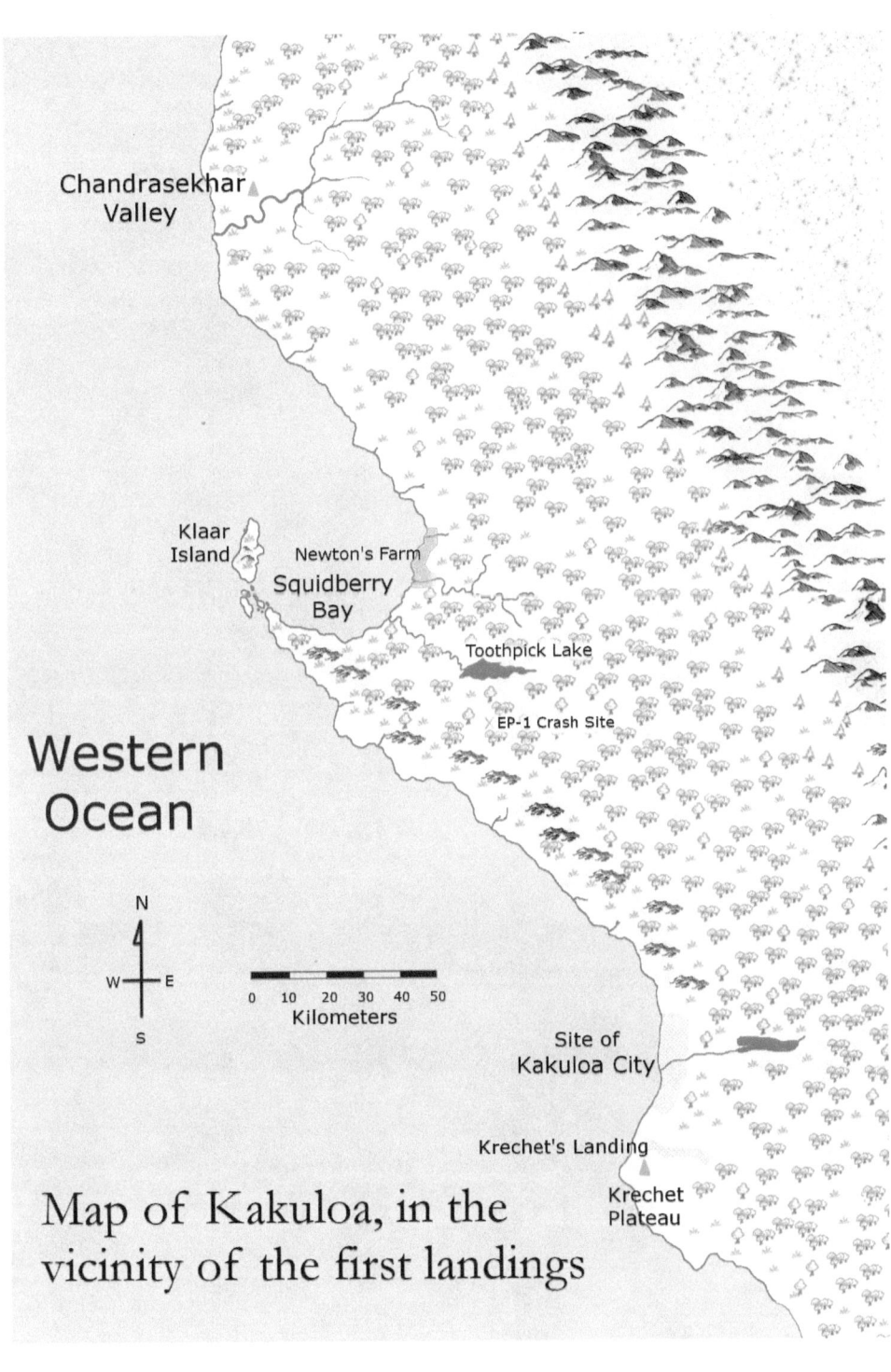

Chandrasekhar
Valley

Klaar
Island

Newton's Farm

Squidberry
Bay

Toothpick Lake

EP-1 Crash Site

Western
Ocean

N
W — E
S

0 10 20 30 40 50
Kilometers

Site of
Kakuloa City

Krechet's Landing

Krechet
Plateau

Map of Kakuloa, in the
vicinity of the first landings

Contents

KAKULOA: A RISING TIDE

Alastair Mayer

Alpha Centauri Expedition

From Wikipedia, the free encyclopedia, extrasolar edition

This page was last modified on 27 May 2083, at 20:07 (UTC)

In the aftermath of The Unholy War, Dr. Algernon Brenke, while investigating force-shield technology[citation needed] instead discovered and developed a working warp drive. At about the same time, China had perfected the compact fusion reactor, coincidentally capable of powering such a drive. In July, 2069, a multinational expedition was assembled to visit the two Earthlike planets discovered[when?] to be orbiting the two main stars of Alpha Centauri. The ships comprised the American flagship, *USS Robert A. Heinlein*, the Chinese *Xing Hua*, as well as three ships capable of landing: the Indian *Chandrasekhar*, the Russian *Krechet*, and the American backup lander, the *Poul Anderson*. A sixth ship, the European *Jules Verne*, had issues on its test cruise[citation needed] and the crew was redistributed among the other ships.

The *Xing Hua* disappeared just as the fleet reached the Alpha Centauri system, presumed destroyed by collision with a comet fragment. It was later discovered that it faked the explosion and returned to Earth so China could reverse-engineer the warp drive.[disputed - dis-

^{cuss]} The rest of the fleet continued with the mission, checking both planets from orbit and landing on Baker, the planet at Alpha Centauri B. The first team landed in the *Chandrasekhar*. The *Krechet* landed later about 250 km away.

The explorers found evidence that the planet—renamed by the landing team to Kakuloa because of the landing site's similarity to Hawaii—is Earth-like because it had been terraformed. The lifeforms show genetic divergence from Earth life approximately 65 million years ago.[citation needed]

Tree squids and squidberries.

During a flight in an ultralight between the *Krechet* and *Chandrasekhar* sites, the plane struck multiple birds and went down midway between the two ships. The pilot and passenger, Doctors Fred Tyrell and Ulrika Klaar, were forced to hike overland the rest of the way. During that trek, they discovered a grove of trees by the coast where octopus-like creatures were climbing the trees and eating a berry growing on a vine in the tree. Tyrell dubbed the creatures tree squids. They took samples of the so-called squidberries.

Aftermath

Later, the crew of the *Krechet*, which had no fuel to reach orbit, transferred to the *Chandrasekhar* for the return to space.

In light of the discovery that the planet has been terraformed, Elizabeth Sawyer, the mission's second in command, took a crew of volunteers in the ship *Anderson* down to the surface of Able, the planet orbiting Alpha Centauri A, to investigate it in detail. They did this knowing they would not immediately be able to return; their refueling module had been lost with the *Xing Hua*. The plan was for the *Heinlein* and *Chandrasekhar* to return to Earth, obtain the backup refueling module, then return to pick up the *Anderson* crew.

Complications arose.[clarify] Neither of the returned ships was considered reliable enough for another interstellar mission without overhaul, and the Chinese were no longer providing fusion reactors. Planet Able (later, Sawyer's World) turned out to be terraformed, and the *Anderson* crew settled in to survive as best they could until someone returned to pick them up.

Follow-up Expedition

On Earth, one of the pharmaceutical companies[which one?] examining specimens returned by the original expedition discovered a potential anti-aging drug, cephalomycin, in a yeast growing on the squidberries. Commodore Drake leveraged this[citation needed] to get the company to help finance a return mission, which required developing new ship technology. Four years after that, in 2074, the three-ship return expedition arrived at Alpha Centauri. The *Endeavour* and *Vostok* landed on Able (Sawyer's World), and found that the *Anderson* crew had all survived, and five children had been born during their isolation. The *Victoria* continued to Kakuloa to further investigate squidberries. [See Alpha Centauri: Second Expedition]

[See also: Kakuloa, Sawyer's World, Terraformers, Treaty of Alpha Centauri]

Prologue: January, 2070

Dive boat Sea Squirt, *Earth*

Ellie Greystone handed up the camera and then her flippers to the man at the top of the dive ladder, then, ignoring the weight of the rest of her gear, hauled herself up and climbed aboard. Her dive buddy and boyfriend, Patrice Beauchamps, was right behind her, handing his own fins up before climbing out.

"How was it?" Ron, the dive-master, asked as he helped Ellie off with her tank.

"Fantastic! I got some great footage of three octopus coordinating a hunt; at least that's what it looked like. I want to analyze their skin patterns and see what I can sort out."

"*Oui*, she spent most of the dive chasing those octopus. I should 'ave known better," Patrice said.

"Octopuses? Coordinating?" said Ron. "Humboldt squid do that, but I've never heard of that in octopodes. Are you sure you're not reading more into it than was there?"

"I t'ink she was," said Patrice.

Ellie glared at him. "We'll know for sure when we get another look at the video. I suppose it's possible there was something else going on, but it looked like two of them chased the prey to a third."

"Did it share it with the first two?" Ron asked.

"Well, no." As she said that, she realized that the third cephalopod might just have made an opportunistic grab for the prey, with no real coordination. That made more sense. Octopus tended to be loners; it was squids that swam in schools.

"You need to be careful to eliminate all the likely explanations before going for the unusual," Ron said. "Especially if you decide to go for your doctorate. Even your master's thesis will be torn to shreds if you don't."

He was right, she knew. Although he was "just" their dive boat captain, Ellie knew Ron had a background in academia before giving that up. She still had plenty of research to do before finishing her master's, let alone applying for a PhD track.

Patrice gestured to the powered-up datapad perched on the console. "You are surfing porn while we're down?" he said. It was a joke; the screen showed a news feed.

"It gets lonely," Ron said, playing along. "But no. There was an announcement on the radio. The Alpha Centauri mission has returned. I was trying to find out more."

"The Alpha Centauri mission?" Its departure had been big news the previous summer, but Ellie hadn't been following the details. She grabbed a towel to dry her hair.

Ron nodded. "Part of it, anyway. *Heinlein* and *Chandrasekhar* have entered the solar system. They'll be landing on the Moon in a couple of days. No word yet on the other ships, that's why I was checking the news feed. But so far very few other details than that."

"There were five ships, *n'est ce pas?*" Patrice said. "What 'appened?" He was an engineering student, and he had followed the story of the departure closely.

"They haven't said yet. But they did say the planets were remarkably Earth-like, and they brought back biological samples."

"Earth-like?" Ellie, who had been buried in the towel as she dried off, raised her head. "Do you suppose they have anything like cephalopods?"

"I'm sure they found invertebrates. But anything more than that would be an incredible coincidence, don' you t'ink?"

Ron nodded in agreement. "Assuming they found animal life at all, invertebrates make sense."

"I suppose you're right. Still, it will be interesting to see what they did find."

"Don't tell me you are thinking of switching to exobiology?" Patrice said.

"Ha, no." She shook her head. "Let me finish *this* degree first."

"I would love to visit another planet," Patrice said. "Maybe I will switch to exobiology." He grinned broadly. He had met Ellie through the school's dive club.

"So would I," Ellie said.

"If they find intelligent aliens," Ron said, "maybe you'll learn to talk to them."

Ellie laughed at that. "Somehow I doubt a background in cephalopod behavior would have much use at Alpha Centauri."

"There's a job title for you," Ron said. "Speaker-to-Squids."

Patrice looked at him, shaking his head slowly. "You read too much science fiction."

Ron grinned back. "There's no such thing as too much."

Ellie laughed.

∞ ∞ ∞

The call came as the *Sea Squirt* approached the dock. Greystone's omniphone chimed, and she dug it out of her bag to answer it.

Patrice had been admiring the lines of her face as they cruised back from the dive, both of them sipping on post-dive beers. He watched her now as she glanced at the screen, a slight frown wrinkling her brow. Must be a junk call, he thought.

"Hello?" she said, holding the omniphone up to her ear. "Yes, this is Ellie Greystone." A pause. "Yes, she is. Why, what's happened?"

Patrice sensed the stress in Ellie's voice. He put his beer down and sat forward.

"Is she all right?" Ellie continued. "She what? Was anyone else hurt?" She listened for a while, then shook her head. "No, no, not that I know of." She slumped forward, propping her head up with her free hand, elbow on knee. "Oh. I see...No, I'm out of town. I can be back tomorrow evening..."

Tomorrow? That caught Patrice by surprise. They had planned another day of diving. Whatever it was must be serious.

"Yes. You're sure she's okay?...I...Thank you. Goodbye." She thumbed off the omni and molded it around her wrist. She looked up. Her eyes were haunted.

"What's wrong?" Patrice asked.

"I have to get back. I'm sorry, we need to cut this short. My mom was in a car crash."

"Oh no!" Patrice wanted to ask, 'Is she all right?' but that was a stupid question; they wouldn't have called if there was nothing wrong. "How is she?"

"Shaken up, but not seriously injured. They want to keep her in overnight for observation."

"*Quoi?* But if she's not injured?"

"Apparently she blacked out before the crash. A witness said it was like she was asleep, but with her eyes open. She's never done that before. At least, not that I know of..." Her voice trailed off. Was she remembering another incident? "Anyway, they want to run some tests."

"It's an old car?"

"What? Why...oh, right. No, it's not autonomous. Mom doesn't trust them."

Patrice stepped over and put his arm around her shoulders. "The important thing is she is not hurt, right? And nobody else was?"

Ellie nodded. A short, hesitant nod.

"*Bien.* Let's gather up the gear. We check out tonight, we can be there in the morning."

Ron had obviously been aware of the conversation but had stayed out of it, focusing on docking the boat. Without a word, he started gathering their dive gear and putting it ashore.

Ellie looked at the gear, then back at Patrice, her brow furrowed. "You want to drive overnight?

It wouldn't have been his first choice, but under the circumstances, he didn't have a problem with it. Besides, he was an engineer; he *did* trust his car's autonomous systems. "You want to get back as soon as possible, I understand."

"I... thank you." With Patrice's help, she stood up and started to disembark. She stopped abruptly, one foot still on the boat and the other on the dock. "Wait, my video."

Patrice had already grabbed the camera. He held it up to show her. "Right here."

PART I - Second Visit

Alpha Centauri System, 2074

(NOTE: The details of Endeavour's *(and later* Vostok's) *landing on Sawyer's World to rescue the Anderson crew are given in the book* Alpha Centauri Volume 3: The Return.)

Chapter 1: Krechet's Landing, 2074

Kakuloa (Alpha Centauri B II)

The starship *Victoria* sliced through the atmosphere above the Western Ocean, heading toward a broad basalt plain near the coast where, just over four years earlier, the *Anderson*-class ship *Krechet* had landed the second team of the Alpha Centauri expedition. *This is it,* thought William Blake, observing from the third seat in the cockpit.

"You're sure this is a good landing area?" The captain, Kat Coleman, asked him. "I don't want to run into the same trouble that *Krechet* did."

"Absolutely sure," Blake said. "After that, the crew did a thorough geological survey of the plateau. It's safer than Chandrasekhar Valley." The latter, where the first team had landed, turned out to be flood-prone.

Victoria had orbited the planet Kakuloa just long enough to locate the original landing sites, two hundred fifty kilometers apart near the west coast of the main continent. It was between those two sites that Fred Tyrell and Ulrika Klaar, on an overland hike, had discovered the mangrove-like trees in a small river estuary, together with the white berries that grew on a vine in those trees. When they'd stumbled across them, the berries were being eaten by cephalopods that Tyrell promptly nicknamed tree squids. Thus, the berries become known as squidberries; they were the whole reason *Victoria* was here.

"Coast is in sight," the navigator, Retta Flint, said. "Altitude 8,000 meters, range thirty kilometers."

On the horizon a gray line of cliffs rose up from the ocean surface. To the north, the cliffs lowered to a thin line, dark near the cliffs, lightening to a near white further away from them. As the ship drew closer, they could see waves smashing against the cliffs in huge clouds of spume and spray. Toward the beach, where the ocean floor sloped more gradually, the rolling waves began breaking a kilometer or more from shore, lines of surf advancing one after the other to surge up the sand.

"Are those waves as big as I think they are?" Coleman asked idly.

"Probably bigger," Blake said. "That's one of the things that reminded them of Hawaii, and why they named the place Kakuloa."

"Which means what, giant surf?"

"It doesn't mean anything," Blake said. "George Darwin said he made it up. It does sound Hawaiian though."

"If you say so," Coleman said. "Is that surf pounding the cliffs going to be a problem?"

"No. The reports said they're stable, and the landing area's a kilometer inland from the edge."

By now *Victoria* was coming up on the shore line, its altitude a mere 2000 meters. The plateau showed scattered vegetation growing in pockets of soil on the otherwise bare rock. A few kilometers further inland, a forest wall rose. In the middle of the rocky plain, and to their north, stood something clearly artificial.

"I see *Krechet*!" Blake said. "Look to port, ten-o'clock."

Two kilometers off, a roughly conical ship stood perched at a slight angle. Around its base, and again towards the forest, lay scattered equipment. There was no sign of the tents the original crew had pitched to house field laboratories and extended living space.

Flint looked up from her console briefly. "It's at more of an angle than the pictures they brought back. And some of the gear is gone."

The captain had seen it too. "Four years out in the weather will do that," she said. "I'm surprised it's still standing."

Blake wasn't. He'd gone over all the reports carefully. "They double-anchored it with guy-wires and propped up the leg that punched through the cave roof. It's probably more solid than if they'd had a normal landing."

"We'll check it out later. Historic monument, that," Coleman said, then added: "Okay, prepare for landing."

Victoria slowed to a near hover, and the whine of the ventral jets rose. There came the c*lunk-clunk* of the gear doors opening and the landing gear extending.

"Engage autoland," said Captain Coleman. "Flint, read it out for me, please."

"Roger that," she said. "Altitude fifty meters, speed zero. Coming down at five."

"Copy."

"Twenty-five, down at three," Flint said.

"Surface looks good. Some dust." Coleman checked the landing radar display. The ground return was fuzzy; this wasn't a paved landing pad, but the irregularities were within tolerance.

"Ten, down two."

Coleman nodded. "Go to land."

"Five. Two. Contact!"

Victoria settled on the surface with a slight bump, taken up by the shock absorbers in the landing gear.

"Thrusters off. We're down."

The captain turned to Blake and said formally: "Colonel Blake, we've landed. The mission is now yours."

"Thank you, Captain," he said. "Please call *Endeavour*. Tell them, '*Victoria* is on the beach'."

Coleman nodded to Flint. "Go ahead."

"Aye, Ma'am."

The message wouldn't reach the other ship for nearly four hours. *Endeavour* and *Victoria*'s sister *Vostok* were at the other terraformed planet in the system, orbiting Alpha Centauri A, currently almost as far from this planet as Neptune was from Earth. Earth itself was more than four light-years away.

"And, Captain? I'd like preliminary checks," Blake said. "I doubt that the air here is any less breathable than it was four years ago, but let's be sure, eh?"

"Completely agreed." She turned and tapped a sequence on the console keyboard.

"All right," Blake said. "Secure from space. As soon as the atmosphere checks out, I want the aircar assembled and ready to go." That would be their primary medium-range transport, replacing the ultralight airplanes the first expedition had used.

"Also," he continued, "the satellites we left in orbit. Mr. Fenety needs to fine tune the GPS systems and start downloading sensor data." The previous expedition had made do with the *USS Heinlein* and *Anderson* remaining in orbit, but Blake had insisted on more extensive coverage.

Which reminded him, there was something the first expedition left behind. "When the aircar is ready, the *Chandrasekhar* landing site needs to be checked. Their refueling module reactor was left in safe mode. Telemetry says it's still that way, but I want a visual on the site."

"If we can bring the reactor back online," Flint said, "the power will come in handy for recharging batteries if and when we explore further north."

"My thoughts exactly," Blake said. "Speaking of which, Flint, you're in charge of the boat." The boat was a rigid-hulled inflatable, able to cope with all but the roughest seas. "Figure out how you're going to get it assembled and down to the beach."

Flint grinned. "I think *not in that order* would work best."

Blake laughed and nodded. "Agreed. Use the aircar as a sky-crane if that helps." It could carry the unassembled parts, at least.

He assigned a few other tasks to different team members, then a soft alert chimed from the captain's console.

"Atmosphere checks out," Coleman said. "No significant differences from four years ago," he said.

"Good," Blake said. "Let's go get this little camping trip set up."

Chapter 2: The Next Resort

Chitiri Resort Development Co., Earth

Paul "Parry" Cohen pivoted his desk monitor around so that his associate, Lauren Hewitt, could see it. It showed a long stretch of sunlit beach, with clean white sand and above that, tropical trees. The sea was a gin-clear blue with huge rollers breaking in the distance. The point of view was from some altitude above the beach, with enough land in the foreground to suggest the image was taken from a cliff. "What do you think?"

"Gorgeous," she said. "With that cliff, is that Noronha? And how come there's nobody on the beach?"

"Hah," Cohen said. "The first answers the second. No, it's not Noronha. This is Kakuloa."

"Somewhere in Hawaii? Is it a private island?"

"Don't you pay attention to the news? It's another planet, orbiting Alpha Centauri B. You know, our first trip to another star? And our second, now that the *Endeavour* and company are headed back there. That's why these pictures are in the news again."

"Oh, *that* Kakuloa. I thought it sounded familiar. They should be there by now, right? They left a few weeks ago. I hope they found the *Anderson* crew all right."

"So, you *are* paying attention."

"But why are you showing me this? It's a nice beach, sure, but nobody's going to be travelling to another star system for a vacation, let alone building a resort there."

"A hundred years ago you could have said the same thing about some of our best properties. Think of it, this place is literally untouched."

"More like a hundred and fifty," she said. "Okay, so maybe there'll be a tourist business to Kakuloa in the twenty-third century. I'm not going to hold my breath. There's not a lot of tourist traffic to the Moon, and that's right next door."

Cohen sighed. "Come on, Lauren. The Moon doesn't have beaches and oceans. But you're right, it's too early. The new *Endeavour*-class ships are a lot better than the *Heinlein*- and *Anderson*-classes, but they're still not civilian cruisers. Maybe the next generation. It will be interesting to see what the current expedition comes back with."

"Hopefully, the crew of the *Anderson,* or maybe what's left of them. Isn't that why they went?"

"That's the official reason. But you've heard the rumors."

"You mean about an alien plant that's the source of an immortality drug? Don't tell me you believe that!"

"Anti-aging, not immortality. And an assortment of other pharmaceuticals besides. That's why Centauri Pharmaceuticals was formed. It's jointly held by a half-dozen of the biggest biopharmaceutical companies. Did you know they contributed a major chunk of the funding for the current expedition?" That wasn't strictly secret, but neither was it well publicized. The companies involved were playing that close to the vest.

"So? I imagine a new ecosystem means good odds for new biochemicals. I'm sure they're looking, but the *Heinlein* couldn't have brought back enough of anything to even begin to develop new drugs."

Parry Cohen shook his head to himself. It was amazing what they could do with computer modeling of pharmacokinetics these days. He understood hardly any of it, but his sister's husband was in that business. When Parry had asked him about the immortality drug rumor, he had merely smiled knowingly and said something like: "even if there were such a thing, it would be too early to tell for sure." But there was no point in getting into an argument with Lauren over it.

"You're probably right," Cohen said. He looked at the image on the monitor again. "Still, it is a pretty beach."

"There are still a few of those on Earth, Parry, and they're a lot easier to get to. They also don't have huge question marks about what sort of governing regulations the place will have. Speaking of, how is the Noronha Project going?"

"I've got the latest here," Cohen said, bringing up the project data on his screen. She had raised a good point. Would the Outer Space Treaty (as Amended) even apply to Alpha Centauri the way it did on the Moon? Questions for another time. He put that aside and started briefing Hewitt on the latest with the Noronha Project, their current in-development resort on an island off the Brazilian coast.

Chapter 3: Greystone

The Greystone House, Earth

Ellie Greystone sighed and folded her omni. The paper she'd been reading, "Contextual traits and correlation with biological characteristics in *Illex oxygonious*," was drier than most, which was saying something. She stood up, stretched, and picked up her empty coffee mug to take it to the kitchen.

"Mom," she called out, "I think I'm going to go into the lab to work on my research." She was now working on that sought-after PhD.

There was no immediate answer. *Uh oh.* Ellie rounded the corner into the kitchen. Her mother was standing at the counter. "Mom? Did you hear me?"

Her mother turned and looked at her, or rather, a little past her. "That's nice, Cheryl. Yes."

Oh, crap, not again. "Mom, it's me, Ellie." Cheryl was her aunt, her mother's younger sister, who lived two states away.

Her mother nodded, still not quite looking at Ellie, with a far-away look in her eyes. She nodded again. "Uh huh." She began to slowly rock from side to side, taking little shuffling steps without really moving from her spot by the counter, and muttering almost inaudibly.

"Mom?" Ellie knew that there was nothing she could say to snap her mother out of it, or even if it would be a good idea if there were. This little spell, or *petit mal*, or whatever it was, would pass in a few moments. She had seen it before. It had started a few years after her father had died, although there wasn't necessarily a connection there beyond age. Ellie had been a late child, her parents in their forties when she was born. The spells didn't happen often. After one passed, her mother would be fine, sometimes for weeks. That didn't make it any less disturbing when it happened.

The doctors had made some vague diagnoses, hooked her up to an electroencephalograph, done scans, and prescribed drugs, but until they caught one of these little microseizures while she was wired up to an EEG or in the middle of a PET scan, they couldn't say anything definite and didn't want to give her anything stronger. After all, most of the time she was just fine. Except for the AVO restriction she now had on her driver's license: Autonomous Vehicles Only. Ellie didn't get the point of that; why issue the license at all? Although, there was less of a stigma to that than to having the license pulled altogether.

"Ellie! There you are." Her mother was back from wherever it was she had gone. "Just put your coffee cup in the sink, sweetie. I'll take care of it."

"Uh, thanks, Mom. Are you okay?"

"Of course I am. Why wouldn't I be?"

"No reason." Ellie knew from painful experience that her mother would have no memory of the episode, and it would only stress her to bring it up.

"And why are you moping around the house? You should get out."

"I've got studying to do."

"Well, then go study on campus. Go to your lab. You're not going to meet people sitting at home."

Ellie wondered how much of what she had said earlier about going to the lab had filtered into her mother's subconscious. This wasn't the first time something she'd said while her mom was seemingly oblivious had come up in conversation minutes later. Nor was it the first time that her mom had broadly hinted that Ellie ought to be "meeting people," code for "finding a boyfriend." Not that she had time for one right now. Her last one had been a massive time-sink, although she hadn't thought so at first. She smiled at the memory. Nor was it entirely his fault.

"Ellie, did you hear me?"

"Yes mom, I was just thinking about it." Her mother did seem fine now. "That's a good idea. I'll go to the lab. Do you need anything before I go?"

"Don't you fuss about me. I'll be fine. Go, have fun."

Fun? Even when her mother was all there, she was still a bit out of it. But then Ellie figured that was true of most moms.

∞ ∞ ∞

At the University

"Hey, Ellie, you're going to want to hear this!" Jaydon Phillips said, bursting through the door to the lab, waving his omniphone.

Ellie Greystone looked up, annoyed. Since it was a Saturday, she had hoped to have some peace and quiet. "Unless it's directly related to my thesis, no, I'm probably not." Jaydon was a fellow grad student who shared the lab.

"Would you settle for indirectly related?" he said, grinning.

Ellie sighed. When he got like this, he was insufferable. Or maybe it was her being stressed out. "Okay, what it is it?"

"Another batch of announcements from the Alpha Centauri expedition."

"They just left. Surely they're not back already."

"No, the first expedition. They finally got around to reviewing and releasing some of the footage shot on personal omnis. I didn't even know they had copies of that from the *Anderson* crew. Apparently some of them documented things with whatever camera was handy. They got video of life-forms that's not in the official recordings."

Ellie perked up at that. There'd been considerable buzz around the biology department about how Earth-like the life-forms were that the first expedition had found, both plant and animal. But the expedition hadn't been equipped to do much in the way of marine biology beyond taking a few samples from the ocean surface. "So, what have you got?"

Jaydon turned his omniphone towards her and said: "Take a look."

Ellie looked. The video was shaky, unsurprising if someone had captured it with a hand-held omni rather than the usual cameras the expedition had used. It showed leaves and branches against sky. It was difficult to make out detail because of the contrast, but the trees looked like a kind of mangrove or banyan, with aerial roots. There was something moving in the branches, although it wasn't clear what.

"So, they found some sort of monkey, or whatever that is in the trees," she said. "So what?"

Jaydon grinned widely. "Keep watching, it gets better."

She knew he wasn't going to leave her alone until she'd watched the whole thing. She focused on the screen again. The animal, whatever it was, moved along the branch much like a monkey, hanging beneath the branch by its limbs. The tail was obviously prehensile too. While hanging there, it reached with two arms towards what might be a cluster of fruit. Wait, two arms? But it was holding onto the branch with...she could see at least four, no, five other limbs.

"What the..." She grabbed the omni from his hands to look at it more closely. She froze the image. Despite the low contrast, she could just make out the arms or legs. One, two, three...that thing had seven limbs, all as prehensile as its tail. It couldn't be! She hit play, and a moment later an eighth limb came into view. "No freaking way!"

"Keep watching."

The scene changed. Whoever had been recording it had stopped and restarted, the scene was now better lit. There were more animals in the trees, moving fluidly, swinging from one branch to another, grabbing and eating whatever that fruit was. Greystone had seen enough cephalopods in enough different conditions, the conclusion was inescapable. "Octopus? In *trees*?" There was another explanation. "This is a hoax, right?" She felt her temper rising. "You did this with computer animation." She didn't need this waste of time.

"No, no, I swear! Keep watching."

She looked back at the screen. As the image panned around, she caught sight of a human figure, male, starting to climb one of the trees. Someone else, female, with a vaguely Nordic or Slavic accent, was talking in a hushed voice. The voice sounded somewhat familiar, but Ellie couldn't place it.

"*We came across these creatures in a grove at the mouth of a creek about a hundred kilometers south of the* Chandrasekhar *landing site,*" the voice said.

"*They're pretty clearly cephalopods, octopus from the appearance of the body and number of arms, although Doctor Tyrell, who first spotted them, wants to call them tree squids. Not a proper scientific name, of course, but to distinguish them from the mythical northwest tree octopus.*

"*They seem to be feeding on the berries growing from a parasitic vine in the trees. Tyrell is attempting to collect some samples. We hypothesize that the berries may be high in protein, or perhaps fermented sugars, which attracts the cephalopods.*"

The man in the video—that must be Tyrell—turned and called back, "*Ulrika, a hand here?*"

The video changed again, panning around to show the face of the omni's owner. Blonde hair, grey eyes, and pale—if dirt smudged—skin. Ellie recognized her. "*This is Doctor Ulrika Klaar, signing off.*" The video ended.

"Well nuke me," Ellie said. "that *was* Klaar! I met her once, at a conference, and watched her interviews before the Centauri mission."

"I told you it wasn't faked."

"But, but, octopus? On another planet? In *trees?*" She wasn't sure which of those things surprised her more.

"Yeah. Weird, huh? I thought you'd be interested. Anyway, I'll let you get back to your thesis work."

She shook her head. This wouldn't affect her thesis, except that she was beyond focusing on it now. She was done for the day. She started packing up her gear. "Are you kidding? After that? I won't be able to concentrate." She stood up from the bench. "This is all your fault." She was miffed at Jaydon, but her comment was more in the way of the usual back-and-forth banter between them than actual anger.

He raised his hands in supplication. "*Mea culpa, mea maxima culpa.* I figured you'd be interested."

"I am. *Too* interested. That's the problem."

"Fair enough. Can I buy you a beer to make up for it? We can talk about alien biology in the pub."

"As long as you stick to *alien* biology," she said. They were just friends, with nothing between them beyond working in the same lab, and she thought it best to keep it that way. Her mom might disagree. "Sure, let's go."

"Uh, of course. Um, Ellie?"

"What?"

"Can I have my omni back?"

Chapter 4: *Vostok*

Kakuloa, Alpha Centauri system (a week later)

The starship *Vostok*, which had left Sawyer's World just hours earlier, made a final micro-jump to bring it within the orbit of Kakuloa's larger moon. Captain Tsibliev contacted the ground and announced their arrival.

"*Victoria*, this is *Vostok*. We are currently 300,000 kilometers out. Plan is to come straight in. No parking orbit."

"*Roger that*, Vostok. *Welcome to the neighborhood. We have a landing area cleared and marked for you. Give us a heads up when you're close.*"

"Affirmative," he said, then added in an amused tone: "You *are* knowing I have been here before, *da*?" Tsibliev had captained the *Krechet*, four years and some months earlier. He had called in quite a few favors to be on this return mission. "Anyway, ETA is approximately six hours."

"*Copy ETA six hours. And in that case, welcome back.*"

∞ ∞ ∞

Tsibliev settled *Vostok* onto the basalt plain two hundred meters from *Victoria*, and two kilometers from his old *Krechet*.

"Welcome to Krechet's Landing," said William Blake as *Vostok*'s airlock door opened.

"Last time, Darwin was welcoming me to Kakuloa," Tsibliev said, "You are changing name each landing?"

Blake chuckled. "The planet is still Kakuloa. We decided to name this plateau after your old ship. The valley to the north where the first landing took place is now Chandrasekhar Valley."

"Ah, *da*. I take it you have checked that out?"

"Only briefly. There's a bunch of junk that the first expedition abandoned, like what they, or you, stripped out of *Chandrasekhar* to save weight. The fuel processor is still there and intact, with no sign of radiation leakage."

"*Korosho.* Good. What about squidberries?"

"We did a preliminary survey of the coast. We found a number of inlets with mangrove trees, many of those with what look like squidberries, but we found other berries too. Or maybe they weren't ripe yet. We didn't see any tree squids, but we were surveying from the air. So did Doctor Klaar decide to come along to show us where she found them?"

"*Nyet.* She begged off. Her daughter, Susan, is only one year old. Klaar didn't want to be travelling with her, and she wasn't going to leave her and young Poul behind while she came to Kakuloa. We brought next best thing, Fred Tyrell."

"But Tyrell is a geologist, not a biologist." Blake had studied the biographies and mission reports of all of the first expedition crew.

"*Da*, and he was with Klaar when they found the tree squids and the berries. He will recognize spot. He and Klaar confirmed it from your aerial photographs."

"Yeah, we got that. There just isn't any convenient spot to land an aircraft there. No problem, we'll find it from the sea. The GPS system has nearly completed its calibration."

The navsats *Victoria* had deployed in the days before landing were still making fine positioning adjustments to their orbits and otherwise tuning their systems. The data that Drake's expedition had brought back had been helpful, but lacked the resolution for navigation satellites to give meter accuracy that agreed with ground truth. The satellite network would help them find their way to the squidberry grove from the sea, and also let them refine the maps they had of the rest of the planet.

The area the first expedition had covered, from a few kilometers north of Chandrasekhar Valley southward to the Krechet Plateau, and from the coast to the mountain range in the east, was less than one-tenth of one percent of the land area of the planet. Very little of that had been actual boots on the ground.

Even ignoring the polar icecaps and the mid-continental desert, there was plenty left to explore. Had they gotten lucky with the squidberries, or were there even more interesting things to find? The GPS satellites all sported sensor suites to augment the extensive photomapping both *Heinlein* and, more recently, *Victoria* had done from orbit. The photos had revealed a lot worth investigating, and the newcomers looked forward to that.

∞ ∞ ∞

Fred Tyrell grinned as he disembarked from the Vostok. He certainly hadn't expected to be back here. He had always assumed that if they ever were rescued from the planet now known as Sawyer's World, it would be to return to Earth, not a side trip to Kakuloa. Not that he minded. It would be interesting to see how things had changed in the four years he'd been away.

As he stepped down the ramp, he was promptly surrounded by a small group of crewmembers from the *Victoria*. They had come straight to Kakuloa after the *Anderson* landing party had been spotted from orbit, so he guessed he was a bit of a celebrity. And everyone had questions.

"Dr. Tyrell! What's Sawyer's World like?" asked one.

"How did it feel when you realized the *Heinlein* wasn't coming back? What did you think when the *Endeavour* landed?"

"Welcome to Kakuloa!" said someone else, who had clearly forgotten that Tyrell had first landed here four and a half years ago.

"Did you have any idea what the squidberries were when you found them?"

"Whoa," Tyrell said, somewhat amused and a little intimidated by the crowd. Between the *Endeavour* and *Vostok* crews, he had gotten used to seeing faces other than the same few he'd spent the last four years with. To the *Victoria* crew, however, he was more the returning hero than the rescued castaway. "It's good to see you all, but one at a time, please."

Will Blake made his way through the small crowd. "All right folks," he said, "give the man space. He'll be here for a few days." He looked around at them. "Don't you all have work to do?"

The small crowd slowly dispersed. "Sorry about that," he said to Tyrell. "I'm Will Blake. I trust Drake or Tsibliev told you about why we're here?"

Tyrell nodded. Drake had told the *Anderson* team about what Skrellan Pharmaceuticals had found in the samples he and Ulrika had gathered, and how they'd helped finance the return mission. "Yes. That's pretty amazing."

"Indeed. So, are you ready to go find some more squidberries?"

"Sure. And I don't mind the crowd. It's nice to see more new faces. Was it like this for the others when they got back to Earth?"

"Sometimes worse," Blake said, "but the time in quarantine gave people a chance to get used to the idea that they were back."

"I'd forgotten that. I guess we'll have to go through that too." Tyrell wasn't looking forward to it. "Are they equipped for children?"

"Uh, probably not, but I'm sure that can be rectified quickly."

"We'll work something out. Most of us aren't in a rush to go back, and kids are adaptable." He'd been pleased with how quickly the children had grown used to the newly arrived strangers. "Now, you were saying about squidberries?"

"Yes. How do you want to do this? We have the RIB set up —"

"Rib?"

"R.I.B., rigid inflatable boat. It's a modified Zodiac, an inflatable with a rigid hull."

"Got it. We had something similar, only without the rigid hull. But let's fly over first," Tyrell said. "It will be easier to recognize from the air than from off shore."

"You want to revisit your crash site?" No doubt Blake knew the story of how the earlier expedition's electroplane had crash-landed and Tyrell and Klaar had had to hike back—discovering the squidberries on their way.

"Hell no," Tyrell said. "Especially not if it's still home to flocks of birds. But I know the route we took from there to the coast. There's a lake that makes a good landmark; from there we followed the outflow stream down to near the shore then north to a larger creek."

"Then what? We can't land in the trees or the creek."

"No, but we can drop a beacon. It's a technique we used several times both here and on Able. On Sawyer's World," he added, correcting himself. "You do have locator beacons?"

"Of course, and we can fab more if we need to." Blake said. "So we home in on that from the ocean side?"

Tyrell nodded. "Yep."

"Very well, let's do it your way." He raised his wrist and tapped a sequence on his omni to call the ship. He talked as they walked. "*Victoria*, this is Blake. We're going to want to go for a flight first, to survey the area from the air. We're on our way over. Is AC-1 available?"

"*How long do you need it for?*"

"A few hours. Is it charged?"

"*Fully. But have it back well before dark. Flint needs it later, and we'll need to top it up.*"

"Roger that."

"So who is Victoria?" Tyrell asked. "I assume your ship is named for somebody?"

Blake grinned. "Officially? *Victoria* was a sailing ship in Magellan's fleet, the only one to successfully complete the first circumnavigation."

"Ah," Tyrell said. "Krysansky told me that the *Vostok*, among other things, was the first ship to discover and circumnavigate Antarctica. And *Endeavour* was Cook's ship. I sense a theme. But, there's an unofficially?"

"All I know is that there's a Skrellan Pharmaceuticals vice president, who played a big role in persuading them to fund this mission, named Victoria Holmes," Blake said. "What do you think?"

Tyrell chuckled. "I think I'm going to put the question to Commodore Drake over a drink sometime. It sounds like there's a story there." Drake, who had commanded the first expedition, had returned on the *Endeavour*, and—to hear the others tell it—

was almost single-handedly responsible for getting the new ships designed and built on a compressed schedule.

Blake nodded. "There is. Franklin and I go way back; I've heard some of it."

"Really?"

"We were in the service together, before he transferred to the Space Force. In fact, he recommended me for this mission."

"I thought it was a civilian mission."

"It is. I had already retired. The *UDT* grumbled a bit, but the pharmaceutical companies leaned on them. That might have been Frank's doing too; I didn't ask."

∞ ∞ ∞

As they approached the *Victoria*. Dusty Jenkins, one of the junior crew, was trundling something out from under a tent canopy. It was an open metal framework, with two seats in an obvious open cockpit area in the center, and six horizontal fans arrayed around it.

"What in the world is *that*?" asked Tyrell. "It looks like an oversized drone."

"That's our aircar," Jenkins said.

"A flying car? Seriously? That can't have much range."

Blake explained. "The batteries are good for five hours flying time. Six hundred kilometers, plus reserve."

"How does it recharge? You can't possibly stow enough solar panels, I don't see where you could."

"No, that's one advantage your planes had. We have to recharge at the ship," said Blake. "Maybe one day they'll get the fusion plants down small enough to fit inside one of these, but not yet."

"So it flies like a drone? Or a helicopter?"

"Either. You can program the controls to emulate almost anything and the computer figures it out."

"Fantastic. So what are we waiting for?"

∞ ∞ ∞

Blake climbed into the cockpit's left seat and gestured for Tyrell to take the other.

"I can't wait to try flying this," Tyrell said. "I assume the computer can compensate if I do anything stupid?"

"Yes, but I'll take it up," Blake said. "It's mostly idiot-proof, but does have a few quirks. Technically it's still in beta. We got a couple of prototypes for this mission; we wanted something more flexible than the planes your expedition had."

"Yeah," Tyrell said, looking over the vehicle as he climbed in.

It looked something like an open-topped car, except that the outline, from above, would be more of an elongated hexagon than a rectangle. The open cockpit had two seats abreast. At each of the fore and aft corners of the cockpit was a horizontally-mounted fan, making four of the six corners of the hex. Directly in front and behind, making up the fore and aft corners, were two slightly larger fans. The whole thing was connected and sur-rounded by a framework of what looked like graphite composite tubing, with each of the fans surrounded by a shroud.

"Do the ducts improve the efficiency of the fans?" Tyrell asked.

"Slightly, but they also protect the blades and too-close by-standers."

"Good. It's hard to imagine a bird strike that would take this out."

Blake nodded. "If it did lose a rotor, you can still land fine on the other five, even fly for a while if you had to."

"That beats a forced landing on bad terrain," Tyrell said, re-membering his own experience.

"I can imagine," said Blake. "On the other hand, if you hadn't crashed, you and Klaar might not have stumbled across the tree squids and those berries, so we might not be here at all. At least not yet."

"There is that."

Blake settled into his seat and watched as Tyrell did the same. While Tyrell fastened his belt, Blake grabbed the spare headset and handed it to him.

"Noise canceling headphones," Blake said. "You'll want these."

Tyrell slipped them on and adjusted the boom mike. "*Sound check.*"

"I hear you fine. All set?" Blake had the console on and was running the computer through a checklist.

"Let's go."

Blake touched a control and the rotors spun up with a whine.

Even through the noise-canceling headphones came the slightly muffled sound as of angry hornets. *Big* angry hornets.

Blake checked the console again then pulled up on the stick in his left hand. The aircar leapt in to the air like a fast elevator. "Which way?"

"North northwest. Take it up to five thousand meters and we should see the lake." Tyrell said, then added "Uh, what's the ceiling on this thing? Can it go that high?"

The ground dwindled away rapidly, and they headed north. "Something like that," Blake said, then added: "uh, I think, even in this gravity and atmosphere. To tell you the truth, five kilometers is a bit higher than I'm comfortable with. Not that we should ever need to, but this thing doesn't glide well. Or at all, really." Blake sounded a bit embarrassed. "I know there's no rational reason five thousand would be any worse than one thousand if something went seriously wrong. In fact, it would give us more time to try to recover." He paused, then added "I know it doesn't make sense, it's just me."

"No problem. Whatever you're comfortable with." Tyrell said.

"It's been over four years; do you still remember the way?"

"I flew the route between the *Chandrasekhar* and *Krechet* landing sites enough times, before my crash-landing. Yes, I recognize the terrain. Geologist, remember?" Tyrell pointed a fist's width to the left of dead ahead. "Set your heading ten degrees more west. What's our speed?"

Blake glanced at the display. "Airspeed is 120 kph, ground speed 125. We have a slight tail wind."

"Good, we should be able to see the lake in about forty minutes."

"Copy that."

Blake let the computer do most of the flying as he kept an eye out for birds and watched the terrain go by. He was aware of Tyrell watching the ground for a while, then watching Blake's own hands on the controls.

He had it configured like a helicopter, with a collective and a cyclic. Tyrell's side had matching controls. Unlike a helicopter, though, there were no pedals. Yaw control was built into the stick, like the rotation controller on a spacecraft.

"So how does it handle?" Tyrell asked.

"Smooth as silk. The computer's the real pilot, I just make suggestions. Watch this." So saying, Blake reached forward and tapped a control on the console screen.

"Okay, our course is locked in." He released the controls and held up his hands. "Look, no hands!"

"Uh, okay..."

Blake rested his hands back on the controls. "Now, since it isn't a plane, we don't actually have to point in the direction we're going. He raised his right hand so the fingers were gripping the top of the cyclic handle from above, as though it were a dial.

He twisted the handle slightly. The aircar turned in that direction but kept its same track over the ground. He turned it more. Now the car was flying sideways.

"That explains the lack of yaw pedals." Tyrell said.

"You've flown helicopters?"

"Mostly in them as a passenger, not as pilot. It comes with the territory of being a field geologist. But this flying sideways is just a tad disturbing. Not usually much call for it."

Blake gave the handle a final twist and then released it. The car, still flying in straight path over the ground, rotated sideways in a complete circle, facing west, then backwards, then east, finally coming around to center itself on its original north-by-northwest heading.

"Okay," Tyrell admitted, "that is cool. I'm not sure what you'd use it for, but cool."

∞ ∞ ∞

Not long after that, Tyrell spotted the landmark he had been looking for in the distance. "There it is, Toothpick Lake."

"Toothpick Lake? Why that name?"

"It's a joke. Ulrika told me about toothpick fish, which live in the Amazon, when we reached the lake. There's no reason there would be any in the lake, it was a cautionary tale about unknown wildlife. And no, I'm not going to explain toothpick fish. Look it up."

"Uh, okay," Blake said, wondering what the deal was with toothpick fish. They sounded harmless. "What do we do when we reach the lake?"

"At the west edge of the lake there's a natural dam formed by a rock dike," Tyrell said. "The stream we want flows out of that. We follow it to the line of hills before the sea shore, then turn north."

"We don't go to the shore?"

"That's not the stream you want. Well, there might be squid-berries on it, but there was a storm coming in when we were here, so we sheltered on the lee side of the hills."

Something in Tyrell's tone made Blake turn to look at him. He wore a grin as if at some private joke. What was that about? Then Blake remembered that Tyrell and Ulrika Klaar had married a couple of months after the *Anderson* landed on Sawyer's World. *Oh*. He grinned.

"North of that is the larger creek we followed to the shore," Tyrell continued. "That's where we'll find the banyans."

"Banyans? I thought they were mangroves."

"Is there a difference? I'm not a biologist. Something with branching roots above the waterline. Could be both, for all I know."

"All right." Blake twisted the throttle on the collective and pointed the cyclic slightly down. The aircar tilted forward and the rotor pitch rose as they sped up. He was anxious to get there.

Chapter 5: Mangroves

Kakuloa, west of Toothpick Lake

"There they are!"

It was both oddly familiar, and yet not, for Tyrell to see the banyan grove from above. The last time he'd been here, four years ago, he and Ulrika had been stumbling their way along the bank of the creek, hungry, tired, and him still suffering from the mild concussion he'd gotten when he'd crash-landed their plane. He remembered the elation they had both felt when they spotted the banyans, or mangroves, a sign that the fresh water of the stream was turning brackish, a sure indication that they were almost at the shoreline and an easier trek north to the *Chandrasekhar* landing site. Tyrell grinned to himself. That had been the day after Ulrika had gotten friendly in the tent. He remembered *that* well, and was amazed he remembered as much of the next day as he did. *And now we have two children. How awesome is that?*

Blake dropped the aircar lower over the trees. There was a frenzied rustling and splashes in the stream as tree squids dropped to the safety of the water.

"I think we startled them," Blake said.

"Interesting behavior. They didn't care about us when we were on foot. I wonder if there's an aerial predator."

"They're pretty big, it's hard to imagine a bird big enough to carry one off."

"Something like a large eagle could carry a couple or so kilos, maybe?" Tyrell said. "Anyway, unless you want to try landing on the beach, we need to drop a couple of beacons."

"No. We don't have the time, and landing on sand kicks up a blast," Blake said. "Here, take the controls for a moment while I get the beacons."

"I've got it," Tyrell said, taking the controls.

Blake rummaged briefly in the bag beside him and pulled out a couple of fist-sized electronics packages. He clipped small parachutes to them. "These should get caught in the branches. That's what we want."

"They aren't waterproof?"

"They are, but water cuts the range on the signal."

"Oh, sure."

"Here we go." Blake reached back and hurled a bundle out over the trees, the parachute opening after a dozen meters. The beacon's arcing flight came to an abrupt halt as the 'chute grabbed air, and the package floated down into the trees. A gust of wind took it as it touched a branch and blew it sideways. It cleared the branch, then dropped through, somehow managing to avoid getting hung up on anything and falling with a visible splash into the stream.

"Oh, come *on*." Blake shook his head in disgust. He readied a second beacon and threw it.

This one arced out, the parachute trailing behind it but not opening. The arc continued down through the trees and out of sight. The sound of any splash was lost in the whine of the car's rotors.

Tyrell grinned. "Want me to try?"

Blake swore. He checked something on his omni. "There's a signal. It's on the ground, not in the water. But yes, let's do another one. Stupid things."

"I have an idea," Tyrell said. "Take the controls, then do what I tell you."

Blake passed the third beacon/parachute combo to Tyrell and took the controls. They couldn't simply drop it over the side without risking it being sucked into the rotors. "What did you have in mind?"

"Keep it a couple of meters above the trees and moving forward about 15 kph. And keep it steady." Tyrell unfastened his seat-belt as he said this.

"Don't be climbing out. I don't want to have to explain to your wife how I lost you."

Tyrell grinned. "No worries, just standing up." He did so, holding on to the top of the windshield with one hand to keep his balance. In his other hand he held the beacon. Raising that arm, he let the parachute open into the wind as they moved, holding the beacon tightly.

"Not too fast, now. Okay, over those trees."

As the aircar moved over the densest part of the grove, Tyrell tossed the beacon upward, its open parachute grabbing the air and pulling it back over the rear of the car. He turned to watch it, and was pleased to see it drifting down to get snagged in the upper branches of one of the trees.

"Done. You can turn us around."

Blake turned the craft and looked down to where the beacon hung tangled in the tree. He slowed to a hover, off to one side so as not to disturb the chute with their downdraft.

"Interesting," he said. "It *is* both."

"What?"

"The tree is a mangrove, or something similar. The berries are growing from an epiphyte, a plant growing on the tree."

"Right, so?"

"So the epiphyte itself has dropped aerial roots down to the ground, which is a characteristic of banyans. On Earth they're a kind of fig."

"And here?"

"Not figs. Too many millions of years of separate evolution. But they're both flowering plants, so there's a common ancestor somewhere."

Tyrell sat back down and shook his head. Even though he'd been living with it for over four years now, the idea that life here, and on Sawyer's World, and on Earth, all had a common heritage still boggled him sometimes. Rocks were so much simpler.

Blake flew the aircar out toward the ocean.

"Where are we headed now?"

"I wanted to see what the coast looks like from out here. Even with the beacons it will be easier if we know what to look for, and I want to be sure we can bring the boat in."

"That shouldn't be a problem. It's a sandy beach away from the mangroves."

It was. A thin strand of white sand stretched north and south away from the inlet, punctuated here and there by other groves, with the occasional spit or offshore sandbar. To the south, near the horizon, the coast curved westward, backed by a ridge of hills. That would be the northern side of the peninsula that jutted out between the original two landing sites.

"Good. It looks like there are other places the berries might grow. Maybe we can plant them if they're not growing there naturally."

"There may be wetlands back from the beach. The terrain is relatively flat, and you'll get seawater coming in during high-tide storm surges."

"Any crocodiles?" Blake wondered.

"Maybe. I mean, not that I ever saw, but George Darwin said he'd seen things that looked like alligator nests on one of his flights. They could have been some other animal, though. The squids would probably avoid the area if there were crocs. Maybe elsewhere on the planet—we barely scratched the surface—but not near the beaches."

"One less thing to worry about, then. Good." He pulled the aircar up to higher altitude, still heading westward.

"Where are we going now?" Tyrell asked. "I thought we had to get back?"

"Eventually, but I want to check out that headland." He pointed forward, to where the hills on the tip of the peninsula showed twenty kilometers away. "By the maps, it looks like it's roughly two-hundred kilometers by sea from here to Krechet's Landing, what with going around the peninsula. That's a four-hour trip each way, plus recharging time for the boat's batteries."

"So, you're looking for a spot for a camp?"

"Exactly. There's not much beach by the inlet, and the low ground would be subject to flooding by storm surge. Those hills look like a better option."

Tyrell tapped the panel in front of him to bring up the map. It had been too long since he'd been here before to remember all the details. The bay formed by the peninsula was thirty kilometers across, and the peninsula itself broke into a short archipelago at its tip. The largest island, about fifteen kilometers long and eight across, had a low mountain that sloped gently to the east or lee side, facing the mainland across the bay.

"Yes, that looks good," Tyrell said. "We never explored that, but geologically it looks like an extension of the coastal ridge that extends to Krechet Plateau. Probably nothing biologically unique there; the islands aren't separated from the mainland by much. There should be a good beach on the lee side."

"That's what I'm hoping." By now they were close enough to make out details of the islands, a few smaller ones scattered be-tween the tip of the peninsula and the larger one Blake was headed toward.

Several of the small islands were only separated by shallow, rocky straits, but there were enough larger channels that coming this way by sea shouldn't be an issue. "Good," Blake said. "The boat can cut through here. We won't have to go all the way around."

The verdant hills and lush vegetation on the short coastal plain leading up to them reinforced the feeling that they were somewhere near Hawaii, although Tyrell knew that these hills were not volcanic. Perhaps more like the Oregon coast, if that were warmer, he thought.

As the approached the larger island, Blake put the aircar into a gentle descent.

"It looks good," he said. He flew a few hundred meters above the eastern shore, heading northward. There was a broad, sandy beach that rose into an area of low scrub and then forest. A line of dried seaweed and other beach litter marked the high tide line, still leaving plenty of room for a camp above that. "How often do you think the water gets above that tide line?"

Tyrell considered the question. "Take us lower," he said, and Blake did. "Obviously it does sometimes," Tyrell continued, "or there wouldn't be sand here. But there's some vegetation growing up through it. Probably not very often."

"How weird are the tides, anyway? This planet has two moons."

"The smaller one doesn't have much effect. As a rough rule of thumb, the tidal effect is proportional to how big the object looks in the sky. The second moon is much smaller and further away, so the effect is lost in the noise. The sun—well, Alpha Centauri B—has a bigger effect." Tyrell was no astronomer, he was repeating what the astrophysicists on the first expedition had said. But he hadn't seen anything to the contrary.

"All right, excellent."

"Mind, the shape of the coast has the most influence over local tides."

"Right." Blake increased power and began to climb. "Oh," he said, and fished out another beacon. He didn't attach a parachute to this one "Toss this over the side. Above the tide line."

"You're not going to land?" Tyrell asked as he took the beacon and threw it overboard, watching it arc toward the sand below.

"Not this time. We'll be back," Blake said, and started to turn the aircar south.

"Before heading back, do we have enough time and power left for a side trip to the *Chandrasekhar* landing site?"

Blake checked the instrument panel. "We should, and I can recharge when we get there."

"How?"

"The *Victoria* crew came out earlier to check it out. Your reactor unit was in good shape, so they started it up again, for just such use. We're going to want to explore further up the coast. Any particular reason you want to head up there?"

Tyrell shrugged. "Old time's sake. Curiosity. I'm wondering how much it's changed."

"Fair enough." Blake turned the aircar north, climbing as he did so.

Chapter 6: Chandrasekhar Valley

280 km north northwest of Krechet's Landing

They flew northward up the coast towards the broad river valley where, years earlier, the *Chandrasekhar* had made humanity's first landing on a planet of another star. They stuck to the coast, in part because Blake wanted to survey for other potential squid-berry-suitable mangrove inlets. The river that flowed through Chandrasekhar Valley was much wider with a greater flow than the tidal creeks they'd seen earlier. That fresher water meant there were no mangroves here; the lack of salt let other species out-compete them.

They turned inland as they reached the mouth, rising above the range of coastal hills. The river had long since eroded its way through the landslide-created dam that had given Sawyer and Fin-ley so much trouble, and the river was much as it had appeared when they'd first landed. The *Chandrasekhar* itself was long gone, of course, but the landing area was obvious. Prominent was the refueling module, the nuclear-powered module that Blake's team had powered back up. The lack of one of those, with its ability to synthesize rocket fuel from the water and air, is what had meant the *Anderson*'s landing would be a one-way trip, as the *Krechet*'s had been. The spare had been destroyed when the *Xing Hua* had hit something in warp and exploded.

Except, Tyrell thought, remembering what Drake had told them, *that wasn't actually what happened.*

There were also piles of equipment, unnecessary panels, even crew couches that had been ripped out so that the *Chandra* could launch with both its original crew and that of the Krechet, plus as many specimens as they could possibly carry. And even at that, reaching orbit had been a close thing. *Fun times*, thought Tyrell. *Someone should write a book.*

∞ ∞ ∞

Blake verified that the reactor module was still generating power—he didn't care about rocket propellants—and plugged the aircar into the reactor module to recharge. "All right, let's take a look around. You guys sure left a mess."

"We did, but it wasn't this bad when we left. Between the blast from our rockets and four years of weather, what did you expect?"

"Fair enough. Anything you left behind that you want to recover? Or anyone else left behind, for that matter?"

"My favorite geologist's hammer. The *Anderson* had a spare but this one I'd had since college. Not the end of the world if we can't find it though."

"You guys really were paring down the weight."

"It was that or another kilo of biological specimens. Ulrika was willing to give those up, but I insisted."

Blake smiled at that. "No wonder she married you."

"Heh, I suppose."

"Well, look around. Do you remember where you tied down the plane?"

Tyrell looked around, trying to remember. The scattered jetsam didn't help. "Over there, I think. But I'm not seeing anything that looks like a plane."

"Like you said, jet blast and four years of weather."

Blake found it, or what was left of it, a few minutes later. He found one of the tie-downs first, screwed into the ground, and followed the cable to a tangle of carbon tubing and torn film.

"It doesn't actually look that bad," he said.

"You're kidding," Tyrell said, looking over the remains of what had been electroplane-02. "My *crash* didn't look that bad."

"No, look," Blake said. "Most of the tubing is intact, it only looks bad because the wing fabric is all torn and wrapped around it. The motor seems fine, and I don't see anything wrong with the propeller."

"I wouldn't trust it."

"We can fab a new one. The console seems all right; rain wouldn't hurt it. I'm not sure about the batteries."

He was right about the electronics, they were sealed and waterproof. So were the batteries, in theory, but: "After four years without maintenance I'd be surprised if they held a charge," Tyrell said.

"So would I. We have spares."

"Why? What do you want to do with it?"

"Another aircraft would be useful. Let's finish disassembling it, then secure it to the aircar. Leave the fabric, but let's bring the rest. We can fab any other parts we need."

"Isn't this now a historic site?" Tyrell asked. He didn't really care; to him it was just a place he and his team-mates had spent a few months exploring.

"Take lots of pictures," Blake said, smiling. "If someone wants to restore it to the way it looked, they can."

Tyrell shrugged. "Sure. Now it's only a—what's the archeology term? —midden heap anyway."

"Oh, I have no doubt someone will put up a commemorative plaque. *Here people from planet Earth first set foot, blah, blah, blah.*"

Tyrell grinned at him. "*All* life here originated from planet Earth. We may be the first *humans*, but I'm not so sure about the first people."

Blake looked at Tyrell. "What are you... Oh, shit. You're right. Terraformed."

"Bingo. Although I don't really think the Terraformers themselves were from Earth."

∞ ∞ ∞

They took off half an hour later, with the frame and electronics of the old EP-02 strapped to the aircar, and headed south.

Tyrell had found his hammer, slightly rusty but in otherwise good shape, having been protected by a now-worn specimen bag. He was more intrigued by the remains of the EP-02. "So even if we can repair the frame," he said, "how do you propose to recover the plane? Don't tell me you brought a few rolls of aircraft fabric."

"Even better, we brought a machine to make fabric."

"Really? Out of what?"

"The local trees. Or grass, or whatever goes for grass on this planet. Anyway, cellulose."

"You're going to make it out of wood? Or paper?"

"Hah, no, altered cellulose," Blake said. "You've heard of rayon, right?"

"One of the first synthetic fabrics. Flammable, I think."

"Yes, first synthesized from wood cellulose almost two hundred years ago. We—well, the engineers—modified the process some, tossed in a few other chemicals, and came up with something similar that's stronger and less flammable. It comes out as a fine fiber, which the machine spins into a thicker thread. There are knitting and weaving attachments for the fabber."

"Well I'll be darned. That would have come in handy on the other planet."

"The process has been around for a while on Earth, replacing oil-based synthetics. I guess nobody thought you'd be here long enough to be making fabric."

"Horribly short-sighted of them," Tyrell said sarcastically. "Speaking of fiber," he added, "The Krechet landing area sits on a very large basalt flow."

"Way ahead of you," Blake said. "The next ship here will be carrying a small pilot-plant for producing basalt fiber and fabric. That's another reason we chose the plateau as our base; a ready supply of construction material."

Tyrell was impressed. The folks involved in planning this follow-up expedition so far seemed to be anything but short-sighted. *Which just means,* he thought cynically, *that when this planet springs its surprises, they'll be doozies.* He didn't for a moment believe there wouldn't be any.

Chapter 7: Boat trip

Krechet's Landing, that evening

"It's nearly two hundred kilometers by sea from here to the squidberry grove that Tyrell and Klaar discovered." Blake said to the assembled group. "That's at least four hours each way by boat, so we're going to set up camp on an island across the bay from Squidberry Inlet. We'll foray from there first to gather what we can from that grove. Most of that will go back to Earth for the pharmaceutical companies. Dr. Reyes will retain samples to examine here."

"Why?" Tyrell asked.

"Primarily, so we know exactly what to look for elsewhere. We're going to survey up and down the coast to find other places the squidberries are growing naturally. We know there are other mangrove areas, some with berry vines, but we don't know yet which of those are the same species or have the same kinds of fungus growing on them."

Tyrell nodded. "Fair enough, and secondarily?"

"As a baseline for comparison. Assuming we do find other squidberry patches, we'll want to compare their yield against what you and Klaar found. It's entirely possible we'll find somewhere even better, either in terms of berry yield per hectare or in terms of pharmaceutical yield per berry. Or both. Cooper Reyes here will be looking at that, at least as best he can with the lab facilities we could bring with."

Tyrell nodded. "That makes sense. Will you want me here for that survey, or can I get back to Camp Anderson?"

Blake grinned. "I understand you're anxious to get back to your wife and kids. That's fine. You've pinpointed the original berry patch. I would like your help for a couple more days while we do the initial harvest. Even if you've only done it once, you're the closest thing we have to an expert on that."

"Sure, no problem."

"After that, we can give you a lift on *Vostok* on its way back to Earth. I understand that you and the rest of the *Anderson* crew have elected to stay?"

"Pretty much. We plan to return to Earth briefly for family visits, medical checkups, and at some point, to give the kids a decent education, but mostly Sawyer is working out the details of that with Commodore Drake, such as he can."

"Sure. That's outside my purview anyway. I work for Centauri Pharmaceuticals. But speaking for them, there will probably be consulting jobs for any of you who want them, whether here or back on Earth."

"Does *here* include Alpha Centauri A? Sawyer's World?"

Blake didn't answer immediately. Obviously from Centauri Pharmaceuticals' point of view, Kakuloa or the labs on Earth would be best. "I'll have to take that up with my bosses. Until we have more experience with the ships, and more of them, we don't want to be running a taxi service between there and here. It may be only a minute in warp but there's still the take-off and landing at each end. However, if we can get reliable high-bandwidth communications between there and here, then probably." He paused for a moment, then looked at his engineer, Jim Fenety. "What is the radio communication lag anyway?"

"That depends where Alpha Centauri A and B are in their respective orbits, and where the planets are. At their closest it's approximately a two-and-a-half hour round-trip. Right now, though, the two stars are only a little past their maximum distance, so five-and-a-quarter hours each way."

"And it will stay that way for another decade or so." Blake sighed. "So, no real-time conversations. Email could work, if kind of slow. I guess I've had slower email exchanges even on Earth. No promises, but I'll pass that on up the line."

Blake continued: "But you've gotten me sidetracked. Back to our immediate plans. We'll need a tent, gear for four of us, and supplies for at least a couple of days. It will be Fred Tyrell, me, Retta Flint piloting the Zodiac, and Dusty Jenkins as an extra hand. Make it three days. We should be in frequent contact via the aircar, but it doesn't hurt to be prepared for contingencies."

"You've got that right," Tyrell said.

"Indeed. I think between the aircar and the RIB we can manage all that in one trip each. Let's get the gear together today and set out at first light tomorrow. Make sure everything has a full charge, and don't forget to stow the solar chargers. We'll need them to get back."

"Yes," Tyrell piped up, turning to face the rest of the group. "Trust me, you don't want to walk back."

That drew a few good-natured chuckles. By now they all knew the story.

∞ ∞ ∞

They set out the next morning, three of them in the boat, a modified large rigid-hulled inflatable with a powerful electric outboard motor. Blake and Reyes would be taking off in the aircar in a couple of hours, to rendezvous at the island around the same time the boat got there. If necessary, it could guide the boat through the channels between the islands.

The boat was six-and-a-half meters long, a rigid shallow V-shaped hull. The bow and sides were large, bright orange, inflated tubes, with a solid stern plate to which the dual 75kW motors attached. The floor was flat; the deck boards covered the battery compartment. Tyrell had ridden in similar, but smaller, boats on Earth, and it resembled a big brother to the inflatable boat they'd had on the first expedition.

"This is a rigid hull? How did you get that aboard the *Victoria*?" The starships were cramped. The warp equations put an upper limit on a ship's size, and much of that volume was taken up with deuterium fuel for the reactors, as well as general spacecraft and flight systems.

"In pieces," Flint said, and grinned. "Some assembly required. I wasn't too thrilled with that, but from what we were told about the waves here, I wanted a rigid hull. Zodiac did a semi-custom build for us. It went together pretty easily and, although it's a bit heavier, it's every bit as strong as if it had come from the factory in one piece. Should give us a nice smooth ride when we get up to speed."

Tyrell could appreciate that. Soft inflatables had a tendency to hammer the surface in anything more than a very light chop, and one had to hang on to the handles like a rodeo bull rider. Not that he'd ever done the latter; he wasn't crazy.

There was a stand-up console midships with a windshield, ship's wheel and other controls. Calling it a wheelhouse would be a gross exaggeration, but it gave the captain a better view than sitting at the stern would. Tyrell looked at the others on the boat, and eyed the large, empty plastic drums on the floor of the boat alongside their camping gear. "Exactly how many squidberries are you expecting to collect?"

"As much as we can. The samples *Heinlein* and *Chandrasekhar* came back with were barely enough to do much more than preliminary assays. From what I heard, if they'd followed a normal testing regime, they wouldn't have had enough to get to the mouse trials. Apparently, the PI—principal investigator—was so intrigued by the preliminary results that he skipped steps and stretched out the few milligrams of cephalomycin that he had."

Tyrell thought back. They had gathered a few bunches of the berries, something like small grapes, when they'd first discovered them. No more than a couple of kilograms, if that. But these barrels, filled, might be close to a ton.

He gestured to them. "So all that might yield a gram of your wonder drug. How many doses is that?"

"I have no idea, that's not my department. They told us to bring back as much as possible, while being sure to leave enough for the crop to survive."

"That shouldn't be a problem. There were a lot of trees and berries. So long as they're not too seasonal."

Flint took her eyes off the water and looked at him. "You mean there might not be any berries now?"

"Relax. We saw some from the air yesterday, and the squid were feeding on them. In this climate there's probably a more or less continuous cycle, although Jennifer Singh would be the expert on that." Dr. Singh had been the botanist on the first expedition, and had stayed with the *Anderson* landing team on the planet they were now calling Sawyer's World.

"Ah." Flint turned her attention back to piloting the boat, alternately scanning the water ahead, the coast, and the beacon locator app on her omniphone. "Did Doctor Singh visit the site? Maybe we should have brought her."

Tyrell thought. Had she? "I don't think so. We were down to one plane after that and beginning to wrap up the expedition. I'm sure she studied our samples, though. You could ask. But her daughter, Chantal, is only six months older than our Susan. I don't think Jennifer would want to come here with a toddler."

"There is that. I must say you folks surprised us. We were afraid of what we'd find when we finally got back here. A thriving colony with—five is it?—kids was a pleasant surprise."

"Hah. We had our scary moments. And Doctor McFadyen thinks there's something in the environment that countered our birth control implants. We didn't *intend* for it to be a colony mission." At least, thought Tyrell, nobody had ever come out and said that. Given Elizabeth Sawyer's actions both before and after the landing, she might have been at least considering the possibility, as had others on the crew. Not that he had cause to complain.

"Ha, then I'm glad *Victoria* didn't land. Blake said something about sending a team there to investigate. There might be something else Centauri Pharmaceuticals can turn a profit on."

"I'm sure they're going to find all sorts of interesting possibilities. I'm no biochemist, but two planets that started out with Earth-based life and then evolved separately for sixty-five million years must have all kinds of useful pharmaceuticals. Although I imagine the companies are getting pretty good at synthesizing whatever they want by now."

"Yes and no. Again, not my department. I'm a pilot, not a scientist. From what I understand, though, they can eventually come up with a way to synthesize a molecule once they understand the structure, but designing one from scratch to do something specific is orders of magnitude more difficult. There are way too many possibilities."

"This is why I like geology. I started to take an organic chem class once, thinking it might be useful for petroleum geology—this was before the bottom fell out of *that* market—but gave up on it. Gave me headaches, and not from breathing the fumes."

Flint chuckled. "I hear you. Unfortunately, unless you've found something like unobtainium, I'm not sure there's anything to mine that's worth hauling four light-years back to Earth."

"No, probably not. But there are geological differences, so there are some new minerals. Nothing worth bulk shipment, but I'm sure there's a market for exotic alien gemstones."

"Have you found any?"

"Different minerals? Yes. Exotic alien gemstones? Nothing yet, but we've literally barely scratched the surface," Tyrell said. "Oh, we did find obsidian spear points."

"You *what?* Are you kidding me?"

"It was in the reports. Oh, but I guess those haven't gotten to Earth yet. This was not long after the *Anderson* landed on the other planet. Finley and I found a couple in a ravine; we've found a few others since. We figured they were maybe a half-million years old, give or take a couple of hundred thousand. No sign of whoever made them."

"But that's huge! Proof of intelligent aliens, even if they're no longer around."

"I would have thought two terraformed planets would be proof enough of that."

Flint turned to Tyrell, her expression blank. Then her eyes slowly widened. "Well, nuke me."

Tyrell chuckled. "It finally sunk in, huh? I don't blame you. Nobody gets it the first time. It's too big and too abstract. It sounds like science fiction."

"You're right." Flint shook her head. "Terraformed planets," she said, mostly to herself. "With life *from Earth*. Somebody had to have done that. Any idea who? Or what?"

"No clue. After a while you just come to accept that maybe we'll never find out. Or maybe the Terraformers will show up next week. Best not to think about it and focus on the here and now."

"Uh, yeah, I guess so." Flint shook her head again, as if to clear it. After a few moments of silence, she said: "So those spear points. That's not abstract, people can relate to that. *Those*, my friend, are going to be worth a fortune."

The thought startled Tyrell. He'd never thought of them as anything but interesting archeological specimens, destined for a museum somewhere. But he realized that Flint was right. There had always been a market for rare artifacts, sometimes legitimate, more often not. And how much rarer than artifacts made by actual aliens could you get?

"More than squidberries?" he asked.

"Well, no, probably not. Collectibles are one thing, life-saving drugs another. But the thing about artifacts is that you don't need a huge and expensive processing facility to refine and manufacture them, nor years of clinical trials before they *can* be marketed. Anyone with a shovel can go looking for artifacts. You might want to pass the word to your friends on Sawyer's World to brace themselves for a gold rush."

Tyrell shook his head. He realized that, while Flint might be exaggerating, she was likely not wrong. Who'd have thought that one of the first things an alien colonial government would need would be a Department of Antiquities?

∞ ∞ ∞

Flint now had the Zodiac out beyond where the waves were breaking—that had been interesting, given the size of some of them—and opened up the throttle. The Zodiac surged forwards with a whine, and Tyrell tasted salt as their passage kicked up spray. Soon they were going too fast even for that, their speed leaving their spray behind them, and the wind roaring in his ears. This was almost as much fun as flying.

They stayed five to ten kilometers off the coast, close enough to remain in sight but more than far enough to avoid any rough water. They'd seen no unexpected reefs or shallows in their aerial survey; the bottom sloped gradually but steadily offshore to the edge of the continental shelf another twenty or so kilometers further. The steady rush of wind, the splash of their wake and the repeated gentle thumping as they crossed the swells soon had Tyrell nodding off. He sat down on the deck, leaned back against the inflated side tube, and went to sleep.

∞ ∞ ∞

The thumping grew louder. Tyrell could now feel it as well as hear it. It reminded him of something. What *was* that? *Girranos!* He awoke with a start. "Giranno stampede!" he shouted, leaping to his feet. As he came fully awake, he realized he was not back at Camp Anderson. Flint was staring at him. Dusty Jenkins, now driving the boat, also looked over at him. Tyrell grinned sheepishly at them.

"And what," Flint asked, "is a giranno?" Of course, Flint, as part of *Victoria*'s crew, hadn't landed on Sawyer's World and wouldn't have heard the story. "And how would they stampede at sea?"

"Sorry about that." Tyrell shook his head, taking a moment to clear it. "A giranno is a Sawyer's World animal, like a cross between a giraffe and a rhinoceros, but without the horns. Twice as big as an elephant. I guess the thumping of the waves reminded me of a stampede." Tyrell realized the thumping had changed, now more frequent. "Did we change course? The waves feel different."

"Slightly. We're angling in to shore, so yes, they would. Tell me about this stampede?"

"Bad news. Destroyed one of our cabins, knocked over the *Anderson*, and nearly killed Sawyer. She saved my son, Poul." Tyrell didn't want to talk about it. The memory of what could have happened still choked him up.

Flint noticed his discomfort. "Oh, that sounds grim. I'm sorry I asked. Everyone made it through okay, though?"

"Sawyer still walks with a slight limp, but yes, it could have been worse. So why," Tyrell said, changing the subject, "are we angling in to shore? It doesn't look like we're there yet."

"We're not. It'll be another hour and a bit. But I'm getting hungry and we cleverly packed the food where it's not easily reachable while we're at sea. Dusty is putting ashore at the beach yonder." She pointed at a strip of sand a kilometer away. "We could use a break anyway. Or at least, some of us could."

"I guess I've had my nap. But food sounds good."

∞ ∞ ∞

It took a few minutes to beach the boat and dig around through the gear for the food. While most of it was pre-packaged rations, someone had thoughtfully packed what passed for sandwiches and cold drinks for the first meal.

"Sandwiches. This is luxury!"

"Enjoy it while you can. The fresh food we brought from Earth won't last more than another few days, and then we're all on rat-packs unless there's something local we can eat."

"Even the rat-packs are better than survival rations. Ulrika and I decided they were deliberately made to taste the way they did so people wouldn't binge on them. As for local food, there's probably plenty that is edible, but we never really tested for that here."

"And yet you set down in the *Anderson* without knowing if you could eat the food?"

"By then we had a pretty good idea that the biochemistry was similar to Earth's, from the orbital surveys and the drones. We also knew that Kakuloa's life was Earth-derived, so it was a fair bet that Able's was too. But we had a set-up to digest and ferment local biomatter and convert it to something humans could survive on, if it came to that. Fortunately it didn't. The sludge that comes out of the processor tastes even worse than survival rations."

"Well, we should have regular re-supply missions from Earth once things get rolling, but it wouldn't hurt to investigate the local flora and fauna for what's edible. It will save shipping it all in."

"Who knows, you might even find something tasty. I imagine these oceans are well-stocked with fish. Apparently, so was Earth before we invented fishing trawlers. And I know for a fact there are lots of birds. Too many." Tyrell added, thinking back on the multiple bird strike that had crashed his plane four years earlier. The sky had been almost dark with them when they'd startled from the treetops and surged around the plane.

"Speaking of birds," Jenkins spoke up, "are those seagulls?" He nodded down the beach, to where several large birds were circling and occasionally diving at something in the shallows.

"Something similar, sure, but not actual seagulls. Life here would have diverged millions of years before current Earth gulls evolved, but convergent evolution and similar environments produce similar-looking animals. There's a lot of that, both here and on Able."

"You mean Sawyer's World."

"Yes, that. I'm still getting used to the name."

They watched the gulls for a while. Tyrell was sure that Ulrika, or any other zoologist, could as easily tell these birds from Earth seagulls as they could tell the various species of Earth gulls and similar seabirds apart, but in Tyrell's view, if these birds were suddenly transported to an Earth beach, most people wouldn't notice anything unusual about them. For that matter, he mused, the gulls probably wouldn't notice anything unusual about the beach, either, except perhaps the number of people.

The small flock was closer now, having gotten used to the strange bipeds below them. Dusty Jenkins tore off a piece of his sandwich and tossed it to where the waves lapped on the sand. One of the birds peeled off and dived for it. A meter from the water it spread its wings wide and flapped, braking to a near halt, as if not sure what to make of the piece of bread floating there. It flapped again, hovering for a moment, then dipped its head, snatched up the bread and climbed back to rejoin the others circling above.

Amused, Jenkins tore off another piece and tossed it on the beach, closer this time.

"I don't know if feeding the local wildlife is a good idea," Tyrell said.

"If Earth birds can eat bread, I'm sure these can. You said yourself the biology is the same."

"It wasn't really the bird I was worried about," Tyrell said, watching as two birds this time swooped down on the bread, fought over it briefly, and flew off.

"What do you mea—" Jenkins was interrupted in mid-sentence as another bird, or perhaps the first one again, swooped down and grabbed what was left of the sandwich from his hand. "Hey, what the...?"

"*That's* what I mean."

All the birds were now circling lower over the three humans, and two more swooped down low over them, looking for this wonderful new source of food.

"Ow! Dammit, that one pecked me!" Jenkins said, lashing out with his free hand as he pulled the other back to his chest. The bird whose feathers he'd brushed let out a loud *SQUAWK!* and took to the sky.

Another two dived at Flint, then veered off as she flailed her arms at them, losing half her sandwich. A third came in low, checking out what Flint had dropped. She kicked at it. "Okay, guys, lunchtime is over," she said. "Pack up."

"For us or the birds?" The gulls were swooping lower now, emboldened. One tried to snatch food out of Tyrell's hand. Dodging, he threw what was left of his meal as far down the beach as he could.

"For us. Toss the rest of the loose food, that will distract them."

Jenkins was already doing that. Tyrell did the same and joined him in hastily loading whatever gear they'd unloaded back into the Zodiac. Most of the birds went after the scraps the men had thrown, although a couple continued to buzz the team as they struggled to push the boat back into the water.

"They're just birds, for crying out loud," Jenkins said.

"Do you want to sit here trying to fight them off while you eat? And how's your hand?" Flint said

"No, and I'd swear that bird had teeth. Let's get out of here."

"Just birds?" Tyrell said. "I've got an Alfred Hitchcock movie for you." The *Anderson*'s video library had been well stocked, and movie nights had been a popular pastime for the crew for the first few years.

"A who what?"

"Never mind."

The boat was half in the water now, and Flint climbed aboard and went forward to the console. "Shove off!"

Tyrell and Jenkins each had a side of the inflated bow tube and were pushing the boat out to where it was fully afloat. The birds had finished off the scraps they'd tossed and were coming back for more. Tyrell felt an impact on his head and claws raked his scalp as the gull tried to take his hair.

"Ow! Stupid bird!" he swatted at it, then heaved again on the boat.

The water was now knee-deep, and Flint yelled "Clear!" as she switched on the motors. "Get aboard!"

Tyrell and Jenkins dived onto the side tubes, grabbing the hand ropes, then rolled into the deck. "We're on! Go!"

Flint shoved the throttle into full astern and they surged backward with a whine, the birds flapping around them in confusion. One attacked Jenkins again as Flint pivoted the boat around, pointing the bow offshore. Then the boat came up on plane and shot away from the shore, the gulls following briefly before giving up in confusion.

"Everyone okay?" Flint called back.

Tyrell took stock. His scalp and hands were scratched, but he had no serious injuries.

Jenkins said: "Only scratches. I see what Tyrell meant about not worrying about the bird. Sorry."

Tyrell chuckled. "Yes. Remember, the wildlife here has no concept of humans. They haven't learned to be afraid of us. Some will stay away because we don't smell right, but others won't." He put his hand up to his head again, then looked at his palm. There a red smear of blood on it. He had definitely had worse, he thought, remembering the crash. "And for the record? I am *really* starting to hate birds."

Chapter 8: Rendezvous

Aboard the aircar, north of Krechet's Landing

Blake pushed the aircar as fast as he dared, keeping in mind the need to balance battery reserve against speed. He had wanted to be at the peninsula by now, in case Flint wanted him to scout a path through the islands to the bay side, but aside from Reyes taking longer than expected to get his gear loaded, there'd been that trouble with *Vostok*'s water couplings.

Each ship had a processing unit to extract deuterium—heavy hydrogen—from any convenient water source, which in the case of Krechet's Landing, was the ocean below the cliffs. *Victoria* had deployed her pumps and hoses with no issue, but somehow the hoses on *Vostok* had come up twenty meters short.

Captain Tsibliev could have lifted the ship and moved it that much closer to the plateau's edge, but it was surrounded by un-loaded gear that could have been damaged by the ship's thruster down-wash, and would take time to move. After some discussion and improvisation, they'd tapped a T-junction into the water line feeding *Victoria*, which would suffice.

Blake looked forward to setting up a more permanent refuel-ing facility. It would be needed to handle the traffic he expected if the squidberry extract proved out. Meanwhile, that had put him an hour behind schedule. He checked the console and nudged the throttle up a notch.

∞ ∞ ∞

The island opposite Squidberry Inlet

"Man, that's a long haul," Jenkins griped as they hopped out into the shin-deep water to pull the boat ashore. "Why did *Chandrasekhar* and *Krechet* land so far apart anyway?" he asked Tyrell.

"It wasn't my call," Tyrell said. "But there was no point in both of the ships landing in the same place, and the plateau was one of the nearest spots with obvious geological and biological differences. The *Krechet*'s crew wanted to put down even further away, but Drake insisted that, if necessary, they be able to hike to the *Chandrasekhar* to take off."

"Hike? That's got to be over 200 kilometers!"

"And Ulrika and I hiked nearly half that when our plane crashed." Well, more like only a third before Tsibliev had picked them up in the other plane, but he wasn't going to tell this whiner that. "They could have done it in four or five days, if they'd had to. Maybe less."

"Oh. I guess five hours in an open boat isn't that bad, if you put it that way."

"Besides, if we hadn't made that hike, we'd have never discovered your precious squidberries." They were about out of the water now. Tyrell took a few more steps onto dry land and said, "I hereby dub this Klaar Island."

"Did that a lot, did you? Naming geographic features after each other?" Jenkins said as they finished hauling the boat above the tide line and began to unload it.

"Hah, no. Mostly we assigned numeric or whimsical designations. What I just did is hardly official."

"Careful," Flint said, "names have a way of sticking."

∞ ∞ ∞

There was no sign of the boat as the aircar approached the channel separating the big island from the tip of the peninsula. That probably meant they'd made it through safely. Blake had confidence in Retta Flint's skills.

Sure enough, as they flew over the hilly backbone of the island, the bright orange inflatable came into view on the beach. It looked like the crew had just finished unloading. Blake grinned.

He slowed the aircar to a hover as he reached the beach about twenty meters from the boat and landed with a spray of sand. As the rotors spun down he heard muttered shouts from Flint and company about being blasted with grit.

Blake and Reyes climbed out, and as Blake secured the aircar, Flint said, "Welcome to Klaar Island."

Blake looked at her, then at Tyrell. "Oh?"

Flint turned to Tyrell and grinned. "I warned you."

"I need to learn to watch what I say," Tyrell said as he came over to speak to Blake. "Anyway, you're timing is perfect, but if you're going to be flying in and out of here much, we're going to want to make a landing pad to keep the sand down."

"Out of what?" Blake asked. "We could lay leaves or branches down, but they'll just get blown around too."

"You have fabbers back on the ship. Could they make a mat, a woven mesh? That rayon you were talking about?"

Blake nodded. "I suppose. I'll talk to Fenety, our engineer. I guess we should have brought a plane after all."

"Has he looked at our old electroplane, EP02? Figured out what it would take to make that flyable?"

"Not yet. We had other issues to deal with this morning." At Tyrell's raised eyebrow, Blake added: "A minor plumbing issue. Nothing serious, but that's why we're late. I'll fill you in later." He grabbed a bag from behind the seats. "Anyway, let's get the rest of the gear out of the aircar."

∞ ∞ ∞

With the camp assembled, there were still several hours of daylight left, enough to reconnoiter Squidberry Inlet, as they now called it, by boat. Blake and Reyes joined them.

It was another forty minutes from the island to the mangrove swamp, homing on the beacon Blake and Tyrell had left the day before. They could see others patches of mangrove, but until they'd secured samples of known squidberries they'd focus on those first.

There wasn't much beach on either side of the creek to pull the boat up, so Flint reduced the throttle and maneuvered upstream. "Is there anywhere to put ashore?" she asked Blake and Tyrell.

"We couldn't see much of the creek through the canopy," Blake said. "Tyrell?"

"Not that I recall, but forty or fifty meters in, the creek is only knee-deep. You can tie up to the trees."

"No carnivorous fish to worry about?"

"Not that Ulrika and I encountered, at least nothing big or numerous enough to bother us. Of course, we weren't here for long, so I'd keep an eye out."

"Fair enough," said Flint.

Blake examined the tree branches overhead. If there had been any tree squid, they had scattered at the approach of the boat. There were clusters of berries, though. Perfect. He looked over the branching trunks of the mangroves and the thick aerial trunks of the vines, or banyans, or whatever they were that the berries were growing on. There were plenty of hand and foot holds.

"So, you guys just climbed up into the branches?" Cooper Reyes asked.

"Yeah," Tyrell said. "By then, we'd slogged through so much different vegetation we weren't worried about whatever the local equivalent of poison ivy might be. Maybe we were lucky. The branches were certainly strong enough."

Blake came to a decision. "All right, fair enough for now. We may want safety harnesses, or a pole-and-hook to reach, before filling the barrels. It'd be embarrassing to have someone break something falling out of a tree."

"Good point," said Tyrell.

"There's plenty of rope," Flint said. "We can rig temporary harnesses from that." She gestured to a coil of rope on the deck near the bow. "We can spare a few meters."

"All right. We'll take it in shifts. Two in the trees and two in the boat. We'll cut bunches of the berries and toss them down.

Cooper, if you want to look around to get a feel for what a proper squidberry grove looks like, go ahead." Identifying other groves would be largely Reyes's responsibility. "Don't get lost."

"Ha, not likely."

Flint found an area where the tree roots gave her enough clearance to get the boat in close to a large tree trunk, one that had aerial roots wrapped around it to make climbing easy.

She tossed one end of a line to Jenkins. "Hop out and secure us to the tree."

"Roger that." Jenkins climbed over the tubular side of the boat and slid into the water, which indeed barely came to his knees. The inflatable had a very shallow draft.

"All right, I want to go see what all the fuss is about," Blake said. "Tyrell, Reyes, care to join me?"

∞ ∞ ∞

The labyrinth of branches and roots actually made the climb easy; there were plenty of places to grab hold or place a foot. In others, it was almost too crowded; the tangle in places grew so close together that they had to go around. At one point, Blake found himself hanging from hands and feet, monkey-like, beneath a branch. His grip was solid, but he was still thankful for the harness and the rope tied to it and draped over a higher branch, being belayed by Jenkins in the boat a few meters upstream.

"Don't tell me you and Ulrika did this for a few berries," Blake said.

"We found an easier place to climb, and Ulrika was so fascinated by the tree squids that she just kept crawling. There were more berries then too, I think. Or maybe I'm misremembering. It has been over four years."

"Huh." By now Blake had reached the cluster of berries he'd being going for. It looked very much like several large bunches of small white grapes. The berries were actually a pale yellow, but with a powdery surface coating that made them look more whitish. *This must be the yeast they want*, Blake realized. Some of the berries were starting to turn brown and wrinkle.

"Didn't you say the squids were eating fermented berries? I don't think these are as ripe yet. Maybe that's why there aren't any squids, not enough booze in the berries."

"Ha!" Tyrell barked a short laugh. "You may be right. Or they've already eaten all the good ones."

"We'll have to spend some time studying the growing cycle of these things." Blake had pulled himself around so he was lying on top of the branch, his legs still wrapped around it, while he worked on cutting bunches of berries free. He held a bunch in his left hand while cutting through the stem with a knife, careful to keep his weight centered over the branch.

"Ahoy below, more berries for you!" he called when he freed a couple of bunches.

Flint had a large, long-handled net, the kind used to land fish, and held it outstretched beneath Blake. "Ready."

Blake tossed the berries into the net. "Three points!"

"You're too close, that's only two points." Jenkins said.

"I get an extra point for making the shot from a tree."

"If you say so. Not that anyone's keeping score."

By now Flint had transferred the berries from the net to the collection barrel. "If I hadn't moved the net to catch them, you wouldn't have scored anything," she said.

Blake started to protest, then thought better of it. "Actually, with that net it's more like lacrosse. What do I score for that?"

"You get an assist," Flint said. "I dunked it. But I have no idea on the score. That there was the closest I've ever come to lacrosse."

Tyrell, who was wedged into the fork of a tree branch, called from behind Blake. "If you guys are through with your sportsball game, don't we have more berries to collect?"

"Roger that," Blake said, and began to crawl along the branch to another cluster. "Haul that barrel ashore, I don't want to keep crawling back out over the boat."

∞ ∞ ∞

After another half-hour, they had one of the large barrels half-filled and had the harvesting technique down to where their speed had considerably improved. Blake called a halt.

"We're just hitting our stride!"

"Yes, but I want to get a batch back with Cooper tonight."

"And I'd rather not be flying in the dark," Reyes said. "We still need to get back to the aircar at the campsite, and that's across the bay."

"I don't want to be at sea at night either, not until we're more familiar with this place," said Flint.

"All right." They climbed down out of the trees.

"Do we want to haul that back aboard?" Tyrell said, gesturing at the barrel.

"No need," Blake said. "We'd only have to drag it back the morning. But give me a small container's worth, though," said Blake.

"Right," Reyes said, "I didn't come all the way out here to go back empty-handed tonight. I've got work to do on that."

"Works for me." Jenkins reached in grabbed a bundle that he handed to Reyes, who put it in a large sample bag. Jenkins then picked up the barrel's lid and began fastening it on with a broad nylon band.

"Will that barrel be okay overnight?" Blake asked Tyrell.

"It should be. The only thing around here that we've seen that eats berries are the squids, and maybe birds. Neither should be able to get the lid off, nor would have any reason to."

"Fair enough. It does beat dragging it back and forth."

They shoved the bright yellow plastic barrel further back from the water, between the trees, far enough back that waves or tide wouldn't disturb it, but still visible from the Zodiac.

"These are going to be bloody heavy when they're full. I'm not looking forward to getting them in and out of the boat," Jenkins said.

"A couple of hundred kilos. You getting weak in your old age?" Blake grinned. Jenkins was in his early twenties, a decade or more younger than Blake.

"Yeah, but the gravity is higher here," Jenkins protested, also grinning.

"By less than three percent," Tyrell said, shaking his head. "Kids these days."

"When the debate club is quite ready," Flint said, "I'd like to cast off. Time's a wasting."

Tyrell turned to look up at the sky to the west, just visible through the branches towards the mouth of the creek. "Whoa, the sun's lower than I expected."

"You're not on Sawyer's World anymore. The day here is almost three hours shorter than what you're used to, remember?"

"Yeah. There's something to be said for a twenty-six-hour day."

A few minutes later, Flint had the Zodiac zooming at high speed across the bay toward Klaar Island. The name had stuck.

∞ ∞ ∞

The campsite, evening

Alpha Centauri B was nearing the western horizon when Cooper Reyes lifted off in the aircar, heading back to the Krechet Plateau with his bag of squidberries. It would be dusk before he got there, but the landing area was well lit, and if needed, the vehicle was quite capable of returning home without any input from a pilot, even in the dark.

None of the others were particularly sleepy, although they were all worn out from the days exertions. Everyone was still adjusting both to Kakuloa's 23-hour day, and the fact that the landing site's local time had been several hours off from the Earth-clock the ships had been keeping.

After a quick meal from the self-heating ration packs, they had gathered branches and driftwood to make a small bonfire on the beach.

"So where's Sol?" Jenkins asked, looking up at the sky, bright stars visible through large gaps in the sparse cloud cover.

The others all looked up and around. After a moment, Blake said "I have no clue, I'm not an astronomer. Flint? Tyrell?"

"I recognize constellations, they're not much different from Earth. But I'm not seeing one with an extra star. Fred?"

Tyrell looked up and around. A week earlier, back on Sawyer's World, it had been a night like this when they'd spotted the trio of ships in orbit. Earlier they had been pointing out stars to the kids. But the sky looked different here. He realized why.

"It's the wrong time of year here. Sol is an extra star in Cassiopeia, in fact we were looking at it when we spotted you in orbit. That was a surprise. But the seasons are different between here and Sawyer's World. The year there is nearly twice as long as here. I'm not exactly sure, but we're probably on nearly opposite sides of our respective suns. You'll have to give it a couple of months, or check from orbit."

"Cassiopeia. That's why I'm not seeing it," Flint said.

"If it's any consolation," Tyrell said, pointing to a very bright star rising above the bay, "that is Alpha Centauri A. Sawyer's World is orbiting that. It'll be bright enough to read by, and we're nearly at our furthest distance apart."

"How far is that?" asked Jenkins.

"What were you doing during training, sleeping?" Flint asked, amused.

"No. I know the numbers. Twenty-seven AU. What's that in the Solar System?"

"Almost as far as Neptune. At its closest it's no farther than Saturn. I imagine it's really bright then."

"There are two moons, right?" Jenkins said. "I only saw one last night."

"Big or small?" Tyrell had had other things on his mind the night before.

"Uh, big, I guess. Roughly the same as Earth's moon."

"Yes, that's the bigger one, Mahina Nui. The small one, Mahina'uku, probably rose later."

"What does it look like?"

"Well, it's obviously a moon, but it barely shows a disk. More like a pin head. Darwin and Sawyer said it's smaller than Phobos as seen from Mars, but bigger than Deimos. It's actually bigger than those, but further away."

"I haven't been to Mars, so that doesn't help."

"Me neither. Anyway, I've been away from here for a few years; I don't have the local lunar calendar memorized, so I can't tell you when it will rise."

"It should be in your omni," Blake said. "Did you get the download?"

"Yeah. I can check later. I just want to watch the sky."

"I hear that. It never gets old. There aren't many places on Earth where the sky gets this dark anymore—campfire and Alpha Centauri A notwithstanding."

The conversation dropped for a while as they lay on the sand looking at the sky and listening to the lap of waves on the beach.

Eventually Tyrell sat up and said: "I don't know about the rest of you, but I'm not planning on sleeping on the beach. There's a much nicer tent set up than what I had the last time I camped out on this planet, so I'm going to take advantage of it. Good night, folks."

The others stirred themselves and agreed with the sentiment. Blake checked that there was nothing flammable near the now-glowing coals of the campfire, and then joined the others.

Chapter 9: The Treaty of Alpha Centauri

Chitiri Resort Development Co., Earth

Parry Cohen looked up from his newsfeed when Lauren Hewitt arrived at the office.

"What do you know about the Treaty of Svalbard?" he asked her.

"Nothing at all. Should I know something?" she said.

"How about the Outer Space Treaty?"

"Thinking of going into international law?" Hewitt asked. "What's all this about?"

"'Going into'?" Parry echoed. "Do you know how much I get involved in international law when we develop a resort?" It was a lot, although usually it was more the local laws than actual international law.

"Isn't that what lawyers are for?" She walked over to the autochef to get coffee.

"They're for crossing T's and dotting I's. I have to know enough to tell them what I want. At the rates they charge I don't need them giving me lessons on what I can look up on the net."

"So, what is this all about?" she asked again.

"The *Endeavour* just got back from Alpha Centauri. Well, they're in the solar system; they'll be landing on the Moon for quarantine. I've been reading through the reports."

"Yes, the news said that they were in-system. Not only did the entire *Anderson* crew survive, they had kids! Isn't that wonderful? I can only imagine how happy they were when the *Endeavour* landed."

Cohen grinned. "Maybe not as happy as you think. They declared independence."

"They what? Can they even *do* that?"

"Interesting question. The talking heads are having a field day over it, of course. Apparently, there's nothing in the Outer Space Treaty that explicitly forbids it, because back when it was written nobody thought the matter would come up. Of course, if they go through with it, they might have to give up the four-plus years back-pay they're due."

"They must have something to trade, then."

"Information, for one," Parry said. "I don't know what else." But that was a good point. Or maybe they figured public sympathy would be on their side if it came to a challenge.

"What was that other treaty you mentioned? Svalberg?"

"Svalbard. It's an island north of Norway, in the Arctic Ocean." He'd had to look it up himself, although by now the talking heads on the new feeds would be cheerfully glossing over the details as they explained it to their subscribers.

"You are *not* thinking of a resort there. Unless the Arctic has suddenly warmed up a whole lot more than anyone expected?"

"What? No! The *Anderson* crew came up with a Treaty of Alpha Centauri based on the Treaty of Svalbard."

"Treaty with who? Who has the authority to agree to that?"

"That's the fun part. Nobody, and everybody."

She studied him for a moment. "Have you had your coffee yet? You're not making sense."

"Actually I am. The Outer Space Treaty says no nation can claim sovereignty over a space body, or words to that effect. So presumably that means no country has authority to approve or deny their claim. On the other hand, the Terran Union, the successor to the United Nations, *does* have authority in that regard, since they aren't a sovereign nation."

"Okay, so why this Treaty of Svalbard and not whatever treaty governs Antarctica?"

"Excellent question. The Antarctic Treaty limits what anyone can do on that continent. No mining, no agriculture—although that's kind of a moot point—no permanent residents. You can visit, do scientific studies, but that's it. On the other hand, the Treaty of Svalbard lets any signatory nation do pretty much whatever the hell they want, subject to Norwegian law—but it only lets Norway spend taxes collected there on supporting the islands themselves. They can't spend money collected in Svalbard on, say, building a new bridge in Oslo, or contributing to the general Norwegian welfare fund."

"Oh. *Oh.* That's brilliant. So, if somebody wants to emigrate to Alpha Centauri, or set up a mine there—"

"Or more to the immediate point, harvest local plants for their pharmaceutical properties," Cohen said, grinning and nodding.

"—then they have every right to. Or at least it would depend on Alpha Centauri law, whatever that is."

"Exactly."

"That makes too much sense. The *Union de Terre* will never approve it."

"Apparently Commodore Drake, senior representative of the *UDT* in the system at the time, already signed it. He may well face another court martial for that, but it takes the pressure off of the *UDT* representatives. None of them have to be the first to favor it."

"They'll repudiate it, though, won't they?"

"Some of the members will try, I'm sure. But others will have more sense, or be willing to listen to lobbyists. And just wait until the PR starts. Have you *seen* the pictures of the kids? They're adorable, and they were born on that planet. Would you take their home away?"

"But that's not—"

"That's *exactly* how it will be spun." It was certainly how Parry would spin it. "I'll bet you Centauri Pharmaceuticals has PR firms working on that campaign right now. The last thing they need, with all the money they have invested, is the *UDT* imposing something like the Antarctic Treaty or declaring that any money

CentPharm makes of their drugs is 'the common heritage of mankind'."

"No wonder you're smiling. Your chances of building your New Noronha, or whatever you want to call it, just went up. If you live that long."

"Not that name. But who knows? Maybe the rumors of Cent-Pharm's anti-aging drug are true. Or maybe it will become possible a lot sooner than you think. If there's money to be made, people will follow. And where there's people, there are people who want to take a vacation."

"Now you're starting to sound like ad copy. And speaking of that, I've got the revised layouts for the new hotel to review."

"Ah, right. Back to work." As he turned back to his desk, a poster on the wall caught his eye. It was an ad for a combination hotel and casino he'd opened a few years earlier. He smiled. He was willing to bet that it would be a long time before the Alpha Centauri government, whatever it turned out to be, got around to imposing laws about gambling. Or laws about any number of other things, for that matter.

Chapter 10: Berry Harvest

Kakuloa, Squidberry Bay

They left camp shortly after first light the next morning. Squidberry Inlet was still deep in shade when the big Zodiac hummed up the creek.

"Where's the barrel?" Blake asked, looking for it.

Flint had been focused on maneuvering the boat. She glanced up and left, towards the bank. "It should be there," she gestured, "by those trees." She went back to concentrate on bringing the boat in as close to the shore as she could.

"I'm not seeing it." Blake looked again. Since the morning sun was still behind the inland hills, it was dark between the trees, but not so dark that the bright yellow barrel wouldn't show up. He was sure they'd left it beside that tree there, with a banyan root curled into an S-shape.

"There it is," Jenkins said. "Looks like it fell over."

Blake looked where Jenkins pointed. Sure enough, there was a glimpse of yellow behind two tree trunks.

"That's weird. Does the tide come up that high?"

"I wouldn't have thought so," Tyrell said. "Not without a storm surge, and it was calm last night. Maybe the bay makes for a strange tide here? It's not like we were ever in this spot long enough to worry about local tide tables."

While it was true that variations in coastal geography could make for fluke tides, especially in bays where they tended to focus and channel the water, but Blake didn't think that was the case here. Then he realized why not. "No, look, there are leaves and such growing nearer the ground. If the tide were ever that high they probably wouldn't grow there. Anyway let's get ashore."

By now Flint had the boat with its port side up against the bank, or rather a tree growing near the bank.

Jenkins jumped out and took the line to tie it off. While tying it, he said "Alien planet, alien biology? Maybe the leaves don't mind salt water."

"It's not that different," Tyrell said. "More likely an animal knocked the barrel over. Let's go see." He climbed out of the boat.

Blake was right behind him. "Did you see any animals big enough to do that? That barrel was heavy. I don't remember any-thing like that in your reports."

"Not close up. We did see a few large animals from a dis-tance, or caught them on camera. Not here in the mangroves though. Might be something nocturnal."

By now they'd made their way around the trees to where the barrel lay on its side. The lid was off. Blake spotted it a few me-ters away. The barrel itself was empty, with only a few stems and juice stains to show that it had been half full of squidberries the evening before.

Blake uttered a curse. "What the? Something stole our berries!" He looked sharply at Jenkins. "I told you to make sure the lid was secure!"

Jenkins shook his head. "I did! Put the lid on, put the snap band around it. Checked it. It was solid!"

"Maybe it came off when something knocked over the bar-rel?" Tyrell said, half-asking.

"It wouldn't if it had been put on right," Blake said, still glar-ing at Jenkins.

"It was." Jenkins pointed at the lid, a few meters away past a tree. "And it wouldn't have ended up over there if it had just fallen off when the barrel tipped."

Blake looked at the lid, and at the barrel. Jenkins had a point. He walked over to the lid and picked it up. It was scratched, but otherwise intact. Where was the band? The lid secured to the bar-rel with a wide nylon strap that clamped it to the lip of the barrel, then latched with a lever mechanism. A band clamp. It would take something with dextrous fingers and reasonable strength to open the clamp. He looked around for it.

"Anyone see the locking strap?" The others started looking around for it. "Tyrell, would the squids be strong enough to un-latch it?"

"That assumes they'd even have a reason to. But I don't know. Their tentacles can be strong but without bones I'm not sure they'd have the leverage. You think it was tree squids?"

"I don't know what to think, but so far as we know they're the only animal around that eats the berries. I know octopus can be smart, do you suppose these things are?"

"I have no idea. You'd have to ask Ulrika, but it's not like we studied them very closely or very long."

"Found it!" Flint's call came from behind another tree. She reached down and picked something up, then held it up. It was the locking strap. The clamp was still locked shut. But the nylon strap itself had two ragged edges, like it had been torn or chewed through.

"Let me take a look at that," Blake said, as Flint brought the strap over. The tough plastic locking clamp was indeed still closed, although there were several scratches and gouges on it. The strap itself showed signs of having been chewed on or clawed at, with the marks concentrated around where the strap had parted. Blake took a piece of the strap between two hands and tugged experimentally, then pulled hard. It held.

Blake handed the strap to Tyrell. "What do you make of that?"

Tyrell repeated the same tugging that Blake had. "It's cer-tainly strong enough. It didn't break by itself." He looked at the rest of the strap, and the clamp. "Quite a few scratches. This is new gear, right?"

"Yes, it wasn't scratched up like that yesterday."

Tyrell examined them closer. "Claw marks? Tooth marks? This is almost something a bear might do, except that a bear could probably open up the side of the barrel with a swipe of its claws."

"Yeah, that was my thought," Blake said. "Whatever it was probably smelled the berries inside. Your landing teams didn't see any bears, did they?"

"No. Ulrika and I joked about it during our hike from the crash site, but we never saw anything like that, or any signs of that."

"The tree squids, the octopus, they don't have claws, do they? Or teeth?"

"No." Tyrell started to shake his head then stopped and looked straight at Blake, frowning. "They have beaks."

"Beaks?" Jenkins said, disbelieving. "Like birds?"

"Tyrell's right," Flint said. "On Earth, squids and octopus have beaks."

"Yeah. As for what bird beaks can do, take a look at a parrot," Blake said.

"No need," Jenkins said, holding up his hand. "I have personal experience, remember? Oh, wait, you weren't there."

"Where?" Blake asked, puzzled.

"We stopped ashore for lunch on the way up yesterday," Flint said. "Dusty here thought it might be a good idea to feed the birds. They got greedy."

"You should have told me. You okay?"

"It was no big deal," Jenkins said. "Just a nip. And my fault."

"All right, but in future anything like that should be reported. If your hand swells up or you keel over from toxic shock, we'll want to know what to avoid."

Jenkins eyes grew wide. "What? Do you think...oh, I get it."

Blake tried, unsuccessfully, to suppress his grin at the younger man's expression.

"Very funny."

"Well, I'm kidding and I'm serious," Blake said. "Even on Earth there are still a few dangerous critters. So be careful."

"Copy that. So what do we do about the squidberries?" Jenkins said, changing the subject.

Blake sighed and righted the barrel. "We get to work and pick more. And from now on we don't leave them unattended. Looks like maybe the tree squids can chew through the straps. I wonder what else they can do."

Chapter 11: Road Trip

Kakuloa, Squidberry Creek

Blake was still helping with the harvest, although this time from the ground, when his omni chirped. They were out of direct range from Krechet's Landing, but the satellite constellation they'd left in orbit could relay the signal. He checked the screen; it was Jim Fenety.

"Blake here. What's the problem?"

"Not exactly a problem, at least I hope not. I found something unusual in the data being relayed from the GPS satellites."

"Unusual how? And which data?" Blake didn't know whether Fenety meant the positioning data or the images and other sensor information. The former could be serious, the latter just puzzling.

"Sorry, the image data. The computers tripped on a linear feature."

"Rivers are linear features. What's special about this one?" Blake said.

"It's a straight line."

"What? Show me."

"Sending." Fenety uploaded the image to Blake's omni, together with its coordinates.

Blake opened the file. The image showed part of a coastline. It wasn't anywhere near here, as far as he could tell from the vegetation and the fact that the water was to the east of the shore, not the west, although that could just mean it was part of a bay. No, the coordinates suggested a considerable distance north and east of here. But there was no linear feature except the beach, and not even that. He zoomed in. Wait, what was that? There *was* something, a faint light line crossing the beach at an angle, extending into the water at one end and the tree cover at the other. If it weren't for the scale, Blake might have dismissed it as a random micrometeor trail the camera happened to catch from overhead, but this wasn't that. Probably just some geological feature, like the dike damming Toothpick Lake that Tyrell had pointed out.

"That *is* weird. Probably nothing, but have the satellites take more pictures of that area when their orbits take them overhead. Speaking of which, we'll probably lose our connection soon."

"Roger that, sir. About fifteen more seconds. I'll make the programming change you want. Anything else?"

"Not for now. I'll take a look when we get back. Blake out." He shook his head as he disconnected. *Just so long as it's not some alien landing strip*, he thought, then chuckled at the idea.

Krechet Plateau, two days later

The barrels were filled, at least to the point where they were almost too heavy to get into the boat, and the team had returned back to Krechet's Landing the night before. Fred Tyrell looked forward to returning home to Sawyer's World. *Home*, he thought. *Funny that I think of it that way now. But that's where my family and friends are.*

Will Blake came up to him as he finished packing his gear. "Doctor Tyrell," Blake said, "I'd like to take you on a little side trip today. You're the only geologist we have at the moment."

"I thought I was going home today. The *Vostok* is ready to leave."

"We'll be taking *Vostok*. We're going to be making a stop before heading to space."

"So out of range of the fliers, then. Where and why?"

"We spotted something on the orbital photographs that I want to take a closer look at. An odd geological formation. At least I hope that's all it is."

"Something the first expedition didn't pick up? We mapped the place pretty thoroughly from orbit."

"Higher latitude than most of your coverage. Also, different sun angles and cloud cover. I went back and looked at the images from *Heinlein*. They show it, but not clearly. There was no reason to take a second look until now."

"So far, you've avoided telling me what exactly you want to take a look at, and where."

"Other side of this continent, and about twenty degrees further north. As for what," Blake pulled a data pad out of his pocket and unfolded it, then handed it to Tyrell. "Take a look."

Tyrell took the pad and studied the image. It was clearly an overhead shot, from orbit. The image was highly zoomed in, showing a stretch of coast. There was a linear structure extending from inland, where it was concealed by vegetation, out into the water until the water was too deep to see it clearly. On Earth, it might be an old quay, or submerged road. "What the...?"

Tyrell zoomed the image in further, but it only made the pixels bigger. He compared the shadows of trees near the feature. It was perhaps five meters wide, and at least a hundred long before being obscured at either end.

"Probably a volcanic dike. They often form linear features. There's one forming a dam for Toothpick Lake north of here. Although they're not usually flat on top."

"Yeah. That was my first thought too, and I'm no geologist. Look at the next picture."

Tyrell glanced up at Blake, then back at the data pad, and swiped it to the next image. This was from a slightly different angle, and with more detail. Either taken with a telescopic lens or in a lower orbit. The dike, or whatever it was, showed a smooth upper surface divided into rectangular sections. They were different sizes, and a few were irregularly shaped, but still gave the impression of large paving stones. Tyrell looked for signs of what the rock might be made of. "What's the surrounding province? Igneous, sedimentary, or metamorphic?"

"Hard to tell, between the vegetation and the ocean. No obvious volcanoes or basalt plains nearby. There are hills, they could be granite or limestone, they're all tree covered. Like I said, I'm no geologist."

"This is the eastern coast?"

"Yes. What do you remember of the geology?"

"Not enough, damn it. Too many years ago. So you want to go take a closer look?"

"That's the idea."

"Is there somewhere to land the ship?"

"A kilometer away. Easy walking distance."

"I'd love to have Sawyer and Finley here," Tyrell said, referring to the other two geologists on the first expedition. "Twenty degrees further north? That would have been out of our landing range anyway. Of course, it's probably just a Bimini road."

"*Just* a road?"

"Not a real road. There's a feature on the island of Bimini on Earth, in the Bahamas. It looks very much like this. It stirred up all sorts of Atlantis stories, or tales of ancient Roman outposts. But it's really a soft limestone with natural faulting that happens to look like a road. At least, that's what I've read about it. I've never visited it. It's mostly underwater."

"Oh."

Tyrell wasn't sure if Blake sounded disappointed or relieved. Perhaps a bit of both. "But sure. If you've got a good place to land and it's an easy hike, we can take a look."

∞ ∞ ∞

Three hours later the *Vostok* descended over the shoreline where the road, or whatever it was, jutted into the sea.

Tyrell watched a magnified view on the screen. "I'm not seeing much in the way of limestone in the surrounding area, but it's hard to tell with this vegetation. I'd say there haven't been many recent geological changes, though. Fjords are well to the north, whenever the last ice age was it didn't come through here. Probably."

"How does the landing zone look?"

Tyrell panned the image around. There were a few short scrubby trees in the field, and some fallen trunks, silver with age. But there was enough of the right kind of low vegetation to be confident that it was dry land and not swamp.

"I think we're okay. The ground might be kind of soft. Also, watch out for branches sticking up from those downed trees."

"*Nyet problem*," Tsibliev said. "I will hover for a while to blow anything loose away, and landing gear has good clearance."

He followed words with actions, and the blast from the ventral jets sent up clouds of dust and super-heated steam, scorching the scrubby vegetation. The ship settled slowly, hesitating for a moment, then dropping the last half meter with a THUMP. He shut the jets and the roaring faded.

"What was that last?"

"Port landing skid crushing log. It's tough, *nyet problem*."

Tsibliev then picked up a mic and announced, "Secure from flight." Then he turned to his XO. "Sergei, as soon as it's cool, go out and check landing area."

He turned to Blake. "We will give it a few minutes for things to cool down. I put out extra heat in the down-jets to burn anything off."

"All right," Blake said. "Tyrell, let's gear up. We've got six or seven hours of daylight left, that should be plenty of time."

∞ ∞ ∞

The vegetation here was more temperate forest than the subtropical of the original landing area, with a mix of evergreen and deciduous trees. The latter weren't like anything they recognized, most of the trees having a leaf shaped something like a cross between an oak and maple.

"Interesting trees," Blake said. "I wonder what the wood is like?"

"Take samples," Tyrell suggested. "Leaves, twigs, whatever it has for seeds, if you can find them." It was still summer, but with the year here being shorter, there might be seeds. "Nobody brought a chainsaw?"

"No, but there should be something at the ship." Blake called Tsibliev to have him send a couple of people out with tools to get wood samples. "Just a slice off a branch, don't have them cut down a whole tree. If it looks worthwhile we'll send a properly equipped team out later."

"Da. Roger that."

"Thinking of going into the lumber business?" Tyrell said. "We had pretty good wood at Camp Anderson. Maclaren even managed to rig up a sawmill. That's how we made our cabins, and the aqueduct."

"We may want a good local source of building materials. This place is too far from Krechet's Landing or the squidberry groves, Maybe we can find something like it closer," Blake said. "Although it is a whole lot closer than Earth."

"How much further to the beach?"

Blake checked his omni. The GPS system they'd put in orbit still had minor gaps, but between what there was and the tracking signal from *Vostok*, it would do for this short trek.

"We should see it in another couple of hundred meters." He gestured at a slight angle to their path. "That direction."

They came to the road before the beach, at where it emerged from under the soil and scrub. There were loose leaves and dirt blown over it, but it was clearer closer to the sand and rocks of the beach.

"Found it!" Tyrell said, as he stopped and stooped down to examine it. "At least it's not made of yellow brick."

The stone was mostly a pale grey, fine grained and worn smooth. It did look suggestive of paving stones, with slight rounding of the rock at the joints or cracks where it had preferentially worn, and dirt and sand in between. Tyrell bent right down and sighted along the stones, his head touching the ground.

"Well?" Blake asked.

"The good news is, I don't see any wheel ruts." He grinned. "Nor did I hear a train coming."

"But is it natural or artificial?"

"I'm not even sure what kind of rock it is yet, but I don't think it's igneous. It looks more like limestone than granite, but it's not that. Pretty sure this isn't a volcanic dike." He took out his hammer—it had cleaned up nicely—and scratched at the stone with the pick end. It left a slight mark. "Softer than steel." He stood up. "Let's see where it goes."

They followed the structure down onto the beach to where it angled into the water. Tyrell strode out on it until the water lapped around his ankles, not bothering to take his boots off. The rock was more worn, and the gaps between blocks wider, as he got further out in the water.

"Well?" Blake asked.

"It's surprisingly straight. Did you extrapolate the path out?"

"Yeah, it didn't seem to go anywhere. No islands or anything."

"What about inland?" Tyrell wondered.

"Ah, no. Nothing but forest."

"You've got radar aboard? You can scan through the vegetation?"

"Yes, why? Do you think there's something there to find?"

"Well, the thing of it is, I'm pretty sure this is a carbonate, some sort of limestone," Tyrell said. "But it's out of place. For it to be straight, it should be a horizontal bed. There could be folding, which tilted the layer up on its edge, but right now I'm not seeing obvious signs of that. Or maybe there was a layer of sandstone above and below and that's eroded to this beach sand and whatever is under those trees. But that's a maybe. And this doesn't look like limestone that's been tipped over sideways." He waded back onto the beach and hammered at the corner of a stone, breaking a piece off. He held it up and examined it closely. It had grains, but too small to make out clearly. *I'm getting farsighted. I didn't think I was that old.* He tapped the omni on his wrist and held the rock up to its camera, then looked at the enlarged image on its screen. There were small grains of darker material in the pale gray matrix, dark green and black. *Interesting.*

"The thing is," he continued, pocketing the rock, "on Earth, odds are there'd be fossils, even if only bits of shell, in most limestones. We only find that here in limestone less than sixty or so million years old. Earth years."

"Okay, sure."

"What bothers me, is how there's any limestone older than that. We think—at least, the conclusion the first expedition geology team came to—that the bulk of the oceans were formed about the same time this planet was terraformed. Most of the water came from somewhere else. So there shouldn't be any limestone older than that."

"Do you need life to form limestone?"

Tyrell paused, considering the question. Under the right circumstances... "No, but it is more difficult. And you *do* need water. You can get other carbonates, like oolites, or travertine around hot springs, but that's not what this is. Maybe we were wrong about when the ocean formed." Tyrell knew he was simplifying his answer, but he didn't think it mattered to what he suspected the rock might be. "The thing is," Tyrell continued, "from what I recall, the original Bimini road is mainly beachrock, a kind of loosely consolidated limestone made of crushed shells cemented together with carbonate. It erodes quickly, and the Bimini stones are only a few thousand years old, although they look much older. This is nothing like that."

"So, back to my question. Natural or artificial?"

"No frigging clue. Well, that's not quite true. For this to be artificial, somebody would have had to build it. It wasn't us, and it wasn't the ancient spear-point makers from Sawyer's World, at least not likely. Unless there's other evidence of local intelligent life here at some point, I'd say natural." He paused, remembering Blake's earlier disappointment. "Although if you're trying to attract tourists, you can keep it mysterious."

Blake shook his head. "No thanks, I'd just as soon not attract that kind of crowd yet. Natural it is."

Tyrell didn't mention what Elizabeth Sawyer had said she'd seen a few months after the *Anderson* first landed. It might have been nothing, and even if not, why would spacefaring aliens be building crude stone roads? This couldn't have been their home planet. "I *would* like to do more research into how it formed." He pulled the rock sample out of his pocket to look at it again. "I have suspicion that this isn't sedimentary at all. I could be wrong about it not being a dike."

"But granite is harder than steel, isn't it? And pink?"

"Granite is harder than steel, yes. There is white granite, but that's not what this is. Do we have any hydrochloric acid back at

the ship? Or even vinegar? I want to test this." If it contained carbonate, the acid would fizz as it released carbon-dioxide.

"Probably not; we weren't planning any geology exploration
yet. Cooper might have something in his kit, back on *Victoria*.
Shall I call?"

Tyrell shook his head. "No need. I want to go home and see
my wife and kids. We've got vinegar back at Camp Anderson, the
result of a failed wine-making experiment."

Blake laughed. "Fair enough. I'm anxious to get back to
Earth myself."

"I thought you were staying here?"

"I'll be back in a few weeks. *Victoria* is staying here. I need to
get the samples back to CentPharm and organize the next phase.
Your time of being alone in this system is over, I'm afraid. *Endeavour* should be back on Luna by now. That's going to be big
news. *Vostok* will be back there a week after we drop you off. I
don't know how soon *Endeavour* will turn around, but there will
probably be a ship coming out here every couple of weeks from
now on. Maybe more here than Sawyer's World."

"Well, there goes the neighborhood," Tyrell said with a smile.
"Of course, if this rock is what I think it is, it's going to get
worse, too."

"Oh? What is it?"

"There *is* a kind of carbonate rock that's igneous, not sedimentary. And it usually forms dikes. Carbonatite."

"Okay, and what's special about carbonatite?"

"Because along with sodium and calcium, it also comes with a
whole laundry list of other elements, often in useful quantities."

"Such as?"

"Oh, stuff like rare earth elements, copper, fluorine, phos-
phorus, titanium, niobium, thorium, uranium, and zirconium," he
rattled off. "Among others. Some of those don't show up in useful quantities in asteroids; they need planetary-sized geochemical
processes to concentrate them. Depending how this assays out,
somebody might want to set up a mining and refining operation
here. For in-system industries, anyway. Probably not worth shipping to Earth." Also, Tyrell realized, there *weren't* many asteroids

in the Alpha Centauri system. The multiple suns made orbits at the distance of Sol's asteroid belts unstable.

Blake had stopped and turned to Tyrell. By now they were a short way back into the forest, near where the "road" disappeared under the soil. "Could I borrow your hammer? Or could you break off a few more chunks of that for me? I think I want to take some samples back to Earth."

Tyrell grinned. "Sure. I'll do it."

A few minutes later, Tyrell gave Blake a double-handful of rock fragments from different parts of the road. "That should do you. Don't forget where you found them." It was sloppy practice; normally Tyrell would have insisted on separately documenting each sample and the precise location it came from. Instead, he settled for Blake taking a few pictures with his omni. This wasn't a normal field trip.

"Thanks," Blake said. "Come on, let's get you back to your family. You might as well enjoy the peace and quiet while you can." He turned and headed back towards the ship.

Tyrell fell in beside him. "Peace and quiet?" he said, then laughed. "You haven't met my kids."

Chapter 12: The Return of Franklin Drake

Skrellan Pharmaceuticals, Earth

The desk speaker announced: "*Ms. Holmes, there's a call from Commodore Drake for you.*"

"Thank you. Put him through," Victoria Holmes said. Her assistant passed the call through to Holmes's omni. "Franklin, welcome back. I take it your mission was a success? And did you bring me some more squidberries?"

"Victoria, it's good to hear your voice. Yes, my mission was a success. The entire crew survived, with a bonus: five kids. Dr. McFadyen wondered if it might be something in the environment."

"I should have someone check that out. And the berries?"

"Should be about a week behind me aboard *Vostok*, along with Dr. Krysansky and Will Blake."

"Good to hear. So now, tell me why you really called."

"I'm hurt. I still owe you dinner. Can't I call to offer you a chance to collect?"

Holmes snorted. "You have a habit of only talking to me when you need something from me. You're still in quarantine on the Moon, aren't you?" She knew he was from the delays in the conversation.

"I'll be on Earth in just over a week. I'm planning ahead." There was a brief pause, but no indication that his end had stopped transmitting. "But now that you mention it..."

"Aha! I knew it. What is it this time?"

"Something you should find useful. Are you aware of the political situation with respect to Alpha Centauri?"

"You mean Sawyer's team declaring independence? So long as that doesn't affect Kakuloa, why should I be interested?"

"Because the Treaty of Alpha Centauri *does* affect Kakuloa. Or at least, you probably want it to."

"Why? The Outer Space Treaty already gives us the right to harvest resources from it."

"But it doesn't do much to protect you from claim jumpers. Nor does it give you any way to incentivize your berry farmers by way of, say, land grants."

"Berry farmers? Aren't you getting ahead of yourself?" They hadn't yet confirmed that the cephalomycin was a useful anti-aging drug. Although they would need a regular supply for all the necessary trials, and if it did prove out, they would need to greatly expand farming on the planet. Drake might be on to something.

"You don't want that door closed before you get there. There's some talk of the *Union de Terre* not only repudiating the Alpha Centauri Treaty, but the Outer Space Treaty as well."

"What about the deal with us, with Centauri Pharmaceuticals?"

"*Our* government will stand by it," Drake said. "Some members of the *UDT* are talking about resurrecting the *common heritage* clause from the defunct Moon Treaty. They may let you produce the drug, but they'll tax all your profits away."

Holmes knew it wouldn't be that easy. The *UDT* itself had no direct taxing authority, that was up to the member nations. But it would make international sales a nightmare. She sighed and rubbed her forehead with her fingertips. *Politics!*

"And the Treaty of Alpha Centauri stops this how?" she said.

"It recognizes Sawyer's World independence and treats Kakuloa essentially as neutral territory administered by Sawyer's World. The latter makes sense, it's only a few light-hours away instead of four-plus light-years."

"And what do you get out of it?" There had to be something.

"Well, it would make it much less likely I'll be court-martialed for signing the damn treaty in the first place."

"*What?* You signed...on what authority?"

"It was a *UDT* mission. I was the commanding officer, therefore also the senior representative of the *UDT*. Also," Drake said, "I had to ask for permission to land."

That was a story she wanted to hear. "All right, tell you what, I'll buy *you* dinner if you promise to tell me the details behind that."

"Deal, but there's more."

"I'm listening."

"If you like the Treaty, you're going to want to mobilize your political connections to ensure it gets ratified. And to help you understand the treaty, I brought back an expert."

"What, who?" Any news regarding the *Anderson* crew had mostly focused on the fact that they'd had five children among them, and that they wouldn't be returning immediately because of concerns about the effects of deep space travel on rapidly growing infants. The latter was probably safe, but nobody had foreseen a need to include a pediatrician in the *Endeavour*'s crew.

"Elizabeth Sawyer. I had to bring somebody back, and it made most sense to bring her. And speaking of that, I might need some additional political help to make sure she doesn't get arrested. Some people aren't happy about the team declaring independence."

Holmes shook her head. "Do you ever do things the easy way, Frank?"

"I prefer to do them the *right* way," he said in all seriousness.

"*Touché*. Okay, I appreciate the heads-up about the Treaty, but it sounds like I'll be doing you a favor too."

"So what do you want in return?"

"Oh, don't sound so wary. You'll like the idea." She gave it a moment, then said: "When can we get ships with more cargo space? The three you've got are kind of cramped, aren't they?"

"They are, but I'm not the person to ask for bigger ships. You're right, I do like the idea, but it's not up to me. And you know that. So why are you asking?"

"You did a great job overseeing the development of the *Endeavour*-class. If there were a program to develop larger ships, or even the same size ship but with more interior volume given over to cargo, would you be willing to help manage it?"

"I was the Assistant Director. Admiral Howard was the lead."

"And we both know you did most of the grunt work; you were motivated. What do you think, is it doable?"

"If we can make the engines or reactors more efficient, we can shrink the fuel tanks," Drake said. "But starting that project is a big if...or is it?"

"Call me when you're back on Earth. Let's do dinner. And let's invite Elizabeth Sawyer along too. I'd like to meet her."

"Uh, roger that."

As Victoria Holmes disconnected the call, she pondered what Drake had said. He certainly gave her interesting problems. She wondered if anyone on Skrellan's legal team had any experience with the Outer Space Treaty, or any treaties for that matter. There must be somebody; Skrellan was a multinational company.

She picked up her omni again. "Get me Legal."

Chapter 13: Reassignment

Washington, DC

The summons to Admiral Howard's office didn't surprise Franklin Drake. Holmes had dropped additional hints about it at dinner with him and Sawyer.

"You wanted to see me, Sir?"

"Frank, welcome back. Congratulations on recovering the *Anderson* crew, even if you didn't bring them all back with you."

"There were, uh, complications," Drake said, seating himself at Howard's gesture toward a chair.

"Five of them, right? That's amazing. Sawyer deserves another promotion for keeping them alive and thriving all those years. Not that she'd get one with that independence stunt."

Drake started to say something, but Howard cut him off. "Don't say it. Off the record, I think they did the right thing. It set a nice precedent, and better to do it now rather than in fifty or a hundred years where it might call for some kind of revolution. But you didn't hear that from me, and it's not what I want to talk to you about."

"What did you want to talk about, Sir?"

"You did a great job putting getting *Endeavour* and her sister ships completed on a compressed schedule. They're a fine class of ship, but we need something bigger."

"Making the warp field bigger cuts the efficiency. Eventually you can't hold enough fuel to make up for it. But you know that."

"The boys and girls at Jackass Flats are working on improvements to the power systems and warp modules. That will overcome some of the efficiency losses. We need ships with more range, and I know CentPharm wouldn't mind ships with bigger cargo bays. What do you think, would the same hull work for both?"

Drake considered the question. The shape of the hull was driven first by warp field geometry, and second, if it was intended to land and take-off from an Earth-like planet, by aerodynamics. The *Endeavour* class deltoid was a good compromise, and there was room for improvement. That dorsal warp pod didn't really need to stick up like that, that had been a last-minute fix for some warp instability issues. If the upper deck were raised to enclose the warp module, that would add cargo—or fuel—space right there. As for the admiral's specific question, Drake didn't see a reason that volume couldn't be designated as either cargo or fuel tankage. It was just a matter of adding cargo hatches or tank insulation. Liquid deuterium would be less dense than virtually any cargo.

He told the admiral that. "So yes, that would work. How much extra range are you looking for?"

"At least twenty light-years."

"Twenty?" That was enough to go to Alpha Centauri and back twice, with fuel left over. And if there were terraformed worlds at any other destination, a ship could refuel there. Deuterium—heavy hydrogen—could be extracted from seawater.

"We might want to go someplace where there aren't likely to be terraformed planets," Howard said, guessing the reason behind Drake's puzzled expression.

"It should be possible to rig something to extract deuterium from an ice moon or comet." *Or even the atmosphere of a gas giant*, although Drake would happily leave that to younger pilots. "But why?"

"Just keeping our options open. I've got a couple of scientists who are curious about Sirius and Procyon. If they ever did have Earth-like planets, they'd have been roasted when their companions entered their red giant stage."

He was right. Sirius, the brightest star in Earth's night sky, was less than nine light-years from Earth, and had a white dwarf companion that had gone through a red giant phase a hundred million or so years ago. Procyon's companion had become a white dwarf a billion years before that. Procyon itself was a yellow-white F5 star, likely too hot and short-lived for the Terraformers to have had any interest; it would become a red-giant itself in another fifty million years, give or take. "So what is the scientists' interest? Trying to figure out if the Terraformers were ever there?"

"No, not exactly." He looked as though he wanted to say more, but thought better of it. Then he said: "Your man Vukovich worked out at the Propulsion Research Lab at Jackass Flats, didn't he?"

"Yes, he was working on upgrades to the warp drive and fusion engine. Why?"

"Did he ever mention another scientist out there, a Doctor Lisa Delany?"

The name wasn't familiar. "If he did, I don't recall it. Why?"

"Never mind. No reason. Now, about this larger hulled ship..."

What was that all about? Drake wondered, only half listening as Admiral Howard went on about the new project. The admiral didn't mention things for no reason. Drake resolved to look up this Delany person when he had a chance, and find out what her field of research might be.

∞ ∞ ∞

When he did look her up, shortly after his meeting had concluded—and he'd accepted the job to oversee the new starship project—he understood the interest in Sirius or Procyon.

Not that Lisa Delany's background had anything to do with astrophysics as such, but if someone wanted to put her work to practical use, they would want somewhere with plentiful energy —such as rocky planet orbiting nearby bright star—and away from centers of human habitation. While Drake hadn't turned up anything on Delany's recent work, which was all classified, her PhD thesis had been on the synthesis and storage of antimatter.

Chapter 14: Lab Report

Skrellan Pharmaceuticals, Earth, a few weeks later

True to Frank Drake's word, a much larger batch of squid-berries arrived with the *Vostok*. The labs at Skrellan had been working with the extract as soon as it cleared quarantine.

"So, bottom line, what's the progress on the cephalomycin?" Victoria Holmes asked her head of research.

"Coming along nicely," Dennis Lodgson said. "The second batch of extract gave me a lot more to work with. I'm going back and doing the trials I skipped with the first batch, although that seems like a waste of time."

"You know the FDA will want to see our testing protocols. We can't skip steps."

"But we already know it works in mice." Lodgson had been so enthusiastic over his initial findings with microbial studies that he'd confirmed the anti-aging properties of the drug, in its pre-liminary crude form, in mice. If he hadn't, Skrellan might never have helped finance the expedition. "But I understand, the paper trail is important."

"So, the drug is worth pursuing?"

"Oh, absolutely. And aside from the squidberries, we've found a number of other potential useful biochemicals. Things we haven't found on Earth but fit into common metabolic path-ways. It's like we found a whole lost continent of new species."

"That's not a bad way of putting it. All right, I'll look over your detailed report. You included recommendations?"

"Yes. There's an appendix that lists all the useful biochemi-cals we've found, and which of those our partners know about, as far as we know. The main body covers the squidberry extract. I think we're going to want to set up a system of squidberry farms or plantations. Harvesting them in the wild isn't going to yield nearly enough for any kind of production scale up."

"What about growing them, or the fungus, on Earth? Or synthesizing the compound?"

Lodgson shook his head. "So far no success on either front. The compound has a complex structure that has no easy precursors. Partway into the synthesis process the molecule starts falling apart, or folding on itself in ways that poison the reaction. It's an organic chemist's nightmare."

Victoria shuddered at the thought. She'd had to take organic chem in college, and some of the labs had almost given *her* nightmares. She hated to think what would give someone who *understood* this stuff nightmares. "And growing it?"

"No luck. We've had limited success growing the berries themselves, under careful controlled lighting and mimicking the Kakuloa environment as closely as possible, controlling the atmosphere and the day length, but the fungus refuses to grow on Earth-raised squidberries. We're obviously missing something, but none of the grow team has any idea what."

Victoria sighed. "Very well, have them keep on it. But at that rate it might be just cheaper to import it from the source. Reproducing that environment doesn't scale easily."

Besides, she thought, after persuading the Board to pay for a long-term lease on a starship, she had better get some use out of it. And yes, bigger ships would be better, so long as they could get enough squidberries to fill the holds.

Part II - Squidberries

Two years later, 2076.

Chapter 15: The Squid Problem

Newton's Berry Plantation, at Squidberry Inlet

Dave Newton looked up from his desk as Rob McWhirter, his foreman, rapped on the door frame and entered. McWhirter's face had a dour expression, his hair was wild, and his trouser legs from the knees down dripped water.

"What's happened?" Newton asked.

"Och, it's the damned squids again," McWhirter said, running a hand through his hair. "The wee bastards hae been into the trees on the south-west lot. The berry crop is devastated. I swear those squids are getting smarter."

"What did they do this time? Find another way through the fences?"

Although capable of surviving out of water, and even climbing trees, the misnamed squids normally kept to the ocean, only swimming up the inlets to the roots of the trees when the berries were ripening. The plantations had fenced off the creek mouths to keep them out, resorting to ever finer meshes of fencing wire as it was discovered that the Kakuloan cephalopods had the same ability to squeeze through tiny openings as their distant terrestrial cousins.

"I dinnae ken. The screens we're using now have a smaller opening than chicken wire. Any smaller and we're going to start damming the river. I didnae see any tears or openings in it when I checked, by I've got my lads going over it with the proverbial fine-toothed comb. Maybe the squids found a gap, or a way under it. Och, maybe they figured out how to climb over it."

"That shouldn't be possible. There's nothing for them to get their suckers on and the wire would dig into their tentacles if they wrapped around it to pull themselves up."

"Aye, well, they got in somehow."

"What's the damage?" Newton asked. Small losses they could live with. It might be cheaper than beefing up their defenses further.

"Still evaluating, but there's damned little left on the vines in that sector. Maybe eighty percent gone."

Newton couldn't believe that figure. "What? How? They couldn't have eaten all that; that would take a small army of squid. How many intoxicated squid did you find?"

"Only a few. Plenty of squid-sign though. There could have *been* a small army, from what we could tell. And I think they've learned to carry the berries."

"What? How?"

McWhirter said nothing, but opened the field bag whose strap was slung over his shoulder. He reached in and pulled out a worn and wet plastic bag, filled with pale yellow berries. "One of the drunk squids we found had a tentacle wrapped around this."

Newton got up and strode around his desk, taking the plastic bag from McWhirter so that he could examine it without dripping on his console. There was nothing remarkable about the bag, it was a common plastic specimen container. This one looked worn enough that it could have been from the first landing, although after six years he'd expect any such would have biodegraded by now.

"So, one bag. It would take several hundred this size to carry off that much of the crop. There's no way the squids would find that many just lying around."

"Aye, that's what I though too," McWhirter said. "But do we know what the first landing teams left behind? I dinnae see how squids could get up the cliffs to Krechet's Landing, and they'd have been seen, but Chandrasekhar Valley is just that, a broad river valley. We know the crew stripped all excess weight out of the *Chandrasekhar* for launch. Probably they left a box or two of unused specimen bags."

"If they did, I hope to hell it drifted downstream after a rainstorm. The landing site is ten kilometers upstream from the ocean. I'd hate to think the squids were smart enough to go looking for something like that."

"I dinnae think so. And that's a hundred kilometers up the coast from here. Even if they were that smart, and I cannae believe that, why would they look there?"

Newton shrugged. He didn't think it was likely either. "Maybe they smelled something in the water? Run-off from the landing site? But no, something the rain washed down is more likely, if that's even what they used." He considered his options. "All right. Keep checking the fence lines, on all sectors, and also set up cameras. I want recordings of whatever it is those squids are doing. Maybe we can get the okay to just shoot the damn things."

The Colonization Authority frowned on the unnecessary killing of Kakuloan animals, except in self-defense or for elimination of vermin. The argument went that until the ecosystem was more completely understood, they wanted to minimize the chances of disrupting it catastrophically. They were mostly concerned with non-territorial species, unconfined to any one settler's property. Since the squids hadn't presented any direct threat to humans, and since their behavior in the open ocean was poorly understood, they were on the forbidden list. However, if Newton could document them causing significant crop damage, maybe he could get them classed as vermin. The Authority *was* sympathetic to the squidberry farmers, since they were not only a major source of revenue for the young colony, but most of the *raison d'être* for it existing at all.

∞ ∞ ∞

Later

"Well, we figured out how they got past the fences. They went around them."

"Around them? What do you mean?" The fences extended upstream well beyond the mangroves.

"They paralleled the northern fence, following Darwin Creek. Then they crossed overland to Kaytee Creek upstream of our fences and came back downstream. They went back the same way."

"That's a four-kilometer trip. How did they pull that off? How did they even know they could?"

"The land is marshy, and with the rains we've had its wet enough they wouldn't have had to go more than a hundred or so meters overland in any one go. As for the rest..." McWhirter shrugged elaborately. "I dinnae ken."

"Well, hell. I guess we're going to have to fence off the east side too." That would take time and money, and additional manpower to periodically inspect and maintain the extended fence. "Are any of the other farms having these problems?"

There were several other berry farms scattered up and down the coast, wherever the squidberries had been found growing. Calling them farms at this point was something of an exaggeration. They were areas of preexisting tree and berry growth, and beyond fencing them to try to keep the tree squids out, little had been done yet in the way of deliberate cultivation. That was changing; there were ongoing efforts to increase the berry yield, and to expand the domains of the mangrove trees by planting more. So far, attempts to grow the berry vine alone had failed.

"Aye, to some extent. I've nae aware of any large-scale raids like we've had. No doubt that will change if we make it harder for the squids to get to our crop."

"Well, not to sound callous, but that's their problem."

"For the now, at any rate," said McWhirter.

"If and when Centauri Pharmaceuticals does manage to produce a successful anti-aging drug, the demand for squidberry extract will skyrocket. We'll be hard pressed to keep up, all the farms together."

"Aye, that's probably true. That means higher prices for us."

"It also means more incentive for them to find a way to synthesize it, or to look for another area on Kakuloa to create berry plantations. They won't all have problems with tree squids."

"There is that. Aye, it's probably better to form a berry marketing co-op now to keep CentPharm from pitting us one against the other. It's something we've been discussing online." McWhirter was more into that than Newton was. Since the berry farms were geographically separated, it was one of the social channels by which they kept each other informed.

"And in the meanwhile," McWhirter added, "we can put our heads together over this squid problem."

"I'm going to talk to Will Blake about it," Newton said. "Perhaps there's a squid repellent or something we can put in the water, or on the trees."

"Or maybe Mr. Blake will let us shoot the damn things."

∞ ∞ ∞

Administrative Office, Krechet's Landing

"No, I can't let you shoot them," Blake said, his temper wearing thin. McWhirter really seemed to hate the tree squids.

"If ye dinna, ye'll have nae squidberry crop at all before long." McWhirter all but shouted.

"Easy, Rob, easy," Dave Newton said, putting a hand on McWhirter's shoulder. "Let's hear him out."

Blake nodded his thanks to Newton. At least he had some sense. Blake had been over this before, probably with all the berry farmers at one time or another, after a tree squid raid or some other calamity had befallen their crop.

"Look, legal niceties aside, we don't know what effect killing of the squids will have on the ecosystem." Since the tree squids came and went across property boundaries, and the ocean, they were considered part of the commons. While the Treaty of Alpha Centauri allowed for privatization of land and resources contained therein, that simple approach didn't work for air, or water, or animals that roamed wide. Any taking or private use of those commons had to be compensated, weighing benefits and costs.

That was one of William Blake's heavier burdens, and the simplest solution was usually just "don't." With modern technology there was no need to dump effluent into the air or water. Taking animals for food for one's self, family, or workers was fine, but taking them for resale was taxed. Killing them because you considered them pests was only allowed if they didn't range beyond your own property, which tree squids clearly did. There was also some language in the CentPharm contracts about not destroying potentially valuable biopharmacological resources, but even though one of Blake's hats was as a CentPharm representative, he generally worried less about that one. Although it might also apply here.

"Sure we do," McWhirter said. "It'll mean more berries because the squids are nae eating them."

Blake sighed. "And if, say, something that squids excrete is an essential ingredient to growing the cephalomycin fungus on the squidberries?" It was possible. The fungus wouldn't grow on Earth, and nobody yet knew why not. "Your berries are worthless if the mold doesn't grow on them."

"It's nae something from squids."

"And you know that how?" Blake persisted.

"Bah." McWhirter shook his head.

"Look, Will," Newton said, "I know we just can't shoot them. But we need to do something. The problem really is getting worse. Isn't there some repellent that won't actually hurt the squids? Or the fish in the creeks?"

Blake wasn't aware of anything like that, but he was no expert. "I'll check with the other farms and see how they're doing. Maybe someone has a solution. I can also pull in an ecologist to look at some other options. Maybe there's a predator that will scare off the squids, or yes, some chemical that will repel them without being toxic to whatever else lives in those creeks."

"And how long will that take?"

"There's a fellow doing research for CentPharm on Sawyer's World. I think I can pry him loose, so that should just be a few days." Blake thought for a bit. They'd be lucky if an ecologist knew enough about tree squids, or any other kind of octopus, to really solve the problem. That was a stopgap to keep Newton and McWhirter happy. Any real help would have to come from Earth, and that would be at least a couple of weeks to get a message there, have CentPharm find and hire someone, and get them back here.

"I'll also put in a request to Earth," Blake continued. "What we probably need is an expert on cephalopods. I'm sure they can find someone to come out here for a couple of months."

"I guess that will have to do," Newton said. "Rob?"

Rob McWhirter didn't look happy—he'd probably been looking forward to shooting a few of his nemesis—but nodded grudgingly. "Aye, I suppose that'll have to do for now."

Blake stood up, and the others rose too. "Great," he said. "I'll get a request off to Sawyer's World for that ecologist straight away. There's a ship due in-system tomorrow, maybe we can get him here by the end of the week. I'll send the request for a squid expert back with it."

"Thanks, Blake," Newton said. "Keep us posted, will you?"

"Of course."

Blake watched them go. He'd known them both for a while, since they'd arrived on Kakuloa. Newton, he knew better, and generally trusted his judgment. That McWhirter, though. Back in Blake's military days, he had known a few men who had an element of the troublemaker about them. Never insubordinate, and capable enough to get things done, but while perhaps never *in* trouble they were never far from it. McWhirter reminded him of that sort. Blake shook his head and shrugged. Newton seemed to have him under control, if indeed control was needed.

Chapter 16: Preliminary Survey

Krechet's Landing

Parry Cohen had just arrived in Kakuloa, and already was in loud discussion with William Blake about what he wanted to do.

"It's a preliminary survey, dang it!" Cohen said. "I just want to walk over the land, get more details on the geology, the hydrology, topography, vegetation, all the things that make up a standard physical analysis for a new resort."

"Isn't all that in the reports that *Heinlein* brought back?"

"That was just enough to keep me interested. They were doing a scientific survey, not focusing on what a resort developer needs. Anyway, I don't understand what your objections are. It's just a survey. Other than what I need for that I'm not even going to lay out site markers. No construction yet."

"If it were up to me there'd be no construction ever," Blake said. "I don't want anything that might interfere with the squidberry farming."

Parry doubted the former but believed the latter. "I don't want that either. The squidberry farms are going to be a mainstay of the Kakuloa economy for quite a while. I certainly don't want to mess that up. And I won't. Look at my resort on Noronha, off Brazil. That area is designated a category five conservation area, and we built a luxury resort within the guidelines for protecting the land and seascapes." Parry was justifiably proud of that, but had fully expected things to be more relaxed here.

"Anyway," he continued, "the nearest squidberry farm is a hundred kilometers up the coast from where we want to build Kakuloa City."

Blake swung his datapad around. It showed a map of the coastline with the various berry farm plots marked out on it. He pointed to one, about thirty kilometers north of Krechet's Landing. "Oh yeah? What about this one?"

Parry looked at the screen, at where Blake was pointing, and laughed out loud. "Ha. Look at your records. You'll see that one doesn't produce squat."

"And how would you know that?"

Parry grinned. "Because it's mine. I arranged it through a shell company." Over the past two years he had spent much of his time, when not focusing on the Noronha project, setting up such shells, doing as much research as he could, and making other arrangements for this Kakuloa project. "I got a great deal on it just because it didn't look like it would produce. The creek doesn't even have mangroves." In fact, Parry thought they might be able to transplant mangroves and squidberries, but he was thinking more of it as yet another tourist attraction—"visit an authentic squidberry farm"—than as a viable farm.

Blake swung the datapad back and tapped at the screen, bringing up several spreadsheets.

"You son of a bitch," he said after a few moments. There was no anger in his voice, more admiration. "How long have you been planning this?"

Parry smiled. "Since I first saw the photographs of the place, after the *Heinlein* returned. At least in my head. Serious planning didn't start until the first reports from the *Endeavour* came back. Then I cleared it with the Sawyer's World government, such as it is, and CentPharm."

"Well, well. But I still can't spare anyone to go out there with you. Everyone on my meager staff already has tasks assigned. Maybe you can hire someone, but people here generally have their hands full with their own businesses."

"Nobody available? Well, I'll do it myself if I have to." He did have the man minding his shell company's farm, but a third person would be helpful. "The Kakuloa GPS system is operational, yes?"

"Yes, we finished the upgraded constellation eight months ago. But surely that isn't accurate enough for what you need. Resolution is still plus or minus a couple of meters."

"How's the differential resolution?" The absolute position a GPS receiver reported was subject to vagaries of atmospheric and other distortion of the signals from the satellites, but a nearby receiver would be subject to the same vagaries. The differences in position could be highly accurate, even if the absolute position wasn't.

"Centimeters, but you'll need a good baseline."

And that was the rub. All the relative accuracy in the world didn't help if you didn't know the absolute position of at least one station.

"True enough. I still know geometry, so I can get pretty close by hand." As long as his measurements were internally consistent, they could be adjusted later to a known baseline. "Still, it would be easier with an extra hand. Are you sure there's nobody?" Parry felt like he was getting a runaround.

Blake sighed. "I might be able to swing something. I assume you want to do this as soon as possible?"

"I'd like to start tomorrow morning."

"What's your transportation?"

The site Parry was interested in started about twenty kilometers up the coast from the spaceport. His non-productive "squidberry farm" was in the middle of it.

"Helicopter."

Blake sighed. "We don't have any helicopters, either. I *might* be able to find an aircar, in a day or two. There will be a fee."

Parry grinned. He knew something Blake didn't. He'd anticipated this. "No need. I brought one with me. They're unloading it from the *Vanguard* now."

"You brought—? That must have cost. I keep asking for more gear." Blake shook his head, obviously wondering how Cohen had managed this feat. "No wonder there weren't as many new people arriving on *Vanguard* as usual. They needed the space." The latest V-class ships weren't much different from the *Endeavour*-class ships Blake had first come out here on. Cramped.

"I wouldn't know about that, this is my first trip out. They said the cargo bay on this ship was bigger than usual. I guess they took the space from somewhere else. Sorry about that, but the helicopter's yours to use when I don't need it. Part of my deal with Sawyer's and CentPharm, but I get to use it when I'm back here."

Blake's expression changed. The frown went away, and he smiled broadly. He leaned forward in his chair. "Well, Mr. Cohen, why didn't you say so? I can think of a few uses for a helicopter that an aircar just can't handle. For that, I think I can pry some-one away from another job for a couple of days."

"Excellent!" Parry said, and then pushed his advantage. "By the way, I'd appreciate access to whatever updated data you might have on the local meteorology and oceanography. Tides, water and air temperatures, rainfall, things like that."

Blake hesitated, then said, "All right. We don't have a lot in the way of ocean data, but we keep weather records for the spaceport and some of the farms."

"Thanks. That helps not only with physical planning, but also planning the high and low tourist seasons, so we can adjust the rates."

"Tourist seasons," Blake echoed, and shook his head again. "Personally I think you're throwing your money away, Mr. Co-hen, but it's yours to throw away and so far you have approval from my bosses. I'll have someone to work with you in the morn-ing."

"Thank you. And call me Parry."

Blake rose, as did Parry, and they shook on it. Then Blake added, almost as an afterthought: "By the way, how are you with a firearm?"

"What? Why?" Parry hadn't heard anything that would sug-gest a need to go armed.

"Nothing really to worry about, but there a couple of shallow swamps in that area. Away from the coast where the water stays fresher, there are critters something like crocodiles or alligators.

We call them alphagators, or just gators. Usually nothing to worry about, but sometimes they need discouraging."

Cohen wondered about the emphasis on "nothing to worry about." In his experience, that usually meant he should be worried. "That's a bit out of my area of expertise," he said. "I've done development in my share of pretty wild places, but we usually just hire some locals to act as lookouts and guards. Can I get someone like that here?"

Blake nodded. "Sure, I'll take care of it."

"Will that be a problem with development?" Dangerous animals could be dealt with, but it added time and expense.

"What? No, not likely. Just chase them off. It's not like they're endangered. There are plenty more, mostly south of the Landing."

"Ah, good." Idly Parry wondered if they'd make good eating, or if their hide could be made into boots or purses. Given the level of protectionism on Earth, such things might make a profitable souvenir sideline. Heck, maybe even make a friendly logo or mascot out of it. But not alphagator; that was a dumb name. Something crocodile? That was it, *The Kakuloa Kroc*. It had a nice ring to it.

∞ ∞ ∞

Kakuloa Spaceport

Blake made a few calls to set things up for Cohen, then went out to see *Vanguard*. There were a couple of items he needed to discuss with its captain, and he was going in person because Captain Greg Vukovich was an old acquaintance. Blake wanted to find out more about this new ship. As he strolled across the landing field, he looked it over. From the outside, it was the same fat deltoid lifting body as *Victoria* and other starships he'd flown on, but with the upper warp pod now enclosed. His discussion with Cohen made him think the interior layout was quite different. He also wondered where the captain planned to stow the deuterium load he'd asked for, twice the usual amount, and why he needed it.

Various pieces of the helicopter had already been unloaded, and Cohen was there overseeing the reassembly of same. The techs working on it, and Cohen, were all wearing augmented-reality goggles to guide them through the steps. He'd take a closer look when he got done talking to the captain.

He stepped up to the main hatch and called inside. "Port Authority," he said. "Request permission to come aboard?"

"Sure, come on in." Captain Vukovich said, meeting him just inside the hatchway. "Port Authority, William? You wear a lot of hats."

Blake did. He was the general manager for both CentPharm and *UDT* operations on Kakuloa, as well as being a duly authorized representative of the Sawyer's World government. Not only did he wear many hats, he had three different bosses. Fortunately for him, they all generally wanted the same thing: keep things running smoothly. He had help, of course, but the settlement was still small enough at this point, barely a thousand people, that his assistants and deputies were part-time, with other projects to keep them busy.

"I wear whichever one I need to at the time," Blake said. "You're no slouch yourself, Greg. I see you've made captain. Last time we met you were Drake's XO on *Endeavour*, right? But I thought you were primarily an astrophysicist. What are you doing out here as a glorified taxi driver?"

Vukovich nodded. "Right, and right. But I go where the service sends me. What's the Port Authority's interest?"

"I had a couple of questions, and I wanted to see the ship. Was this *Vanguard*'s maiden voyage?"

"No, we did a shakedown cruise two months back. To Sirius, of all places."

"Sirius? What's there?"

"Not much of anything, really. A couple of colleagues wanted to check that system out. That's one reason I got picked as captain; because of my astrophysics background. We didn't expect any terraformed planets, and we didn't find any, but the star is so bright and massive they couldn't tell from a distance. But you said you had questions. Was that one of them?"

"No, just making conversation. What I'm really wondering about is your fuel requisition. That's more than twice the usual amount of deuterium for a ship this size on the Earth-Alpha Centauri run."

"Will that be a problem?" Vukovich said, looking concerned.

"No, we have plenty of reserve." There was a heavy water extraction facility at the far end of the field, processing water pumped up the cliff from the ocean. "But I'm wondering why you need that much, and where you're going to stow it all."

"This ship has extended range tanks. We had to, for the Sirius trip, especially since we didn't know if there'd be an accessible source of water or hydrogen to refuel from."

"Was there?"

"Not really. We located a couple of frozen comets far out in the system, but I'm glad we didn't have to try. Which is why for this trip we're converting the cargo bay to another fuel tank as soon as we're done unloading."

"Are you going to have any room for people?"

Vukovich grinned. "Just a couple of crew. No passengers or cargo this trip; we're not going straight back to Earth."

"I guessed that," said Blake. "Can you tell me where?"

Vukovich looked thoughtful and then shrugged. "No particular reason why not, seeing as it's you, but don't spread it around, all right?"

Blake nodded, puzzled at the mystery.

"We're going to Procyon."

"So basically, Sirius all over again?" Procyon was another bright star, not quite as big or bright as Sirius, but also with a dwarf star companion. And probably just as unlikely to have terraformed planets. "Why?"

"I think somebody wants to know if it has any rocky planets at all. In particular, anything close to the main star."

"If it does, they'd be pretty toasty, wouldn't they? Like Mercury, or worse?"

"That's the idea."

"That's crazy," Blake said.

"I'm inclined to agree with you, but there's a construction project underway on Mercury right now."

That didn't make any sense. Mining might make sense, Mercury was metal-rich, although surely asteroids were easier. But a construction project? "What are they building?" he wondered aloud.

"Officially, I have no idea."

"Officially?" Blake said, now very curious. *What else does Mercury have going for it?* Then he realized. "Solar power? But why, when we have controlled fusion? You can get all the power you need from a tank of deuterium, or heavy water. And what do you do with that power on Mercury. Or at Procyon, if that's the connection?"

The captain shrugged. "They didn't tell me. I can make an educated guess, but I don't want to speculate."

Blake had read some science fiction—practically everyone who came out here had—and he tried to recall some of the fictional reasons one might want such a power source. A laser for launching interstellar light sails made no sense, not with warp-capable starships. A laser for defense against hostile aliens? Were there any? That didn't make sense anyway; what would you do when Mercury is in the wrong place in its orbit to defend you? What else? Wait... "*Antimatter?* They're building an antimatter factory on Mercury?"

"Well, you wouldn't want one on Earth, would you? But as I said, I don't know, so I can neither confirm—"

"Nor deny. Yeah, I get it. If someone has figured out a reliable way to store the stuff, it would be a perfect starship fuel. But don't you need dilithium crystals?"

Vukovich laughed. "This isn't *Star Trek*. At a guess, it'd use tech derived from our solid-state fusion reactors, but I've been out of that field for a couple of years now. Assuming there even *is* any antimatter, and again, I can neither—"

"—Confirm nor deny," Blake finished for him. "Yeah, I got that. But wait," he said, remembering something about the positions of nearby stars. "Isn't Procyon closer to Earth than to here?"

"Slightly. A bit over a light year."

"So why come all the way out here if you're going to Procyon? Unless somebody didn't want it too obvious where you were going?"

"To be honest, CentPharm or somebody wanted to get Mr. Cohen's damn helicopter out here, and we had the biggest cargo bay. But you might have a point."

"I'll be damned. So, are you going straight back to Sol after Procyon?" Blake still had some logistical issues to deal with, like a cephalopod specialist for Dave Newton.

Vukovich nodded. "That's the plan."

"Okay then. I'll give you what message traffic we have." It was the only way to get information to or from Earth in any reasonable time.

"The next ship out here might make it back before we do."

"So I'll give them a copy of it too. No harm done." At least, he hoped not. He wondered just how critical the tree squid problem was. He might have to let McWhirter shoot a few of them after all.

"All right then. Sure, I'll take your messages. Was there anything else?"

"Not right now. I want to go check out Cohen's toy. See you later?"

"Yeah. I'll swing by when I get the ship buttoned up."

∞ ∞ ∞

Blake was duly impressed with Cohen's helicopter. He'd been expecting something relatively small, a two- or four-seater, that could have fit into the cargo bay with very little disassembly. What Cohen had arranged to bring was more like a helicopter kit; it was the only way it could have been squeezed in. It looked to Blake a lot like the venerable UH-1Y, itself a descendent of the original UH-1 Huey. It had a four-bladed main rotor and a large crew/cargo area behind the cockpit seats. The rotor blades, tail boom, motor housing, main cabin, tail rotor and various bits and pieces had been stowed separately, then carefully reassembled on the spaceport field. When Blake came back out of *Vanguard*, Cohen was going over the whole thing very carefully, helped no doubt by the augmented-reality visor he was wearing.

"I was expecting something a little smaller," Blake told Cohen when the latter had finished his inspection.

"That's what *she* said," Cohen replied, then at Blake's blank expression, said "Sorry, old joke. Yes, I wanted something that could be helpful in construction. Construction tower cranes don't assemble themselves. Well, actually they do, but they need help at first. This baby will simplify things."

"I thought you were just doing a survey?"

"This trip, yes. I hope to be back. If my plans don't work out, somebody will find a use for it. Anyway, like I said, CentPharm and Sawyer's World are together the majority owners, so I'm not too much at risk. Just don't break it while I'm gone."

"Break it? I'm not sure we have anyone to fly it."

"Nothing to it. If you can fly an aircar, you can fly this. The flight computer is the same, it'll figure out what you want. I'll be happy to check you out on it, not that that's really necessary. We did do some customization for Kakuloa."

"Such as?"

"Well, it was surplus, so we ripped out any military systems that hadn't already been removed. Lightened it some to give it better range and payload. Uprated the motors."

"What about the power source? What's the range?"

Cohen smiled. He patted the side of the helicopter affectionately. "You, my friend, are looking at one of only half a dozen fusion-powered helicopters in existence."

"*What?*"

"Apparently CentPharm has some powerful friends. There are a handful of prototypes, all based on upgrades like this one, although not quite so demilitarized. The same solid-state fusion technology the starships use, just in a smaller package and a lower power output. They're still big—you won't be fitting one in an aircar—but it will run the helicopter all day on a few liters of heavy water. It's got a top speed over 300 kph." Cohen paused and looked right and left as if to see if there was anyone else nearby, and lowered his voice. "I strongly suspect that the military interest comes as much from possibly using fusion to power a rail-gun or laser as it does from extending the range, but I'm just speculating." He held up a forefinger and tapped the side of his nose.

Blake could see how that might be possible. The *Union de Terre* certainly hadn't made conflict go away on Earth, but it was more vigorous about enforcing the peace than the old United Nations had been, with the United States' military a not-insignificant part of that.

"So," Cohen said, "want to go for a flight?"

"I thought you'd never ask."

Chapter 17: Greystone

Marine Institute, Earth

Doctor Ellie Greystone brought a cup of coffee from the office autochef back to her desk and opened her email app to scan her in-box. There was the usual. A reminder of this morning's staff meeting. On the Monday after a long weekend? Whose silly idea was that? There was more. Something from a name she didn't recognize but at a university she did—that could be anything from a conference announcement to a request for a copy of one of her papers, she'd look at it later—spam from a fishing website that had made it through the email filters, something from Skrellan Pharmaceuticals, which was probably more spam, and a couple of others whose content wasn't obvious from the sender or the subject line. She flagged and discarded the spam and began to work her way through the other messages.

The first was from a middle-school student, asking her how to become a marine biologist. Ellie wondered if this were a class assignment or something the kid was really interested in, and how she'd found Ellie's contact information. Probably from the Marine Institute's web site. She flagged that one for later, it would require some thought.

"Morning, Ellie," Jim Roland said as he came into the office. "How was your tricentennial?" Saturday had been July 4, 2076. There had been partying.

"I survived. We saw some spectacular fireworks. Yours?"

"Much the same. We took the kids to one of the fireworks shows. We were all pretty wiped out yesterday," Roland said. "So, anything exciting going on today?"

"The usual. Staff meeting at ten."

"Oh, joy. Speaking of meetings, I'm going to have to leave early tomorrow. We're still looking at schools for young Jessica. Any problem with that?"

"No, that's fine."

"How's your mom doing?" Jim was somewhat aware of her mother's issues, which had worsened over the years.

"She was fine this morning, but I have to admit I'm getting worried about her. I don't like leaving her on her own." There had been a few occasions where Ellie had taken time off to take care of her.

"I thought you had someone looking in on her."

"A neighbor, but I don't want to keep imposing."

"I understand. I remember when my dad had to put his dad into an assisted-living home. It was tough all around at first, but Grandpa was really better off for it. So was Dad."

Jim wasn't much older than Ellie, but then his parents and grandparents all had children young, not like her own parents. She barely remembered her grandparents.

"In her better moments I don't think my mom would sit still for that, and I'm not ready to try to force it. Anyway, I'm not sure I could afford it, at least not the kind of place I'd be comfortable leaving her."

"You mentioned an aunt once. Younger or older?"

"Younger, and in better health. But she lives a thousand miles away and has young grandchildren. I wouldn't want to impose on her."

"Sometimes you're too nice for your own good. I hope you can work something out." He looked around, as if trying to find a way to break off the conversation, which had wandered into un-comfortable territory.

"Yeah." Ellie picked up her coffee mug. "I need a refill," she said, standing up. "You want anything?"

"No, I'm good. Thanks." His relief was obvious.

He has a point, Ellie thought as she refilled her coffee. *Sooner or later I'm going to have to deal with Mom. Hopefully later.*

∞ ∞ ∞

The staff meeting was the usual mundane stuff. Welcome back after the holiday, status reports, who had publications recently, schedule adjustments. Ellie stifled a yawn, and then mercifully the meeting broke up.

"Doctor Greystone, could I see you for a moment?" Doctor Charles Wood, her director, said to her as the group disbanded.

Doctor Greystone? Ellie thought. *Am I in trouble?* "Certainly, sir. What's up?"

Wood waited until everyone else had cleared out of the conference room. "Ellie, this isn't exactly work-related."

So it was back to Ellie now. "Okay, go ahead."

"You might be getting contacted about doing some outside work. An old friend of mine asked me if I knew anyone with any expertise on cephalopod behavior, and I mentioned your name."

"Oh? Who? And what kind of work?" It wasn't unusual for outside companies to arrange for contractual research; that was part of how the Institute kept the bills paid.

"Well, that's the thing. She didn't want to tell me too much about it. Apparently it's related to something that's still rather hush-hush because of competitive interests. And I don't want to say any more than that in case she contacts someone else."

"Okay. So I may or may not be hearing from someone about something?"

"When you put it that way, it does sound rather mysterious and cloak-and-dagger, doesn't it? Well, if you get a call or an email from someone named Victoria, you might want to pay attention to it. I'm not saying you have to take the job, whatever it is. That's up to you of course, and I don't know what's involved. I just wanted to pass that on."

"Oh, all right. Thank you. I'll keep an eye out."

"Right, then. That was all. Keep up the good work." With that, Wood turned and left the conference room, leaving Ellie standing wondering what had really just happened.

Wait, Victoria? Hadn't she seen that name recently? Yes! On what she'd thought was a spam email from Skrellan Pharmaceuticals. A pharmaceutical company. No wonder they were being se-cretive. But why on Earth would they want an expert in cephalo-pod behavior?

∞ ∞ ∞

"No reason on *Earth* at all," Victoria Holmes said when Ellie put that exact question to her.

Ellie had managed to retrieve the email from her trash folder. It hadn't said much, it had just mentioned Director Woods's name and a potential contract, and would Doctor Greystone please contact Victoria Holmes at the enclosed number. Ms. Holmes hadn't wanted to talk on the phone, but rather agreed to meet her for lunch, which was where they were talking now.

Ellie shook her head. This wasn't making sense. "Then why —" and the pieces fell together. The slight emphasis on *Earth*. Skrellan Pharmaceuticals. The biggest stakeholder in Centauri Pharmaceuticals. Ellie had, of course, done her research before the meeting. She had even recognized Holmes's name, but dis-missed it as a coincidence. "Wait, you're *that* Victoria Holmes?"

Holmes smiled, but said nothing.

"This isn't about Earth, is it?" Ellie said.

"I see you've done your homework. Good. That will save some explanations."

"My gosh. I was still a grad student when I saw that first video that Ulrika Klaar made. This is about—" Ellie paused, not sure how much she should say out loud in a place like this, even though there was nobody sitting nearby "—what I think it is, isn't it?"

Holmes nodded again. "Squids, yes, and I appreciate your dis-cretion. We seem to be having a slight problem with them, and would appreciate some expert help. Charles mentioned your name."

"Well, certainly. They seem like a fascinating species. What kind of help do you need?"

"What do you know about squidberries?"

"Discovered at the same time the squids were, and so named because the squids—they're not really squids, you know, more like octopus—were eating them."

"Yes, I know, but the name stuck. Go on."

"I know the pharmaceutical companies have an interest in the berries, presumably they—you—found a potentially useful drug in them, and you helped finance the return expedition to the Centauri system. So whatever you found must be worth quite a lot."

"Potentially, yes. Any new drug is something of a gamble. That's why we're concerned when something might disrupt the squidberry crop."

So that was it. "You can't keep the squids out of the farms." That's why they wanted a specialist on cephalopod behavior.

Holmes's glance darted right and left. This was the news she didn't want overheard. "We can," she said, and then in a lower voice, "but it's getting more difficult."

Ellie nodded. "Octopodes are highly adaptive. So you'd like advice on keeping them out."

"More than that. We'd like you to go to Kakuloa, visit the farms, study the, ah, octopodes, and make recommendations. Are you up for that?"

The words echoed in Ellie's brain. *Go to Kakuloa. Study the octopodes.* Was she up for that? Of *course* she was up for that. Ever since she had heard about— Oh, crap. *Mom.*

Holmes had been watching her face. "What happened? You got all excited there for a moment, and now not. You don't want to go?"

"I would *love* to go. But I can't." Ellie's next words were difficult. "I'm sorry, you'll have to find somebody else."

"Can't? Why not? Don't tell me you have a possessive boyfriend."

"No, nothing like that, no boyfriend. Or girlfriend, for that matter. It's...it's my mother. She's...ill. I can't leave her alone for very long."

"Oh. I'm sorry to hear that." Holmes looked down at the table, tapping her fingers, then looked back at Ellie. "I'll tell you what. I wouldn't expect an immediate answer anyway, and I haven't made a formal offer for you to refuse yet. I can say that we would pay very well, as well as cover your expenses; that's standard. So why don't you think on it for, say, forty-eight hours. Maybe you can find a way to make it work. Unfortunately, I can't give you any longer than that. I'd have to find someone else and we've got the ship schedules to consider. The next starship leaves in a week, and then it's a while to the one after that."

Ellie nodded, feeling slightly numb. It was a rare opportunity, but she couldn't leave her mother alone. She didn't see how she could *find a way to make it work* in a week, much less forty-eight hours. "Yes, all right. Thank you." She rose to leave. "I'll be in touch."

Holmes stood too, reaching out to shake hands goodbye. She held Ellie's hand longer than necessary. "Please, think about it. I think I understand what you're going through, I really do. If you have any questions, please call. But I'm afraid I really do have to find someone in the next week." She released Ellie's hand.

"Thank you." Ellie turned and left the restaurant before Victoria Holmes could see the tears of frustration Ellie felt threatening to well up. *Damn it!* There was an uncomfortable conversation she had to have with her mother. She couldn't put it off any longer, although it was unlikely to help.

∞ ∞ ∞

Victoria sat down as she watched Ellie go. She was exactly what Holmes needed. Intelligent, resourceful, and knew her subject. And, aside from her mother, no ties. But either way, Holmes needed an expert, any expert. She picked up her omni and called her assistant.

"*Yes, Ms. Holmes?*"

"Contact my second candidate. Also, get me everything you can find out about Doctor Ellie Greystone's family, especially her mother, and especially her mother's medical condition. I don't care how."

"*Yes ma'am. Understood.*"

There were certain advantages to being a vice-president of a huge biopharmaceutical company. She might as well use them.

Chapter 18: Tourist Trap

Webster and Schloss Financials, Earth

"You want to build a *resort* hotel," Jim Griffin, the financier, said.

Parry Cohen squirmed slightly in his seat. This meeting was going to be tougher than he'd thought. Unfortunately, he needed access to more cash to make the Kakuloa resort a reality, and now that he was back on Earth, he was trying to make that happen. "That's right," he said.

"On Kakuloa." Griffin frowned.

"Yes."

"You do mean the planet at Alpha Centauri, and not some other Kakuloa? Somewhere in Hawaii, for example?" He raised his eyebrows hopefully at the last.

"No, I mean Alpha Centauri. The potential—"

"Mr. Cohen, all due respect, but *are you out of your mind?* Even if there were potential clientele, it would cost a fortune! How do expect it to ever pay back?"

"Have you ever been to Hawaii? Or Cancun? Or Noronha? Or any of dozens of other tourist hot spots? They're money factories."

Griffin shook his head slightly. He always did his homework. The real numbers were good, but not that good. "They're on Earth," he said. "It takes a few hours to get to them. They have civilization."

"Now, sure. They didn't always. Look at their history." In addition to his own personal experience, Cohen had studied this extensively; that's what his plan was based on. "All they had going for them was climate, gorgeous scenery, and great advertising campaigns. They were in what was then the middle of nowhere. Hawaii was a Navy base in the middle of the Pacific. The village of Cancun was three people in the jungle. They had to build the isthmus and the road from the mainland to the island, then build the airport. There was nothing. In less than fifty years they went from nothing to a world-class resort with 500,000 inhabitants, 27,000 hotel rooms and two million visitors a year."

"Yeah, but they weren't coming by starship."

"Then scale it back. Of course, it won't be that big that fast, but it doesn't have to be," Parry said. "Kakuloa, especially the coast near Krechet's Landing, has the climate and the scenery."

Parry had brought a datapad. He keyed up an image and turned the pad to show Griffin. "These are some pictures from my preliminary scouting of the area. Beautiful, isn't it?" The pictures showed empty beaches with crystal blue waters, the surf breaking in the distance. An aerial shot showed the beach extending away for what must be kilometers, ocean on one side, tropical forest on the other.

"The advertising campaign writes itself," Parry said, blanking the screen. "I'll leave you this, by the way. The business plan is on it, and all the images. Best surf in the galaxy; visit historic Chandrasekhar Valley, site of humankind's first landing on an extrasolar world; see the mysterious tree squids—you get the idea."

"I thought tree squids were off-limits." So, the financier had done some homework. This actually encouraged Cohen.

"Not exactly. Anyway, that's just details. Look, the economy on Kakuloa is on the verge of a boom. The pharmaceutical companies are dumping a ton of money into the place. The Kiahuna company is planning an orbital shipyard there. There's talk of a mining operation at Bimini Bay. I want to get in on the ground floor!"

"But who is going to want to travel there for a vacation? A week out, a week back, that's half a month shot right there."

"The new ships coming on line can do it in half that. Besides, the clientele we're aiming at isn't limited by three-week vacations. It would be high-rollers looking for novelty. It will be a status thing. We'll probably pick up trade from Sawyer's World too, but that's minor. Tourists and executives from the bio-pharmaceutical and spacecraft industries, that's our other market."

"And precisely how do you propose to build anything? As I recall, starships are volume limited. You'd be lucky to get a bulldozer in one, let alone a construction crane. Or a cement mixer. And where do you get the concrete, or the girders?"

"There's already infrastructure there. it's not as primitive as all that. Most of the construction will use basalt fiber rebar," Parry said. "We use that some places on Earth where steel is expensive; it's actually lighter and stronger. Krechet Plateau is mostly the right kind of basalt. For the rest, bigger ships are in the works. One is already flying. Heavy construction equipment can be broken down to sub-assemblies that will fit in a ship. I've already got a heavy helicopter out there to use as a skycrane. When we're done with equipment, we can either sell it or lease it out. There will be demand. Hell, that's almost a business in itself.

"This isn't my first development project," Parry continued. "I've done the research." He touched the datapad. "This proposal includes everything you need: capacity studies, land-use diagrams, feasibility analysis, functional relationship diagrams, cash-flow projections, pertinent regulations, architectural drawings, the lot. This can be the next Cancun. Better, even."

∞ ∞ ∞

Jim Griffin sat back in his chair, appraising Cohen. His enthusiasm was infectious, but Griffin still had his doubts, Cohen seemed to have considered all the construction angles, but had he really thought about the market?

"Hmm. All right, Perry, suppose—"

"Parry," Cohen said.

"Sorry, Parry," Griffin said, not sorry at all. "Suppose I'm a potential tourist. What's your pitch? There are plenty of places on Earth where I can lie on the beach sipping my beverage of choice. Why travel all the way to another star system to do that?"

"Do beaches on Earth have an orange sun?" Cohen asked. "Okay, it doesn't really look orange, but there's less ultraviolet, so there's a lower risk of sunburn. Do they have two moons in the sky? If you thought a moonlit beach was romantic, imagine it with *two* moons."

Parry warmed to the topic, leaning forward in his seat and waving his arms. "Then there are all the sorts of things you can do at an Earth resort—water skiing, surfing, para-sailing—"

"Golf?"

Parry paused. "Well, the gravity is a tad higher; your drives won't go quite as far. We can adjust the course, or use smaller balls. But plenty of other things to do, especially on the water—jet-skis, jet-packs, and diving. The latter with exotic alien sea-life."

"Well not really alien, right? Earth-descended."

"But with sixty-five million years of divergent evolution. It's *different*. The same goes for the land animals, even the plants."

It sounded good, but not great. Something as far away as a week's travel, even half a week's, needed a better hook. How luxurious could starships be? "Is that the best you've got?"

"Well, there's also the detail that Kakuloa is governed under the Treaty of Alpha Centauri, nominally under joint administration by Sawyer's World and the *Union de Terre*." Cohen looked at Griffin, who stared back at him noncommittally, and then he added: "It's like the Treaty of Svalbard, only instead of Norwegian law, Sawyer's World law applies. With limits."

"Meaning what, exactly?" Griffin had never heard of the Treaty of Svalbard.

"Meaning that aside from the essentials like laws against murder and robbery, a couple of regulations covering the native life-forms, and for enforcing contracts, there really isn't much that's illegal on Kakuloa."

Griffin had been sitting back in his chair. At Parry's last comment he jerked upright. Had he heard that right?

"Wait, say again?" Griffin said.

"Since most of the residents are connected with the pharmaceutical and other companies, or are researchers and the like, they're generally subject to the terms of their contracts," Cohen explained. "But outside of that, there really isn't a lot of law enforcement, because there isn't a lot of law. Some security, sure, but as long as nobody is getting hurt, or wrecking the commons, it's pretty much hands off."

"So, there's no prohibition on gambling?"

"Not on gambling, not on most recreational drugs, so long as it doesn't interfere with work, and not on sex for hire between consenting adults."

"You should have led with that." *The hell with the beaches or golf,* Griffin thought. "*Anything?*"

"Well, don't hurt anyone and don't scare the horses."

"Horses?"

"Just a saying. Don't do things in public that would disturb the peace."

"So why isn't this place already the new Las Vegas or, wherever?"

"Because it's mostly been a company town, and most of the folks are under contract. Corporations aren't huge fans of activities that might interfere with productivity. It won't last, though. I'm not the only person who can figure this out. I'm probably not even the only person with a resort hotel background."

Griffin wondered about that last. Did Cohen really think that, or was he just trying to appeal to Griffin's sense of urgency? "Really? Interesting. You mentioned a business plan?"

"It's all in here," Parry said, tapping the datapad. "I'd welcome any input you have, of course. This is based on other projects I've done."

"What about the governments?" Griffin thought Cohen had said something about pertinent regulations, but the fact was the financier hadn't really been paying attention at first; the whole idea had seemed crazy. "Are they going to crack down on this just as it gets rolling? Or tax it to death?"

"Not so long as it doesn't get too out of hand. The dual administration helps; neither side can act unilaterally. Taxes, such as they are, can only be spent supporting Kakuloa. There's a local governor of sorts; he doesn't have many duties. Sawyer's World is mostly worried about Sawyer's World, and the Terran Union is more worried about Earth, and exploration further out. I think they'll appreciate the traffic, so long as it doesn't become an embarrassment."

"Hence the public emphasis on more conventional tourist activities," Griffin realized.

"Exactly. You mentioned Vegas. That boomed then busted as a sin city, then recovered again when the hotels started adding more family-friendly activities. Still plenty of the former, but enough of the latter to put a semi-respectable face on. It's not like we're planning a Kakuloa Disneyland here."

"Well, certainly not with that name, anyway. But you're right. All right, what dollar figure were you thinking?"

"You're the money guy. Why don't I leave you the plan and let you look it over?"

"Give me a ballpark."

Parry gave him a number. It was high.

"*How much?* Are you serious?"

"Skrellan Pharmaceuticals invested five times that in their Centauri project, and that's not counting what the rest of the Centauri Pharmaceuticals combine put up."

"Well yes, but if the rumors are true they're looking at a trillion-dollar business."

"Over the long haul. They won't be out of the red on this for ten years or more. We can be in the black in three. Less with pre-sales."

"Pre-sales?"

"We start taking reservations a year or more out. We pre-sell business suites to interested businesses."

"You can't count that as income." That wasn't quite true; there were different approaches to the accounting.

"That figure covers a lot of initial capital expenditures. Land rights, construction equipment, long-term leases on starships."

"Land rights. You don't have those yet?"

"I have some formally. Informally I've talked to the appropriate people. I've been out there and done preliminary surveys, including a couple of sites I'm not really interested in, just to keep people guessing. The Sawyer's World and Kakuloa governments both think it's a good idea. They're willing to commit on land

rights when it looks like I have financing. They're already cooperating with me.

"I've also got associates, ah, homesteading key locations. I've
got a squidberry farm that is absolutely hopeless at producing
berries but is near a stretch of prime beachfront with a source of
fresh water. It's all in the paperwork." Parry nodded at the pad.
"So why don't you look it over and tell me what you think will
work."

Griffin raised his eyebrows. "Are you looking for a loan or
for an investor?"

"Either way, as long as I keep control. I think at this stage an
investor makes most sense, no?" A loan backed by unbuilt properties on another planet would be tough.

"Perhaps. It would depend in part on what other assets you
have to back a loan. It does sound like you have some already. All
right, Mr. Cohen," he stood up, reaching across the desk to shake
hands, "I'll look at what you've got. Of course, I'll also be looking
at your own financials too. That's routine."

"Naturally. I should tell you, I have lined up other meetings.
Without mentioning specifics, of course. Also there are folks on
back on Sawyer's World and Kakuloa who have an idea of what
I'm up to."

"I see. Well, I hope you will contact me before you mention
this to anyone else. If we should decide to work with you on this,
best not to stir up potential competition too soon, eh?"

"Oh, absolutely. I look forward to hearing from you shortly,
then?"

"We tend to reject more quickly than accept, so no news
could be good news. But do feel free to call me."

"Thank you."

∞ ∞ ∞

Parry Cohen had a bounce to his step as he left the office. It
was far from certain, but his gut feeling was that he had snagged
the support he needed.

Chapter 19: Mother

Marine Institute

Jim Roland looked up when Ellie Greystone came into the office later than her usual early self. Her shoulders were slumped, and her eyes were red.

"Rough night?" he asked.

"You could say that." She sat down heavily at her desk.

"Are you okay?"

"Yeah, I'm fi—" she began, then stopped and shook her head. "No, not really."

"Want to talk about it?"

She sat for a while. Jim wondered if she'd heard his question and was about to repeat it, when she spoke up. "Jim, you mentioned your dad had a difficult time of getting his father into assisted living. How did he deal with it?"

"Is this about your mother? Is she getting worse?"

"Yes. I mean, no, not worse, but it's about her. Remember Woods asking me to stay after the Monday meeting?"

"Yeah, but I don't get the connection."

"I've been offered a research contract, but it means being out of the country for...an extended period."

"That's great! What kind of research?"

"I can't say. I'm under a non-disclosure agreement. But I can't take it; I can't leave my mom alone that long."

The non-disclosure was uncommon but not unheard of. Jim shrugged that off. But turning down a contract? "What did Woods say?"

"I haven't told him yet. I've got forty-eight—well, less than that now—hours to make a final decision. I raised it with Mom last night. She insisted that she was fine, and I should *go and have fun.*"

"But you don't think she is."

"I know she's not. She had another spell while we were talking. She never remembers them, and is mostly in denial about them even happening. I think she thinks we're all conspiring against her to make her think she's crazy. Was it like that with your grandfather?"

Jim thought back. He'd been a teenager at the time, and generally oblivious to anything that didn't directly involve either himself, or girls. "Yes, I think so. My parents, especially Dad, tried to put a good face on it and keep it from us, I think. But yeah, I remember one time when Granddad thought I was his son and my dad was some stranger out to get him. It was scary." It had been. Jim remembered wondering if his grandfather were drunk, except that he rarely drank.

"Oh, I'm sorry."

"Not your fault, and you have your own problems. I'm inclined to say that your mother is an adult and if she says go, you should go, but I know you don't feel that way."

"No, I don't. Besides, I'd worry the whole time, and feel guilty, and not be able to do anything about it."

"Could you send her out to live with her sister? Just temporarily, while you're gone."

"I don't want to impose. I've hinted at it before, but my aunt is in a small apartment."

"She's as much family as you are," He said. Then, trying to lighten the mood: "You both share fifty percent of your mother's genes. Have you even asked?"

"No, not yet."

"Do you *want* this assignment?"

Ellie's head jerked up and her eyes lit. Whatever it was, she was interested. "Yes!"

"Then call your aunt. Look, you probably have more time to make arrangements, it's just that whoever wants to hire you needs time to find someone else if you can't take the job, right?"

She nodded. "Yes, a few days."

"But they need an answer. Call your aunt. Surely you can sell that to your mother, especially with your aunt's help."

Ellie hesitated, then nodded decisively. "You're right. Thanks Jim."

∞ ∞ ∞

The call did not go well. Aunt Cheryl would be happy to look in on her sister regularly if she were local, but didn't have the space in her apartment and wasn't up to giving Mom the level of care that she probably needed.

On the upside, Cheryl would be happy to try to talk her sister into coming out to "visit," and she could "stay at this nice little place nearby where they took care of all your needs."

Of course, there was a waiting list, and Ellie wasn't sure she could afford it, even if she could arrange to sell her mother's house in the short time available. At least she had power of attorney. Or did she? She'd gotten her mom to sign a medical power of attorney after one of her more serious spells, and there had been other papers since. She'd have to check.

That would also mean Ellie would have to find somewhere else to live, but that could wait until she got back from Kakuloa. Except that it didn't look like there was any way she could go. There were too many obstacles. She'd have to call Victoria Holmes and tell her no. Ellie heaved a sigh. Holmes, now there was someone who wouldn't let a few obstacles get in her way. Wait, that might be it. Maybe there *was* a way she could go. First, she needed to research Skrellan Pharmaceuticals.

∞ ∞ ∞

"Dr. Greystone!" Holmes said, answering her omni. "I was hoping to hear from you. What have you decided?"

"That's partly up to you, Ms. Holmes. I'm certainly interested, but under ordinary circumstances, I don't see any way I can leave town, much less Earth, for any length of time. Making conventional arrangements for my mother is proving impossible."

Holmes sighed. That was disappointing. But there was something in Ellie's tone. "Wait, what did you mean by *ordinary circumstances* and *conventional arrangements*?"

"That's why I said it was partly up to you. Skrellan has access to resources that I don't. It depends on whether I—and your squidberries—am worth it to you to help me out."

Holmes had certainly had her share of negotiating new-hire contracts, but this was a new twist. "I'm certainly open to discussion. What did you have in mind?"

"My mother needs an assisted living facility. Anything local is out of the question. My mother refuses to go, and besides, I'm not sure I'd trust any of the local places I could afford."

"I understand. They're not all bad, but evaluating them takes time. You said local was out, so what are you thinking of?" Holmes quietly opened the file her assistant had gathered on Greystone's family.

"My aunt—Mom's sister—suggested a facility near her. She isn't able to take care of my mother herself, but she could visit regularly. There are just a couple of logistical snags that you might be able to help me with."

"Ellie, if I may, dealing with the logistically impossible is what I do." If anything, the Kakuloa project ought to prove that. "What are the issues?"

"Two things. One, there's a waiting list."

Holmes almost laughed aloud at that one. "Give me the name of the place. I can make that go away, or if not, find as good or better a place nearby. Skrellan is in the health care business, we have contacts."

"I thought you might," Ellie said.

Oh? Interesting. "And the other?"

"The cost. I can cover it if I sell the house...but that will take time, and I know you're anxious to get someone out there."

Holmes thought about that for all of five seconds, and that long only because it was her habit never to respond to a favorable offer too quickly. Let Ellie think that was a big ask. "Very well, here's what we'll do. Don't worry about the cost. We'll cover it as long as you're working for us; consider it a family health benefit. We'll make sure the transition is easy after that. We can even arrange to sell the house if that's what you want. We do it all the time when moving executives around." That was true enough, although usually only for executives above a certain level. "Was there anything else?"

Ellie didn't answer immediately. Perhaps she had expected more of an argument. "No, that covers the logistics. I still have to convince my mother to go along with it. My aunt thinks we can convince her to take an extended vacation to visit her sister, but there didn't seem to be any point bringing it up if there was no place for her to stay."

"Of course." Holmes paused, debating her next statement. What the heck, it might simplify things. "Ellie, your mother's medical condition, she's had a number of tests, I assume?" Holmes knew that she had. She had Mrs. Greystone's medical files open on the screen in front of her. Another advantage of being in the health care business.

"Yes, why?"

"Is she cooperative about going in for tests, or treatments?"

"Yes, usually. What does that have to do with it?"

"Look, Ellie, I'll be honest with you." *Mostly.* "I'd really like to get you out to Kakuloa. There are other cephalopod specialists but frankly, most of them are even more tied down than you, or are not who I want to work with. We're a big company, we have a large number of subsidiary companies. I guarantee you that whatever it is that your mother has, we have some kind of treatment or experimental treatment for it. Maybe not a cure, but we'd be willing to enroll her into a relevant study. She'd get full medical care and periodic scans and tests. Maybe an experimental drug, maybe a placebo. Do you think she'd go along with that?"

"I, I'm not certain. Probably."

"Do you have medical power of attorney?"

"I do." Ellie said slowly. "Why?"

"Then you don't really need her permission."

"But.... That's for if she's incapacitated."

Holmes didn't say anything, but let the silence stretch out.

"Oh," Ellie said, as the realization sunk in. "You know what she's got, don't you. You have access to her medical records." It wasn't a question.

Greystone's ability to put two and two together was the whole point of hiring her, so her deduction didn't surprise Holmes. "We're a health care company," she said. "We take mental health very seriously, both that of patients and that of our employees, or contractors. You know this stress isn't good for you either, Ellie. Go to Kakuloa. It's like Hawaii."

That got a chuckle. "The whole planet?"

"Well, no, obviously. But near the landing sites. Look, what we're working on—what we need your help to ensure we can *keep* working on—has the potential to help millions of people. Eventually it could prevent anyone from getting what your mother has."

"Could it reverse it?"

Holmes was tempted to say yes, but in truth that was unlikely. "Probably not, no. The damage is done. Some improvement, perhaps. I'm sorry."

"Then what good does it do my mom?" Ellie snapped.

Holmes bit back her own response. Ellie was stressed, give her a moment.

"I'm sorry," Ellie said, "That was uncalled for. I appreciate what you're trying to do."

"Never mind. I understand. Look, the offer still stands. We'll take care of the facility and the expense. Talk to your aunt and your mother. If you're interested, we'll find a treatment plan. I can't promise any positive outcome on that, obviously, but we'll do what we can. Let me know if it's a go. I can let you have a couple more days to complete the arrangements, but I need to know you're taking the job. If you need any help or advice—financial, legal, whatever—give me a call. I have people."

"Thank you, I will."

After the call ended, Victoria sat back in her chair. What she had said about Greystone being her first choice was true. A mentor had once told her, on the advantage of having money: "If you have a problem and money will fix it, then it's not a problem."

The question is whether money could fix the problem on Kakuloa, with the damn tree squids literally eating into the squid-berry crops. She reached for her omni.

Three days later, Ellie Greystone was on her way to the Moon.

Chapter 20: High Finance

Chitiri Resort Development, Earth

Parry Cohen answered his omniphone with some trepidation, recalling Griffin's comment about rejecting more quickly than accepting. "This is Parry."

"Mr. Cohen? This is Jim Griffin with Webster and Schloss Financials."

"Call me Parry. I wasn't expecting to hear from you so soon. Is this bad news?"

"Well, Mr. Cohen, Parry, it's like this. We started doing our due diligence—your own financials look great, by the way, no problem there—but we ran into a couple of surprises."

"Surprises? Such as?"

"Have you talked to anyone else about this project?"

"Not since talking to you. Why?"

"It turns out there are at least two other companies looking to build a resort on Kakuloa, for similar reasons to those you mentioned."

"I told you it was a great idea," Parry said, outwardly cheerful but cursing his rotten luck. He was sure he'd been the first mover on this.

"Apparently so, which is both encouraging and discouraging. It seems like a solid idea, but we don't know if it can handle two or more competing businesses in that market. In the future when it proves out perhaps, but...."

"So you've got to pick a winner. I'm guessing I'm not it." *Shit.* All that work down the drain. Maybe he could sell his share in the helicopter and what property rights he had there. Or perhaps hold the latter; they might be worth more in future.

"Oh, no. Sorry, you misunderstand. Your proposal is actually the most advanced of the three we've heard about. There may be others, but I'm sure if they were as far along as yours we'd have heard about them."

Parry didn't know how to react. Did Griffin just say that he'd won out over the other two? He felt his pulse pounding. "So, just to be clear, are you telling me I've got my financing?"

"Well, yes and no."

"What does that mean?"

"How do you feel about taking on partners? We, ah, we've had a few backroom chats with some of the potential backers of the other projects, and, to be frank, we're all still a bit leery of the level of risk. We think it has a much better chance of success if the three of you partner up, and leverage each other's synergies, as it were."

"Partners? Who?" Parry was afraid he'd be relegated to some minority position with a couple of the resort megacorporations he was always competing against.

"I can't give you their names right now, this has to be negotiated carefully. I can say that from Webster and Schloss's point of view, you would be the major player. Like I said, your project is furthest along. If you're amenable, we'd like to set up a meeting between all the various players. The best approach would be to create a new company, Centauri Development Corp or some such, and allocate the shares appropriately between the principals and the money people."

"Fifty percent for you and me and twenty-five each for the other two?" Parry said, knowing that was unlikely.

"Ha. I like your optimism, but more likely forty, thirty, and thirty. But we'll know better when we all sit down in a room together."

"How soon?"

"What?" The question caught Griffin by surprise.

"How soon can we all sit down together? At least to get a preliminary agreement and letters of intent. I'd like something I can take to Sawyer's World. I've got land commitments pending."

"You do move fast."

"We're talking about a lot of money, and now the cat is out of the bag, we don't want one of those other companies to back-stab us with a cut-out deal." Cohen knew the dirty little tricks of the business. He'd resorted to a few of them himself.

"I see your point. All right, I can get preliminary papers, especially non-disclosures and non-competes, drawn up by tomorrow. We can meet electronically first, then arrange a face-to-face at a convenient time."

"That sounds terrific. Get a copy to me and to my lawyer as soon as you can. I need to arrange another trip. And, thank you."

"No, thank *you*, Mr. Cohen. We look forward to a prosperous relationship."

Chapter 21: To the Moon

Earth

"The Moon? Why?" Ellie Greystone had asked when Victoria Holmes had told her.

"That's where your ship will depart from. Starships that have landed on terraformed planets aren't allowed back on Earth. Quarantine Directorate regulations. I think it's silly myself. Nothing is going to survive the trip on the outside of a ship, and in more than six years we haven't found anything that was potentially harmful to Earth that we couldn't contain or control. But those are the rules for the foreseeable future.

"And speaking of quarantine, I'm afraid you'll be required to be a guest of the Lunar Quarantine Facility for two weeks when you return. Same overabundance of caution, but you'll have access to the labs there, so you can get work done, and of course you'll be paid."

"You get a lot of marine biologists on the Moon, do you?" Greystone couldn't help blurting out.

"Well, no, but you wouldn't be the first. There is quite a team up there. The focus is split between checking for organisms that might be hazardous, and general research on the Kakuloa and Sawyer's World biospheres and how they've differentiated from each other, and from Earth, over the past sixty-five million years. But you'll have to ask someone else about that, my team is focused on the biochemical research."

"So, I'm an anomaly for you, then?"

"You could say that. But William Blake tells me he needs you, or someone like you, to help them with their squid problem, and

I need the farms to supply us with enough squidberry extract for us to ramp up production, so here we are. We engage specialists where we need them: botanists, agronomists, even climatologists and geologists. We try to integrate vertically, everything from growing precursors to distribution and marketing. We're a big company."

"I would have thought most of your pharmaceuticals were synthesized."

"Where we can and it makes sense, yes. But it's not always easy. If you're really interested I can give you a link to some background information on the corporate web site."

Greystone realized she was getting the discussion off track, and this was Holmes's polite way of redirecting her. Well, she was their research director; she'd be used to getting her scientists to refocus on the task at hand rather than chasing rabbits.

"That's okay," Greystone said. "You were saying, about the Moon?"

"There's a shuttle departing the Texas Spaceport every few days. Have you ever been to space?"

"No, but I logged over four hundred dives before I stopped counting. I'm used to that kind of weightlessness and wearing life support gear."

"It's not exactly the same, and there shouldn't be any need for you to suit up, but you shouldn't have any problem with the orientation. And we have a great anti-spacesickness drug."

"Ha! Why am I not surprised? But I never get seasick."

"That doesn't necessarily mean you won't get spacesick, but again, good to know. How soon can you be ready to leave?"

"I just need to finish packing. My mother is already at her sister's, they're going to check her into the facility in the morning."

"That's great news. And Ellie?"

"Yes?"

"Welcome aboard."

∞ ∞ ∞

Luna

The trip to the Moon had been uneventful, and quicker than Greystone had expected. The days of boosting on chemical engines to a three-day transfer orbit had come to a close. The same compact fusion power plants that had made interstellar travel—routine wasn't quite the right word yet, but nearly so—allowed plasma thrusters to cut the trip down to a half a day. From low Earth orbit, the ship accelerated at a constant one-tenth gee, turning over at the midpoint and decelerating the rest of the way. The turnover maneuver, halfway into the twelve-hour trip, gave them a few minutes of zero gee.

Greystone remembered a time, when her research took her to the Great Barrier Reef, when it took longer than that to fly to Australia. Mostly it still did; supersonic passenger jets were only marginally cheaper than suborbital hops. There was still plenty of subsonic air travel, but that was changing too.

She didn't see much of the Moon itself. Travelling to the Lunar Quarantine Facility from the landing area no longer required suiting up and crossing seventy-five meters of sintered regolith. Now, a bus-like vehicle hard-docked to the Moon shuttle to ferry them the distance, and then docked in turn with the LQF. A similar arrangement would take her to the starship when the time came. Over the past few years, concern about cross contamination had eased, although not faded completely.

∞ ∞ ∞

After a short tour of the Quarantine Lab, Ellie Greystone caught her first glimpse of the starship that would take her to Alpha Centauri. She'd been briefed on it, of course, but the view out of one of the few windows on the base caught her breath. Some hundred meters away, against the stark gray backdrop of the lunar surface, sat the gleaming white delta of the starship *Valiant*.

"Why is it streamlined? Are we not landing on Kakuloa's moon?" Ellie asked when she saw it. There would be no need for a smooth shape in that case.

"Kakuloa actually has two moons, Mahina Nui and Mahina'uku, and no, there's no need to land on either of them. There *is* a quarantine base on Mahina Nui, but that's for any ships returning from other systems. *Valiant* will do a direct descent to Krechet's Landing, hence the aerodynamics. There's not much concern about cross contamination in that direction. Isolation here on Luna protects the exoplanets as much as it does Earth."

"Do the moon names mean anything? Somebody told me that Kakuloa was a made-up word."

"It is. The moon names are actually Hawaiian; they mean *Big Moon* and *Tiny Moon*. Mahina'uku is a bit smaller than the asteroid Ceres. The namers weren't very imaginative."

"Could have been worse, I suppose. They could have used English."

"There is that."

Chapter 22: Shipboard

Starship Valiant, *above the Moon*

"*All hands,*" the Captain announced over the ship's PA, "*we will be cutting acceleration shortly and rotating into position for the warp to Alpha Centauri. For those of you who haven't made the trip before, there will be a few minutes of microgravity, then when we go to warp we will have full apparent Earth gravity. Please make sure you and everything around you is secured for free-fall, and remain strapped in until we're in warp and I give the you the all clear. Once again, free-fall in one minute. Please stay strapped in and stand by.*"

Ellie Greystone lay on the bunk in her "stateroom" aboard the *Valiant.* By comparison, a sleeping compartment on an old-fashioned train would have been spacious by comparison; this room wasn't much bigger than a closet. She'd had similar-sized, or smaller, accommodations in sea-going boats, and those had sometimes pitched and rolled far more than any maneuvers the *Valiant* had so far done, so it wasn't a great hardship. On the other hand, it wasn't like she could go above decks once they were under way.

It was a pity there wouldn't be time to play in weightlessness; turnover on the way to the Moon had been brief and she'd been strapped into her seat. Ellie was no stranger to the neutral buoyancy of diving, and she wondered how that compared with microgravity. She looked around. The compartment was small; how much trouble could she get into? She loosened her shoulder straps and undid her lap belt.

"*Engine cut off coming up. Zero-gee in five, four, three, two, one. MECO.*"

There was a brief feeling of falling as the acceleration stopped, and silence as the sounds of the engines and pumps faded. Ellie shrugged off her straps and floated free of her bunk. *This is awesome!* It wasn't like being weightless in water. There, her inner ear and the fluids in her internal organs constantly reminded her she was in a one-gee field, just being buoyed by the water, its drag impeding her motions. But here, in real microgravity, it was different. She pushed away from a bulkhead, picking up a slight rotation. As she drifted to the middle of her compartment, she tucked her arms and legs, increasing her spin, then stretched them out to slow herself down. She was living a physics lesson in angular momentum. Ellie grinned so widely she felt her cheeks hurt.

Then came the thumps of the maneuvering jets pulsing. The bulkhead moved and the room rotated about her. Her cabin wasn't in the exact center of the ship, so there was some sideways motion as well as rotation, but it was close enough. *Wow, that's a little disorienting, kind of like a bad virtual reality experience.* She realized the ship was twisting and turning to line up on Alpha Centauri. She reached out, touching the overhead to steady herself relative to the room. *This could take some getting used to.* There was a strange feeling in her guts, as though something wasn't quite right. *I wonder if this is what seasickness feels like?* She'd never experienced that herself, but then, *she* wasn't doing the moving, it was everything else. *Just like VR sickness*, she realized, although she was beginning to adapt.

Then more thumps as the jets stopped the rotation, and Ellie found herself tumbling away from the walls. There were a couple of gentle thumps as the crew adjusted the alignment, which Ellie didn't feel but heard, and saw as short sudden movements of the room around her. She remembered that one didn't steer while in warp, one simply pointed and went.

"Secure for gravity, thirty seconds."

Oh, crap. Her bunk was now *above* her. That wouldn't do. She reached for one of the straps that were drifting from the bunk like strands of kelp above a seabed. She touched one and it bounced away from her hand. *Damn it.* If gravity came back while she was in this position, she'd fall headfirst. She might be able to cushion the fall with her arms and prevent a broken neck, but she could still break a bone. *I should have stayed strapped in.*

She bent sharply at the waist and tucked her knees up, putting herself into a slight tumble, then snapped straight as she came to a more upright position. She pushed herself down from the overhead and her feet touched the bunk—*Whew!*—and bounced off.

"Going to warp in five seconds. Stand by."

Nuke this shit! Ellie shoved herself back from the overhead again, and as her feet neared the bunk...

"Three."

...managed to grab a strap between her feet. Keeping them tightly together, she bent her knees to pull herself down towards the bunk...

"Two."

...and bent over to grab the strap with her hands. She quickly pulled herself towards the bunk's surface...

"One."

...and managed to get her body at least near the bunk.

"Warp."

Gravity came back in full force, and Ellie thumped awkwardly onto the bunk. "Ouch," she said aloud, rubbing the elbow that had slammed into the bulkhead as she fell. Her stomach muscles were a little sore, too. It took surprisingly more effort to bend at the waist without gravity helping. She lay on her bunk, contemplating the wisdom of following instructions in an unfamiliar environment.

A short while later, presumably after they had run systems checks, another announcement came.

"All clear. We're in warp for the next thirty-six hours. You're free to move around the ship, but please stay clear of the bridge and other restricted areas."

Ellie rolled out of her bunk. That didn't leave a lot of other space, beyond the mess and the head, but it was worth checking out.

∞ ∞ ∞

"Hi, my name's Parry, Parry Cohen. You don't look like one of the crew or the usual CentPharm employees. What takes you to Alpha Centauri? Scientist? And are you headed to Kakuloa or Sawyer's World?"

The middle-aged man smiled broadly and stuck out his hand.

"Oh, uh, hi. Kakuloa. And yes, scientist," she said, shaking the proffered hand. "Actually, I'm on contract with CentPharm. My name's Ellie Greystone. Marine biologist. And you, Mr. Cohen?"

"Parry, please. We're on this boat for the next few days. I'm, ah, I'm involved with construction. With more people heading out there, I keep busy."

"So, this isn't your first trip out there?"

"No, it's my second, and I'll be going to both Kakuloa and Sawyer's World. It's a bit of a headache. Most of the work is on Kakuloa, but nearly all the administration is on Sawyer's. It'll be worth it, though. I just got the next round of financing approved for the next stage of the project, I just need to finish the paperwork at Sawyer's."

"Couldn't you just do that by email—" Ellie started to say, then realized her error. "Oh, no, of course you couldn't. All messages have to go by ship if you don't want to wait nine years for an answer."

"Right, so it's either send a courier or hand-carry it myself. And there's no good interstellar courier service yet. But enough about paperwork. What's a marine biologist doing for CentPharm, if I may ask?"

Ellie realized she may have already said too much. Why would CentPharm want a marine biologist if not for something to do with the tree squids? Could news of a potential problem have a negative impact on CentPharm stock price if it got out? That was outside her expertise.

"Well, technically I'm under a non-disclosure agreement until I'm ready to publish any discoveries. But you can imagine that pharmaceutical companies have considerable interest in the biological sciences in general." All true, if uninformative.

"Oh, sure, no problem. There's parts of my work I can't talk about either. So, marine biologist? Do you SCUBA dive?"

Ellie laughed. "Sorry, I shouldn't laugh. I suppose there are marine biologists who don't dive, but I'm not one of them. Yes, I've been diving for years. You?"

"I do, as a matter of fact. Oh, nothing fancy, but I've been to a few resorts. Do the tourist thing, see the fancy reefs and the pretty fish. It's strictly recreational; I hire professionals if the construction requires water work."

"I don't think I've ever been on a tourist dive like that. I've dived reefs, of course, but it's usually off of a converted fishing boat after living in a tent or a run-down hotel on the beach. I couldn't afford the fancy resorts."

Parry grinned. "I'll let you in on a secret. The diving you get to do is probably way better than anything the tourists see. But here," Parry fished out a business card and handed it to Ellie. "When you get back to Earth, if you're interested, give me a call. I have a few connections in the resort business. It's worth staying in a luxury hotel at least once just to see what it's like. I can probably arrange a comp. For that matter, if you ever want to make a working vacation of it, I might be able to get you a temporary job as a dive guide. Not your usual thing, I'm sure, but something to think about."

Ellie took the card, surprised. Who used business cards anymore? "Ah, thanks. That's a kind offer. I'll keep it in mind." She looked around. Parry was pleasant enough, but she didn't want to spend the whole trip talking to him. Besides, Victoria Holmes had given her a stack of files to review. "You've been on these trips before. How do meals work?"

Parry looked around too. "Well," he said, "you've come to the right place. This is the mess, or the galley. Both, actually."

"Ah. I thought it might be." She'd already known that.

"Sure. Generally, there are snacks available through the autochef, but there's usually a sit-down meal once a day, typically dinner. There should be another couple of passengers aboard, but if they've been on the Moon for a while they still may be getting used to Earth-strength gravity."

Ellie hoped they'd come in and rescue her soon.

Chapter 23: Kakuloa Arrival

Krechet's Landing Spaceport

As Ellie Greystone reached the foot of the ship's ramp, a fit-looking man, with short, salt-and-pepper hair and a piercing gaze, extended his hand to her. "Doctor Greystone, it's good to meet you," he said, and smiled. "I'm Will Blake, your liaison with Cent-Pharm and kind of the general administrator here. Welcome to Kakuloa. How was your trip?" Overhead, Alpha Centauri B shone brightly.

"Oh, Mr. Blake. I wasn't expecting to be met, I thought I'd have to call you." She'd been briefed on who he was, but like Parry Cohen's contracts, other details couldn't be worked out at interstellar distances.

"We were half-expecting you, or somebody, anyway, and we knew the ship's schedule. *Valiant* dumped its messages when it entered the system; that gave me a heads-up."

"Oh, of course." The last few hours of the trip had been in partial-gee as the ship maneuvered in-system, alternating between normal space and short jumps to warp.

"Anyway, things are pretty informal here. No worries about customs or immigration. You're working for Centauri Pharmaceuticals, so that's all taken care of." He ushered her away from the ship and toward a small building a hundred meters away, the spaceport terminal, such as it was. Around her, servicing vehicles were starting to swarm around the ship like remora around a shark.

"I've made arrangements for you to stay at Dave Newton's farm. His is the largest and one of the worst hit by the tree squids. It's centered on Klaar and Tyrell's original find. I hope that's all right?"

"That sounds fine. What sort of facilities does he have, and how do I get there?"

"He'll be along shortly to take you up there. His family has a relatively big place, and a lab. He's got a CentPharm ecologist-agronomist working up there now."

They reached the terminal building. It was clearly a temporary structure, but there was construction going on nearby. It was set against the spaceport fence, but that fence was currently more a suggestion than an actual barrier, just enough to let people know where there might be a hazard from arriving or departing space-craft, or their service vehicles. Inside the door was another man, older and more weather-worn than Blake, clearly waiting for them.

"Administrator Blake," he said, extending his hand, "good to see you again. Is this our squid specialist?"

Blake shook the man's hand and then turned to Ellie. "This is Dave Newton. Dave, may I present Doctor Ellie Greystone, marine biologist and yes, cephalopod expert."

Newton and Greystone shook hands.

"Welcome to Kakuloa, Doctor Greystone. I hope you can help us with our little problem."

"Ellie, please, Mr. Newton. That's what I'm here for."

"Just Dave is fine." He turned to Blake. "Are there any formalities we need to go through?"

"It's all taken care of. No worries."

"Great." Newton turned back to Ellie. "Then as soon as we collect your gear we can head up to the farm."

"Oh, okay." Ellie had thought she might get a chance to see the local settlement first.

"You're not missing much here," Blake said, sensing her dis-appointment.

"He's right," Newton said. "This is mostly just the spaceport, with a few admin buildings, warehouses, and so on. Things are pretty distributed on Kakuloa right now, although that's chang-ing. Anyway, we can come back to town, such as it is, later in the week. If there's something you forgot to pack, we can probably take care of it. The farm is a hundred-fifty kilometers north of here. The quickest way is by air, but our aircar is down for maintenance this morning. My boat's down at the docks if you don't mind a trip up the coast. It's longer by boat, we have to go around a peninsula, but the boat is pretty fast too."

Ellie Greystone smiled at this. She was a marine biologist, that was why she was here in the first place. "That's fine. That will be a nice change from being cooped up on the starship. Boats are like a second home to me, why would I mind?"

Newton shook his head. "No, of course you wouldn't, what was I thinking? Let's get your gear."

∞ ∞ ∞

Ellie had a backpack with the changes of clothes, toiletries and other items she'd needed with her for the three-day trip. She hoisted it onto her shoulder as Newton grabbed for it. "I've got this, but there's a suitcase checked into the *Not Needed on Voyage* cargo area," she said.

"Fair enough. I'll show you where that gets unloaded." He gestured toward the terminal building. "It's across the field. This way."

There were two other starships besides the just-landed *Valiant* on the field, similar in design.

"Busy place," Ellie said. "I'm surprised. I didn't think there was that much traffic between here and Earth. Or is it between here and Sawyer's World?"

Newton looked over at the starships. "Neither," he said. "Those ships are about to head out into deeper space. Alpha Centauri is something of a jumping off spot. By an accident of stellar geography, we're some light-years closer than Earth is to several of the nearer stars likely to have terraformed planets."

"Oh?"

"Well, Epsilon Eridani and Tau Ceti are about the same distance from Earth, but Epsilon Indi and Delta Pavonis are nearer to here," Newton said as they walked. "An expedition to Epsilon Indi left a couple of weeks ago."

"Why from here and not Sawyer's World?"

"A mixture of politics and practicality. On the practical side, Krechet's Landing is a better spaceport, although they're building one on Sawyer's. From a political standpoint, Sawyer's World is technically independent of Earth, whereas this place is neutral. Those two," he nodded at the ships on the field, "are *Union de Terre* exploration ships. I think they're heading out to Delta Pavonis in a few days, or maybe 82 Eridani. I hear the star names tossed out in the local news, but I don't follow it closely. Too many things here to worry about.

"Speaking of that," Newton continued, changing the subject, "what do you know about why you're here?" he asked. "Ms. Holmes must have told you enough to interest you, since you are here, but I don't know what else."

"To tell you the truth, Mr. Newton—"

"Just Dave, I told you, please."

"—Dave, she had me at *tree squids*, although I had to get a few issues resolved before leaving." That was an understatement, but she had managed. "Anyway, Kakuloa's arboreal cephalopods have fascinated me since I first heard of them, and nobody has really studied them yet."

"That's a mouthful, *arboreal cephalopods*."

"Well, they're not really squids. More like octopus."

"Oh, I know that. Too many syllables though. Although often as not it's more like *damned tree squids* or *bloody tree squids*. Or worse."

"Yes. Elizabeth Holmes said you were having a problem with them and hoped I could help. What sort of problem?"

"They've taken to raiding the squidberry crops. At first it was sporadic. They'd make their way past our fences and harvest the ripest berries. They eat them, sometimes they seem to get drunk on them."

"I'd heard that the squidberry juice had many interesting chemicals in it, and that it could ferment on the vine."

"'Interesting.' Yes, that's one word for it. How much did Holmes brief you on exactly what we're doing here?"

"You're raising squidberries and providing extract so that the pharmaceutical companies have enough for pilot projects and drug trials. Apparently, they won't grow on Earth."

"That's the gist of it, anyway. Did she make you sign a nondisclosure?"

"Limited. I get to write up any scientific findings on the cephalopod behavior, but everything else is trade secret."

"Okay. Plenty of rumors about it anyway, but the main interest in squidberries is a biochemical with anti-agathic properties."

"Anti-aga...an anti-*aging* drug? Seriously?" So *that's* what Holmes had been hinting at.

"Serious enough for the pharmaceutical companies to have ponied up several billion dollars to complete development of the *Endeavour*-class starships and help launch the return expeditions here."

Ellie knew they'd been involved, but the extent of that had been downplayed. The news hype had been the planned rescue of the crew of the *USS Anderson*, whose voluntary stay on Kakuloa's sister planet had turned out to last four years longer than anyone had expected. Meanwhile, the biopharmaceutical companies had been investigating samples returned by *Anderson*'s sister ships with, it would seem, amazing results.

"No wonder they don't want anything happening to your crop. So, you want me to find a way to keep tree squids out of it? How hard could that be?"

Newton barked a short laugh. "You of all people know how smart cephalopods are."

"Very intelligent for invertebrates, yes. And octopus are flexible enough to squeeze through very small openings."

"Smart enough to figure out how to carry berries in a bag?"

"*What?*"

∞ ∞ ∞

Newton explained how McWhirter had discovered the drunken tree squid after the raid on the berry farm.

"Octopuses are smart," Ellie said. "Some even use tools, if you can call building walls around their dens tool use. It's a stretch, but I could see where one might figure out how to carry things in a bag. Did anyone see any others with bags?"

"No, they were gone, except for a few that were too drunk, or high, or whatever it is they get, to move. But of those only one had a bag."

"A fluke, then."

"Not with eighty percent of the crop gone. They didn't eat it all there, and they couldn't carry that much without containers of some kind."

"But where would they get the bags?"

"We don't know for sure, but we think they were left behind by the first expedition. The *Chandrasekhar* landed in a broad river valley, and they had to jettison excess weight to bring the crew of the *Krechet* back with them. An unused carton of specimen bags, left out in the weather for six years? Maybe they washed downstream. Maybe the squids swam upriver to find more."

"How far from your farm to that valley?"

"Roughly a hundred kilometers."

"That's a very long way for an octopus to travel. Real squids, perhaps, since they're more efficient swimmers. Is there a long shore current? Which way does it travel?"

"The wave current is usually from north to south along that stretch. I'm not sure about away from shore. But I really don't care where they got them, I just want the damn tree squids to stay out of my mangrove trees and away from the berries."

"Okay, that probably doesn't bear on your immediate problem. It is a long way, though. Perhaps it shows what the cephalopods—" she still couldn't bring herself to call them squids "—are capable of.

∞ ∞ ∞

They arrived at the dock where Newton's boat was tied up. It was close to a dozen meters long, with a sleek shape that looked like it was built for speed. It was bigger than what she was expecting. The name was also unusual.

"The *Disco Volante*? Flying disk? What's the story there?"

"Flying saucer, actually. It's an old movie reference," Newton said. "You'll find out. Mind you, she's not as big or as fancy as her namesake."

"She's still big. How did you get it here? That's too big for a starship, isn't it?"

"It is. The motors, controls and fittings were brought in, but the rest of it was built locally. There are a couple of large three-dee fabbers in town, and they do a good business. The decking and trim is local hardwood."

A third of the way fore and aft on each side there were side mounted pods or modules. Greystone wasn't familiar with the design. "What are those? Outriggers?"

Newton grinned. "Something like that. I'll show you when we get out past the breakers, where the water is smoother."

She stowed her gear and helped Newton cast off, and the boat surged away from the dock with the hum of heavy-duty electric motors. In a few minutes they were a kilometer off shore and Newton turned the boat northward.

"All right, now I'll show you what those are." He activated a control and she heard a muffled *clunk* of machinery deploying.

She leaned over the rail to look at the pods, which now extended streamlined struts down into the water, with horizontal planes unfolding at the ends. Not outriggers. "*Hydrofoils?*"

Newton grinned broadly at her. "Hold on to something." She grabbed the rail, and he shoved the throttles forward. As the motors' hum rose to a whine, the boat surged forward, lifting almost immediately up onto the foils, now flying through the water like wings. Ellie staggered not only against the acceleration, but against the ever-increasing force of the wind.

"How fast will it go?" She had to yell over the noise.

"Top speed is about 150 kph, I usually keep it to one-twenty. We'll be there in just over an hour."

Ellie grinned. She could get used to this.

Chapter 24: Newton's Berry Farm

Kakuloa, Western Ocean

They continued north, paralleling the coast. The basalt cliffs near Krechet's Landing gave way to broad beaches, occasionally lost to view as huge rolling waves swelled between the boat and shore. A few tens of meters inland, the ground rose slightly, revealing lush vegetation, similar to, but different from, what one might find near the shores of the Hawaiian islands on Earth. There were fewer palm trees here, and more of something like Norfolk pine, as well as other broadleaved trees Greystone didn't recognize. Where streams met the shore, there were often the multi-rooted mangrove trees that the squidberry vines—themselves banyan-like—grew upon. The first landers had been right. This part of the planet, at least, reminded her of Hawaii.

"Take a look." Newton pointed to the shore as they passed one small mangrove-choked creek. Back from shore, through the trees, Ellie could just make out a small structure, possibly a house.

"That's a small squidberry farm, Jim Lofgren's. See how close the hills come to the shore?"

"Yes." The thickly forested hills started rising just one or two hundred meters back, with the ridgeline perhaps a kilometer inland.

"The creeks along this stretch are relatively short and narrow, not the best habitat for the trees and squidberry vines."

"So why does he have a farm here?"

"Lower cost. Also, he doesn't have as many problems with tree squids. It balances out. Something to keep in mind."

"Good to know. I wonder if it's at the edge of their range or there's something about the creeks or the berries they don't like."

"It might be the range. It's another sixty or seventy kilometers to my farm, and very little to interest tree squids between there and here."

"At least at the shoreline," Ellie said. "I wonder what the bottom's like."

∞ ∞ ∞

The farm.

Newton angled the boat toward shore, toward a cove formed by a short spit of land and the outlet from a creek, lined with the ubiquitous banyan-like trees. A few kilometers back they had rounded a peninsula, so the coast here did not see the kind of massive waves that they'd seen nearer Krechet's Landing.

As they pulled closer to shore, Greystone spotted the floating dock along one bank of the inlet, with a couple of smaller boats tied up to it. A gangway connected it to a wooden walk leading up towards the large house, which was on higher ground back from the water.

Newton brought the boat alongside with practiced ease. Two men, one who looked to be in his forties, the other much younger, —barely out of his teens, if that— were standing on the wharf waiting.

"Toss them a line, would you?" Newton said to her, nodding at a rope coiled on the deck, near the stern.

Greystone had spent enough time aboard watercraft of all sizes to know her way around. She picked up the coil, double checked that one end was secured to a cleat, and tossed it to the younger man on the wharf, who deftly caught it and began pulling the boat in. At the bow, Newton had done the same, throwing a line there to the other man.

"Bumpers!" Newton called, but Greystone had anticipated this and was already pushing the fenders over the edge to provide a cushion between the hull and the edge of the wharf. Newton nodded approvingly.

When the moorings were secure, Newton gestured to Greystone, and addressed the two men on the dock. "Gentlemen, may I present Doctor Ellie Greystone. Doctor, my chief hand, Rob McWhirter and my son, Gulliver."

"Call me Ellie," she said, and stepped down onto the wharf to shake hands.

"You can call me Gully, almost everyone else does."

"Gully," the elder Newton said, "come give me a hand with her bags."

Before she could object, Gulliver had leaped aboard the boat and grabbed the pack and the suitcase his father had pointed at.

"Here, I'll take my pack," Ellie said as he reached across the narrow gap between boat and wharf, grabbing it as she did so.

Gulliver slung the suitcase onto the wharf and followed behind it, picking it up again before she could.

"Take her on up to the house," Newton told the others. "I'll secure the boat, unless one of you were planning on taking it out?"

"No, Dad, that's fine."

McWhirter gestured at Greystone's pack. "Are you sure I cannae take that?"

"I'm fine, thanks," she said. She walked the length of the dock, looking at the mangrove trees and the numerous thick roots extending into the water on both sides of the creek. The bark was smooth. A motivated octopus would have no problem climbing that. Ellie had seen a common octopus climb up a smooth concrete wall, its suckers gripping the surface. Even the smaller-diameter roots, a few centimeters across, would provide plenty of grip for an octopus with an arm wrapped around one.

"Something wrong, lass?" McWhirter asked.

"Oh, no, I was just curious about the trees. About how easy it would be for an octopus to climb them."

"Verra easy. I can tell ye that from personal observation." McWhirter sounded irked, and his accent had thickened.

"And there are too many connecting roots and trunks to just wrap them all with something they couldn't climb. I'm beginning to see the problem."

"Indeed. But let's get you settled in first."

"Yes, thank you. Please, lead on." She bit down before adding *Macduff*. That probably wouldn't go over well. Besides, the line was "lay on," not "lead on."

"All right, lass. This way." He led off up the path, Gully Newton following with her other bag.

∞ ∞ ∞

The house was surprisingly large, although much of it was pre-fabricated.

"This place is much bigger than I expected. The second expedition was just two years ago."

"Two Earth years. Closer to three in Kakuloa years, and we've been busy. Centauri Pharmaceuticals was very anxious to get this operation going."

"But there are still years of clinical trials yet, surely?"

"Aye, but they're confident. And they need enough product to engineer their pilot production. It takes nearly a ton of berries to produce a gram of pure cephalomycin, and—fortunately for us here—they've nae had success growing them on Earth. Anyway, as to the size, we were all in this one building when we first started setting up the farm. We're spread out more now."

"How big is the farm?"

"We have a fair bit of land, but only a wee part of it is productive. We're slowly expanding the mangrove orchard. You'll see some of that on the tour. We're digging channels to expand the habitat, but it will take a few years to get the new trees to a state where the berry vines bear fruit. That's assuming we can get the damned squids to leave them alone."

"I see."

McWhirter had led her up a stairway to the second floor. That was part of what had surprised Greystone about the place, she had expected something more sprawling and single level, although this was a far cry from the traditional plantation house.

"Why build up instead of out?" she asked.

"Better view from up here. Mister Newton likes to be able to survey his domain, so to speak. We spend enough time in the trees, it's nice to be able to look out over them."

There was a short hallway at the top of the stairs, with several doorways leading off it. McWhirter opened one of them and waved Greystone into it.

"This is one of the guest rooms. It's yours while you're here." McWhirter said. "There's a separate dorm for most of the regular hands, and I have a wee hut of my own. The Newton family lives in the house, of course, and you'll be meeting Juliette de la Paz and Henry Caporale. Juliette is the accountant, bookkeeper and general paper pusher. Henry is up here from Krechet's Landing. He's a biologist, well, more an agronomist, doing studies on the local ecosystems to make sure we don't accidentally do anything that would interfere with our crop."

Greystone nodded. "Yes, Mr. Blake mentioned something about that."

"Centauri Pharmaceutical's idea. They have a lot of money invested in the whole Alpha Centauri project, they dinnae want to mess it up." McWhirter said.

Ellie felt his tone suggested that he didn't care one way or the other, but just nodded.

"Anyway, Henry and Juliette are each in their own guest rooms, just down the hall. I'm afraid it's a communal bathroom, like a boarding house. It's not exactly luxurious here, but it keeps the rain off."

"Mister McWhirter—"

"Rob, please."

"Rob, I've lived everywhere from aboard ship—sea-going, not just starships—to a tent on a beach. I'm sure this will be fine."

"Aye, of course. We have a large dining room, usually everybody eats together."

Dave Newton, who had caught up from securing the boat and reached the top of the stairs in time to hear McWhirter's comment, said: "Of course you're welcome to help yourself to what's in the kitchen at any time. As I said before, if there's anything else you need, just let me know and we'll arrange to get it for you."

"Thank you." Ellie was anxious to find out more about the tree squids, but she was also feeling overwhelmed from the events of the last few days. "If you'll give me a few minutes to put things away and get cleaned up? Then we can get started."

The men all suddenly looked like they'd remembered they had somewhere else to be, which they very likely did.

"Take your time, Doctor," said Newton. He glanced at his omni. "Dinner's in three hours, at six. Why don't you come join us then? If you're hungry now, I can have the kitchen rustle up a snack."

"Aye lass," McWhirter said. "I've got other work to do now. I'll just be off." He turned to leave, then paused to look at Gulliver. "Lad?"

Gulliver looked quickly at McWhirter, then at his father, then back to McWhirter. "Ah, right. Yessir." He nodded to Greystone. "Ma'am." He followed McWhirter out.

"Smart boy you have there. Do you have other children?"

"A younger daughter. She's back at Krechet's Landing with her mother. There's a small school there. My wife teaches and does some of Blake's administrative work on the side. They'll be back for the weekend."

"I look forward to meeting them." Ellie paused, realizing that between the days in space and whatever Kakuloa's rotation rate was, there was an important detail she was missing. "Uh, this will sound dumb, but what day is it today?"

"Ha, not dumb at all. It's Tuesday. We keep a seven-day week, so does Sawyer's World, although the day and month lengths are different, so we're not in sync. There's an app."

"Right," she had got some of that from the briefing, but this planet's similarities masked the differences. "Thank you. That's going to take some getting used to."

"No worries. Anyway, I'll leave you to settle in. Feel free to roam around the house. Closed doors are bedrooms or offices, please respect their privacy. I'll have someone show you around the grounds later, I suggest you keep to the house until then. There shouldn't be anything really dangerous out there, but it is a working farm on a wild planet." He paused, as if wondering to bring up another point. "Do you have any weapons training?"

"Weapons? I've caught dinner with a spear-gun a few times, but no. I thought you said there wasn't anything really dangerous?"

"Not so much around these parts. The first landing crew didn't find anything either, surprisingly. A few smaller predators that kept the babbits in check, and something like a hawk, but nothing big. Further south and away from the coast there are crocodilians, but they don't seem to like the salt water. I've never seen them around here. Don't worry about it. I was just curious. We do have a range and McWhirter or I would be happy to give you some instruction. Might be worthwhile if you're going to be out on the frontier."

She shrugged. She didn't have strong feelings one way or the other. Weapons were tools, and Newton had a point. She just didn't know how much she might be "out on the frontier" after this job. But large animals weren't the only potential danger.

"What about snakes or spiders?" she asked. "Anything venomous?" The octopuses were likely venomous, of course, but very few species were dangerously so. And she knew how to be careful with them.

"Nothing we've had trouble with. Do they bother you? I wouldn't have thought a biologist—"

"Oh no, not at all. Just checking."

Newton chuckled. "Okay then. There are a few critters that can be a nuisance; here, I'll give you the link to the newcomer orientation page." He tapped the omni on his wrist, and her omni beeped in acknowledgment.

She checked it. "Got it."

"Here, while I'm thinking of it," he said, tapping his omni again, "this should give you access to anything you'll need here in the house."

"Ah, thanks."

Newton nodded. "I think you'll do all right here. Again, welcome, and I'll see you at dinner."

"Six o'clock," she confirmed, setting an alarm on her omni. "Thank you."

∞ ∞ ∞

Ellie unpacked a few things from her bag and went down the hall to check out the bathroom. The place was no hotel, but it was far ahead of some of the old boats she'd spent days at sea on, or the wooden huts on tropical beaches.

Back in her room she flopped on the bed. The furnishings were simple. The chair and bedside table were constructed from rough-hewn local timber, while the bed and combination desk/dresser were kit-built from flat-pack furnishings. The latter were of the sort one could find in almost any apartment on Earth. That wouldn't take up much space to transport. It was better than she'd been expecting. *So this is Kakulo*a, she thought. It didn't *feel* much different from Earth. She knew the gravity here was three percent higher, and the sun more orange, but those differences were below the threshold of human perception. The vegetation beyond the window wasn't anything she specifically recognized, but it was close enough to Earth life that she could as easily be in some semi-tropical area there that she hadn't visited before. As she thought about it, she realized that at night, even the stars wouldn't look much different. Alpha Centauri was close enough to Sol that the constellations were essentially the same. Although, she realized, instead of two bright stars to the west of the Southern Cross, there'd be just one.

She unwrapped her omni from her wrist, straightened it out, and unfolded it lengthwise twice, then touched the control to lock it in that position and expand the screen to the entire surface, turning it into a small info-pad. On the trip out she had reviewed general information about Kakuloa, but she might as well review the orientation brochure for specifics.

"Welcome to one of Centauri Pharmaceuticals squidberry farms," she read.

The material was a mix of planetary data she had already learned from reading about the First Expedition's findings, although then she had glossed over the astronomical details, being more interested in the biology.

Kakuloa orbited Alpha Centauri B, the smaller of the two major stars in the Centauri system, not counting Proxima, the distant red dwarf. Kakuloa orbited closer to its sun than Earth or Sawyer's World did, compensating for the star's slightly cooler temperature, and consequently it's year was only 243 days long. *Is that Kakuloa days or Earth days?* she wondered, then scrolled up the page to reveal the answer in a neat little comparison table. 243 local days, about 234.45 Earth days. There was a section on the local calendar: the year was eight months of alternating 30 and 31 days. There was an app, which she downloaded to her omniphone, that helpfully kept track of the current local time, Earth time, and Sawyer's World time. Ellie was beginning to get a headache just thinking about it: biology was so much simpler than astronomy. She wondered how the local lifeforms had managed to adapt from the day and year they had been used to when transplanted from Earth. If had been shortly after the end-Cretaceous impact, Earth's climate would have been so messed up that anything still surviving probably wouldn't have had too difficult a time of it. Then she remembered something she'd read about how days were shorter during the Cretaceous anyway. It had something to do with the Moon's tidal drag gradually slowing the Earth's rotation down. *Hah, they never mentioned that in time travel stories.*

Most of the biological details, such as they were—the article was written for intelligent laymen, not biologists—were data she already knew from the data the *Heinlein* expedition had brought back. Local lifeforms were based on terrestrial biology, having diverged sixty-five million Earth years earlier, as best as they could tell. Kakuloa had no native grasses, or at least none discovered so far, and other plants had evolved to fill that niche. The opposite was true on Sawyer's World, and some native Sawyer's World cereals were beginning to be raised as crops for human consumption. Ellie considered this of passing interest, she was more into zoology than botany.

As far as local pests went—and local here meant the area within a couple of hundred kilometers of the original landing sites, since most of the planet remained to be explored in detail—there were few. A few biting insects, one species of mildly venomous spider. Ellie chuckled to herself at that. *All* spiders were venomous, it was just that most of them had venoms that were at worst mildly irritating to humans or had mouth parts too small to puncture human skin. Presumably the article meant that there was one local species that managed to overcome both those limitations.

On the other side of the inland mountain range the climate was much drier, because of the rain-shadow effect. Probably the deserts held nastier species. Deserts usually did. She wondered if that was why she liked the ocean so much. On the other hand, the ocean had some pretty nasty lifeforms too. That was probably also true of the ocean here. She remembered something about jellyfish. There it was, she saw as she skimmed the page. Something like a bright green man-o-war. Okay, she had packed a lightweight wet suit. She had expected—hoped—to be doing some diving.

Ellie yawned. Much of this was review, and it had been a long day. She skimmed further.

The mangrove swamps, in addition to the trees providing a habitat for the berry-bearing vines, were also a hatchery and nursery for several local species of fish. That made sense, the same was true of mangroves on Earth. The brackish water in and around the roots provided natural shelter from larger predators, so the hatchlings had a chance to grow to where they could more easily survive in open water. Newcomers were warned not to disturb these, as the local ecosystem was still only poorly understood. Ellie was surprised at that enlightened view, but as she read further she recognized the company's self-interest at play: it was unknown what other valuable pharmaceuticals might be discovered. Sure, they'd hate to discover something only to realize its source was on the brink of extinction because they'd messed up its habitat.

She flipped through the rest of it. Much of it related to administrative details, safety procedures, and the usual sorts of things in a new employee orientation. Given her position as a consultant rather than a full-time employee, a lot of it was irrelevant. Just as well, she could barely keep her eyes open. She skipped ahead to the end.

"You will be given specific instructions and additional information relating to your particular job responsibilities," it read. She could hardly wait. "Enjoy your stay." She chuckled at that. *With no mint on the pillow?*

Ellie checked that she had already set a reminder alarm, then, based on the wisdom learned from dozens of field trips, rolled over, closed her eyes, and fell instantly asleep.

Chapter 25: Dinner

Newton Farmhouse

Ellie came down to the dining room at six. She was ravenous, and the aroma of cooking wafting up had made her more so. Since the *Valiant* was destined next for Sawyer's World, then back to Earth, it had kept Earth time, rather than spending the trip slowly synchronizing itself to Kakuloa local time. Her body clock was seriously out of whack, but the nap had helped.

The large dining room held two long tables, with seats for eight to ten at each. Ellie recognized several of the people seated at one table. She presumed the others were mostly field hands, or whatever the appropriate term was.

McWhirter had a seat to the right of the empty seat at the head of the nearer table. The seat to the left of that was also empty. "Doctor Greystone," he said, gesturing at the seat across from him, "please have a seat." He looked at Gulliver, sitting nearby. "Gully?"

"What? Oh!" The young man leaped out of his chair and came around the table to pull back the chair for her. She smiled as she sat down and he adjusted her chair.

"Thank you, but that's really unnecessary."

"Aye," McWhirter said, "but it's polite. It doesn't hurt to teach the youngsters manners, although it probably won't happen once your novelty wears off."

She laughed at that. "I see." She looked around at the unfamiliar faces, many of whom were staring back at her. "Uh, are you going to introduce me?"

"Mister Newton will be in shortly, he'll want to do the honors." McWhirter said. He looked toward the door. "Ah, here he is now."

"Gentles," Newton said, moving to his place at the head of the table but remaining standing. "My apologies for being late."

There were mutterings of "no, not at all" and the like, but Newton raised a hand to silence them.

"I'm sure most of you are wondering about our newcomer. Allow me to introduce her to you." In an aside, he asked Ellie to stand up. "This is Doctor Ellie Greystone, just arrived from Earth. She's a marine biologist, a foremost expert in cephalopods, octopus and squid."

That last prompted a few murmurs around the table.

"She's here to help solve our marauding tree squid problem. Please make her welcome and extend her every courtesy and assistance she needs."

There was a brief round of applause. Ellie nodded and said "Thank you. I'm looking forward to working with you."

"All right," said Newton. "I'm not going to slow dinner down any further by introducing all of you individually. You'll have an opportunity to introduce yourselves in the rec-room after dinner." He looked at Ellie. "Is that all right with you? We can put it off if you're tired."

"No, that's fine, I look forward to it."

"Right then." Newton looked toward the kitchen, which was behind Ellie, and nodded to someone. "Let's eat. I'm sure everyone is hungry."

∞ ∞ ∞

"So, Doctor Greystone—" Newton said conversationally as they began eating.

"Ellie, please," she said.

"Ellie, then. I noticed you examining the roots of the trees down at the dock. Did you come to any conclusions?"

"Only that there are too many to consider wrapping them in something the tree squids can't climb. In aquariums on Earth, we often have a problem with octopus climbing out of the tanks, so we've come up with a few solutions, but it's a more complicated problem here."

Newton nodded. "We tried something like that at first, but the squids either climbed up a different tree and then crawled across the branches, or somehow managed to just tear the material off."

"Octopus have chemical receptors in their suckers, it's part of how they search for food, tasting as they go. Maybe we can find something that tastes terrible to them and spray that on the bases of the trees. Collectors will sometimes squirt something like that into an octopus den to force it out."

"I don't think so," Henry, the ecologist sitting to her left, said.

"Why not?"

"Several reasons. Foremost, we'd have to study it extensively to be sure the chemical doesn't have any adverse effect on the squidberry crop itself, or on the squidberry fungus they extract the pharmaceuticals from. Better to lose a few berries to squids than all of them to the squid repellent."

"Oh, well, of course, but—"

"Secondly," Henry continued, "we'd have to research its effect on the fish hatchlings that make their homes around the roots. We don't want to accidentally poison a population, at least not until we know how it fits into the local ecology. Ethical considerations aside, we could be killing off something that could yield the next pharmaceutical marvel."

"Yes, it would have to be something harmless, just bad-tasting."

"And finally," Henry said, "it does rain here fairly often. The chemical would get washed off and have to be reapplied regularly." He paused, then added: "Sorry to rain on your parade, so to speak."

Ellie groaned. "Are your puns always that bad?"

Before he could answer, Dave Newton said: "No. Usually they're worse."

Ellie had been about to ask Henry whether he was just floundering around or doing it for the halibut, but at Newton's comment, she refrained and took another bite of her dinner.

Chapter 26: Orientation

Newton Farm, next day

Breakfast was again in the communal dining room, served buffet style. Ellie was expecting something like the fare she'd had at conference hotels, with emphasis on pastries and toast and less so on protein, but what she found was the opposite. There was a large dish of scrambled eggs, another of sausages, some smoked fish, but no bacon. There was toast, thin slices of a grain-heavy bread, but no pastries or breakfast cereal.

Henry Caporale joined her in the buffet line and eyed her plate. "You might want to take it easy on the sausage, it's spicy."

"I don't object to spicy. I wouldn't mind more toast though."

"Most flour is imported from Earth, so that's kind of a scarce commodity. There are no grasses on Kakuloa, so no cereal crops." He gestured at the toast. "The flour in this is probably from Sawyer's World. The *Anderson* team started cultivating grains soon after they landed, although they don't have anywhere near the starch content of typical Earth crops yet."

"Oh. And the eggs?" By now she and Henry had both filled their plates and made their way to a table. The seating at breakfast was also informal.

"Also from Sawyer's or Earth. So far nobody has had any luck trying to domesticate any local birds. There's been discussion of bringing in chickens, but we want to be sure they don't get loose and mess up the local ecology. The sausage, though is local."

Ellie cut one in half and raised it on her fork to examine it. It looked like sausage. She took a bite. There was a savory flavor to it, rather good, with a taste that wasn't like pork or beef, more like slightly fishy chicken...and then the spice took hold. It was *hot*. She felt herself breaking out into a sweat as she grabbed her glass of water and chugged it down.

"Wow! You weren't kidding about it being spicy!" she said between breaths. "Why do they make them that hot?"

Caporale grinned. "They don't add any spice. That's the way the meat comes."

"What? What kind of animal is this from?"

"Alphagator, the local alligator equivalent, a kind of crocodilian."

"But how is it spicy?" She took another drink of water, her mouth still burning. "This is more like hot peppers than horseradish. It's not toxic, right?" Ellie wondered who had ever decided this was edible, although the taste had begun to grow on her. She took another bite.

"No, no. It's something like the capsaicin in chili peppers. Nobody has quite figured out yet if it's from something in the gator's diet, or something they synthesize. It does get stronger in older animals."

"Surely they're carnivores. What could they be eating with capsaicin in it?"

"No idea. It hasn't been a high priority. But birds and reptiles aren't bothered by it the way mammals are, and maybe they're not exclusively carnivorous. Just like the tree squids."

"That's a weird thought. Anyway, if they developed it as a defense, I'd hate to meet the mammal that preys on them."

Henry grinned. "Pleased to meet you."

Ellie got his point—they were both eating alphagator sausage —but gave him a dirty look. "You don't look nearly old enough to have co-evolved with these things."

"Ha, fair point. And humans are quirky enough to enjoy spicy food."

"It is good," she said, "but it does take getting used to." She took a smaller bite of sausage, following it with a large bite of scrambled eggs. She looked around the dining room. "Is there coffee?"

"There's a vague analog of coffee, in that it's hot, brown, and contains caffeine. We get real coffee when a ship comes in, if we're lucky. If there was coffee in your ship's cargo, it wasn't destined for here, alas."

"If I'd known, I'd have packed some in my luggage. Damn."

"You get used to the other stuff. If you can eat gator sausage, you can drink the coffee. It's from Earth, but instant, not beans. And the list of things that you might have wanted to pack in your luggage is very long, but it's better than in the early days. I'd still kill for a pizza."

"No pizza?"

"Crust, cheese, tomato sauce, they're all in scarce supply here. Plenty of sausage, though." He grinned broadly. "Don't get me wrong, we eat well enough. Last night's dinner wasn't specially laid on for you. But most of the cargo coming from Earth is in the way of equipment, construction gear, and the like, rather than food. We can get by on eating what grows here far easier than we can make machinery from it."

"That's not too different from some tropical areas I've done research at. I was telling McWhirter yesterday that I've stayed in far worse accommodations than this. I'll survive."

"Well, I'm glad to hear that. We'd hate to lose you just because there's no pizza."

∞ ∞ ∞

After breakfast Newton sought out Greystone. "Come on, let's go for a ride," he said to her.

"A ride? Where to?"

"A flight, actually. Just around the farm, to give you an idea of the place. It's faster than walking, and I want to look over the squidberry trees anyway. Maybe you'll see squids."

"Okay, that sounds good."

Ellie followed Newton out to a pad between the house and the farmhands' outbuilding, where the vehicle was parked. The vehicle was an open-cockpit aircar, a multirotor.

"Have you flown in one of these before?" Newton asked, as Greystone looked the open-framed aircar over with apparent skepticism.

"Not exactly. Helicopters a few times, and an enclosed multi-rotor a couple of times, but nothing quite like this. It's usually boats." She looked the vehicle over again. Newton was already climbing in on the left side, so she climbed into the passenger seat.

"Nothing to worry about. It is noisier than a closed-cab, though." Newton reached down and came up with two sets of headphones. He handed one to her. "Here, this will keep the noise down, so we can talk."

Newton flipped a few switches, checked the display panel in front of him, and twisted the handle on the lever in his left hand. The rotors spun up with a whine, and the craft climbed into the air, kicking up a light spray of dust.

"This is the main compound," Newton said, hovering the craft just above the house's rooftop level and pivoting it around slowly. "The house is obvious. That way," he pointed, "is the path to the dock." He rotated the car further. "The dorm for the farmhands there, and that other building beside it is the garage and vehicle maintenance shed. We have a couple of ATVs and space for the aircar if the weather is coming up. There's a heavy-duty fabber and some other equipment for working on the vehicles as needed."

He let the car drift toward an area beyond the shed. It was surrounded by a tall, fine-meshed fence and contained several rows of trellises or racks, about half with vegetation draped over them.

Her first thought was that they were trying to grow the squid-berry vines on them, but the ground was dry and the vines were just hanging there, not touching the dirt. "What is that?" Greystone asked.

"Drying racks. We don't actually dry the berries too much, but if we let them get drier, kind of like raisins; the fungus is still active but the berries are smaller. Since space is at a premium on a starship, we can pack more in. Although," he continued after a short pause, "if we can't get this marauding squid problem under control, we won't have enough berries to worry about that."

"Have the squids ever tried to raid the drying area? You've got some pretty heavy duty fencing around it."

"Generally not, they don't seem to like crossing dry ground, and this is too far from the water. We did find a couple up against the fence during a heavy rain, though."

"Really? That's interesting. I wonder how they knew the berries were even there."

"Beats me. They might be able to see them from the treetops, but I'd be surprised if their vision was that good. Maybe they tasted something in the runoff water. They can't smell, can they?"

"Not the way you or I would, no. At least, terrestrial cephalopods can't. They can detect chemicals in the water, but I think *taste* is a better word for it than *smell*, so you may be right."

Newton looked thoughtful. "Huh. Do you suppose you could come up with any kind of squid repellent?"

Ellie considered that. Even if she could identify a suitable chemical, it might have to be continually added to the water, and who knew what side effects it could have. As Caporale had pointed out at dinner, the mangrove roots were a nursery for many kinds of fish, and she wouldn't want to add something that would harm them. "I'll certainly investigate that possibility. That's assuming I can even identify something that would repel them. I'll need to look at what predators they have. We can't just dump poison in the water, for one thing it might harm the berry crop." She didn't know if Newton would care about fish, but he would certainly care about that.

"Right, wouldn't want that," he said.

"Do you know anything about what might eat the cephalopods?"

"Not in the water. I'm sure something must, we have some pretty big fish here, but it hasn't been studied much. Something for you to do, if it helps solve the problem."

Greystone noted the conditional. They were definitely expect-ing her to focus on their specific issue, this was not just an academic investigation into the ecology and life cycle of arboreal cephalopods. Well, she could live with that.

"Wait, what did you mean, *not in the water*? Are there other predators?"

"I'm pretty sure there must be. Not that I've seen any, but at first they were very skittish with the air cars, and would drop into the water whenever one flew over the mangroves. We figured there was a bird of prey that had a taste for calamari, but I don't know that anyone has seen one, and eventually the squids started ignoring us."

"That's interesting. I wonder if your presence has scared off whatever predator it is. That might be worth checking into."

"What are you thinking?"

"If we can mimic the behavior of the predator with a small drone or ornithopter—"

"—it might scare the buggers off," Newton finished her thought. "Well, you've got access to the network, see what you can find."

While talking, they had continued flying and were now over the mangrove patch near the dock.

"Meanwhile, we're here. No squids today, from the looks of it. Sometimes they'll leave when we show up, but it's not like the panic before they got used to the aircars."

"What did they do then?"

"They'd just drop out of the trees, like it was raining squid, splashing down into the creek. There's probably video of it somewhere."

"I'd like to see that."

"I'll see what I can find. Let's head up the coast to the next patch."

"Just how big is your spread, anyway?" she asked.

"I've got twelve kilometers of coastline, and two kilometers back. There are four creeks in that with squidberry groves. We don't really need the two klicks back, the water is too fresh for the trees long before that, but it's a round number."

He turned the aircar to head north. "I give you a quick over-flight. Manning's farm to the north has ten kilometers of coast and three creeks, and there are other farms beyond that. This one is the biggest and probably the best. It certainly cost me."

"Cost? Doesn't CentPharm own the farms?"

"Not exactly. I'm not an employee of Centauri Pharmaceuticals. The agreement they came to with the various Earth and Alpha Centauri governments was that the company got certain rights to the berry areas up and down the coast. In turn, they did a lease-purchase deal with people who wanted to settle and farm it, but we bid on the parcels. It wasn't a cash deal, we bid based on offering a certain quantity of the berries at a certain agreed price. They also looked at our qualifications and likelihood of success, just like any other contract. I won't bore you with all the details, but it's like a farmstead. Eventually the property becomes all mine—or rather, my company's—and I can sell the squidberries for whatever the market will bear."

"That sounds like a sensible arrangement. It gives you incentive to tend the resource for the long haul, not just grab and go."

"Exactly. And since Centauri Pharmaceuticals wants us all to succeed, their self-interest extends to making sure we get as good a crop as we can, which is why you're here."

"So, whatever I come up with can be used by the other berry farms too?"

"Yes. CentPharm is getting a concession from us on price, of course, they're not completely altruistic, but they're fronting your fees and expenses."

"I'll do my best to make it worth your while, then."

"I never doubted it."

"Will I be able to visit the other farms?"

"Certainly, if you feel you need to." He checked his omni. "Probably not a good time to just drop in on Manning. I'll coordinate with the other owners, but we all agreed to bring in an expert. I'm sure they'd welcome the opportunity to meet you, at least. But as I said, this is the biggest farm, so you can probably do most of your work here."

"Sure."

They had passed over a couple of other creeks with groves of the "squidberry trees," as some people called them, at the creek mouths. Newton had then swung the aircar inland for a bit, to where the seashore vegetation changed to a lower, more swampy terrain.

After a few more minutes, Newton checked his omni again and turned south. "I need to get back, other things to do. McWhirter can answer pretty much any other questions you have about the farm, he pretty much runs the day to day ops."

Ellie was sure she had questions, she just had to figure out what they were first.

Chapter 27: Cephalobots

Newton Farm

After an informal lunch of sandwiches made with the mealy, Sawyer's World bread, Ellie Greystone sought out McWhirter. She'd thought of some questions.

"So how do you harvest the berries?" she asked, after she'd caught up with him and made sure he had some time to answer. "I know in some kinds of orchards they spread nets under the trees then use a mechanical shaker to shake the fruit off, but that seems problematic with the trees growing out of the water. Surely you don't pick them by hand?"

"Och, no. Well, we did at first, but that's impractical. Now we have small robots, like mechanical monkeys—although they look more like spiders—that climb the trees and harvest the berries. I can show you them if you'd like. They're better than humans, they can get out on the smaller limbs, but they're not perfect. There's nae a lot of room for on-board intelligence and trying to control the lot of them remotely tends to drive the central artificial intelligence schizophrenic. The last thing we want is a crazy AI on the network."

Greystone shuddered. That had happened on Earth a couple of times back in the day. The results were...bad. "No, that wouldn't do at all." But the idea mechanical versions of the tree squids—cephalobots—picking the berries intrigued her.

"Gulliver's a bit of a whiz when it comes to this stuff, he's working with a roboticist back at Krechet's Landing on tweaking things. Maybe they'll come up with improvements."

"Do the cephalopods ever interact with your harvesting robots?"

"Aye, they did at first. They seemed afraid of them and would flee the area whenever we sent out a swarm. That was great, we thought we had our wee tree squid problem solved, but after a while, when the bots just ignored the squids, the squids started ignoring the robots. They generally still do, although sometimes if a bot finds itself isolated, nearby squids will gang up on it and try to throw it out of the tree. We've lost a few that way. We did consider implementing a self-defense mechanism for them, but practical aspects aside—we're nae sure what would work—that runs into a mess of regulatory issues."

"Regulatory issues?"

"Aye, so I've been told. I'm not certain how much of Earth law applies here, but the *UDT* has strict regulations about arming autonomous robots, and the local authorities frown on molesting the local wildlife. We could probably make a case for self-defense on that last, though."

"Mr. Newton told me that the cephalopods, the tree squids, had been found carrying off berries in old sample bags. Is that right?"

"Aye, that's right. I caught that one myself. Only the one, but they'd carried off enough of the harvest to suggest many of them were doing it. Why?"

"Cephalopods are smart. Some can be trained. I was wondering if we could turn two problems into a solution and train the squids to harvest the berries for you."

McWhirter didn't say anything, just stared at her for a long time. Several expressions flashed across his face, he was clearly chewing over what she had just said.

"Mr. McWhirter?" she prompted.

"I do like the way ye think, lass. That's brilliant..."

"But?" From his expression, Ellie was pretty sure there was a *but*.

"Well, that seems to me that would take some time. How would we train them to do that? What's the reward that's better than just slithering off with the berries? And how long afore we have enough trained squid to both replace our robots and keep the wild squid away? And, how much of our crop do we lose in the meanwhile?"

He was right, she realized, feeling her enthusiasm drain away. That would have been a fun and challenging project. "Those are all valid points," she conceded. "Especially about coming up with a way to actually train them. That's not my specific expertise, but I know a few people whose focus is animal behavior and training. Octopodes can be trained to do simple tricks, but I guess I'll just have to work on a deterrent in the meantime."

"Sorry to disappoint you, lass. As I said, it's a brilliant idea, I just dinnae think it's practical in this situation."

"No, I suppose not. Maybe someone can look at it as a longer-term solution."

"Perhaps." McWhirter didn't sound very enthusiastic at the prospect. Greystone wasn't entirely sure why. Of course, the farm needed an immediate solution, but in the long run, wouldn't trained animals, already well adapted for gathering berries, be better than mechanical devices with their AI limitations and maintenance needs? Oh well. It was Newton's farm; she could only make recommendations.

Chapter 28: The Flight Video

Newton's Berry Farm

The call came while Ellie was sitting in the otherwise-unoccupied dining room, going through her notes. It reminded her of doing homework at the kitchen table as a teenager, back when her Dad had been alive and her Mom healthy. The chirping of her omni was a welcome intrusion to that line of thought.

The display announced her caller as William Blake. She tapped the phone. "Ellie Greystone here."

"Doctor Greystone, this is Will Blake. First, I just wanted to check that you were settling in all right. Any issues?"

"Oh, thank you. And call me Ellie. No, everything is fine. This is luxury compared to some of the field trips I've been on."

"Glad to hear it. The other thing is, Newton mentioned that you were interested in seeing any videos of the tree squids reacting."

"That's right. Anything that could give me insight into their behavior, especially anything that seems to frighten them."

"Sure. I have some of that video, from our first overflight of the mangrove patch." Blake said. "I'd almost forgotten we had it, but I dug it out of the archives."

"The one from when you and Tyrell checked it out? Great. There was a mention of the cephalopods just dropping out of the trees. Can I see it?"

"Sure, I'll play it now and give you a voice-over, it's better without sound. Feel free to capture the stream."

"Okay," she said, unfolding her omni's screen to full size and tapping a control to record Blake's transmission. "Go ahead."

The scene was clearly an aerial view, shot from a downward-facing camera on an aircar. It showed an overflight of the creek, then a thickening tangle of mangrove branches and squidberry vines.

"This is where we first approached the grove, coming from upstream," Blake said as the image played.

There were several tree squids in the trees. As the aircar drew closer, the squids suddenly all dropped from the trees, splashing into the creek below, with a few that had been above land swinging to where they too could drop into the water.

The video continued, but the cephalopods were all gone. Blake stopped the playback. "I know it's not much. There might be more from later flights. The aircar always has a camera running, but we don't always upload it to storage."

"That's a good start, though," Ellie said. "Clearly the aircar frightened them off. That was as fast a reaction as a flock of birds taking off. Faster, even. Is there sound?"

"Just the whine of the rotors. Want to hear it?"

"No, there's probably nothing useful. But let's see it again."

Blake restarted the video. Again, just as the aircar drew overhead, the tree squids bailed.

Clearly the cephalopods had an ingrained reaction to something flying overhead, which suggested a potential predator. Could it be a transferred reaction from marine predators? Octopus on Earth were mostly bottom-dwellers; in the open, any predator would come from above. "You said they eventually got used to the aircars?"

"That's right. The first few times we flew out over the trees, if there were squids in them, exactly the same thing happened. They just all plummeted to the water. As soon as a few started, they all did, from what we could see. But after a while it became more sporadic. Sometimes they'd drop, sometimes they wouldn't. Eventually it just stopped altogether."

"Interesting. That first reaction, that must be almost instinctive, a kind of flinch away from something overhead. But it wouldn't be just anything, or even harmless birds would set them off. So they reacted to the aircars because they were unfamiliar. And once they learned that aircars didn't hurt them..."

"They stopped reacting to them, just like they were seagulls or something."

"So we need to find out just what predator they are really afraid of. If we can modify an ornithopter drone to look like that, it should scare them off."

"Won't they just get used to that, too, if it doesn't attack them?"

"That depends how deeply ingrained that response is. It would have to be almost hard-wired to be that fast, but with an ability to learn to inhibit it. Are there large birds of prey around here?"

"Certainly not around the spaceport, our activities would have scared them off, and there's not much prey. You'll have to ask Newton or Caporale about up where you are. And again, the farm activity may have spooked them. If they were keeping the tree squid population in check, that may explain why they seem to be more of a problem now."

Ellie nodded. That made sense. "What about elsewhere? Do you know?"

"As I recall, the *Chandrasekhar* team reported something further north that preyed on their runny babbits, a Kakuloa equivalent to a hawk or eagle," Blake said. "That would be big enough to prey on a tree squid."

She considered this. The size would be right, but perhaps not the behavior. "The babbits are an open field animal?"

"Yes, like a rabbit, but not."

"Then it's probably not the same predator. Swooping down on prey in a field is different from prey in a tree. It's possible, though. Is there something that feeds on fish?"

"I'm not familiar with any bird like that around here, but there must be something. Wouldn't they have the same problem? Open water versus tree branches?"

Ellie nodded. "You've got a point. I'll go through the reports. There's a chance that this behavior evolved a long time ago and the predator has moved on, or gone locally extinct. It seems unlikely though. I guess we could always try rigging a drone with different silhouettes and see what works best."

"That sounds like it could take a while. I think Newton was hoping for something sooner and more reliable," said Blake.

"Of course. I'm just thinking out loud. There are several other possibilities I can look into."

"Excellent. Let me know what you find," Blake said. "I'll send you a link to any more video I find, and I'll have my computer guy see about allowing you direct access to the archives."

"That would be great, thanks." She was already thinking of different lines of research to pursue.

"All right. That's it for now. Blake out." The connection clicked off.

Ellie was amused rather than offended at the abrupt end to the conversation. She knew people like that; intelligent, focused, and horrible at small talk. She was a bit like that herself.

She picked her things up from the dining room table. She wanted to go over the video again, and if Henry Caporale was in the lab, get his input, especially about possible predators.

As she walked back up to the lab, she thought about Blake's comment about Newton wanting a quick solution. She couldn't blame him for that, but these things took time. She should brainstorm to come up with a list of all the possible approaches to deterring or repelling the tree squids. *Arboreal cephalopods, dang it*. It would be useful to set up remote cameras in the trees to see what else might trigger different behaviors. She'd talk to Henry about it, maybe he already had useful data.

∞ ∞ ∞

Newton's Office

"Boss?" McWhirter's rap on the door frame was hesitant.

Newton waved him in. McWhirter came in, shut the door behind him, and sat down.

McWhirter didn't usually close the door, this must be serious. "What's on your mind, Rob?"

"The Greystone lass. I'm nae sure inviting here was a good idea."

"Why not? If she can figure out how to keep the squids out of the berries, what's the possible harm?" He tried to think of what the downside might be. Mostly he'd been worrying about his son, Gulliver, doing something that might offend her. She was several years older than him, but attractive, and there weren't many females near Gully's age on the planet, let alone at the farm. Newton felt they'd raised Gulliver well, but.... "Anyway," he said, "it's not like this is an eighteenth-century plantation where a woman is going to rile up the natives."

McWhirter frowned. "Funny you should put it that way."

Uh oh. "What are you talking about?"

"You and I both know those squids are smart. She knows it too. And maybe they're smarter than we think."

This wasn't going where Newton had been afraid it would. He relaxed. "How smart could they be?" Newton said. "They're invertebrates."

"She was thinking they could be trained to harvest the squid-berries for us. They'd be better at it than our robots."

"They probably would, at that," Newton said, and chuckled. "It's an interesting idea, but not a solution to our immediate problem. It would take too long."

"I think training them to do *anything* would nae be a wise idea. It makes them look even smarter," McWhirter said.

"So what? It's not like they have a language or make fire. Seriously, what are you worried about?"

"I cannae put my finger on it. I just cannae help but feel that showing the squids to be intelligent would be a bad thing."

Newton scoffed. "You've got a bad feeling? And next you'll be reminding me of your heritage and that your entire maternal line was fey. Don't worry about it."

"Dinnae joke about such things," McWhirter said with a scowl. He stood up, then added: "And it was nae my entire maternal line, just my wee old granny. Mind, she's as far back as I know about." With that, McWhirter grinned, winked, and left the office.

Chapter 29: The Lab

Newton Farm, the Lab

"They're in groups?" Ellie asked. She and the ecologist, Henry Caporale, were in the lab—another spare room in the house, with basic laboratory gear, a microscope, chemical equipment, computers, a collection of various plant and insect specimens—watching a video on the large monitor. It showed a group of squid climbing through the branches of the mangrove trees, collecting and eating berries from the parasitic vines. She had first assumed that the animals just congregated individually on the rich food source, but the behavior of these seemed somehow more organized than that.

"Yes. Herds, flocks, whatever the right term is. We call it a squad of tree squid."

"It would be a school of squid, but these aren't squid. They're octopodes. Eight legs, soft bodies—but octopus are usually solitary; they don't gather in groups."

"Maybe not on Earth. They do here, at least this species does."

"They do when they're eating squidberries. Maybe there's something psychoactive in them."

"Well, alcohol. They prefer the ones that are starting to ferment. I assume octopus are affected by alcohol?"

"Yes, in fact it's sometimes used to anesthetize them. But I was thinking of something else."

"Like what?"

"There were some experiments done, oh, decades ago, before the war, on how octopus reacted to certain psychoactive drugs.

There was one, MDMA—methylene-something, an amphetamine variant sold as a party drug—that made octopus much more social." The similarity in reaction between the octopus and humans had been surprising. "It had something to do with serotonin levels, I don't recall all the details." If that were the case here.... "Is that why CentPharm is interested? They're looking at a potential recreational drug?"

Henry's eyes widened, then he shook his head. "No way. They wouldn't spend all this money on something like that. Plenty of easily-synthesized drugs in that market, and the whole recreational drug business is too risky for the companies backing CentPharm. It wouldn't even be a good cover story for what they're really after." He stopped abruptly, as if unsure how much he could reveal.

"Don't worry, I've signed the non-disclosure. I know about the potential anti-agathic."

"The rumor is, it's more than just *potential*. But that's not why the squids are after the berries. It definitely leaves them intoxicated, we've just assumed it was the alcohol. Surely CentPharm would have noticed anything else?"

Ellie shrugged. "You're probably right. Still, it is odd behavior for octopus. I wonder...." she trailed off, lost in thought.

"Wonder what?" Caporale asked.

"I wonder if they're something else, neither squid nor octopus. We can't call it *Octopus arboris* if it's not even genus *Octopus*. Although, they're obviously not cuttlefish or any other kind of Earth cephalopod either."

"There are other cephalopods, right?"

Ellie nodded. "Oh sure, but with only one or a few species in each genus. There's nautilus, but they have shells and way too many tentacles, and they're small.

"Then there's *Vampyroteuthis*," Ellie continued, warming to the subject, "the vampire squid, although it's not a true squid. In fact it has a lot of features in common with octopus, but they're very different in their own way. It's so dark at the depths they live that their eyesight is poor, and they have photophores more than chromatophores."

"They glow?"

"They can. In fact, they don't squirt ink, either, but rather a cloud of luminous fluid. We really don't know much about them, they live at depths of about 750 meters. They're small, too." Ellie thought *Vampyroteuthis* was a fascinating animal, although it was virtually impossible to study in the lab. But yes, it was neither true octopus nor true squid. Its arms mostly didn't have suckers, as such, but peg-like cirri.

"Then vampire squids probably diverged around the same time as tree squid ancestors, but in a different direction?" Caporale said. It was half statement, half question. "When did squids and octopus diverge, anyway? I assume there's a common ancestor somewhere, but that was never my specialty."

"That's actually hard to say. I mean, sure, if you go back far enough, the common ancestor to squids and octopuses was likely a kind of ammonite." Ellie paused, thinking. She hadn't thought much about cephalopod paleontology since grad school. It had had a ridiculously obvious scientific name for an intermediate species. *Oh, of course.* "Got it, *Dissimilites intermedius*, 128 million years ago. The history is sketchy. Soft invertebrates don't fossilize well, although squids and cuttlefish each have different internal shell remnants. If I remember right, there are a couple of Cretaceous genus from circa 95 million years ago that were intermediate between squids and octopus. But that's still 30 million years before the Terraformers collected specimens from Earth, or whatever it was they did."

"Could there have been another species, or genus, from 65 million years ago that's a missing link between squid and octopus?" Caporale asked.

Ellie shrugged. "There's no evidence of that. But then again, octopus don't fossilize well, so it's certainly possible. There's a genus, *Palaeoctopus*, from the late Cretaceous, but that's most likely pure octopus." She thought a moment, then continued. "Our tree squid friends here could be descended from something that went extinct shortly post-Cretaceous on Earth." That reminded her of something. "In fact, there's reported evidence that a species of ammonite survived into the early Paleocene, after the extinction, but they had shells, so no relation. Still, there could have been an intermediate squid-octopus species not represented in the fossil record. I'll have to see what their insides look like to get a better idea."

"It's not impossible," Caporale said. "Did you know we have coelacanths, or something like them, in the sea here?"

"Really? Well, they managed to hold out on Earth, why not here?"

"They're a bit bigger here. Nearly six meters."

She turned to look at him. "Now you're telling fish stories, Henry. Six *meters*?"

"No, I swear. But so far as I know, nobody's found sharks yet, so maybe they fill that niche."

"Sharks fill lots of niches. I'd be surprised if there are none at all here."

He shrugged. "Perhaps the Terraformers didn't import them, or they didn't take."

"It would be interesting to see what replaced them, if so."

"You may get a chance to find out. I assume you brought dive gear? If not, we have some here."

"Of course. Did you ever know a marine biologist who didn't bring their gear when they travelled?"

"Well, no, but then I don't know many marine biologists. You can get the local decompression tables off the net."

"Local? Oh, of course." Between the slightly different gravity, air pressure, and quite likely air composition and sea-water density, there would be differences in the depths and times for no-decompression dives and for decompression stops if one stayed down beyond those. Shallow dives, like around the mangroves, would be fine, but she'd have to pay attention for any offshore dives.

"You can just download them if you have a standard dive computer, or you can borrow one. I'd be happy to do a checkout dive with you, or you can get Newton or McWhirter. We don't do much offshore diving, but we're all qualified."

"Okay, good to know. Thanks." Ellie was sure she had more dive time than all of them put together, but she wasn't so stupid as to think she couldn't learn something from someone who had dived the local waters.

Ellie shook her head. There was a lifetime's worth of work here for a marine biologist. Many lifetimes' worth. Probably for every other kind of biologist too. It was like having, no, it was *exactly* having a snapshot of Earth life taken just after the end of the Cretaceous and transplanted to different but Earth-like worlds, then each left to evolve in their own ways. The implications were incredible. Species, even genera, that went extinct on Earth might have been transplanted and survived here, or on Sawyer's. Others would have evolved differently. Was there such a thing as comparative paleontology? There was now.

Just as she started getting used to the idea, the enormity struck her again. How many terraformed worlds? Two here in the Alpha Centauri system, one per star. There was a scattering of sun-like stars within range of the latest starships, how many of them might have terraformed planets too? Telescopic observation showed hints, and whatever the Chinese had found at Epsilon Eridani, although a more primitive planet, could also have had Terran origin. She wondered if humans would ever know just who or what had done this. She envied the first landing team. She herself had been surprised when the news came back, but she could only imagine the feelings of the biologists on that first team as they slowly came to the realization that the lifeforms they were looking at had to have come from Earth those many millions of years ago. She felt the hairs rising on her arms. She rubbed them to get rid of the goosebumps.

"Are you getting the feeling you've just walked into a haunted house?" Caporale said.

"How did you— I don't believe in ghosts."

"I've seen that look, and the goosebumps, before. Still get them myself occasionally, if I let myself think about it. You're wondering about the Terraformers, right?"

"Yes, I guess I was."

"Anyone with any imagination does, and then the implications sink in. It hits most newcomers sooner or later. We have a dumb name for it: terra-shock."

"As in terror, or Terraformer?" She'd had more a feeling of awe than of fear.

"Terraformer. Whoever they were, they're as long gone as the dinosaurs. Non-avian dinosaurs, that is, not birds."

"I figured that's what you meant. You don't suppose...?"

"That intelligent dinosaurs were the Terraformers?"

"Well, of course they couldn't be. No. But..."

He smiled. "Everyone comes up with that when they realize the timing coincidence. But you're right, they couldn't be. There's no evidence either here or in the Solar System, and if there *were* a species of dinosaur smart enough to do this, why did they let themselves go extinct? No, the real Terraformers could have missed the end-Cretaceous impact by a million years and things here would look pretty much the same."

He was right. Even if they found evidence or descendants of a species known to have died out when the dinosaurs did—a living ammonite, say, or even fossils of them, here—it would be taken as evidence that one species, at least, survived the extinction only to die out later, and just not left any fossils on Earth in that time frame. And as she had told Henry, there had been some reported—and disputed—ammonite fossils from the early Paleocene. A dead clade walking, as the phrase went. Not that ammonites walked. She grinned to herself at the mental image.

Chapter 30: The Other Video

Newton Farm

Dr. Greystone watched the video intently. She had found a clip of them reacting to a possible predator. The octopuses—she still couldn't quite bring herself to call them squids, because they clearly weren't, although they weren't exactly octopus either—swung through the tree limbs in a manner that resembled spider monkeys, minus the leaps. Suddenly they all scattered, swinging off in different directions or just dropping into the water below the trees. What had caused that? A few seconds later a predatory bird came into frame, maneuvering through the branches, looking for a meal. That explained the sudden panic amongst the octopus, but surely they hadn't all seen it at once, and there had been no warning cry. Octopus couldn't make much in the way of sounds.

She backed the video up to just before they'd scattered, and watched it again. If one had noticed the predator first, its flight might have triggered the others, in a radiating pattern. No, except for a few stragglers, they all seemed to scatter at once, the stragglers trailing by no more than a second or two. And the stragglers were randomly dispersed. tree squids at the edges of the squad scattered just as quickly as those in the middle.

She watched the video over and over again, focusing on each cephalopod in turn. Their eyes were set wide on the sides of their heads, and, not being constrained by the eye sockets of a vertebrate skull, could redirect for both a wide, almost 360-degree scan, or focused forward together for a binocular view to gauge the distance to prey or, in this case, a tree branch they might grab for. Most of the berry-gatherers had their eyes spread, presumably scanning for more berries or on the watch for predators. She noted the position of the stragglers, rewound, and watched them.

Now that was interesting. Nearly all the stragglers had been in binocular mode, reaching for a branch or otherwise focused. She changed the software so that she could view the video as a sequence of frames beside each other, like a strip of old-time movie film, making it easier to study the progression of events. She scrolled the segment back and looked again. Yes, the squids that had responded quickest were in wide-eyed mode, alert to everything going on around them. Had they all seen the predator at the same time? That seemed unlikely.

Some terrestrial squids were known to use color shifts for communication, could that be it? There were reports of tree squid color shifts, but for the whole squad to respond at once would mean that they could all see each other, or at least see some sentinel squids keeping lookout. That didn't seem possible, they were spread among the tree branches, and sentinels implied too great a level of cooperation for octopuses. She must be missing something.

She pushed back from the desk and stretched. What she really needed was coffee, but she'd settle for whatever was hot, brown and caffeinated that was available in the kitchen. Henry Caporale was working on something on the other side of the small room they called a lab. "Henry, I'm going for coffee, or whatever it is," she said. "Do you want something?"

Caporale turned in his chair to look at her. "You must be desperate. But sure, I could use a break myself."

As they walked to the kitchen, he said: "I noticed you've been reviewing those videos quite a bit. Are you making any headway?"

"Maybe. I think I have pretty solid evidence that they're communicating visually, but that's hardly a surprise. When a predator approached, the ones that were slowest to react were focusing on reaching for a branch or for berries, so their eyes were forward. The others were wide-eyed, and so more alert, although they couldn't all have seen the predator. Some must have been reacting to others."

In the kitchen, Ellie found a mug and went over to the autochef to fill it.

"Do you think they post look-outs?" Caporale asked. "Some herd animals do that."

"Too soon to say," she said. "I've never heard of that in octopuses, but then most of them aren't social to begin with." She took a sip from her mug. It was bitter, burnt-tasting, but at least hot. She made a face. "That's almost revolting. It's saving grace is that it's not de-caf."

Caporale chuckled. "Careful. If you develop a taste for that, you'll never appreciate the real thing again."

"Ha! That's about as likely as developing a taste for squid ink," she said. "No, I take that back. Squid ink doesn't actually taste too bad. Not that I've had it straight, but it's used in cooking."

She eyed the dark brown liquid in her mug. "Actually, this looks a bit like cuttlefish ink. Right color, anyway." She took another sip. "Yep, I'm sure cuttlefish ink tastes better, if saltier." She looked up at Caporale. "Aren't you having anything?"

"After that glowing recommendation? I think I'll try the tea," he said, walking over to the autochef to do just that.

"Is that better?" Ellie asked, when he'd taken a sip.

"No, not really. Just different. Come on, let's go back."

∞ ∞ ∞

Back in the lab, she ran through the video again, but nothing stood out. She took another sip of her coffee. Damn, she *was* starting to get used to the flavor. Either that or her taste-buds were going numb. That was more likely. She thought about what Henry had asked about them posting look-outs. Were they?

She played the video again.

This time, she focused on one part of a single tree. There was a small group of eight or so squids in a branch overhanging the stream. They had all dropped near simultaneously, but most of them couldn't have seen the predator. Again, she expanded the video to multiple side-by-side frames.

She used a slider to scan back and forth across the video frames, which animated the whole sequence. As she reversed the video and slowed it down, the reversed splashes seemed to push the squids out of the water and up into the tree branch, where they curled their tentacles to grip it. Wait, what was that?

One of the squids bore a subtly different color pattern than the others. She scrolled back the video a few frames further. The pattern changed to the mottled green of the other cephalopods, blending in to the tree leaves. It had changed its pattern just before the group dropped – and it had been the last to drop. A signal?

Now that she knew what to look for, or thought she did, she scrolled back to the start again and watched the whole tree. Unfortunately, the octopodes' camouflage was excellent, and she was having trouble finding other examples of the pattern the sentinel squid had shown. She'd think she had spotted one, but then when she focused on it, it seemed not quite there.

At least in the trees, squirting ink wouldn't help. She remembered one of her early dives, when she'd reached for a small swimming octopus. It had squirted a cloud of thick ink that held together. Ellie had assumed it was still in the cloud and reached for it, only to come up empty handed. It turned out the octopus had simultaneously changed its skin color to match the background and jetted off. It had been floating there, all but invisible, a meter away from the ink cloud. Human vision, like other animal vision systems, was too easily distracted.

"Hey, Henry, is there a way to have the computer search within a vid or an image for a specific pattern?"

"What, you mean like face recognition?"

That wasn't what she'd meant, but that would be an obvious use-case. "Well, not faces. An arbitrary pattern that one squid made, I want to see if there are any others but there's too much clutter."

"Oh, sure," he said. "*Where's Waldo*." It wasn't a question.

"What?"

He came over to her desk. "That's what it's called. I'm not sure why. Here, select what you're looking for."

Ellie drew a rough circle around the squid that she thought had warned the others, being careful to omit any of the background.

"Okay," Henry said, gesturing at the screen. "Now go to *Search*, then *Advanced Options*, then select *Waldo*."

"Ohh... I always wondered what that was for."

"Yeah. It does a smart match, like face recognition, not an exact pixel match."

"Perfect!" She okayed the search.

And there it was. A half dozen other squid, scattered throughout the treetops, had similarly changed pattern, all within moments of each other. And the others had dropped when they saw that.

∞ ∞ ∞

Newton's office

"It took a while," Greystone said to Newton and McWhirter, "but I finally tracked it down by going through frame by frame. The octopus – squids – react fast. They can switch their chromatophores in thirty milliseconds. It's quite remarkable. So is their intelligence."

"Intelligence?" Newton scoffed. "A white-tailed deer warns the herd by flashing its tail, that doesn't take much intelligence."

"Deer don't set out sentinels in a regular array. Look at this." She highlighted several individual squids in the image of a tree full of them. "These are the ones who pattern-flashed." She touched a control and straight dotted lines appeared, connecting the sentinels. "These are lines of sight. Each sentinel can see and be seen by at least two others. From the first one spotting a threat to all the sentinels 'lighting up' took barely a second. If I go through this frame by frame you'll see the one who spotted the predator light up first, then those that can see it, then those that can see *them*. It's almost as effective as a warning cry. I'm a little puzzled as to why they don't make a pattern with more contrast, like your white-tailed deer, but maybe that would just make them a target for the predator. That's why I didn't spot it sooner."

"You said you had good news. How does this help?"

"We've just learned the squid word, or color pattern, for *danger*," she said.

"You're saying they have a language?" McWhirter interjected. "Are ye daft?"

"No, no. Not any more than a deer's tail-flash is a language. It's just a signal," she said, sensing McWhirter's hostility to the idea. "That behavior is a more squid-like than octopus-like," she added. "We've seen something similar in some Earth squid species. Anyhow, given how fast they react, this may not even be conscious, but rather an instinctive reaction. Just as many insects and poisonous animals use a characteristic black-and-yellow pattern to warn off other creatures, and some harmless species mimic it to that same end."

"So how does that help us?" Newton asked.

"What if we post placards, or even decoy squid, painted in that scheme to warn them off?"

Newton sat back. "On Earth, I've seen fake owls used to discourage birds from frequenting areas where they weren't wanted," he said thoughtfully. "And I have to admit that I'm wary of any black-and-yellow flying insect, although I know some of them are just harmless flies. It might work." He looked up. "McWhirter?"

"Aye, it might at that."

"It's worth a try," Newton said. "We'll do placards and tape first. If we have to, we can see about fabbing up a few decoys." He looked over at Ellie. "What do you think?"

"Yes, hopefully that will do it. At the very least we'll get more information on their behavior."

"I'll be surprised if it's that simple, but let's go ahead with it." Newton looked at McWhirter again. "Rob?"

"Aye. I'll get on it."

Chapter 31: Dive Trip

Newton Farm, a couple of days later. Dinnertime

Tomorrow promised to be a slow day. The placards had been printed up and, after Ellie Greystone had shown what she wanted, the farm hands were placing them in and around the different squidberry groves, along with adding additional cameras to observe the reactions. Now they just had to wait for the cephalopods to show up and react.

Dave Newton was going to head into Krechet's Landing to pick up some gear, a task that any of the others could also have handled but he planned to head down that evening to see his wife and daughter, then return the next day.

"Are you taking the aircar or the boat?" Gully asked between bites.

"I don't have much to pick up, I figured the aircar. Why?"

"We were thinking of taking the *Disco* out for some diving, if that's all right. Miss Ellie, I mean, Dr. Greystone, wants to check out what the squid's offshore habitat might be like, and just generally get some diving in. Dr. Caporale would be coming along too, and I can pilot the boat."

Newton looked over at Greystone and Caporale. "Is that right?"

"We'd been talking about it in abstract terms, nothing definite," Ellie said. "But the weather looks good, and I don't have much to do here until we see the results of the placards."

"I've already briefed her on the local dive tables. Aside from that, she's probably got more hours underwater than the rest of us put together," Henry Caporale added.

"Please, Dad?"

Newton took a sip of his coffee and made a face. "I'll have to see if I can get some real coffee today too. All right, Gulliver. Take your gear, but you're not going in the water unless there's some emergency that absolutely requires it, and if so, call me first. You stay with the *Disco*, and make sure the boat doesn't go anywhere while you have divers down."

Gully made a face. He'd obviously heard all this before. "Yes Dad."

"And don't use the foils. There isn't anywhere you need to get to that far or that fast. Keep it within a few kilometers of here. In fact, stay in sight of shore. Got that?"

"Yes, Dad."

Newton looked at Greystone and Caporale. "He's in charge of the boat, but you have my authority to override him if he breaks any of the above rules. Understood?"

"Understood, Mr. Newton," Ellie said. "I'm sure we'll all be fine."

"Of course you will. Forgive me, sometimes my inner father comes out and I forget how old Gully is. So go, enjoy your dive." Newton paused, then added, "Gully, you can go out as far as the drop-off, okay? No point in going any further than that anyway."

"Got it," Gully said. "Uh, Dad? I'll have to get out of the bay for the drop-off, that's forty kilometers around the point...."

Newton sighed. "You're right. Okay, you can use the foils, but keep it below eighty."

"Below eighty, got it." Gully turned so his father couldn't see his face but Ellie could, and he smiled broadly. She grinned back.

"And let McWhirter know where you're anchoring and when you've got divers in the water. All right?" He looked around. McWhirter was at the other table discussing something with a couple of the other hands. "McWhirter, did you get that?"

"Get what?"

"The two scientists are going out on a dive tomorrow, and Gully's going to take them in the *Disco Volante*. Does that interfere with anything you had planned?"

"No, that'll be fine."

"Okay. He's to contact you when he anchors, when they're in the water and when they're out again."

McWhirter nodded. "Aye, I understand. No problem."

"Maybe I should send somebody else along with them too."

"Dinnae fuss. Gulliver will be fine, and the *Disco* can pilot herself if she needs to." McWhirter had a point; the *Disco Volante* was fully computerized.

"You're right. Fair enough." Newton turned back to the others. "Okay, you're all experienced divers, I'll stop my fussing. Enjoy yourselves."

With that he rose from the table and left, his son calling "Thanks Dad" after him.

∞ ∞ ∞

Next day, aboard the Disco Volante

"So, this drop-off, what is it?" Ellie after the boat had cleared the shallow water near the creek mouth and was building up speed.

"Just like on Earth," Caporale said. "I'm sure you must have dived some. The water near here stays shallow, no more than fifteen, twenty meters deep until a couple of kilometers off shore, except here in the bay, then starts sloping down more steeply toward the edge of the continental shelf. It goes from twenty meters to sixty or seventy meters quickly, levels out for a while, and then it really plummets, dropping down to a couple of thousand meters. Possibly more; the ocean floor hasn't been mapped very well yet."

"Then there's a lot of life on the drop-off? There's usually a mix of sublittoral and pelagic species." She saw Gully's blank look and added "Coastal waters and open ocean. Different species of fish and other marine life have different preferred habitats. Benthic species prefer the sea floor, whether deep or shallow."

"Oh, sure," he said.

"Yes, *a lot of life* is exactly right," Caporale said. "I've dived out there a couple of times. Can't say that I exactly recognized any species, but then there's no reason I would. They all looked vaguely familiar, though."

"Sure. Earth-descended but divergent. But while octopodes like the sea floor, I can't see our tree-climbers coming forty kilometers or so just to get at the berries. I'll want to do a dive closer to the tidal zone if we're going to look for them."

"Sure, we can do that," said Caporale. "I know a couple of possible places."

"Deep dive first, though," Ellie said. That was a basic rule of diving; it reduced the chances of getting decompression sickness.

"Of course."

∞ ∞ ∞

They waited until they were at the dive site to suit up; the strong wind of the hydrofoil's speed would have made it difficult on deck. Henry Caporale was donning a shorty wet-suit; it covered his torso but had short sleeves and legs.

"How's the water temperature?" Ellie asked, watching him.

"Typically about twenty-three or -four degrees; warm enough." He looked at her full wet-suit. "You'll probably roast in that."

"It's thin. I was thinking more for protection against jellyfish or fire coral."

"I've haven't heard of anything like fire coral here. There are jellyfish, but this is mostly the wrong season for them. It's up to you."

Ellie thought about it. She didn't have to wear the whole thing, it came in two parts, jacket and pants. "Fair enough." She put the long pants aside and donned the jacket, then reached down to grab the beaver-tail and fasten that in front, leaving her legs bare.

As they assembled their packs, tanks and hoses, Ellie asked Gulliver. "Do you have a UWPS?"

"A what? UWPS? An oops? What's that?"

"Underwater Position System. Maybe you call it something else. It's like a GPS system for underwater."

"How would that work?" Gully asked. "Radio signals don't penetrate water."

"You're right, they don't," she said. "It's a set of buoys, or sometimes attached to the boat, that convert the GPS radio signals to ultrasonic ones. A diver has a device that detects those and gives you a location. Some dive computers have the receiver built in." She held up her own. "Mine, for example, although it won't work without the beacons."

"Oh. I've never heard of that," Gully said.

Henry had been following the conversation. "There's not much call for such a thing here. Nearly all the diving at the farm is in, at most, a couple of meters of water, things like fence repair and inspecting the dock and the boats. On Earth I've only seen them on high-end dive boats."

Ellie could understand that. The equipment was specialized, and thus expensive even for dive gear. To work, it needed at least three buoys, and ideally four or more. The things were more common in her line of work, but not universal. On the other hand, marine archeologists wouldn't be without them.

"Never mind, I was just curious. This should be a pretty straight-forward dive, and the visibility looks good."

"If anything, today it's not quite as good as usual," Henry said. "It will probably be clearer past the drop off, without the sand to stir up."

"Sounds good. So, follow the anchor line down, angle upstream to the drop-off?"

They briefly discussed their dive plan, and agreed with Gulliver on when they'd be back.

"All right, let's hit the water," Ellie said as she stepped over the rail. With one hand on her mask and the other stabilizing her gear, she took a long stride forward into the sea.

It was good to be back in the water.

Chapter 32: Construction

Newton's Berry Farm, Kakuloa

Dave Newton landed the old aircar on the pad behind the house in a swirl of dust. He was back from Krechet's Landing.

Rob McWhirter had heard the incoming aircar and was at the pad to meet him. "How was the trip? Get what you needed?"

"Interesting. Yes, that and more. Here." He tossed a duffel bag to McWhirter, who caught it. "There's your supplies. When you have a moment, come up to my office and I'll tell you about what else."

McWhirter cocked his head. Newton seemed agitated. "Oh? Aye. I'll be along in a moment." He turned to one of the outbuildings, calling to one of the other men to take the bag, as Newton headed in to the house.

A minute or two later McWhirter came into Newton's office. "Was there a problem?" he asked. "Is your family all right?"

"They're fine. No problem, at least not yet. By the way, did Gully check in? I spotted the *Disco* from the air as I came in, out near the drop-off."

"Aye. Divers down a bit before you arrived." McWhirter checked the time on his omni. "They should be back up shortly. But what was it you wanted to tell me?"

"At Krechet's Landing, and north of there, I spotted something that might be a problem in future," Newton said. "There was a new ship on the field, unloading heavy gear. Construction equipment."

"That's hardly a surprise. Kakuloa is growing."

"It's the direction it's growing that concerns me," Newton said. He unfolded his omni. "I took these pictures from the air. What do they look like to you?"

McWhirter examined them. The images showed large stretches of the shoreline and adjacent jungle. Several long swathes had been cleared through the vegetation, with what looked like a wide, cleared trail heading south. There were several bulldozers, and what looked like the foundations of at least one large building.

"Where was this?" McWhirter asked.

"About fifteen kilometers north of the Landing. It looks like they're putting a road in between the two."

"Aye." A few of the pictures showed isolated individuals doing something. He zoomed in the image. They were paired up, one with a tripod, the other some distance away with what could be a precision GPS antenna on a pole. A number of areas had been gridded out with stakes and strings or ribbon.

"Surveyors?" McWhirter wondered. "Clearly somebody is building something, but this area is huge."

"Exactly." Newton shook his head. "It's a lousy area for squidberry mangroves, so there's that, but it looks like somebody is investing a small fortune in construction."

"Nae so small, given shipping costs. But given where it is, do you think it will it interfere with our operations?"

"No, I don't think so. It's over a hundred kilometers down the coast. It won't even bother the Lofgren place. But what the hell are they doing? Houses? There's no call for that much housing, probably not for years, and certainly not there."

McWhirter examined the images closely, noting the layout of the paths that had been cleared, and what might be a dock or marina under construction. "Whatever it is, there are going to be boats. It's an odd place to put a dock with all that sand, though. You'd only get shallow draft vessels in there, unless they dredge."

"That makes no sense," Newton said. He paused, looking thoughtful. "Unless..."

"Unless what?" McWhirter asked.

Newton shook his head. "No, that doesn't make sense either. There's no market."

"Market for what?"

"The beach there would be a wonderful recreational area. The waves break a good distance out, but close enough for dedicated surfers. Your shallow draft vessels could be small catamarans or jet-skis."

"Och, don't be daft. Who on Kakuloa has the leisure time or money for that? And it's a long way from the Landing or any of the farms."

"Like I said, there's no market."

McWhirter looked at the images again. There were a couple of large areas laid out, and many smaller ones. Inland, a cleared lane ran in the direction of one of the freshwater lakes beyond the ridge. He zoomed in on a pile of long objects between that lane and the road back toward Krechet's Landing. Pipes?

"It looks like they'll be putting in a pipeline to yon lake," he said, pointing to the image.

"It does. They're clearly expecting a lot of people. If not from around here, then where?"

"Tourists, do you suppose? Nae, that cannae be." On Earth, McWhirter would be sure that was it. *But here?*

"Tourists? To Kakuloa? Most of the third-world countries on Earth are more civilized than this place."

"Aye, and some of those that aren't are still homes to high class luxury resorts. Build a hotel, put in a casino, close off the beach from the local riff-raff...."

Newton nodded slowly. "And there's no local riff-raff here. Well, aside from us, that is. You might be onto something. If that's someone's plan, they are going to be investing a lot of money."

"Aye. Although probably not as much as Centauri Pharmaceuticals." Which raised another possibility. "Speaking of, I imagine the executives would enjoy a nice place to say when they come to visit."

"They don't come to...Oh, but they would, wouldn't they? CentPharm might even want to own a piece of it." Newton leaned back in his chair, putting his hands behind his head. "I'm not sure how I feel about this. If whoever is running this is successful, it could be a good thing. It will bring more traffic to Kakuloa, which means more amenities available, but might also drive up prices we have to pay."

"Aye. At least we're far enough away from this site it shouldn't affect us directly."

"Not at first. If it is successful, I imagine others will try to build on that success." Newton looked thoughtful. "I wonder how much of the land between here and there is spoken for? Maybe we should look at expanding the homestead."

"It might be time for young Gulliver to start thinking about a place for his own." McWhirter said.

"It might be at that. But I'll want to find out more about just what is going on. There may be opportunities even before they get the place up and running."

"We'll want to be careful we don't lose men to them. I'm sure they'll be needing construction help, both for clearing and building. If they start poaching farm workers..."

"That's a good point," Newton said. "I'm sure they'd have no trouble recruiting help from Earth, but there'd be an advantage to hiring locals where they can. Keep an eye on that, McWhirter. Let's see what we can do to encourage our men to stay. Of course, if there are any troublemakers you want rid of...."

"Oh, aye. That thought hadn't escaped me." *Unfortunately*, he thought, *the one troublemaker I'd really like to be rid of is more interested in tree squid intelligence than construction.*

As if on cue, both Newton's and McWhirter's omniphones warbled with an urgent call tone. It was Gulliver Newton.

"Dad, Mr. McWhirter, there's a problem. It's ten minutes past when Greystone and Caporale said they'd be back, and they haven't surfaced. There's no sign of them anywhere."

Chapter 33: Alone

Newton's Farm

Newton looked at McWhirter. "How long?"

"Forty minutes they've been down, if they descended when Gully called last."

"How long a dive were they planning?" Newton asked Gulliver.

"Thirty minutes. They weren't planning to go below 30 meters and wanted to do a shallower dive on the way back."

The numbers made sense. Newton called up a set of tables on his omniphone. That was just within the no decompression limits and would let them do another half-hour dive an hour later to twenty meters, still leaving a safety margin. So maybe they wouldn't do that second dive today. If that forty minutes was all bottom time, they'd have to do a decompression stop of 25 minutes. That would be cutting their air supply close.

"Is there a decompression tank over the side?" It was good practice to hang an air tank on a line at the recommended decompression depth, just in case.

"Yes. Ellie insisted."

"Okay, they probably just overstayed their bottom time and will need to decompress. Can you see the tank?"

"I've got it on the underwater camera now. There's no sign of them." The camera was usually used to check for obstacles or examine the hydrofoils.

Newton looked at McWhirter. "How much air do you reckon?"

"Greystone's an experienced diver. I'm nae so sure about Caporale. I'd worry about his air consumption first."

Newton agreed. Henry would probably run through his air long before Ellie did, and they should start back toward the surface before that. "He'd be running out about now, if they're at thirty meters."

All the gear was equipped with "safe second" backup regulators, letting two divers breath from a single tank without the hassle and risk of passing a single regulator back and forth. They *should* be on their way back.

"What's the visibility?" Newton asked Gulliver.

"Not quite twenty meters, maybe fifteen. Not as good as it usually is."

But still good enough to see the dark outline of a boat against the bright surface, surely? "Take a couple of strobes off the life jackets. Put them on a weighted line about fifteen meters apart, one at the end with the weight. Then lower it over the side. If they're having trouble locating the boat or the anchor line, that should help."

"Got it, Dad. I'll call you back."

"Do ye think that's the problem? They lost track of the boat?"

Newton's expression was grim. "Not really. I've dived with Caporale, he doesn't seem the type to get lost easily, and I'm sure Greystone's not either, not with her experience. Maybe the current's strong today, and they drifted further from the boat. But the lights can't hurt, and it gives Gulliver something to keep him busy." *And less likely to do something stupid*, Newton thought.

"Oh, aye."

"I need to call Blake. Not that there's anything he can do, but he should know. Hopefully they'll show up at the decompression stop any minute now and it will all be a lot of fuss over nothing, but..."

"Aye, *but*. I'll go check out the aircar. If they've surfaced some distance from the boat, they'll be easier to spot from the air."

"Right, thanks."

Newton picked up his omni again.

∞ ∞ ∞

"How long ago?" Blake said, when Newton explained the situation.

"Just a few minutes. They probably just overstayed their planned bottom time, and they'll surface any time now. I wanted to give you a heads up in case that doesn't happen."

"And no Underwater Position System. I'd remember something like that." The surface buoys also received a signal from the diver side of the system, tracking them. But that was moot here. "I'm going to get the helicopter prepped. We can be there in forty, forty-five minutes."

"To what end? To be blunt, if they haven't surfaced by then, they're not going to. Not alive, anyway."

"And if they're on the surface a couple of kilometers from the boat? They can't swim back to your place, and you can't see far from the *Disco*. The helicopter will be faster."

"McWhirter's getting the aircar ready."

"Weren't you just down here a couple of hours ago? You won't have a full charge on that."

Damn. Blake was right, Newton realized. He should have thought of that himself. "All right. If you want to fly out here I won't object. You can stay for dinner and we can laugh about two scientists who can't follow their dive plan and gave us all a scare. While you're on your way here, we'll go out in the aircar anyway."

"Roger that," Blake said. "Stay safe yourself. Call me if anything changes."

"Of course."

As he clicked off, McWhirter came back in, looking unhappy. Newton could guess why. "So how much charge *does* it have?"

The look of surprise on McWhirter's face would have amused Newton more under different circumstances. "Aye, that's what I came to tell you. Maybe an hour."

"That works. Blake will be here in less than that. He's taking his helicopter."

McWhirter nodded. "I hope that's a wasted trip. Any word from Gulliver?"

"No. I'll call him back." Newton did so.

"Hi Dad. I just got the line and the strobe lights in the water."

"Have you checked the camera again? Any sign?"

"Just a moment. No, the tank is still there, no sign of Henry or Ellie."

"Maybe there's a current and they surfaced a couple of kilometers away. I'm going to come out and search from the air."

"Okay. I've got a drift line out but it's only a hundred meters. I don't know how much more line we have." A drift line, sometimes called a tag line or current line, was what it sounded like: a line with a float at the far end that would drift in the current downstream of the boat. It could save a diver a difficult swim if the current had pushed him beyond the boat...so long as it hadn't pushed him beyond the line too.

"Check the aft locker. Use whatever you can find. Oh, and Gulliver?"

"Yes Dad?"

"First, you did the right thing in calling us right away. Second, under no circumstances are you to leave the boat. Stay on board. And keep the boat where it is; that's our reference point."

"Of course."

"All right. I should be overhead in about..." Newton thought for a moment. The drop-off was forty kilometers away, the aircar's cruising speed was 120, but it could do 160. "...fifteen minutes." That was going to chew up the battery; they wouldn't have much time on station. It couldn't be helped.

"Okay, Rob. Everything ready?"

McWhirter nodded. "Aye."

"Let's go."

Chapter 34: Fish

Thirty minutes earlier, underwater

It had been a while since Ellie had dived anywhere like this. The water above the drop-off had been a little stirred up, with fine sediment cutting the visibility to about twenty meters. She'd dived in much worse, but beyond the drop-off, away from the sandy bottom, she could easily see forty or more meters. It was like flying, except for the blue tinge to everything.

Henry was right, there was all kinds of life. The corals and anemones growing along the bottom had that same familiar-yet-not look that the rest of the lifeforms she'd seen so far on Kakuloa had. Fish whose structure resembled familiar species, but whose coloring was wrong, or fish with familiar looking coloring but completely the wrong shape or size.

The variation had its limits, of course. The rules of camouflage, or predator avoidance, or hydrodynamics, didn't change just because the planet was different. To hide, you still had to look something like the background. Eyespots could still confuse a predator. And water was water, even if the ratios of salts were a little different.

She checked her dive computer for the time and depth. There was still plenty of margin. She tapped Caporale's arm to get his attention, then pointed down over the drop-off.

Neither of their gear was equipped with an underwater communication system. While such did exist, it tended to be noisy, short ranged, and something of a distraction. It made sense when involved in some specific task, like underwater construction or repair, but Ellie had always found that for sightseeing or general surveys, their lack made it easier to focus one's vision, and reinforced the need to keep an eye on your dive buddy. The hiss of air in her regulator, the burble of exhaled bubbles, and the distant sounds of some Kakuloan parrot-fish equivalent munching on coral were relaxing.

Caporale moved his head in a slow, exaggerated nod, then pointed down the drop-off himself and made the *okay* sign with thumb and finger.

The edge wasn't sharp, the drop-off was more a steep hill than a cliff, but the clarity of the water below her gave Ellie a momentary, irrational, fear of falling. She let air out of her buoyancy compensator and glided downslope, scanning the nooks and crannies in its side, and, every once in a while, casting a glance at her dive computer or at Henry, who kept pace beside her.

She leveled out at thirty meters and swam slowly along the wall. It was already darker down here, with the reds nearly all gone from the plants and animals growing or swimming alongside. Some of what looked nearly black would probably look crimson in the beam of a dive-light, but she hadn't brought one.

She felt Henry suddenly grab her arm and tug. She turned to face him, and he pointed out away from the wall and down. His eyes were wide. She looked where he was pointing but didn't see anything at first. She looked back at Henry, quizzically.

He made a waggling motion with one hand, holding his palm vertically. The sign for *fish*.

She nodded. Sure, there were fish.

He made the sign again, then stretched both arms wide apart. A *big* fish. He pointed.

She looked again at where he was pointing. The water away from the side of the drop-off was a deep blue, dappled slightly by beams of sunlight from the surface. There was a darker patch of blue, and some of those lighter beams were still, not flickering in and out like the others. Then it snapped into focus as her brain figured it out. There *was* a fish. It was huge, dark blue with lighter blue splotches. Now that she knew what she was looking at, she could make out more detail. Large eyes, a large mouth, bony plates around the face. Fins. Lots of fins. Lobed fins. That was a *coelacanth.*

She swam towards it, slowly, trying to get a feel for how big and how distant it was. Coelacanths on Earth grew to maybe two meters long, although most were smaller. This one was at least twice as big, if she was judging distance properly. What did they eat again? They were benthic feeders, fish and cephalopods. Hopefully not divers. She wondered if they ate tree squids, or if their ranges overlapped at all. She'd have to ask Henry.

Where was Henry?

She turned back to look. She was much further from the drop-off wall than she had thought. The coelacanth had been moving away as she swam toward it. There was Henry, about ten meters away, gesturing at her to come back. Good idea.

She turned to take a last look at the coelacanth, which was now swimming down to deeper water and closer to the wall. It had to have been at least four meters long, maybe five. Ellie realized that she had no idea what *Kakuloan* coelacanths ate. She backed away slowly, checking over her shoulder to be sure she was still swimming towards Henry, and thinking about shark cages.

She lost sight of the creature and turned around, continuing back toward Henry and the wall. He was drifting along it as he waited for her, the current pushing them both southward. At a fair clip, she realized as she saw how fast they were moving relative to the rocks and corals of the wall. Something large loomed behind Henry, a large fish, but not a coelacanth or shark. She waved at him, then made a circling motion with one arm. *Turn around.* It swam slowly closer, seeming more curious than hungry, although it was big enough to do Henry serious damage if it chose. He was oblivious, still facing her. She signaled again. *Turn around, dammit!*

He finally figured it out and turned, just as the big fish—it wasn't a grouper, but similarly shaped, and larger—reached him. He reacted, startled, waving his arms and kicking to back away. The fish in turn reacted to his sudden movement, thrashing wildly before turning and swimming off into the deep blue. It had caught Henry with a heavy sideswipe and bounced him off the rocks behind him, and he hung in the water, limp. Ellie kicked hard and sped toward him.

He still had his regulator in his mouth, and bubbles showed he was breathing. As she reached him, he began to move, reaching up to fix and clear his dislodged mask.

She caught up to him and grabbed his shoulder. He flinched, then relaxed as he turned and saw it was her. She held her hand up in front of him, thumb and forefinger making a circle. *Are you okay?*

He nodded, making his own *okay* sign. Then he shrugged and rocked his hand from side-to-side, palm down. *So-so.*

She looked him over. She saw no obvious scratches or cuts. His gear was askew and his shorty wet-suit scuffed, but otherwise he seemed unharmed. The impact must have stunned him momentarily. She signed *okay?* again, and he nodded.

She checked her gauges and dive computer. They'd gone deeper and longer than originally planned, but not by much. She still had plenty of air, although that last burst of speed would have hurt her normal consumption rate. She pointed at her gauges, then at the surface. *We should ascend.*

Henry made the okay sign, and they began to slowly swim upward. Henry checked his own gauges, then thumped his chest with his right fist and held his console out in his left hand for her to look at. He was starting to run low on air.

She looked at her own again, and at her dive computer. To be safe, they should do a five-minute decompression stop at seven meters, putting their total ascent time at nine minutes. She had enough air, but if they weren't near the boat and the spare tank hanging over its side, Henry would be out. He could use her spare regulator to breathe from her tank. She hoped it would be enough.

They were above the edge of the drop-off now, and had swum a little way up the gently sloping bottom, trying to angle northward against the current, hoping to catch sight of the *Disco Volante*. There was no sign of it, and the sea bottom here didn't look at all familiar. Even though they'd started the dive swimming up-current, they had obviously drifted far south of the boat. That complicated things.

Chapter 35: Search and Rescue

Above Squidberry Bay

The aircar, with Newton and McWhirter aboard, whined over the waters of the bay as fast as Newton could make it go. They were still a few minutes out from where the *Disco Volante* was anchored.

"Any sign of them?" Newton asked Gulliver over the radio.

"Not yet. I've got a drift line out three hundred meters. I looped a couple of life jackets into it with their strobes on, to help them find it."

"Good thinking. They did have DSMBs, didn't they?" A DSMB, deployable surface marker buoy, was often known as a safety sausage. It was an inflatable, brightly-colored marker, about two meters long and maybe a tenth that in diameter, hence the nickname. A diver surfacing away from the boat would inflate it and let it stick up out of the water; it was much easier to see from a distance than just the diver's head.

"Yeah Dad. I'm not seeing any sign of them. I've been looking."

"Okay, sure. We're almost there." The *Disco* was visible now in the distance. A couple of flashing lights showed to the south of it, most likely the life-jackets Gully had tied to the drift line. "Did they have strobes on their gear?" It wasn't standard for a day dive, but he could hope.

"I... I'm not sure. I don't remember seeing them."

"All right, it must be your drift line." There were also dimmer, bluer lights flashing below the *Disco*, marking the decompression tank. "I see your strobes. We'll follow them south and work a search pattern from there."

"*Copy that.*"

McWhirter had been checking the aircar's panel. "We dinnae have a lot of time left on the batteries. We'll have to turn back in ten minutes."

"Then let's hope that's enough time to find them. Set a timer and then keep watching the water."

"Aye."

Newton cast an eye skyward. It was only mid-afternoon, so there were still hours of daylight left, but there was a bank of clouds on the northwestern horizon.

∞ ∞ ∞

William Blake and his pilot roared northward in the big helicopter. Blake had commandeered it, and the pilot, from Cohen's construction site, as well as a couple of his employees with dive experience. He hadn't been able to reach Cohen himself, Blake would sort that out later.

The helicopter's panel showed an indicated airspeed of 315 kph. Unfortunately, an almost head-on breeze reduced that to a ground-speed of only 305, but they were almost at the base of the peninsula, about as far north as Toothpick Lake to the east. If Greystone and Caporale hadn't surfaced by now, they were dead. More likely, though, Blake kept telling himself, they had surfaced some distance from the boat and just hadn't been spotted yet. But part of his mind couldn't help running over what-if contingency plans. He supposed that was why he was good at what he did.

The worst case was that they were both dead, for whatever reason. There'd have to be an investigation, and the loss of their skills and knowledge would set back the squidberry project, especially if the tree squids kept raiding the crops. If they managed to recover the bodies, the investigation would go quickly; whatever the cause was should be obvious. If the bodies were never found...that was the real worst case. There'd be more searches, and the investigation would drag on.

Certainly Blake hoped they'd be found, alive and well prefer-ably, but at least alive, for their own sake and not just that of the project. But he'd lost people before. It always took something out of him, but the mission came first. If cephalomycin proved out, it would extend millions of lives.

They were coming up on the tip of the peninsula proper now, with the islands ahead. Time to check in.

"Newton, this is Blake on Helo-1. Do you copy?"

"*Affirmative. Are you almost here? We're about out of charge.*"

"Just coming up over Klaar Island now. Any luck?" As he said it, Blake knew it was a dumb question. Newton would have let him know already.

"*Negative. We've been doing a zig-zag search pattern straddling the drop-off, south of the Disco. There's a driftline out with strobes.*"

As they flew over the last line of hills, Blake saw what New-ton was talking about. A pair of lights extended in a line south from the *Disco Volante*. Newton's aircar was flying maybe a hun-dred meters above the surface, between the helicopter and the lights. "We see them, and you. Okay, we've got it from here, you get back while you've still got charge. I don't want to have to fish you out of the drink too."

"*Roger that. They have DSMBs, so keep an eye out.*"

"Safety sausage, roger. Let's hope they're deployed. Now get on home."

"*We're on our way. Gulliver's on the Disco, keep him posted.*"

"Copy that."

Blake watched as the aircar broke off from its search pattern and headed across the bay toward Squidberry Inlet, just on the horizon.

"Okay," Blake said to his pilot. "Take it down to a hundred meters and pick up their search pattern." He turned back to the two others sitting in the passenger/cargo compartment. "One of you on each side. They've got inflatable markers but don't count on them being deployed. If you see anything but water, sing out."

"Got it."

∞ ∞ ∞

Ten minutes later, as the helicopter made yet another turn from the ocean side back towards the shallows, one of the observers sang out.

"Marker buoy, eleven o'clock! About six hundred meters off."

The helicopter halted its turn as it came up on the bearing. "Do you see it?" The pilot asked Blake.

Blake scanned the water ahead of them, first with his naked eyes, then with binoculars. All he saw was water and waves. He swept the binoculars back and forth. A flash of yellow poked up from a wave then went out of view as his binoculars swept passed.

"Wait!" he said, and swept back again. "Got it!" He lowered the binoculars, staying focused on the spot. Now he could make it out, just. He pointed to it. "There, about five hundred meters now. Bring us over it and descend to thirty meters."

He raised the binoculars again. Yes, that was definitely a safety sausage. He checked the time. The divers should have surfaced at least fifteen minutes ago. He scanned the area around the marker. There was some light chop, but the divers should be visible floating at the surface. There was no sign of them.

By now the helicopter was above the marker, its downwash blowing it around a bit. The copter wasn't equipped for water landings, but it had a winch. "Who wants to go for a swim?" Blake asked.

"Already on it," said John Rennie, one of the searchers, pulling on fins and a mask.

"Take us down to wave height," Blake told the pilot.

As the aircraft lowered to just above the wave tops, the downwash making a relatively smooth area of water beneath, John stepped over to the door, grabbed a packaged self-inflating raft, and jumped into the water.

As he hit the water, the helicopter pulled up to twenty meters to give him clearance. He looked up at the helicopter and waved, signaling he was okay, then turned and set off toward the marker.

By now the safety sausage had blown or drifted about fifty meters south.

Blake watched as John approached the marker, his head down, breathing through his snorkel, except for the occasional glance up to be sure he was on track. He reached it, then swam around it in a circle, as if looking for something. He dived down, his feet coming up then kicking to push down further. He surfaced about fifteen seconds later. Floating next to the buoy, he started pulling up on the line attached to the base of the marker.

After a minute, he flipped over on his back and waved at the helicopter again.

"Bring us down closer," Blake said.

John, holding the base of the buoy in his left hand to help keep himself afloat, raised his right arm, his hand holding the other end of the line. From it dangled the line's reel, apparently snagged in the line, and clearly not clipped to a diver's gear.

"Damn."

Chapter 36: Washed Up

Above the Drop-Off

Ellie tapped Caporale and signaled him to stop ascending. She had no idea how to signal "we've drifted too far, we should deploy a DSMB," so instead she just grabbed her own. It was attached to a reel of line, in turn clipped to a D-ring on her buoyancy compensator. She pulled the rolled-up, uninflated safety sausage and a meter of line out from its reel and pointed to it with her other hand, then pointed upward.

Henry nodded, getting the idea, and reached to help her unroll the sausage.

Once done, and not wanting to waste unbreathed air, Ellie took it by the base, removed her regulator, and exhaled into it. She did this several times, so that it now took on its sausage shape, floating vertically in the water and tugging lightly on the reel of line.

She took the reel and began deploying the line, the yellow marker buoy rising through the water above them. As it rose, the air inside it expanded, inflating it further. About six meters above them, it was tugging hard on the line, but the reel wasn't unspooling it quickly enough. It began to tug Ellie up with it. She tried to loosen the spool, but the line only seemed to snag tighter. The marker buoy was now acting like a lift bag, pulling Ellie toward the surface, decompression stop be damned.

Henry realized what was happening and grabbed her belt as she rose past him. He dumped air from his BC to try to drag her back down, but by now the air in the marker had expanded it to its maximum, and it was pulling hard.

Ellie had no other choice. She unclipped the reel from its D-ring and let it and the buoy pop to the surface without her. No matter, Henry still had his.

The two of them adjusted their buoyancy to resume a more reasonable ascent rate, watching their gauges as the tiniest of their bubbles drifted slowly upward past them.

At eight meters, they leveled off, both of them checking their dive computers for the time. They needed to drift here while the nitrogen that had dissolved into their blood at depth slowly dissipated, so as not to risk it forming dangerous bubbles when they surfaced. Getting the bends from a dive like the one they'd just done would probably be more uncomfortable than dangerous, but there was no point in risking it.

Three minutes into the decompression stop, holding on to each other and carefully watching their depth, Henry thumped his chest again. Ellie reached for her spare second stage. She was about to hand it to him when he made a throat slashing motion. He was out of air.

He took her spare and spit out his own regulator, then took a deep breath from hers and blew a cloud of bubbles. He gave her a thumbs-up, then an *okay* sign. Ellie looked at her pressure gauge. It was cutting it close, but there was nothing else to do but float there and breath until their decompression time was up or they ran out of air. If the latter happened, they would just surface, it was only eight meters away, and be then be wary of any symptoms of decompression sickness. Which were unlikely at this point, Ellie assured herself.

∞ ∞ ∞

As it happened, they took their last breaths from the tank after they'd done their decompression but were still a meter from the surface. It was no big deal, they just kept exhaling that last few seconds, then both gasped in a huge breath as they broke the surface.

"Well, let's not do that again," Ellie said between taking breaths and spitting out salt water, relieved to be on the surface.

"No argument here. That fish was huge! It really whacked me!"

"But you're all right?"

"Yeah, just knocked about. Maybe some bruises. What kind of fish was that?"

"I have no idea. It looked something like a big grouper, but not." She looked around. There was no sign of the *Disco Volante*, or of the inflatable marker she'd had to let go.

"We should get the other marker up. Gulliver will have no idea where we are, and we overstayed our dive time. He'll be frantic."

"Right." Caporale bent down to grab his own DSMB, frowned, and ducked his head underwater. He came up and said: "I can't seem to grab it, that bump with the fish knocked my gear around. Can you see if you can see it?"

"Sure." Ellie let some air out of her buoyancy compensator, took a deep breath, and ducked down. She checked the straps on Henry's gear, and around the back by his tank. No DSMB. She surfaced again.

"I don't see it. Did you have it in a BC pocket?"

"No. Clipped on, same as yours."

Ellie nodded and ducked under again, paying close attention to the straps and rings on his buoyancy compensator. There was a short, loose, strap by his waist. She tugged on it to pull herself close, and examined it. The stitches where one end had attached to the rest of the rig were torn. The DSMB was definitely gone.

"It must have ripped loose when that fish knocked you against the rock. It's gone," she told him when she surfaced.

"Oh, shit," he said. "Now what do we do?"

"Not panic."

"Got that. I'm not panicking. Yet."

"Sooner or later they'll come looking. Probably sooner; they'll figure we must have surfaced by now."

"We're going to be hard to spot. Do you have any signaling gear? Strobe? Smoke?"

She shook her head *no*. "If we see an aircraft we can try bouncing sunlight off the front of our masks like a signaling mirror. Aside from that, no. Oh, I have a whistle." She showed him the plastic pea-whistle attached to her left shoulder strap.

"Oh, great." He used his mouth tube to blow more air into his BC, inflating it to its maximum to raise him as high out of the water as possible. Ellie did the same.

She paddled herself around in a circle. Mostly it was just water as far as she could see, but in one direction—south-east?—she could see distant hills when the waves took her high enough.

"There," she said, pointing. "Is that land? Where is that?"

Henry turned himself around to see where she pointed, then had to wait until a wave raised him up so he could see.

"Yes, I think that's Klaar Island. If we can see it, we can't be more than a couple of kilometers off."

"The current is taking us south. What's beyond that?"

Henry thought for a bit. He'd seen maps and aerial photographs. "Nothing at all. The current might push us east a little too, but if we miss that island there's nothing but open water for hundreds of kilometers, unless we get lucky and wash into Krechet's Landing."

Ellie didn't like the sound of that at all. Even with aircraft searching for them—and she wondered how long they'd look before giving up—they were too small in a stretch of ocean too big for them to have a chance of being spotted. Their best bet was to make for land, or at least make sure they stayed within Squidberry Bay. Big as it was—about a thousand square kilometers—it was far smaller than the Western Ocean.

"We'd better start swimming. Head east; the current will push us south."

"Agreed."

Still floating on their backs, they began to slowly and steadily kick towards land. Ellie hoped they'd get far enough before the current swept them south of the peninsula islands. She kept watching towards the north. If an aircraft did come, it would probably be from that direction; that's where they'd look first.

∞ ∞ ∞

Every few minutes they checked to see that they were on course. They were, but the current was pushing them south faster than they could paddle east. There was nothing they could do about it but to keep kicking.

After a half-hour or more of this, Ellie remarked, "I'm going to have a hell of a sunburn on my legs. I should have worn a full-length suit. At least the water's warm."

"That's one thing you probably won't have to worry about," Henry said. "Alpha Centauri B is an orange star, so not as much ultraviolet as Sol."

"Oh, well. That's something anyway."

"On the other hand, this water isn't *that* warm. Another hour or two we might have to start worrying about hypothermia."

"Great. Forget I said anything."

For some reason Ellie found herself thinking about her mother, and wondered how she was doing. *Probably better than I am, right now. Oh well, if I do end up washing out to sea and am never seen again, maybe she'll be too far gone to miss me.* Oddly enough, that thought didn't cheer Ellie up much.

Chapter 37: Lost

Above Squidberry Bay

With John Rennie back aboard the helicopter, Blake examined the DSMB reel with disgust and misgiving. It had obviously jammed, and equally obviously it had been unclasped, not ripped loose. If Greystone or Caporale were being pulled to the surface too fast, jettisoning it would have been the correct move. But this was just one. There should be another.

"Get me wind and current speeds. I want an estimate of where that thing was when it surfaced."

"Got it."

Fortunately, the GPS system had been fully operational for a while now. They had a precise fix on where they'd found the buoy, and where the *Disco* was anchored. Logically the divers would have been somewhere on a line between the two, adjusting for however far the buoy had drifted on the surface. That would depend on both winds and water current.

The divers would have drifted away from that point too, but more influenced by water than wind. If they did the math right, they could get a good estimate on where they were now.

Meanwhile, the helicopter had resumed its back-and-forth search pattern. The *Disco* was still at anchor. The GPS was great, but the ship provided a handy visual reference. Poor Gulliver Newton must be feeling pretty miserable by now, but there was nothing he could do, and not really anything he could have done differently.

"Sir? I've got that data."

"Let's see it," Blake said.

Sarah O'Neil was the other of Cohen's crew who had volunteered, at Blake's suggestion, to come along. She held a datapad out for him. The screen showed a chart of Squidberry Bay, the peninsula and the short archipelago off its tip.

"The *Disco Volante* is anchored here," O'Neil said, pointing at the little ship icon on the chart. "Surface current is in this direction." An arrowed line showed the position and direction of the *Disco*'s drift line.

"This is where we found the marker," she pointed out a little orange oval on the map. "Given wind and surface currents it would have surfaced about here." She pointed at another spot, north and west of where they'd found it.

"That's quite a bit further out than I would have thought."

"There's quite a breeze."

"What's the water current at depth there?"

"That's tricky. It's different beyond the drop-off, the wall changes it a bit. But they were obviously south and a bit west of the *Disco*, where they went in. Gully Newton said they were going to head north first, but we don't know how far or fast. The current can be pretty strong."

"So, extrapolate best and worst cases."

"Right." O'Neil tapped the datapad screen, and an elongated ellipse stretching north to south, showed on the map. "Best guess is they were somewhere in this region when they released the buoy."

Blake eyed it grimly. The width of the ellipse bracketed the islands, and he knew there could be rough currents between them. The length of it extended from a bit further north than they were now to a kilometer north of peninsula. Worst case, they were on their way out to sea.

"Show me surface currents and winds." he said.

She did so, tapping the screen so that two vector arrows showed on the screen.

"Give me the most likely average of those for a diver on the surface." That would mostly be the water current, the wind might play a small part.

"There."

"Okay, now displace that ellipse by that much, based on elapsed time." The time estimates varied too, anything from their originally planned thirty minutes, to whenever they'd likely run out of air.

She manipulated the datapad some more. The resultant ellipse was larger and displaced mostly south. Now it clearly straddled the islands, but mostly on the ocean side. They could be in the bay, they could be on an island, or they could be out at sea somewhere. Blake dearly hoped it was the middle option, but the most dire was out to sea. That's where they'd look first.

He pointed to the spot on the map. "Okay, new search pattern. We fly to here," he pointed to the southern extreme the ellipse, on the ocean side, "then zig-zag our way north."

"Copy that."

Blake checked the coordinates again, then relayed them to the pilot. "That way. And keep looking," he said to the searchers. "It'd be stupid to overfly them and miss them on our way the other end of the search pattern."

∞ ∞ ∞

In the water

"Did you hear something?" Henry asked

"Waves. Did you mean something else?" Ellie replied.

"No, shh, listen. Maybe an aircraft?"

Ellie listened. Other than the waves, nothing. She tried to listen for the high-pitched whine of an aircar, or the drone of a propeller. Nope, just water noises. Wait, there was a low-pitched thumping, a bit like a boat pounding over the waves. No, it was faster than that.

"A helicopter?" she said.

They both stopped and turned in the water, scanning the sky. "That's what I thought I heard," Henry said.

"I don't see anything."

"Me neither."

The thumping grew fainter. "I don't hear it anymore," Ellie said. "If it was a helicopter, it's gone."

"If it's flying a search pattern, it'll be back."

"Let's hope so." Ellie turned again to look for the land they'd seen. It was definitely more east now than it had been. "We'd better kick it up a notch, or we're going to miss land."

"Slave driver," Henry said, but he rolled back and starting kicking.

Ellie did the same. They'd both been doing a slow, easy kick, which with their fins propelled them at a steady pace, but her leg muscles were definitely starting to feel it. *Please don't cramp*, she told them.

Chapter 38: Dude, Where's My Helicopter?

Future site of Kakuloa City

Parry Cohen looked up from the computer display he'd been focused on for the past while, going over construction reports and updating his project plans. Mostly things had been going well. There were the usual minor setbacks, but there was slack built into the schedule for that. Nothing on the critical path was delayed yet. He was surprised to note the time. He'd been at this for a couple of hours.

As he got up and stretched, he felt there was something different about the usual construction sounds outside the hut where he'd been working. It seemed quieter. He went outside to see what was going on.

There were still people with heavy equipment moving dirt and grading the roadways, and a team laying a pipeline into a trench that had been excavated a couple of days earlier. That wasn't it. He looked further to where the foundations of the first hotel were going in. The core of the heavy tower crane was now about five stories tall, still being raised.

That was it. It *wasn't* still being raised. Where was the helicopter? It should be acting as a skycrane, lifting the tower segments into place. He looked around, neither seeing it nor hearing it. What the heck?

He called the foreman of that project, a man named Vitruvo.

"Where's my helicopter?" Parry demanded before Vitruvo had much chance to say anything. "Why isn't that crane going up? That's a critical path item! What happened?"

"Uh, Mr. Cohen, Administrator Blake commandeered the helicopter. Some kind of emergency."

"Emergency, bullcrap. That helicopter is mine whenever we need it for construction, and we need it now. What kind of emergency, and why didn't he ask me?"

"I told him he should, but he just grabbed a couple of people and took off. Something about missing divers."

"Missing divers, and he took a helicopter? Wouldn't a boat make more sense? Which way did he go?"

"He headed north, sir. Said something about Squidberry Bay."

"Squidberry Bay? That's over a hundred kilometers from here," Parry said. Wait, wasn't that where that marine biologist from the ship had been headed? Ellie Greystone, that was her name. "He said divers? Scientists, maybe?"

"Yes, that's right."

"You said he grabbed people. Who?"

"John Rennie and Sarah O'Neil."

Cohen knew the names. Both were construction divers, Rennie big and powerfully built, O'Neil almost as strong, smart and with some medical training. Blake must have an encyclopedic memory for personnel to have picked those two on short notice.

"I tried to call you," Vitruvo said, "but your omni kept going to voicemail."

Damn it, it would have. He'd silenced it so as not to be interrupted while concentrating. But the two workers Blake had taken were also divers. They'd been working on the foundations for the marina, although not today. Blake had done the right thing.

"All right. That's on me, but you should have come up to the hut to tell me. If it's what I think it is, I'd have given him the chopper, and the people he needed." He paused, wondering if there was anything he could do. None of the work his own divers would be doing was in more than a couple of meters of water, so he'd had no reason make sure there was a recompression chamber available. No, there was nothing he could do but stand by. There wasn't even any point calling Blake, that would only distract him needlessly.

"Okay," he said. "Find something else to do in the meantime. We'll resume work on the tower when we get the helicopter back."

"Got it, boss."

"I hope Ellie's all right," Parry said, more to himself than to Vitruvo. He clicked off.

∞ ∞ ∞

A hundred and twenty kilometers to the north and west, Blake was hoping the same thing, for both Greystone and Caporale. They'd been zig-zagging their new pattern for fifteen minutes now, working their way slowly north from beyond the southernmost limit the two divers could have reached. He hadn't expected to find them that far south, he just wanted to be sure he didn't undershoot. But it was still frustrating. His gaze kept sweeping the ocean surface ahead of them, while Rennie and O'Neil behind him scanned to the sides.

He had an idea. He called Dave Newton.

"Did you find them?" were Newton's first words when he answered.

"Not yet, still looking. Listen, I had an idea. *Disco* has underwater cameras, right? Can they see the bottom?"

"She does. Gulliver said the visibility wasn't that great today, but we can lower one of the cameras, as long as he keeps the speed down. You want him to up-anchor?"

Blake didn't see any point in the boat remaining where it was. There was no way the divers would be swimming back to it, not given where they'd found the abandoned DSMB. He told Newton as much. "If it's okay with you, I'd like to have him take the *Disco* to where we estimate they released the marker, drop the camera, and do a slow spiral out from there. Maybe he'll spot something. Any objections?"

It took Newton a few moments to answer. Blake could only imagine what he was thinking. "No, that makes sense. I just wish

I were out there with him. And I don't know whether to hope he finds something, or that he doesn't. But he should be able to handle it."

"Good, and I understand your feelings," Blake said. "I hope he doesn't find anything either, but we should look."

"Agreed. Of course if something happened beyond the dropoff, there may never be any trace."

"We'll worry about that when I'm ready to call off the search. That's not going to be for a while yet, unless we find them first."

"Copy that. Okay, I'll call Gulliver and have him contact you for detailed instructions. If nothing else, it'll help him feel useful. Poor kid."

"It *will* be useful. Thanks. Blake out."

The helicopter swung about to the next leg of the search.

∞ ∞ ∞

In the water

"How are you doing, Henry?" Ellie said. Neither of them had said anything in a while, but they were both still plodding along.

"Hanging in there." His voice sounded weak. "You?"

"Tired, sore, and bored. This is not how I wanted to spend the afternoon."

That drew a faint chuckle. "I thought you liked the water?" Henry said.

"Not as much as I used to. By the way, what's the salinity of the ocean here?" She didn't care about the specifics, but since this ocean was much younger than Earth's, it was probably less salty. She couldn't quantify it by the taste, though.

"Too salty to drink, if that's what you're thinking."

"Damn." It had been. She was thirsty. And starting to feel cold. She tried not to think about it. *Just keep kicking*, she told herself.

"I'll buy you a beer when we get back," Henry said.

"Don't tease."

"Sorry. I've just been thinking about that for the last little while. Surprisingly good for a local brew."

"Local?"

"Yeah, one of the other farmers up the bay brews it."

"From what? I thought there weren't any native cereals on this planet." *I can't believe I'm having this conversation now*, Ellie thought, but realized it was better than some of the alternatives.

"Uh, good question. I'm not sure I want to know, but he must import something. Do you have to have cereals to make beer?"

"I'm no brewer, but I think so. Don't you know? You're the ecologist."

"Sorry, I come from a long line of wine drinkers. Ask me about grapes."

"Has anybody tried making wine from squidberries? They look kind of like grapes."

"I don't know. Might be worth a try."

Ellie was about to say something else, when Henry spoke again. "Could make a good sideline," he said. "Think CentPharm only needs skins, not juice."

"We know they ferment well enough. The squids get drunk off of them."

"Yeah. Might be other chemicals in there too. Holmes would know." Henry's voice was getting weaker.

"Victoria Holmes?" Ellie asked.

"Yeah. Smart lady. Like you."

That was an uncharacteristic remark from Henry, and his voice sounded almost slurred.

"Henry? Are you okay?"

"Wha? I'm fine." His voice was definitely slurring.

"Hold up, Henry, stop swimming." She grabbed his BC and pulled him forward to a vertical position. His face and lips were pale. She didn't see any signs of shivering, but he looked drowsy.

"Wha's goin' on?" he asked.

"I think you're going hypothermic." She was feeling chilled herself. She wondered how much longer she had.

"Nah, water's warm."

"Not warm enough." She considered her options. There really weren't any. "We need to drop your tank."

"Wha?"

"It'll get in the way. We should have probably have dropped them a while back." Maybe. The weight of the tanks had helped stabilize them in the water, but they added drag. Now Henry's tank would get in the way of what she needed to do. "Turn around."

He didn't turn, but nor did he resist when Ellie turned him. She disconnected the inflator from his BC. Like hers, his BC was integral to the backpack that held the tank, so she couldn't just take the whole pack off. She pulled his regulator and gauge hoses from over his shoulders, then unfastened the strap holding the tank to the backpack. It came free. Empty of air, the tank was just slightly buoyant, and the weight of its valve, attached regulator and hoses rotated it so that it floated base up, just at the surface of the water.

"Tha's 'spensive gear," Henry protested weakly.

"Shut up, I'm saving your life."

"Oh? Good." He sounded drunk, but it was the hypothermia.

She jettisoned his weights, too, but kept hers on to help stabilize her beneath him. "Okay, lie back."

She wrapped her arms around his chest from behind, his body in front of hers. "Cross your arms, out of the water." He did so, crossing his arms over hers. "Good, now try to kick in time with me," she said, and started to kick with the same slow, deep stroke they'd been maintaining.

It wasn't ideal, but she'd reduced their net surface area, and her legs, when they coordinated, helped keep his warm. His arms were now out of the water, not losing heat so quickly. She didn't know how long she could keep this up, but it was helping her retain body heat too. She hoped. How long would it be before she felt sand beneath her?

∞ ∞ ∞

Gulliver was now on the new station, the *Disco*'s autopilot sweeping the boat in an expanding spiral while he monitored the underwater camera. The helicopter reached the westward limit of its search area and turned back toward the northernmost island beyond the peninsula. Klaar Island, where, two years earlier, Blake had camped along with Tyrell, Flint, Jenkins and Reyes that first night they'd gathered squidberries.

Blake didn't have time for reminiscing. He scanned the water ahead, still looking for any sign of his two missing scientists. It was late in the afternoon now, the sun about halfway down the sky to the west. He'd keep going at least until dark, then re-evaluate. The helicopter had a searchlight.

They reached the eastern limit of the search pattern, and the helicopter began its turn just shy of the island.

"There, on the beach!"

The pilot immediately stopped the turn and stayed in a hover, not changing his heading.

"Where?"

"Two o'clock, just above the water line."

Blake couldn't see past the pilot at that angle. "Bring it back, ninety-degree right turn."

As the chopper swung around, Blake focused his binoculars on the beach, sweeping them back and forth along the limit of the wave's wash. A figure came into sight, lying on the sand. No, two of them together, still in their gear, the water lapping at their feet as the waves surged up the beach. Neither was moving, although they were surely close enough to hear the helicopter.

"There. Set us down there, close as you can."

The pilot eyed the beach. "Those trees are kind of close to the water, I don't think the beach is big enough. How about I hover just off shore?"

"Do it."

The helicopter dropped and leveled out just meters above the water, spray and sand whipping about in the downwash. Still the bodies on the beach didn't move.

"A little lower. That water's shallow." The last thing he needed was for someone to break a leg jumping into water that turned out to be less than knee-deep.

Blake undid his straps and squirmed back between the seats to the cargo area, where John Rennie had the door open and was sitting on the deck, his feet on the landing skid.

As the helicopter dropped to a meter above the water, Rennie leaned over, grabbed the skid, and swung down, splashing into thigh-deep water about five meters from the shore. Blake was a few seconds behind him.

They ran across the beach to where Greystone and Caporale lay, the blast of sand and spray lessening as the helicopter backed off.

They couldn't have been out of the water long. The bodies were still wet, clammy to the touch. Blake feared the worst, then Greystone rolled over and moaned. "Cold," she said.

"Hypothermia. Get their gear off," Blake said, and called the helicopter. "Get back here. I need you to land. They're alive but hypothermic. I need blankets, warming gear, whatever you've got."

"Roger that."

Rennie and Blake finished getting the dive gear off the two scientists and unzipped their wet-suits. The air was warm, it would help. Caporale was shivering now. It was a good sign; it meant he was alive.

Blake and John doffed their shirts, still dry, and used them as towels to help dry the others off.

The pilot, in a skillful bit of flying, brought the helicopter in at literal wave-top level, his skids brushing the water, but the tips of his rotors were below and clear of the tree branches overhanging the beach. Blake thought that the blades could probably have handled a few branches, but he wasn't the one doing the flying.

O'Neil jumped out of the chopper as soon as the skids touched the sand, carrying a bundle of folded blankets. The downwash whipped the sand up, but it couldn't be helped.

Together the three rescuers bundled Caporale and Greystone in the blankets and into the helicopter. John then grabbed up the discarded dive gear and clambered aboard. "Clear, go," he said.

The helicopter edged out away from the trees and then climbed. "Where to?" the pilot asked.

"Newton's farm, it's closest, and he has an infirmary," Blake said. "And keep us low, I don't know what their decompression situation is." As he said that, John handed him the dive computer he'd recovered. Blake looked at him and gave him a thumbs-up. Smart move. He turned back to the pilot. "Call Newton and tell him we're on the way, then call *Disco* and tell Gulliver he can come in. We've got them and they're safe."

That last might be an exaggeration. Hypothermia was serious, and Caporale also had a few scrapes and bruises. Blake wondered what the story there was. He looked at O'Neil, who was tending to them. They were already connected to medical monitors and she was setting up some kind of warm air system. The helicopter had come equipped with a surprisingly complete medical kit. "How are they doing?"

"Serious but stable. Caporale's core temperature is lower. With that bruising I'm worried about internal injuries."

"And Greystone?"

"More exhausted than hypothermic, but still chilled."

"Thirsty" Ellie managed weakly.

Blake smiled. "Give her something. We'll be at Newton's in about five minutes." The helicopter was at full speed now.

Chapter 39: Recovery

Newton's Farm

The next day, Greystone was up if not exactly about. Blake had stayed the night in one of Newton's spare rooms, but the helicopter had taken Caporale back to Krechet's Landing where his possible internal injuries could be dealt with. They turned out to be more internal bruising, not bleeding, so he would be back after a couple of days of rest.

Blake, Dave and Gulliver Newton, and Ellie Greystone gathered in the dining room after breakfast. Greystone still had a blanket wrapped around her shoulders, and she sipped from a hot mug of coffee.

"Still cold?" Blake asked her.

"No, but I want to feel too warm for a while. I was starting to think I'd never feel warm again."

"So, what happened?" Blake asked. "By the way, I want to keep this informal, but consider it an investigation. I need to justify the resources we used. Helicopter time and some of Cohen's people."

"Sure, I understand," Ellie said. She'd expected something like this. It wasn't the first time she'd been involved in a search and rescue, although it was the first time she'd been the subject of one.

Ellie recapped the dive, starting with Caporale and her following the *Disco*'s anchor line down, against the current, and verifying that the boat wasn't likely to come adrift while they were down.

Gulliver confirmed that that had been their plan, and he'd watched them go until they were out of sight.

Ellie then mentioned the coelacanth and the big whatever-it-was fish that had battered Henry, and then noticing the current. Her best guess was that the current beyond the wall was much stronger than it was over the shallows.

"That makes sense," Blake said. "It also sounds like the current is running much stronger there than it usually is. It might be a tidal or seasonal thing."

"I can vouch for that," Dave Newton said. "I talked to some of the other squidberry farmers further north, where the drop-off comes much closer to shore. Jim Hernandez said it seems to be running faster than usual. He noticed it when he was out fishing."

"We should have treated it as a drift dive," Ellie said. "Deployed our surface markers right from the start and had the *Disco* follow us."

"We know that now," Blake said, "but it sounds like by the time you realized how strong the current was, you were already being swept south of *Disco Volante*. Having to deal with Henry's encounter didn't help."

Dave Newton nodded agreement. "I probably wouldn't have done anything different. You had your DSMBs, and you did the right thing by deploying it as soon as you realized your situation. That it got tangled, and that Caporale's had been lost...well, shit happens. I'm just glad it didn't end up as bad as it could have."

Ellie just nodded, still somewhat numbed by thoughts of what could have happened.

Blake agreed. "And you did an admirable job of getting Henry to shore. You almost certainly saved his life, and you risked your own to do it."

"I wasn't just going to swim off without him," she said.

"No, but you would have been justified if you had. Some people would have."

She shivered, and not just from the cold. She knew Blake was right. She had been near the point of doing just that when she'd realized she'd reached water shallow enough to stand in. That had given her the energy to drag Henry out and up the beach before collapsing herself. She had been closer to abandoning him than she wanted to think about.

Blake looked at her, seeming to know what she was thinking. "But you didn't. And in any case, I'd rather deal with one body than two. I'm just glad that this time it was zero."

"As are we all," Dave Newton said. "And Gulliver, I'm proud of you. You followed instructions and didn't do anything to make the situation worse. Under the circumstances, there wasn't anything else you could have done."

"Your father's right," Blake said. "As Milton put it, 'they also serve who only stand and wait', and I know from experience that can be a very hard thing to do."

"Thanks," Gulliver said, apparently not quite convinced.

"Okay," Blake said briskly. "I'm going to call this no-fault. Nobody did anything outright stupid or negligent based on the information available, although yes, in hindsight there were things that could have been done differently. Nobody was seriously injured or died. Caporale was slightly injured but that was the fish's fault. We did lose some gear and Cohen lost some time on his project, but not seriously so. I'll settle with him."

He looked around at the others. "Anything else?"

"About Cohen's project..." Dave Newton began.

"Let's talk about that after. It's not relevant to this discussion, except that it's why we had the helicopter at all."

"Fair enough," Newton said. "That's all I had."

"I just want to thank everyone involved," Ellie said. "I still feel like it was my own stupid fault, and I'm sorry to have caused so much trouble."

Blake shook his head. "That's a normal reaction, don't worry about it. Nobody knew the current was running stronger than we're used to. Another data point for the oceanographers. They're still working things out about this planet."

"Even so...."

"If you want to repay us," Dave Newton said with a half-smile, "find a solution to our damn tree squid problem."

Ellie laughed. "Okay, now that I think I can do."

Chapter 40: Death of a Decoy

Newton Farm

"Well, that didn't go quite as expected," Ellie Greystone said a week later, examining the remains of the shredded decoy she had fished out of the creek beneath one of the squidberry trees. It had taken a couple of days to prepare and print up signs bearing the warning pattern. A day after they had been posted, the squids were back, ignoring the placards as if they were just another part of the scenery. The odd thing was, they still reacted to the live squid displaying that pattern.

Undaunted, she, Caporale—by then back from Krechet's Landing and claiming to be fully recovered—and Gully had worked to model and 3D-print life-sized models of sentinel squid in several different positions, each displaying the warning pattern. They scrapped the placards and deployed the decoy squids in the trees, then waited to see what happened.

What happened was that the presence of the decoys, when the octopodes had seen them in the trees, seemed to enrage them. Several of the larger tree squids had swarmed up the trees, their mantles going dark—a characteristic dominance expression, similar to a gorilla standing and thumping its chest—and ripped the decoys from their perches before proceeding to dismember them with their beaks and arms, tossing them to the ground or creek where others finished the job. Greystone had never seen behavior that aggressive in any terrestrial octopus, and only a few species of squid. Sure, sometimes Earth octopuses were cannibalistic, but this was different.

She had brought the remains of the decoys back to the lab, where she was poking at them now. "Any traces have probably washed away," she said, "but I wonder if they injected any venom while they were biting. Those squids were *pissed*."

"Do you suppose we got the color patterns wrong?" Caporale asked. "Maybe we insulted their mothers."

"Ha," Ellie chuckled. "As if they ever knew their mothers. Octopus moms don't eat while sheltering their eggs, and they die soon after the eggs hatch." She felt a twinge, wondering how her own mother was doing back on Earth. She should send an email. It would take at least two weeks for a reply, or longer, depending on ship schedules. She stared at the decoy on the bench in front of her. Later.

"More likely it suggested a predator species," she continued, wondering about the implications for the intelligence of tree squid. "But the colors were right. Even the polarization was right. I don't know for sure about Kakuloan cephalopods, but on Earth many of them can detect different polarization patterns. Many animals can, it helps them detect prey. Cuttlefish can even change the polarization of their skin."

"Really?"

"They modulate their iridophores, something like chromatophores. These animals can't, though. At least, I looked for it and didn't observe it." She picked up a dismembered decoy. It was a mess. "I'll have to review the videos. Maybe the real squid sentinels animate the pattern somehow. That would complicate things."

"It would make sense, though," said Caporale. "Maybe give a direction of the threat."

"And these decoys could be as annoying as the boy who cried wolf," Greystone said. "I'll have to try some experiments with animated displays if that's the case."

"Fair point," Caporale conceded. "Maybe the almost-but-not-quite appearance triggered something like what we humans experience as the so-called uncanny valley, when an image or robot looks close to, but not quite like, a human face."

"McWhirter said they'd sometimes gang up on a lone harvesting robot. I wonder if that's a similar response?"

Caporale shook his head. "I don't think they've ever been that violent with the bots."

"Oh. Anyway, I don't know how we'd test or fix that. But we can test for having the pattern move. What if we rig up a couple of display panels, or even smart fabric if it's available, show a video of the pattern changing from *nothing-to-see-here* to *danger*, and loop it?"

"Sounds like it's worth a try. You're the behavior expert."

"You know what else would help? If I could keep an octopus or two in a tank here in the lab. I could get quicker feedback on my tests."

"Good idea. In fact, why haven't you done that already?"

"Keeping an octopus in a tank is much easier said than done. They're escape artists, on top of it being all the ease and simplicity of any salt-water aquarium. Which is to say, not easy at all."

"True enough."

"But you're right, I should have started that project already. I'll check with Dave."

"If it helps with the squid problem, I don't think he'll have a problem with it."

∞ ∞ ∞

The only problem Dave Newton had with it was that she hadn't thought of it sooner.

"So you finally come up with that after nearly three weeks of messing about? I'm still losing squidberries, you've been spending quite a bit on your placards and your decoys, and you still have nothing to show for it? And *now* you think it might be worth keeping one in the lab to experiment on?"

"It wasn't my first choice because octopuses are difficult to maintain in captivity. Any marine aquarium is difficult; for cephalopods even more so. And the stress can affect their behavior. Anyway, I'm sorry. As for the cost, I thought CentPharm was paying for—"

"Yes, yes. They'll reimburse me, but it's still an issue in the short term. Plus, there's the trips to Krechet's Landing to pick up the stuff in the first place. What am I going to need to pick up to set up your aquarium? Or your fancy animated displays?"

"I..." Ellie had not been expecting Newton's reaction. She could understand his frustration, she felt that herself. She wondered if the trouble she'd caused on her dive trip was part of it, although he hadn't brought it up since. Unfortunately, investigative science rarely produced solutions to order. At least Cent-Pharm would understand that. "Look, I'm sorry I haven't come up with a solution yet. These cephalopods are far more complex than anything on Earth. They're a new species, heck a new genus, quite probably even a new superfamily. I know it's not what you want to hear, but these things take time, unless I happen to get lucky. I know I'm on the right track, but even if not, with an experimental animal I can test out other options, like a repellent that won't harm the squidberries or the other life in the creeks."

She paused, considering her options, then added: "If you're really not happy with my performance," she continued, "I can talk to Will Blake and he can set up at one of the other farms. They may not have quite the facilities you have here, but I'll be out of your way."

Newton recoiled. She didn't know if he took her threat seriously, or for that matter if she'd really meant it herself, but he understood the advantages of having her here working the specifics of his problem. No doubt she could solve it—if it were solvable—working somewhere else, but it would take longer, and he wouldn't get it first.

"No, no," he said. "You're not in anybody's way here. I apologize if I gave you that impression. I'm just letting off a bit of steam. It's been a rough day." He sighed and, leaning back in his chair, ran a hand through his hair.

"I understand," Ellie said. "I'm kind of frustrated myself. I honestly expected it to be easier."

"'No plan survives contact with the enemy,' eh? Whoever first said that got it right." Newton sat forward again. "All right, tell you what. Pull together a list of what you need, for both your fish-tank and your animated displays. I'll forward that to Blake and I'll have it picked up when he's got it ready."

"Thank you, that sounds fine."

"Sure," He paused, then added. "We're at our wit's end here. They made a mess of what they didn't eat when they savaged your decoys. In the meantime, do what you can, all right?"

"Of course," Ellie said, and retreated to the lab. She'd go over the videos again. Maybe she'd missed something.

∞ ∞ ∞

The Lab, some days later

"Okay, Henry, I think this is it," Ellie said to Caporale. "Look at these frames here." She showed him a sequence of images leading up to the *danger* pattern they had already tried. "See how these first lines are broad, then these thinner lines form a few frames later? There might also be some subtle color shifts but it's difficult to tell with the lighting."

"I see what you mean," Henry said. "That first pattern might be more likely to catch the others' attention. But why not just stick with that?"

"Remember what we said about possibly coding details about the threat into the alert? Either what kind or the direction?"

"You think that's what the second part of the signal is?"

"It would make sense. If you want to warn somebody about, say, a bear, you'd yell *Hey!* to get their attention, then point at it and yell *Bear!*"

"Not me, I'd just run. Leave the other person as a distraction for the bear." He grinned.

She swatted his shoulder. "No you wouldn't. That was just an example anyway."

"Okay, okay. You have a point, but isn't that showing a lot of intelligence, even for a cephalopod?"

"It is a bit farfetched for an octopus. I've heard reports of Humboldt squid coordinating attacks though, so they'd probably be smart enough."

"They're a lot bigger, aren't they? But as you keep saying, these aren't squid."

"They're not, but they have a lot of squid-like behavior characteristics. I really need to capture a couple so that I can test them."

Caporale glanced over to the corner of the lab to where the aquarium setup was nearly complete. "Shouldn't you finish their new home first?"

"Yes, but Newton has been bugging me about making some 'actual progress on the real problem.' I'm multitasking."

In truth she had been working hard. In between bouts of poring over hours of the video they'd captured from the cameras in the trees, she had been building a salt-water aquarium setup using a mix of improvised equipment and pieces laboriously designed and fabricated to connect it all together. It wasn't as though she could just order everything from the local aquarium supply dealer; the nearest one was over four light-years away. Well, she could send an order by ship, and with any luck a few weeks later get a package on a returning ship, and with even more luck it would be the right part, but neither she nor, especially, Newton, wanted to wait that long.

"If I can get a couple of display panels out there and see some effect, that will go a long way to making all of us happy."

"Even if it does, it's going to take a lot of display panels to cover all the groves. Unless we start cannibalizing other equipment, I doubt there are that many available on Kakuloa, and maybe not even then."

"I'll burn that bridge when I get to it."

"Um, I don't think that's how that saying goes."

"No, but that's the way I feel."

Chapter 41: Displays

Newton Farm, the next evening

McWhirter, Gulliver Newton, and several of the other hands had spent most of the day working on Henry Caporale's project. He wanted to try extending the growing area for the berries by planting additional mangroves and the vines that grew on them. Since the existing creeks already had all the trees they could support, this involved digging a canal to divert part of the flow of one creek into a newly dug shallow lagoon. From there, it would connect via another canal to near the original creek mouth. Much of the digging had been hand work; the crew had been at it for several days. Today they had reached the stage of digging through the final sections between the creek and the hitherto dry canal. They'd already installed sluice gates at the up- and downstream ends; Caporale and Newton wanted to be sure they could restore the original flow if the diversion adversely affected the salinity of the water in the main grove and harmed the trees. Now it had been a matter of removing the final soil barriers, opening the gates, and seeing what happened.

What happened was that the water flowed into its new channel as expected and started to fill the new pool, then continued on to the outflow. What was not expected was that a slight miscalculation in gradient meant that the lagoon began to overflow its downslope bank and create a muddy quagmire. They quickly shut off the flow, but the fix was to let the lagoon drain and then level its floor, moving the excavated dirt to the downhill side to raise that bank.

Since the lagoon was already too low to drain completely
without being pumped out, that meant a good deal of muddy
work for some of the men. Gulliver Newton, being the youngest,
was one of those assigned to that particular task. The weather
was warm, and most of them were already working in shorts, so it
was no great hardship for him to kick off his shoes and wade out
into the now ankle-deep water to finish the work.

What Gully hadn't counted on was slipping and falling face
first into the mud when they were almost done. And then the
dinner bell rang.

One of the men gave him a hand up, chuckling. After Gully
wiped the muck off his face with his hands, he grinned along with
the others, none of whom tried to hide their amusement.

"Are ye all right, lad?" McWhirter asked.

"I'm fine. Just thought I'd try going for a swim," Gully said.

Caporale chuckled. "You might wait until we refill it first."

McWhirter raised his voice to be heard by the work team.
"That was the dinner bell, lads. Time to knock off. This will
keep."

As the men started to gather up the gear, McWhirter came
over to Gully. "Let the rest of the men put the equipment away,
lad. You go get yourself cleaned up and change for dinner. I'll tell
your dad you might be a few minutes late."

"Thanks." Gully peeled off his shirt and wrung it out as best
he could, then headed up to the house.

∞ ∞ ∞

Everyone was eating dinner when Gully came back down-
stairs to the dining room. Ellie Greystone was talking with Caporale when Gully entered, and she looked up to see him wearing a
tee-shirt with a cartoon character on it. The character was animated, a superhero striking a villain and then striking a pose.

"What is that you're wearing?" Dave Newton demanded
when he saw it. Ellie had been wondering the same thing.

"Sorry Dad, it's the only clean shirt I had," Gully said, as he
sat down.

"Well turn it off, it's distracting."

"Okay, sure. Sorry." He reached down and did something at the hem of the shirt. The character stopped moving.

It wasn't the first time Ellie had seen animated smart fabric, and the non-screen surface of her omni could do something similar. Not animated, but it could change color and pattern to match a still image; Ellie sometimes used the feature to coordinate with her clothing when she wore the omni on her wrist. But an omni-phone had a lot more computational power, and cost, than a shirt. That gave her an idea.

"Gully," she said to him, "that shirt. How is the picture animated?"

"This? Oh, it's smart fabric, some kind of electronic ink, I think. There's a controller built into the hem."

"What powers it?"

"This one is just batteries. There are other kinds that generate their own power from the wearer's motion. Pretty cool, but more expensive. Haven't you seen shirts like this before? They're pretty new, but I figured they'd be common on Earth."

"Not that common, not yet anyway. I have seen a few kids with them, but I don't work much around kids. Not that you're a kid. But I'm more curious about the details. Does it just do the one sequence?"

"This one, yes. There's a ROM built in to the controller. I've thought about swapping that out, so I could upload a different clip. It wouldn't be too hard."

"Well, not for you maybe," Ellie said, remembering Gully's interest in robotics. "Is it the whole shirt or just part of it?"

"This shirt it's just the front part. But the fabric is flexible enough you could do a whole shirt I suppose. It would cost more. Why?"

"How much of that fabric is available on Kakuloa, do you suppose?" Her question was addressed to the others at the table in general, not just Gully.

"I've no idea," Dave Newton said. "Does it have other uses than fancy clothing? I suppose it might. Why?"

"You want to use it for anti-squid displays," Caporale said. "Right?"

"Exactly," she turned to Newton. "We think that animation plays a part in the squid's warning signal. Making displays out of something like this fabric has got to be cheaper than standard computer screens." For that matter, she realized, they could try making a stuffed-squid decoy out of it, if they wanted to try that again.

"I get it. Okay, I'll ask Will Blake. He should have a database of all the manifests of any ship that's landed, so he should know what's available. Or order it from Earth, if he has to. But will it work?"

"We can test it with regular screens. If Gully is willing to hack the controller in his shirt, we can try that too." She looked at him and raised an eyebrow.

"Uh, yeah, I guess so." He looked at his father.

"It's your shirt. Your call."

"Okay. There's no reason to cut up the shirt, right? Just modify the controller."

Ellie nodded. "Sure, we can just put it over a frame. Or," she grinned, "you could wear it."

"Ha, me, Gully Newton, Speaker-to-Squids. I like it."

Ellie saw McWhirter glance up with a scowl. He saw her looking and smiled. "Aye," he said. "Speaker-to-Squids. But do they listen?"

Chapter 42: Taprobane

Krechet's Landing, Kakuloa

Administrator Blake was just finishing his own dinner when he was interrupted by an alert on his omni. An automated communications relay had just received a signal from a ship arriving in-system. It caught him by surprise. He hadn't expected another ship from Earth for four or five more days. His surprise gave way to concern and curiosity when he realized it wasn't from Earth. It was one of the long-range ships, *Grande Hermine,* returning from a 9.7 light-year trip to Epsilon Indi, a sun similar to Kakuloa's own. But it wasn't due back for weeks. Even if there had been no Earth-like world, it would take a while to do a close-up survey of the system. He patched his omni into the relay.

"*Grande Hermine,* this is Kakuloa, Blake speaking. So, obvious first question, aside from why you're back so soon," he said over the link, "did you find an Earth-like world, and was it terraformed?"

"*That's two questions, but yes, and more than likely.*"

"You know what that means, *Hermine,*" Blake said. "Do you have any emergencies that prevent you landing on Mahina Nui for some quarantine?"

"*Negative on that Kakuloa. We're okay for quarantine, but keep in mind it's been nine days since we left there, so cut our time accordingly.*"

Just as ships heading into the Solar System had to land on Luna for quarantine, any ship arriving from a planet other than Earth or Sawyer's World had to quarantine at the base on Kakuloa's big moon. Nobody wanted to accidentally import something that might devastate the ecology of Kakuloa, and especially not of the squidberries. The difference was that, once it had cleared quarantine at Mahina Nui, the ship itself would be allowed to land on Kakuloa. Earth itself was still paranoid enough to forbid that.

"Roger that," Blake said. "*Grand Hermine* is cleared to land at Darwin Station on Mahina Nui. Anything else I need to know?"

"*Ah, negative, Kakuloa. We'll follow Protocol Seventeen.*"

That caught Blake off guard. Protocol Seventeen? What the hell was that? There were no such things as numbered protocols. "Roger, you do that. Kakuloa out."

Blake immediately went to a secure channel, scrambled to the ship's ident code, and hailed it back.

"Grand Hermine *here. I thought you'd figure that out, Blake.*"

"All right, what do you have that's so secret you didn't even want it known that you had a secret?" Blake had correctly sur-mised the reason behind the cryptic "Protocol Seventeen" re-mark.

"*We found something of particular interest on Taprobane. That's what we named the terraformed planet. You might want to meet us on Mahina Nui to discuss it in person.*"

Whatever it was must have security implications. For what it was worth, Blake was the ranking *UDT* official in the system, al-though there was an ambassador on Sawyer's World.

"Can you give me a hint? Something about the Terraform-ers?"

"*No, not them. But we did find a civilization. Bronze or iron age tech level. We did NOT make contact. I decided that any decisions about that were way above my pay grade, so we came back early.*"

"Ye gods. Above mine, too. All right. You made the right de-cision. We'll discuss this more. I'll come up and meet you at Dar-win Station. Blake out."

Intelligent life? Iron age? The *Anderson* crew had found an-cient stone artifacts on Sawyer's World, but this was something else again. At least these aliens weren't spacefarers. Yet.

Chapter 43: Uneasy Feelings

Newton Berry Farm

Gulliver had worked diligently over the next two days, experimenting with his animated shirt controller. He had replaced its ROM with programmable memory and, eventually, managed to reverse-engineer the encoding for the display. Said encoding, of course, hadn't matched any video standard with which he was previously familiar. Luckily, the Kakuloa network got updates from Earth whenever a ship arrived, and he found enough hints to let him hack together a program that, after some tweaking to get the image blocks in the right order, displayed whatever arbitrary video he uploaded to it.

Greystone had created a suitable file of the tree squid's warning pattern and together they'd programmed the shirt panel to display it. It looked perfect, mimicking the same subtle changes that the real sentinel squids made.

The next step was to test it.

∞ ∞ ∞

Newton's Office

"What's on your mind, Rob?" Newton said to McWhirter. The latter had sought him out privately.

"I'm a wee bit concerned with just where Greystone is going with her octopus studies. This whole *Speaker-to-Squids* thing."

"If she can tell them to go away, and they listen, where's the problem?"

McWhirter frowned but didn't answer right away. "You know I keep tabs on the local forums. Seeing what's up with the other farms, local chatter, and the like?"

"Sure. That's more your thing than mine. What does that have to do with it?"

"What have ye heard about Epsilon Indi?"

"What?" The question threw Newton. He knew Epsilon Indi was a star slightly less than ten light years away, and similar to Kakuloa's own sun. "An expedition to there just got back a couple of days ago, right? What does that have to do with squids?"

"Perhaps nothing. It depends on how smart they are, or seem to be. Rumor has it—"

"Rumor? I know you've got your sources, Rob." Newton made it a point not to ask too much about those sources.

"That's as may be. *Rumor* has it," he said, with emphasis, "that they found intelligent natives, iron age technology."

"Really?" Newton was surprised, but not shocked. At some level he had supposed it was just a matter of time. The artifacts found on Sawyer's World were evidence that other terraformed planets had evolved intelligent species, although that one was apparently long extinct. It was fascinating, but Newton still didn't get the connection. Squids could never develop metal tools; that took fire, and surely more intelligence than they had.

Was that what McWhirter was worried about? "I don't see what that has to do with tree squids," he said. "They don't have technology and couldn't develop it. What are the natives like, these Epsilon Indians?" Newton's eyes widened as he realized what he'd just said. "Please tell me they're not calling them *that!*"

McWhirter shook his head. "Indians? Och, no. Apparently they're mammals, but not ape-descended. Meerkat, or something like it, so the speculation goes. They're calling them timoans."

"Timoans? You said *meerkat?* Don't tell me they look like—"

"I dinnae ken what they look like. But they worry me."

"Why? You're not comparing the squids with them, are you? And even if so, so what?"

McWhirter looked down at his knees, his hands grasped. Then he looked up again. "Did you know they're discussing declaring that planet, at Epsilon Indi, off-limits?"

"What? Who is?"

"*Union de Terre,* or at least a few of the folks on the expedition. People are making noises about the Prime Directive."

Newton scoffed. "You mean that thing from *Star Trek?*" The old video show had made a brief resurgence when a real warp drive had been developed, but it didn't last; the reality was too different. "That was honored more in the breach than the observance, as I recall. Anyway, that ship sailed a long time ago. Haven't we already interfered by landing there? And we probably will on any other inhabited planet we set foot on."

That was an increasing number. Expeditions were launching every few months now, as more ships became available. Expeditions had already visited Tau Ceti, Delta Pavonis, and further out. Settlement on terraformed planets was being encouraged, so who knew where else. Newton didn't pay much attention to that, he was too busy with his own business here. But there was another thing.

"Anyway," Newton continued, "that's Epsilon Indi. *Union de Terre* doesn't have the same authority here. Kakuloa falls under the Treaty of Alpha Centauri, so Sawyer's World gets a say. Even if the tree squids were intelligent, even if they were tool users—"

"What about the bags?"

"Not definitive," Newton said, but the thought gave him pause. "But okay, even if they were tool *makers,* they still don't have a language—"

"Speaker-to-Squids." McWhirter interrupted.

Newton glared at him. "Hypothetical. Even so, there's no way they even come close to your timoans. But even if they did, *even if* they did, *Union de Terre* and Sawyer's World would have to agree on a policy before it came into effect here. The *UDT* won't have even received the news about Epsilon Indi yet, let alone decided anything about it, and Sawyer's depends too much on the traffic that Kakuloa gets to do anything to mess that up. Remember, when people come to Alpha Centauri, they're mostly coming to Kakuloa, not Sawyer's World. It's sheer accident that that place got settled first."

McWhirter nodded, but hesitantly. "I suppose."

Newton sat back, leaning on the arm of his chair. "Of course. Don't take those rumors too seriously; everyone's got their own agenda. And none of it will mean anything if we can't keep the tree squids out of our berries."

"Aye, there's that. I guess the pharma companies wouldn't be too happy if something political threatened their business."

"Now you're thinking. Yes, if it ever came to that, the first whiff of trouble and their lobbyists would be all over it. Hell, when the anti-agathic hits the market, they'll probably put a bounty on tree squids."

"Aye, now there's a pleasant thought," McWhirter said. He rose from his chair. "You're right. Sorry to be a bother."

"No worries. Now, let's get to work on that plan of Greystone's."

As McWhirter left his office, Newton leaned forward and placed his elbows on his desk, clasped his hands, and thought. He didn't really think the tree squids were that smart, but Greystone was an expert on, for want of a better term, cephalopod psychology. She'd already discovered a level of communication between the squids he hadn't expected. It would be for the best if she could find some way of keeping them under control that didn't involve finding out any more about tree squid communication or social organization than absolutely necessary.

Just in case.

Chapter 44: Vision

Newton Farm

It was the day after that when the tree squids showed up again. Greystone and Gulliver had arranged the modified shirt in one of the mangrove trees, near a large cluster of berries. Ellie had set cameras up to record everything, and the warning shirt duly activated as the squids began climbing the trees.

They totally ignored it.

∞ ∞ ∞

The Lab

"What. The. *Expletive!*" Ellie said as she watched the video of the squids grabbing berries, oblivious to the warning pattern flashing nearby.

"You can use stronger language than that," Caporale said. "I won't be offended."

She glared at him, and he retreated to his corner of the lab. "Seriously though," she said, still frustrated but lowering her tone. "It's like they don't even *see* the pattern. They reacted to our decoys, violently, but this? Nothing."

"The decoys were at least squid-shaped. Maybe they thought they were a different species. Pattern aside, that shirt doesn't look like anything."

"But the pattern is obvious," Ellie said. "They'd have to be blind not to see it. I don't get it. We even tried different ones. They didn't respond to the videos of other squid patterns at all the same way they do with live squid."

"Different color receptors?" Caporale asked. "Like, maybe the screens don't reproduce colors the same way the squids see them?"

Ellie shook her head. "That shouldn't matter. Cephalopods are color-blind."

"*What?* But the color patterns..."

"I mean their retinal cells don't distinguish color. They don't even have color receptors."

"But then why do they even make color patterns?"

"Just because they're color-blind doesn't mean their predators can't see color. Camouflage evolves in response to predation."

"Well, sure, I know that, but..."

She understood where he was going. How then did they communicate? "There's a trick cephalopods have. Even without color receptors, they can see color, sort of. Cephalopods have weirdly-shaped eye pupils, U-shaped or rectangular," she said. "Mostly we think that's to help break up the outline of the eye—some have color patterns that help that, extending the pupil beyond the eye. But it does increase the effect of chromatic aberration."

"That has something to do with lenses and colors, right?" Caporale said.

"Yes. Different light frequencies—different colors—focus at slightly different distances. Some cephalopod species can quickly vary the focus of their eyes; they tell colors by how different areas come and go in and out of focus."

Caporale considered this for a moment, then nodded. "Huh. I hadn't noticed the pupil shape, I just assumed they were round. But I haven't looked closely."

As he said that, she realized that she hadn't really looked closely either. So far, all her encounters with the cephalopods were at a distance, or on video, and she'd been focusing on their behavior and skin patterns. Another reason to get the aquarium up and running and capture a few specimens.

"That's weird," Caporale continued. "So they can't really see color? And yet they're so brightly colored."

"Like I said, predators. And they can see the contrast. Although there is one species on Earth, the firefly squid if I remem-

ber right, that lives in the deep ocean. It can see colors in a narrow blue-green band."

"That would make sense. Shades of blue are the only light
that make it to any depth. Could something like that have happened here?"

She thought about it. "I can't rule it out; sixty-five million
years of divergent evolution could have led to a mutation involving color vision. I'll have to do some research on the firefly squid,
but the only way I can think of to determine that definitively in-
volves dissecting out the retinas and doing biochemical and mi-
crobiological analysis, looking for vision pigments or something
like cone cells." She preferred not to sacrifice an octopus just for
that purpose, but it might be the only way to learn. "Do you have
any specimens?"

Caporale had been collecting examples of almost every new
life-form he came across, so long as he found more than one or
two. With the fauna, he would examine their stomach contents to
determine what they ate, if it wasn't obvious from observation.

"A couple of preserved specimens, yes, and you're welcome
to take a look at them. But if you're looking for pigments, the
preservative might have affected the chemistry. I'm sure nobody
would have a problem with you taking a fresh specimen."

"Well, *I* might, but I'll get over it," she said. Then, seeing the
surprised look on Henry's face, she explained. "I'm not particularly squeamish; I generally have no problem taking marine specimens. But these animals seem particularly intelligent. It'd be like
killing a dolphin."

"Really? You think they're that smart?"

"Maybe not. But they do socialize, and apparently communicate."

"Well, so do bees."

"Not the same. Anyway, I'll do it if I need to. If I were *that*
squeamish I'd have quit biology a long time ago."

"Huh. Yeah, I remember back in school there were always a
few folks who switched majors after the first dissection lab. I
don't know what they thought they were getting into."

"I guess simulating it in virtual reality doesn't quite prepare everyone for the real thing."

"No, it rarely does. Now, if they could simulate the *smell*..."

Ellie laughed. Most modern preservatives didn't have much odor to them, but what they did have was distinctive. And fresh specimens could be in a class all their own. Intestinal contents aside, certain squid were known for their ammonia content.

Chapter 44: Here's Looking at You, Squid

The Lab

The aquarium gurgled away in the corner of the lab. It still held no octopuses, but the vegetation and few small fish swimming about in it seemed healthy. It had taken a while to get the system stabilized.

Ellie Greystone was working at the table, bent over a dissection tray holding one of Caporale's preserved tree squids. It was on the small side, under a kilogram and only half a meter long with the arms stretched out. Caporale had collected it from under one of the trees. It apparently fallen out, perhaps drunk on fermented squidberry.

It much resembled the common octopus, *Octopus vulgaris*, of Earth, found in waters all over the planet. Its coloration was unremarkable—the tree squids lacked anything like the stripes of the zebra octopus or the prominent circles of the highly venomous blue-ringed octopus, devoting their chromatophores to camouflage and more dynamic communication. This specimen's color had likely also faded some due to the slow bleaching action of the preservative.

She had already discovered that the funnel and gill structure was more complex that terrestrial octopodes she'd examined. Cephalopods used that both for breathing and as a water jet for propulsion, and in nesting females, keeping debris away from the egg clusters. Neither of the latter two functions explained the complexity. If she had to guess—and without a live octopus to study up close, she had to—she guessed that the side channels and chambers on the funnel interior helped the animal store water to keep its gills moisturized. Even on Earth, octopuses could survive for a while out of water, but the tree squids here seemed able to go a lot longer before returning to the creek. The higher average humidity and oxygen content of Kakuloa's atmosphere no doubt helped, but it couldn't explain it all.

There were the usual large neural clusters at the base of each arm, the "sub-brains" that coordinated the motion of each arm and even each sucker on the arm. Ellie had once watched an octopus lying flat on the seafloor, arms spread, seemingly immobile...and yet managing to creep across the seabed toward a crab, each sucker individually acting as a tiny leg to "walk" the animal in that direction. The sub-brains explained the dexterity, but not this species' intelligence.

The main brain was behind and above the eyes, and its vertical lobe, believed to store learned visual information, seemed larger than what Ellie would expect in a similarly-sized common octopus, or any similar Earth species. Interesting. It wasn't proof of anything; the neural system of octopodes was complex. It had to be, given the level of control they had—conscious or not—over their chromatophores.

Ellie turned her attention to the octopus's eyes. They were misted over, probably from the preservative, and any coloration pattern around them had faded when death relaxed the control over the chromatophores. Thus, the area around the eye lacked the eye-bar she might have expected. As she looked at it closer, the eye pupil itself looked more round than rectangular. That was unusual. Most octopuses had horizontal rectangular pupils, and the eye-bar, when the animal emphasized it, extended that line to confuse and intimidate predators. Some other cephalopods, cuttlefish in particular, had even more-complex pupil shapes. As she had mentioned to Caporale, it helped them distinguish colors despite having a color-blind retina. This animal's pupil was more oval than rectangular. If that wasn't a fluke, or an effect of the preservative, how did it see the warning pattern? Contrast alone?

That could simplify things, but it didn't explain why her displays so far hadn't worked.

She needed a live specimen or two.

∞ ∞ ∞

It took a week, but she finally had her specimen, a smallish tree squid, weighing not much more than half a kilogram. It was probably young, but it was difficult to tell with octopuses.

Trying to catch any in the creek had been an exercise in futility; they swam and crawled in and out of the mangrove roots so that it was impossible to get her collecting net—actually a clear plastic box open on one side with netting across the other—in amongst them. Finally she'd dived on a large coral head in about ten meters of water and managed to extract one. If she needed another, she'd go out again. Keeping two in captivity was asking for cannibalism without separate tanks, however friendly this particular species might seem to be.

∞ ∞ ∞

She had done some simple behavioral experiments first, to establish a standard for comparison. She had the octopus, which she'd nicknamed Otto, learning a simple maze, with a reward of a small crab of the kind she'd seen them eating in the wild. It learned the maze quickly.

She also ran the test with a different maze, this time rewarding the animal with a few slightly-fermented squidberries. It learned that maze even more quickly; the berries were an even better treat than the crabs.

So far, except for the enthusiasm for squidberries, the behavior was similar to many Earth species of octopus. Ellie's next step was to show Otto pictures of some of the different patterns she'd seen on the wild tree squids, and in particular the one she'd decided was the warning pattern. She tried both static and moving pictures. Otto's reaction was the same as that of the squids in the trees; he totally ignored the patterns.

Maybe Otto wasn't as smart as she thought. She tried a few other experiments, then released him and went and caught another, that she named Octavius.

Octavius didn't totally ignore the patterns, but nor did he react as she had expected. He seemed attracted to some, swimming up to the side of the tank where the display was mounted and examining it in detail, but ignoring others. After a while he began to mimic the patterns he found interesting, changing the patterning on his own skin to match. Ellie was intrigued, but this could just be an example of an octopus's normal camouflage reaction. But why did it ignore some patterns? She tried generating random designs. Some were variations on the squids' usual patterns, others were simple geometric shapes.

She tried rewarding Octavius, both with crabs and with squid-berries, when it mimicked a pattern. It learned to respond more quickly, but she couldn't get it to display one of the rewarded patterns on its own. Nor had Octavius ever reproduced a pattern exactly; although the light and dark areas were correct, the colors were a bit off. Interesting, but not definitive.

Maybe Henry had some ideas.

∞ ∞ ∞

"Well, you did say they were colorblind," Henry Caporale said when she explained it to him.

"Their retinas are, yes, but what about chromatic aberration?"

He peered into Octavius's tank. The octopus was hiding in a corner. "What shape are its pupils?"

"Good question." With all her behavioral experiments, she had managed to forget the reason she wanted to collect a live specimen in the first place. "Hang on."

Ellie scooped up a crab from the tank where she kept Octavius's food supply, and activated the display on the side of his tank. He oozed out of the corner and slid over to the display, then mimicked the pattern it was showing. Ellie and Caporale looked closely at its eyes. The pupils were oval, not much taller than they were wide. "Well, nuke me," Ellie said. "They *must* be color blind." She dropped the crab into the tank, where it was seized upon by Octavius.

"Then how do they reproduce camouflage colors?" Henry asked.

"Not very well?" she said. It was true that Octavius didn't reproduce her colored displays accurately, but he had no problem concealing himself against the sand in the bottom of his tank, or against the vegetation. "I don't know."

"Remember what I said before about different visual pigments? Maybe there's your answer. Perhaps it has something to do with the orange sun," Henry said.

"That won't make that much difference; all the colors are still there," Ellie said.

"You're right. So, give it an Ishihara test."

"A what?"

"Ishihara test. For colorblindness. You know, those circles made up of slightly-different-colored dots and some very different colored dots that outline a numeral. Someone who can tell the difference in the colors will see the number, and someone who can't, won't. Or they'll see a different number, depending on the pattern. I don't know how you get a squid to tell you what number it's seeing, though."

Ellie grinned. "But I do."

∞ ∞ ∞

Since Octavius had already been trained to respond to some different simple shapes, like squares, triangles and crosses, it didn't take much more training to respond to those shapes when configured as different patterns of black and white dots, like the Ishihara tests but in monochrome. That was the first step. It was all right that Octavius tended to reproduce the exact spot pattern rather than just the shape outline, it would work just as well.

The next step was more of a challenge. Ellie had to come up with a set of test patterns with enough variations in colors to let her determine which specific ones Octavius responded to. She wasn't sure if a standard display had the color range to do the full job, but it was a start.

That raised another question. If it wasn't enough, how would they build displays that could deter the tree squids? That was a question for an engineer. It was the sort of trivia that her old boyfriend Patrice Beauchamps had always been coming up with. She could ask him, and without giving anything sensitive away. She wouldn't get an answer for a couple of weeks, but she wasn't ready for one yet anyway. She just wished she could see his face when he found out she was at Alpha Centauri.

∞ ∞ ∞

The crude squid Ishihara tests Ellie could do confirmed Caporale's hypothesis. Octavius could see and differentiate colors, but very differently from humans. A color image on a regular red-green-blue digital display might look normal to people, with their red, green and blue color receptors, but would look very different to an animal with different color receptors. The next question was, what colors *were* Octavius's receptors sensitive to? She had narrowed it down some with her tests—blue was a safe bet for one of them—but not definitively.

She had borrowed a set of colored markers from Gulliver to create other test patterns, since ink pigments reflected a much wider range of light frequencies. That narrowed it down further, but again, some ink pigments were mixtures rather than pure colors. Once she had the color receptors pinned down exactly, it shouldn't be too hard to find appropriate pure pigments to match.

The best way to be sure would be to examine the octopuses retinas, chemically extract the photosensitive pigments, and run a series of tests to see which light frequencies excited those specific molecules. The lab here didn't have the proper equipment. She'd have to call Blake and see what facilities were available in town, and how she could get access to them. There was probably something; CentPharm had a small biochemical lab for basic screening, and there was other ongoing research. She wondered how many grams of retinal cells she would need. That would depend in part of the sensitivity of the equipment. Probably several squids' worth.

She looked at Octavius, lying in his favorite corner of the tank. "Not you, buddy," she said to him. "I've put too much work into training you as it is. I'm sure McWhirter will be happy to round me up a couple of others."

Chapter 45: Results

Kakuloa

Three days later, Ellie Greystone was en route to Krechet's Landing in the aircar, with Dave Newton piloting, and with a container of octopus eyeballs in a cooler.

"I've figured out the problem," Greystone had told Newton when she'd arranged the trip. "Why the tree squids weren't responding to my displays."

"Great. Why not?" Newton had asked.

"Because they're not colorblind."

"Wait, did you say because they're *NOT* colorblind?"

"Yes." She quickly gave Newton the same rundown on terrestrial cephalopod color vision that she had to Caporale.

"But," he said, "if they see colors by aberration, wouldn't that fail with displays anyway? They only use three actual colors because human eyes only have three kinds of color receptor: red, green, and blue."

"You're right, and I thought that might be the problem at first. But their pupils are rounded, which blurs out the aberrations. So I ran some color tests using multiple pigments to reflect a fuller spectrum."

"Ah, that explains the colored markers. I wondered. Is there any good news?"

That's why I need to go to Krechet's Landing. Mr. Blake arranged access to a couple of labs there that have the analytical gear I need. A biochemical analysis of different cells in the tree squid's retinas, and measurements of the electrical response of the vision pigments to different frequencies, will tell me exactly what I need to know."

"Thus the eyeballs. I thought McWhirter seemed a bit happier lately."

"He really doesn't like them, does he?"

"I don't think it's as bad as he likes to pretend. He does take their assaults on our berries a bit personally, but I don't think there's anything more to it than that. He doesn't even like calamari."

The plan was for Greystone to stay in Krechet's Landing for the few days it took to complete her analysis. She'd get a ride back then.

∞ ∞ ∞

Gulliver Newton flew Greystone back to the farm after he'd come down to visit his mother and sister, and to pick up supplies.

After settling back in, Dave Newton asked her how it had gone.

"It went well. I found the opsins, vision pigments, that responded to different frequencies. They must have evolved here; they're very different from anything an Earth cephalopod has. Essentially, they're sensitive to yellow-orange, a blue-green, and blue. It's narrower range than in humans, but quite broader than firefly squid. They're totally blind to the red pigment used in our displays, and nearly so to the green. The blue activates both their blue and blue-green cones. The patterns we were displaying must have looked totally different to them."

Newton nodded slowly. "I get it. But I don't see how that helps. Nobody makes displays with, what was it, yellow-orange, cyan and blue color dots. Surely it would cost a fortune to have something like that custom made. And you don't even know if that would work."

"I'm pretty sure it would, but we won't use the usual display technology. I put the question to an old engineer friend of mine a couple of weeks back, when I was looking at different display solutions. I didn't know what colors I'd need then, I figured worst case I'd need a way to mimic the chromatophores in the tree squid's skin."

"A couple of weeks ago? I assume this engineer friend is on Earth. I take it that you've had an answer back?"

"I have. It turns out that e-ink, electronic ink, has a few things in common with chromatophores. The latter work by covering and uncovering pigment cells with a different color. E-ink works by electrostatically rotating tiny spheres with different colors on each side. Turns out those spheres can be coated with almost any color pigment desired. Custom e-ink displays are a lot cheaper than custom LED colors, even than organic LEDs. So, something like Gully's tee-shirt but with custom pigments."

Newton leaned forward in his seat. "How soon can we get these e-ink displays? Is that something we can manufacture locally?"

"I checked with Blake while I was in Krechet's Landing. He's not aware of any capability like that on Kakuloa, but he said there's an electronics facility on Sawyer's World that might."

"Sawyer's World? I'm used to them being a bit behind Kakuloa. I guess they're catching up."

Ellie shrugged. "I have no idea. Just repeating what Blake said. Worst case, getting them from Earth shouldn't take too long. Patrice—my engineer friend—said that kind of custom order shouldn't take more than a week or so if the pigments are commercially available, and they probably are."

"Patrice? He's French? Not that it matters, just curious."

"Québécois. I knew him at college."

"*Très bien*. And that's the extent of my French. All right, get the specs for what you need to Blake. I think it comes under CentPharm business, but he and I can work out the details later. I hate to say it, but after the failures so far I'm not completely convinced this will work either, but it's worth a shot."

"Already on it. And just in case, I'm working on a backup plan."

"Glad to hear it. And thanks."

Ellie rose and left the office. The fact was, she didn't actually have a backup plan, but she was trying to come up with one. That was close enough to working on it that she hadn't lied to Newton. She hoped.

Meanwhile, she had more testing to do, as well as to work out a deployment plan for what she hoped would be the working panels.

∞ ∞ ∞

It turned out that the facility in Sawyer City, on Sawyer's World, could manufacture custom e-ink panels in a timely fashion...except that they only had one of the specific pigments that Ellie needed. They were told to make up a small batch of panels as far as they could without the required inks, while an urgent order was sent to Earth for the others. It still meant waiting almost two weeks for those, having the rest of the fabrication done at Sawyer City would save another week or two over having that done on Earth.

Someone—the rumor was that it was Naomi Maclaren, the engineer from the original *Anderson* crew, but nobody would confirm or deny that—had not only arranged for the initial prototypes to be expedited, but also to have a local chemistry lab custom synthesize enough of the needed missing pigments to make e-ink for five panels. Ellie had them in hand probably before the shipment from Earth had even left.

It was testing time.

∞ ∞ ∞

The first tests Ellie ran, with her test subject Octavius, were the simple geometric patterns. The more complex shapes, and specifically the warning pattern of the sentinel squids, would need the files changed from their RGB format to the OCB—orange, cyan, blue—color gamut the new displays used.

They worked almost perfectly. Octavius seemed a little confused at first, possibly because the colors didn't match what he was used to from the earlier tests. He got the idea, though, especially when squidberries were the reward.

Now for the critical test. Gulliver had duplicated the animation circuit from his tee-shirt to drive the new displays. The dynamic warning signal could be triggered with a switch.

Ellie, Gulliver, and Henry Caporale gathered around the squid tank with the display in place against one wall, but blank. Octavius stayed huddled in his corner.

"I think he has stage fright," Caporale said.

"He's always shy," Ellie said, "but yes, there are probably too many people about. Dim the lights a little."

Gulliver closed the curtains and turned down the overhead light. "How's that?"

"Maybe too dark, we want him to see the display."

Gulliver turned the light back up half-way.

"Good." Ellie reached for a crab, then changed her mind and took a small bunch of squidberries. "These should get him out, and it will be interesting to see if the signal is enough to make him give them up."

She raised the lid at the end of the tank where the display was, opposite Octavius's corner, dropped the berries in, then closed the lid. A moment later, Octavius began oozing from his corner, slowly, either sneaking up on the berries or just not wanting to attract attention. His skin was mottled to echo the sandy bottom of the tank.

He approached the berries, then swarmed over them. Ellie triggered the display. The result was dramatic.

In the blink of an eye, it seemed that Octavius had turned black, disappearing in a cloud of ink, that slowly dissipated. There was no squid within it, and the berries lay on the bottom of the tank.

"Where'd he go?" Gulliver said. "He just disappeared."

Wise to the ways of octopuses, Ellie said, "Check his corner."

Sure enough, he was huddled tight in the corner, pretending to be just another of the weeds near him.

She turned off the display. There was no point stressing Octavius out. Clearly the panel worked.

"I've seen that trick before," she said. "They squirt ink while changing color to blend with the background, then jet away. A predator will tend to go for the ink. I guess that's the default reaction to a threat. Dropping out of the trees is different, but squirting ink would be useless there."

"That was certainly a dramatic reaction," Henry said. "Congratulations, Ellie, I think you've got it."

Ellie nodded. "I still want to do a few more tests, but I don't want to overstress Octavius. We can try it in the wild tomorrow."

Gulliver was still peering into the tank. "Wow," he said, "that was neat."

Chapter 46: Departure

Newton's Berry Farm, two weeks later

"Well, Ellie, it looks like your automated displays are working out well," Dave Newton said. "We haven't had a squid incursion here since we installed them, and the other berry farmers are reporting the same. Congratulations!"

"I just hope the tree squids weren't relying on an unknown essential nutrient they could only get from the berries."

"You have no reason to think that they were, do you? The squid population seems fine, they were just after whatever recreational chemicals were in the fermented berries."

"That's what Caporale says. He hasn't seen any impact on the population. If anything, he thinks the population is healthier."

"Well, there you are then. What's next for you? Your contract with CentPharm is officially up at the end of the month, right?"

"Yes, but that's Earth date, not local, so I have two more weeks. I need to finish writing up my reports for CentPharm anyway, as well as making sure I have what I need for the academic papers I'm working on."

"You're welcome to stay here while you do that, unless you want to spend your time in Krechet's Landing. We have plenty of space, and it's chaotic there with all the construction going on."

"Thank you, that's very generous."

"Nah, I'll bill it to CentPharm. You would be on expenses back in town anyway, right?"

Ellie grinned. She was not offended. "Yes. Go for it, certainly. I will say I'll miss this place." She sighed heavily.

"Problem?"

"It's not that I don't miss Earth, I do, a bit. But it's very different out here on the frontier. On Earth, even on field trips, nothing feels very wild or adventurous, not the way it does out here. Earth is become too much like a park. A very crowded one." The population had long since bounced back from the hit it took during the Unholy War.

"I know what you mean. I've been back a couple of times, and I always look forward to getting out here again, and not just because I miss my family."

Greystone nodded. "Unfortunately, beyond my work with your tree squids, there's not much call for a cephalopod expert here. I'd still love to try training them to pick berries for you, but —"

"But there are a few folks who don't like that idea," Newton finished for her. "I know McWhirter isn't a fan."

"Right. And even of those who don't hate it, there aren't many who would pay for me to try it. So I guess it's back to Earth for me. Besides, I need to get back for my mom. She's in bad shape."

"I'm sorry to hear that. We'll miss you. At least we have you here for a few weeks longer." Newton's voice trailed off at the end, and he looked thoughtful.

"Was there something else?" she asked.

"Yes. What are the chances the squids will learn to ignore that danger signal? I mean, those signs are basically crying *Wolf!*, and very convincingly. Are they smart enough to realize that there's no wolf?"

Greystone had wondered about that herself. "I don't think so. I think that's more of an instinctual response. The lookouts learn what things in the environment are dangerous and when they need to generate that signal, but the other squids respond to it too quickly for it to be learned. Although...."

"Although?"

"I've mentioned this before, but cephalopods have a distributed nervous system. Multiple brains, if you like, including a small specialized brain in each arm. I suppose it's possible that that gives them a reaction-time advantage, although for a visual signal to get through the eye-brain to the arm-brain...no, it must be instinctual."

She paused, considering what might be done if that was wrong. "Worst case," she said, "you know what to look for if they do stop responding to it. You'd need to find out what the new danger signal is; you already know the color spectrum and how to program the signs. Figuring all that out the first time was the hard part.

"Anyway," she continued, "I'm still here for a couple of more weeks. I'll keep monitoring for any sign that the effectiveness is wearing off, but I don't think it will." Her experiments with immature octopuses suggested that the behavior was more instinctive than learned, unless they'd learned it when hatchlings. She still didn't know much about these animals' life cycle, but no cephalopod nurtured its young once hatched. Research for somebody else, she supposed. Or...

"However, feel free to call me back here if you need to," she added.

Newton smiled back at her. "I'll keep that in mind."

Ellie turned and headed back up to her room. She had reports to work on.

∞ ∞ ∞

The Lab

In between her reports, Ellie worked on cleaning up her section of the lab. She released Octavius back into the wild, carefully avoiding McWhirter while she did so. At Henry Caporale's suggestion, she left the marine aquarium for his use.

"Oh, I'm not planning on doing anything with squids," he said. "But I can try keeping some of the species we find as hatchlings around the mangrove roots. I might learn something."

"Consider it yours, then. Have you worked with salt-water aquariums before? They can be a challenge."

"Not in years, but my brother had one. If he could manage it, I can."

"Ah, no sibling rivalry there. Okay."

"Well, in all serious, I helped him with it, so I do know a bit."

"Any of my other equipment you want? I figured I'd give the electronics to Gulliver. Some of them were his to start with anyway."

"No, that's a good idea. You've been in your room a lot lately. How are the reports going?"

"How do they ever go? It's tedious," she said. "Oh! I should give you a co-author credit on the color vision paper; you first suggested different pigments."

"You just want my help editing the paper," he said, and grinned. "Just quote me and cite it as an unpublished conversation."

"Seriously?"

"Really. I didn't contribute that much. I have plenty of other papers I'm listed on. Besides, I owe you."

"For what?"

"Don't be dense. You saved my life."

She shook her head. "I told you before, you don't owe me for that. If you must, pay it forward. Save somebody else."

"I...okay."

"Anyway, I'm going to have to revisit my earlier conclusions in light of that. With the wrong color gamut, some of the tests don't apply. Otto may have been smarter than I thought he was. Octavius too, for that matter."

"You might not want to push that point too hard," Henry said, glancing at the door to the lab.

"What do you mean?"

Henry lowered his voice. "You know how McWhirter feels about the tree squids. He's not the only one. How do you think he'd feel if they were actually smarter than he thinks? Perhaps more to the point, how do you think the *UDT* would feel about that? And what might they do?"

She realized what he meant. The *Union de Terre* had a very Earth-centric view of things, understandably, and there was already plenty of protectionist feeling about animals of varied intelligence on Earth. Some of she felt was justified, but in many cases not. Would they put tree squid habitat off-limits?

"They wouldn't do anything that might hurt squidberry pro-duction, surely?" she said.

"Maybe not. Do you think the McWhirters here—and some of the other squidberry farmers are worse—would wait for them to act or not act? They were about ready to declare a bounty on tree squids when you got here."

"Okay, I see your point. But what if they *are* that smart? Don't I have a moral obligation to—"

Caporale was shaking his head. "Right now you don't have any firm evidence that they are. I'll admit they're smart, maybe even as smart as dogs. I'm not sure I'd go further than that. You don't have an obligation to act on information you don't have, and if you go off half-cocked, that could trigger rash action on the part of some of the farmers and their workers. If the squids were to be wiped out before *UDT* could act...."

"They wouldn't!"

"Have you ever seen what people are capable of if they feel their livelihood is threatened? It isn't pretty."

She felt sick to her stomach. "So you're saying I should just ignore it, and hope the problem goes away."

"The problem *will* go away. Either cephalomycin will fail in clinical trials, or, sooner or later, the pharmaceutical companies find a way to synthesize it that's cheaper than harvesting and shipping squidberry extract across four light years of space. Ei-ther way, the bottom falls out of the market, and the squidberry farmers, through no fault of the tree squids, pack up and go on to something else."

She stared at him. This wasn't some realization he had just come to. "How long have you been thinking this way?"

"I've seen it before," he said, slumping in his seat. "I just tell myself that the drugs will save or improve thousands or millions of lives, and hope the farmers make enough to get by on if the demand for their crop does collapse." He sighed, then straight-ened up. "It won't for years, and it never does completely; there's always some market left. But I'd suggest keeping a low profile on that particular line of research, at the very least until you're back on Earth."

She nodded slowly. He had given her much to think about. "I won't be finished analyzing all the data until then anyway," she said. "But I think you're being too pessimistic. Maybe you should take a break."

"You're probably right," he said. "I think I'll go check if there's any beer, then see how my mangrove lagoon is doing." He got up and went to leave. He paused in the doorway, looking back at her. "By the way," he said, "did you ever figure out how your DSMB reel got jammed?" He turned and left, leaving Ellie staring after him slack-jawed.

That *had* to have been mere bad luck. Even if someone had meant her harm—and she refused to believe that—nobody could have planned anything that elaborate. Henry must still be suffering from some kind of post-traumatic stress. But she decided to keep his comment to herself. She'd be leaving in a few days anyway.

Chapter 47: The Voyage Home

Krechet's Landing

Ellie Greystone sat in the lounge at the Kakuloa Spaceport, a facility much improved since she'd first arrived, awaiting the boarding call for her trip back to Earth.

As she was reviewing the report files on her omni, a voice called to her. It was one she hadn't heard in a while, but it was all too familiar.

"Ellie Greystone! Are you on this ship too? It's good to see you again. How was your stay on Kakuloa?"

Oh no, she thought, and turned to greet Parry Cohen. "Mr. Cohen! What a surprise. I've seen that you've been busy. We saw your resort construction from the aircar on the way down. From the height of that crane that's going to be a tall building."

"Parry, please. Yes, it is," he beamed. "That will be the main hotel, the centerpiece of the resort. You probably noticed the side-roads too, although they're only just being graded. We'll have cabins there. Housing for the staff beyond that, of course, although it doesn't look like much at the moment. And a golf course."

"Golf? Don't you need grass?" Grass and related plants had never taken root, so to speak, on Kakuloa.

Parry looked down at his feet, then back up at her. "Well, we're having to make some adjustments. We found a local plant that will work for the fairways, like what's growing in Chandrasekhar Valley. I'm still working on the greens. Maybe a sterile grass hybrid, if we can get permission, and if it grows here at all. We have a couple of years to figure it out."

Ellie wasn't sure how she felt about that. It would probably be safe, if it were genetically engineered. Or it could turn out like kudzu. She changed the subject. "Are you heading back to Earth too?" *Please say no, please say no.*

"Not this time. I'm only going as far as Sawyer's World, I have business there I need to do in person."

Whew. That was only a few hours away, and most of that on departure or approach. The actual warp jump was less than a minute.

"But I'll be back on Earth in a few weeks," he continued. "You should take me up on my invite to visit one of our resorts there. You'll probably need it after a few weeks of being Earth-side again, it's just not the same as out here."

"Well, I appreciate the offer, Parry, but I don't know what my schedule will be like. I have reports to work on, and I'll need to catch up with everything that's been going on at work while I've been gone."

"Of course, that's why you'll need a break. But no pressure, the offer's open." He paused for a moment. Ellie was surprised, he could usually ramble on for long stretches apparently without breathing. But then he continued. "Anyway, how was your stay? Aside from the diving incident, I mean. I'm glad everything turned out all right. You were doing some kind of marine biology research, am I right?"

"That's right." She really didn't want to talk much right now, but she'd learned a technique for handling that. "I was doing behavioral studies with arboreal cephalopods, and investigating the effect of their ingesting certain indigenous flora on their neuro-physiology. It's quite fascinating, really. Did you know that cephalopods have an incredibly complex neural system for a mollusk? The ganglia for each—"

"That's fascinating," Parry interrupted, glancing at his omni. "Sorry Ellie, I'd love to hear more about that, but I have a couple of calls to make before we head off-planet. I'll talk to you later, okay?"

"No problem," she said, trying to keep from smiling. "You go take care of business."

"Thanks." Cohen turned and beat a hasty retreat. Ellie smiled. She hadn't even got to the boring part.

∞ ∞ ∞

The trip back to Earth was largely uneventful. Parry Cohen might have a more abrasive personality than Ellie was comfortable with, but at least he was a distraction. The few other passengers and crew largely kept to themselves, or watched videos, or played games in the only really communal area on the ship, the mess.

She spent some of the time editing her reports and collating all the raw data she had gathered on not just the tree squids and berries, but the other marine life she had found time to observe and record. It occurred to her, not for the first time, that she'd have naming rights on a number of those species as soon as she described them in a scientific publication. There were already whole journals now devoted to extraterrestrial flora and fauna, but most of the species so far described were land or shallow-water denizens. The oceans on Kakuloa and Sawyer's World had barely been touched, let alone those on the other terraformed worlds being discovered. The papers would make a nice addition to her resume, if nothing else.

By the third day, Ellie was running various statistical analyses on the numerical data she had. It wasn't that she was expecting to find anything, or even really looking, it was just something to do. She also knew that any apparent result of such analysis was probably bogus; run enough statistical comparisons and meaningless correlations will pop up through sheer chance.

Thus, when the correlation between apparent octopus intelligence and dietary intake first popped up, she didn't think much of it. Obviously, any animal probably does better when well fed rather than starving, but this looked different. But having nothing else to do for another day-and-a-half on the ship, she dug into it.

The more she did, the more it seemed there was a relation-ship between squidberry intake, and the social and problem-solving behavior of the tree squids. She'd had that discussion with Caporale back in the beginning, about how social the octopuses were and if there were some MDMA-like drug in the berries. Not that MDMA made people, or octopuses, any smarter. More the opposite. But it did tend to make them more sociable. If there was a biochemical in the berries that affected neurotransmitters in squids, could that also make them smarter?

And if it could do that, what might it do for humans, particular for humans with neurodegenerative diseases like her mother? Ellie dove into the data.

And came up frustrated. There just wasn't enough. She hadn't been looking for anything like that, and Caporale certainly hadn't, so there just weren't enough data points. Heck, she didn't even know for sure if there was anything in the berries that affected neurotransmitters. But she knew who might.

∞ ∞ ∞

Earth, Skrellan Pharmaceuticals

"Great work, Ellie. You got our tree squid problem taken care of, and without having to resort to chemicals that might have had undesirable side effects," Victoria Holmes said at their post-mission meeting.

"Speaking of chemicals with side effects...." Ellie said.

Holmes frowned. "Yes?"

"Oh, no," Ellie said at Holmes's reaction, "I'm talking about something I may have discovered. A good thing."

Holmes relaxed. "Go on."

"I know you've been focused on the squidberry fungus, that's your actual source of cephalomycin. But have you looked at the berries for interesting biochemicals?"

"We did a preliminary assay, of course. And we've looked to see if we can figure out why the fungus doesn't grow on Earth-grown berries. Why?"

"Find anything that might affect neurotransmitters?"

Holmes blinked. "Not that I recall. Where are you going with this?"

"When I first got to Kakuloa, I was surprised at how social the arboreal cephalopods were. Octopuses on Earth are quite solitary, but there were experiments done back in the twenty-teens where octopuses got a lot more social when doped with MDMA."

"That's methylenedioxy-methamphetamine, isn't it? Why would anyone give that to an octopus?"

"They did a lot of weird experiments back in the day. But my point is that I wondered if there was something in the berries like that. More specifically, when I was reviewing my data on the trip back, I noticed a possible correlation between squidberry intake and the octopus's intelligence. It's probably just a spurious correlation, I don't have enough data to back it up, but..."

"But you were wondering if there was something in the berries that had an effect on the neurotransmitter system to somehow make them smarter. And, I'm guessing, wondering if that might in turn be useful in conditions like your mother's."

"Well, yes. I know it's a long shot, but you might be interested."

"Oh, I'm definitely interested," Holmes said. "Can you leave me a copy of your data? If it isn't already included within the scope of our contract?"

"Certainly, and I assumed it would be, since it relates to tree squids and squidberries. But I did write that up separately, with the supporting data and notes. It's in the files I sent you."

"Excellent. When we're done here I'll have a talk with my head of research. I can have him set up another screening of the berries specifically looking for any neurotransmitter analogs, or anything that might mimic the pharmacokinetics of MDMA or anything else that acts similarly. Of course, that doesn't mean it will be anything useful. The last thing we need is yet another amphetamine derivative; we can synthesize variations on that all day long."

"Sure, and the connection to increased intelligence is tenuous, I get that. And even if that proves out, there's no guarantee it will be useful in humans, let alone in someone at my mother's stage. I'm not pinning my hopes on it."

Holmes smiled understandingly. "Welcome to my world. But thank you for bringing it to my attention. We might get lucky."

"Thank you for looking into it," Ellie said. "Okay, you have my reports and data, is there anything else you need?"

"That should do it. Make sure you get your expenses submitted to accounting, and call me if there's any problem with that. Other than that, thank you again for your efforts. Can we call on you again if we need your talents?"

"Absolutely. Especially if it's off-planet."

"Got bitten by the frontier bug, did you? I'll have to get out there myself and see what the fuss is about."

"You should. Have you heard that they're developing a resort on Kakuloa? I met the developer a couple of times."

"Parry Cohen?"

Ellie nodded. "You know him?"

"Oh, we've met," Holmes said. "He hit CentPharm up for some investment money. Quite a character, isn't he?"

"He is that. Means well, though. Anyway, I've taken up enough of your time. You'll let me know what comes of the squidberry investigation?" She stood to leave.

"Of course," Holmes said. "Oh, there is one other thing, that I hate to bring up."

Ellie realized what she meant. "The arrangements concerning my mother."

"Yes. But we don't need to discuss that now. You just got back. Take a few more days to settle in and think about it. We'll work something out."

Ellie was thankful for the reprieve. She wasn't ready to face that yet.

PART III - A New Cephalopod

Just over a year later; 2078

Chapter 48: The Offer

Marine Institute, a year later

Ellie Greystone had settled back into the old routine at the institute. It wasn't nearly as challenging, nor life as interesting, as investigating cephalopods on Kakuloa had been. But she had a few more papers to her credit, and a few queries out. Maybe something better would turn up.

Her mother had succumbed to the terminal stages of her disease three months ago, although she had stopped recognizing Ellie at all several months before that. At least they'd had a few times together after Ellie had returned from Alpha Centauri.

Ellie's omni chimed with an incoming call, startling her. She glanced at the caller info. *Victoria Holmes?* Ellie hadn't heard from her since a condolence message after the funeral.

"Hello?"

"Ellie, it's good to talk to you again. Listen, I had an unusual request cross my desk. Are you still interested in off-planet work? It wouldn't be with Skrellan or CentPharm, though."

"Uh, most likely, depending on what it is." She was now at full alert, and willed herself to relax. "I assume it's marine biology related? And who with?" ·

"Even better," Holmes said, "it's cephalopod related. I'll forward you the file. And it's a university position."

"University? Off-planet? I wasn't aware of any expeditions." Sometimes a professor would extend an invitation to professionals at other institutions.

"Not expeditions, a new college. It's a bit early yet, but they're getting started. It will be in Sawyer City. They're naming it

Drake University." There was a hint of amusement in Holmes' voice. Ellie wondered what that was about.

But, a new university? And Victoria had asked if she was still interested in off-planet work. She felt her heart beating faster. "Are they looking for professors?" she said, trying to keep the hope out of her voice.

Holmes chuckled. "Yes, among other things. This might interest you even more. Read the message, call me back."

Ellie's omni announced the incoming file. "All right, got it," she said. "Thank you."

She thumbed off the connection and opened the file with trembling fingers.

She skimmed it. Yes, the return address mentioned Drake University. Something about a Department of Biology. Her anticipation made it hard to concentrate on the words. Recent marine discoveries...investigate...cephalopods. Ellie gasped aloud at the next sentence.

"*Ammonites!?* Seriously?" She looked up and around, but nobody was paying attention to her.

She called Holmes back, who answered promptly.

Ellie started talking almost immediately. "You read this, right? It's not a joke?"

"I did, and not as far as I know. I got the feeling they'd like you to come out there and either verify or disprove. You *are* the foremost expert on non-terrestrial cephalopods."

Ellie realized that this was likely true. "But, ammonites went extinct with the dinosaurs!" Her mind reeled. This was either a mistake, a joke, or one of the most important discoveries since...well, since the discovery that these planets had been terraformed, at least. "It must be a mistake. They probably just found some cousin of a nautilus." *Which would be something in itself,* she realized. There were only a handful of nautiloid species left.

"Well, who better to straighten them out? But they're also looking for a professor of biology, aren't they?"

"Why me? They've got three biologists from the *Anderson* team alone."

"All of whom are raising young children and involved in local politics probably more than they want to be. Anyway, you have teaching experience, don't you? Recent?"

"Well, yes, but anyone with a PhD would have that, as a teaching assistant if nothing else." A though occurred to her. "And how did they know about me, and my background, anyway?"

"It probably came come up in conversation. You're not exactly unknown in the Alpha Centauri system. They know of our interest in squidberries and the cephalopods. Don't you want the job?"

"Of course I want the job!" she said, "Even if whatever they found *is* a nautilus!" As she said that, she remembered what she'd said to Henry Caporale about possible post-Cretaceous ammonite fossils. They had been found in just in one location, and only one species, which eventually went extinct too. But still.... If they had survived on Earth for a while after the impact, it might help pin down just when the Terraformers had collected their specimens. If whatever they'd found on Sawyer's World *wasn't* a nautilus.... She had to know.

"Did you set this up?" Ellie asked.

"I swear, all I'd heard was that they were establishing a university, and someone had found a new kind of cephalopod," Holmes said. "I just helped put pieces together."

"Thank you, thank you so much. *A new kind of cephalopod*, eh? Or possibly a very old kind." She looked over the message again, her brain still reeling.

"So, who should I talk to about passage to Sawyer's World?"

Epilogue

Starship Southern Cross, *en route to Alpha Centauri*

Ellie Greystone felt gravity come back, and a few moments later heard the announcement: *"Transition to warp complete. Passengers are free to leave their berths and move about the ship."*

She unstrapped and headed for the galley, where typically the other passengers would gather. She had just entered when a vaguely familiar voice sounded behind her.

"Is that Ellie Greystone? Imagine that, we're on the same ship again. Going back to Kakuloa?"

She cringed inwardly, then turned to face a middle-aged man. "Mr. Cohen, isn't it?" Of course it was. "No, it's my turn to go to Sawyer's World this time. Drake University. What takes you back to Alpha Centauri?"

"It's Parry, please, I keep telling you. I'm going back for the grand opening. First resort hotel on another planet, in the luxurious vacation spot of Kakuloa City."

Ellie remembered the construction site from when she'd left Kakuloa over a year ago. It had been a mix of excavations and half-finished structures, looking more like a war zone than a luxury resort. "Wow, you must have done a lot since the last time I was here."

"Oh, there's still plenty to do. Compared to what we have planned, things are still modest. But, we do have one hotel finished, with beach activities, a small casino and a five-star restaurant. You should come for the opening, my guest."

"That's very kind of you, but as I said, I'm on my way to Sawyer's World."

"The *Southern Cross* stops at Kakuloa first. It'll be a day before you head on to Sawyer's. You're not going to stay aboard ship, are you?"

She had planned to do just that. She didn't want to impose on Dave Newton's hospitality, and she had nowhere else to stay on the planet. "Well, I—"

"Look, the grand opening celebration will be after you have to leave. We do have a few early guests, but meanwhile, the hotel is sitting mostly empty. Stay, try it out, let me know if there's anything that needs improvement, and if you like the place, tell somebody. No obligation. You'll be doing me a favor, helping the place get over its start-up pains before too many paying guests arrive. *Every* place has start-up pains."

Ellie wasn't really convinced, but it most likely *would* be nicer than the ship, and she didn't see an easy way to refuse. It was only one night. "Well, since you put it like that...."

"I do. Look, if we miss each other on disembarking—unlikely, but it's going to be crazy—there'll be a shuttle vehicle from the spaceport to the hotel. It's the Hotel Interplanetary. Not a very imaginative name, I'm afraid, but my financial backers insisted. They did let me name the restaurant."

"Oh?"

"Yeah. Top of the hotel. Gorgeous ocean view and to the south you can see Krechet's Landing."

"I'll look forward to it, then."

Parry looked around the galley. Other passengers had arrived and were seating themselves at the tables.

"I guarantee you the food will be better than here. Not that that would be hard, but with my name on it I'll make sure that it's excellent."

"Your name?"

"Yes. The restaurant is called Parry's."

END

The story of Kakuloa, and early T-Space, continues in *Kakuloa: The Downhill Slide*

A review is always appreciated!

The restaurant, Parry's, was first referenced in the 2010 novelette, *Renee*, set on and around Kakuloa some years after the events herein. It is included below (beginning on page 299) as a free bonus in this trade paperback edition.

Glossary

BC: Buoyancy Compensator - A piece of diving equipment, an inflatable vest, jacket or back-mounted device, to compensate for changes in a diver's buoyancy due to compression of their wet suit, emptying of air tanks, etc.

Cephalopod: a class of the phylum Mollusca, comprising squids, octopus, cuttlefish and nautilus, and the now-extinct ammonite.

Chromatophores: pigment-containing and light-reflecting cells, or groups of cells. Cephalopods such as the octopus have complex chromatophore organs controlled by muscles to achieve rapid color changes.

Deuterium: heavy hydrogen, with a nucleus consisting of one proton and one neutron. The hydrogen component of heavy water. Useful as a fusion fuel.

DSMB: Deployable Surface Marker Buoy - also known as a "safety sausage", a bright-colored, sausage-shaped inflatable buoy to show a diver's location.

Kakuloa: Alpha Centauri B II - terraformed planet orbiting the second largest star (B) in the Alpha Centauri system.

omni: Short for omniphone - compares to today's smartphones as smartphones compare to walky-talkies. (Look for "Nokia Morph" on YouTube for a nearly-there concept video.)

omniphone: See omni.

parsec: A distance of approximately 3.26 light-years.

Sawyer's World: Alpha Centauri A II - second planet orbiting the largest star (A) in the Alpha Centauri system, the first extrasolar planet settled by humans. (See the *Alpha Centauri* series.)

Taprobane: Epsilon Indi III - Third planet orbiting Epsilon

Indi, home world of timoans.

thruster: High-efficiency reaction drive, a kind of fusion-powered arc-jet.

timoan: (Analogous to "human") The sentient natives of Taprobane. Descended from the ancestral species of terrestrial mongoose and meerkats the way humans are descended from the ancestral species of monkeys or lemurs.

T-space: Terraformed (or Terraform) space - Usual term for "known space," a spheroid of stars centered on Earth and about 20 parsecs in diameter. So-called because many of the sun-like stars within it were found to have planets that were not merely Earth-like, but deliberately terraformed.

Unholy War: A nuclear war which took place in the first half of the 21st century, involving primarily the smaller nuclear powers, purportedly for religious reasons.

UDT (Union de Terre): Union of Earth, the successor to the United Nations formed after the events of and immediately after the Unholy War.

warp bubble: The thin shell of highly-curved space surrounding a ship in FTL flight. Based on Van Den Broek's lower-energy configuration of an Alcubierre warp metric.

Acknowledgments

Much of the information about Earthly octopus and squid is thanks to the book *Octopus: The Ocean's Intelligent Invertebrate*, by Jennifer A. Mather, Roland C. Anderson, and James B. Wood. It's very readable, and worth doing so if the subject at all interests you. I barely scratched the surface of what these cephalopods are capable of. (Of course, none are known to actually climb trees, the Pacific Northwest tree octopus notwithstanding.)

The report of post-Cretaceous ammonite fossils is not made up. (See: Machalski, M. & Heinberg, C. 2005-12-31. "Evidence for ammonite survival into the Danian (Paleogene) from the Cerithium Limestone at Stevns Kline, Denmark," *Bulletin of of the Geological Society of Denmark*, Vol. 52, pp. 97-111.) If true (the paper is reasonably convincing), it very likely *was* a dead clade walking. Or swimming, in this case.

The "old movie reference" that Newton refers to about the name *Disco Volante* is of course the James Bond film *Thunderball*, in which in the climactic scene, Emilio Largo's yacht (the *Disco Volante)* sheds its cocoon and attempts to escape on hydrofoils. I'd been interested in SCUBA diving even before that movie, but loved it all the more for all its many underwater scenes. Some years later, I was lucky enough to do a couple of dives on what was left of the set for the sunken bomber scenes, by then mostly just scaffolding with landing gear.

The work on octopus exposure to MDMA is very recent, hitting the news when I was nearly finished with this book. (Edsinger, Eric and Dölen, Gül: "A Conserved Role for Serotonergic Neurotransmission in Mediating Social Behavior in Octopus," *Current Biology*, Vol. 28, Iss. 19, P3136-3142.e4, October 08, 2018). It fit very neatly into the story.

As always, I'd like to thank my kids, Robert the paleontologist and Selena the marine biologist, for their early feedback; writer and diver Robert Williscroft (he literally wrote the book on diving, more than one in fact) for checking what I remember from my SCUBA days; and Jill for her several proof-reads (and error corrections) of the manuscript. Any remaining errors are mine, but as I remind my son Arthur the computer scientist, a real programmer blames the hardware. (grin)

— *Alastair Mayer, Colorado, December 2018*

Bonus Story

The following story, first published as "Renee (and the Space Raiders)" in September, 2010, overlaps events in the next novel, *Kakuloa: A Downhill Slide,* or possibly the one after that (*Kakuloa: Crash and Burn*). Among other things, it explains the significance of the restaurant named in the last chapter of this book.

Note that Jason Curtis, who tells the following story, might be a bit of an unreliable narrator. A few very minor edits have been made to conform with established Kakuloan history.

Renee

by Alastair Mayer

'*Starfire, this is Kakuloa control. Are you declaring an emergency?*'

Air hissed out of a bullet hole in my cockpit, yellow and red warning lights lit up my control panel, the fuel system leaked, my heat shielding was probably damaged, and my spacesuit was on the wrong side of a door to an airless compartment. *Was I declaring an emergency?* People can ask some damn fool questions.

* * *

The guard at the station's departure gate had checked my ID and done a single take. "Jason Curtis?" He'd looked at me as though he recognized me, or the name. *Terrific.*

"That's me."

"Aren't you the guy they hauled out of the *Starfire* a couple of weeks ago, half frozen to death? Something about a broken climate control?"

Sigh. "Yep, that was me." The climate control hadn't been broken; I'd overridden it. "It's a long story, you can probably find it online." I really didn't want to tell the story yet again, the details were embarrassing. "Had to do with a close approach to a star."

"Really? That's kind of ironic, isn't it?"

"Any more iron and I'd be haemochromatic. Look, I'd love to chat"—like hell I would—"but there are people behind me." Well, only two, but that legitimized the plural. "Are we done here?"

"Oh, sorry, sure. Go on through."

I made my way through to the docking area where my ship, yes, the *Starfire* was berthed. Both the ship and I were all patched up now and I wanted to get away from Procyon. The friend I'd come here to see had already left; there really wasn't anything to keep me here. Next stop...I really wasn't sure yet. Somewhere warm, but where I could go outside without wearing SPF 250 sunblock.

* * *

By the time I'd cleared Procyon Station I had decided. I contacted departure control. "This is Jason Curtis on the *Starfire*, breaking orbit and leaving the system, heading for Alpha Centauri. No passengers, no flight plan."

"*Roger* Starfire. *Have a safe trip.*"

The formalities taken care of, I themed the ship's entertainment system to "beach". After nearly coming down with frostbite on my own ship, I wanted a tropical beach where I could feel the sand in my toes and go outside in short sleeves. Meanwhile I'd have to settle for a beach vid.

The computer dredged up the expected collection of vids but also a lot of songs by an ensemble named The Beach Boys, from over a century ago. They sang a lot about cars, girls, and surfing. I didn't get the fascination with cars, perhaps you got to drive them yourself in those days. The interest in girls was obvious. Surfing was something I'd never done. I used to fly aircraft for fun before circumstances forced me to take very early retirement. Those same circumstances left me with enough money to buy my own ship. No, nothing illegal, just a corporate buyout and a golden parachute. But surfing, well, I was willing to give it a try.

There are plenty of beaches on the terraformed worlds we've found so far, but Kakuloa's main spaceport was near one of the best. The big moon and long ocean reach make for some great waves. Or so it said in the guide. Kakuloa orbited Alpha Centauri B, and at a shade under four parsecs from Procyon it was just within my range.

* * *

I made planetfall at Kakuloa a week later. I didn't want to stay aboard the *Starfire* at the spaceport so I checked into the Hotel Interplanetary near the beach. Kakuloa City isn't the tourist spot it used to be, and the local Interplan was modest by that chain's usual standards. Oh, they get tourists, it's only three days from Earth, but not just for relaxing vacations on the beach. There are exotic fauna to hunt and archaeological sites whose builders died out millennia before humans arrived.

After I'd settled in, I wandered down to take a look at the beach. I hadn't heard the roar of an ocean in months; it was a nice change from the whir of ventilator fans. I stood there a while, some distance from the waterline, feeling the sand between my toes, smelling the salt air, and watching the waves roll in. There were some small animals playing on the waves, skittering back and forth across the wavefront before it broke. Then my sense of scale corrected and I realized that I was much further from the water than I'd thought. I was looking at *humans* out there surfing. Those waves were mountainous. I began to have second thoughts about the whole thing and turned away from the shoreline. That's when I saw *her*.

To say she was gorgeous would be to render the word useless for anything else. Perhaps I exaggerate. By the current Rubenesque Earth standards she was skinny; slim and athletic. But I like that look, and on her it looked great. She took my breath away, and I heard myself suck it back in. Tall, tanned, with long, straight, pale violet hair that told me she wasn't afraid of body-mods for the look *she* wanted, not what fashion dictated. Self-confidence is sexy. And she was watching me staring at her. Oops.

She smiled at me. "Hello," she said, "you must be new here."

"Uh, yes. How did you know?"

"Something *malihini* about you, and the look of someone who's been cooped up in a ship for a while." She extended a hand. "My name's Renee."

I reached out my hand and shook hers. "Hi, Jas—, er, Jay Curtis." Then my mouth disconnected from my brain and started rambling. "Is there something psychotropic in the atmosphere on this planet? Strange goddesses don't just walk up to me and intro-duce themselves. One of us has to be hallucinating."

She laughed. "I'm no goddess. Should I be insulted for being called strange?"

"We've been introduced, you're no longer strange." My brain kept trying to tell my mouth to shut up, but it wasn't working. At least Renee was amused.

"So, Jay, where you from and what brings you to Kakuloa?"

"Most recently from Procyon Station, originally Earth." That was dumb, most people out here were originally from Earth, we haven't been out long enough for many native-born, at least not adult native-born. "Just visiting, exploring the galaxy, well, T-space, the nearby terraformed worlds, anyway." Brain to mouth: she'd know what T-space meant. "What about you, do you live here?"

"Me? No, well, not really. I've been on-planet for a while helping to organize an expedition, I'm here at the beach for a break before going back to work in a few days." She looked out at the ocean. "Do you surf?"

"I never have. I thought I'd like to try it until I saw the size of those waves."

She laughed again. I loved the sound. "They should be calmer tomorrow. There was a storm that passed yesterday. If you're interested I could give you lessons. Unless you have something else planned?"

If I'd had other plans, they were just canceled. "No, that would be great, I'll look forward to it. I'm at the Interplan just up the beach," I pulled out my omniphone, "here, let me give you my info." She keyed her molded wrist omni—all she was wearing other than a bikini—and we swapped contact data.

"Okay then, Jay." She smiled at me, her violet-gray eyes twinkling. "I have to run now, I'll call you in the morning." She turned and started to jog off down the beach.

"Thanks Renee, talk to you then," I called after her. I stood watching, enjoying the view, before turning back to look out at the waves. Wow.

* * *

Surfing the next day was a fiasco. I don't know what the Beach Boys saw in it.

It started out well enough. Renee had me do some drills balancing the board on a mound of sand so that I could practice getting up and staying on. I felt silly at first, standing on the board, legs apart, crouched, my arms spread. "Hey, this isn't so bad!" I said, pleased with myself, arms waving madly.

Renee laughed. "Yes, but the sand's not moving. We'll see how you do when we get out there."

Before we headed into the water, Renee had me put a band around my ankle, and pressed a button on the board. "That's a beacon, when you wipe out and the board gets away —"

"What do you mean, *when?*" I smiled as I said it.

She grinned. "Okay, *if* the board gets away, after a minute it will guide itself back to you. Let's go over the controls again. Handgrips here." She pointed to the rubberized grips on either edge of the board, about a third of the way from the front. "They control the motor. Use it to get out past the breakline, and to get up to speed to catch the wave. At that point, release the grips, but you can hold on to the edge of the board if you need to."

"Got it."

"And then just stand up and ride the wave, I'll be right beside you."

"Sounds good." Well, that's what I said. The waves had only died down to about three meters high, still intimidating but I wasn't about to let Renee know that.

We waded into the water, flopped down on our boards and started cruising out, the boards' built-in hydrojets pushing us along. I saw a few surfers, apparently purists, paddling their boards out with their arms. With shoulders that big they could probably pull up trees.

I wiped out on the first wave, and I'm embarrassed to say it wasn't the first wave we chose to ride, but the first one we encountered going out. It started to break over me and I immediately forgot whatever it was Renee had told me about getting out over them. Next thing I knew I was underwater, rolling in a maelstrom of water, air, and sand, not sure which way was up. I found my way to the surface and gasped for breath, looking around wildly. My board came gliding up to me like a dutiful puppy dog. I had a strange urge to pat its nonexistent head. Renee sat on her board a few meters away. She looked like she was trying to keep from laughing.

"Are you all right?" she called.

"Only injured my pride," I said, trying to ignore the salt water up my nose and the sand rash on my leg. "Let's keep going."

The rest of the morning was like that. I managed to avoid being stung by a weird alien jellyfish. Renee insisted it was harmless, but I had my doubts. It looked like a Portuguese man-of-war, but three times bigger and with fluorescent green tentacles. Then I asked her if there were sharks (a possibility, the terraformed planets we've found seem to have been seeded with Earth life from sixty or seventy million years ago; scientists are still arguing over the who, what and why).

"No, but there's something like a 20-foot coelacanth that may be worse", she'd said.

"Okay, time to go in now."

"No, it's a deep water fish, they usually don't bother surfers."

"*Usually?*"

We ended up lazing on the beach, talking. I was staring into her eyes, lost, when she said "Don't fall in."

"What? We're on the beach, not on the surfboards."

"No, I mean the way you're looking at me. We both have to go our separate ways in few days, don't get carried away." It may have been too late for that.

"I'm retired, I don't have to go anywhere."

"Well I'm not, and I do. We're having fun now, Jay, don't spoil it."

Spoiling it was the last thing I wanted to do. I changed the subject. "Sorry. So, how did you learn to surf so well?" She'd been amazing out there on the waves when she didn't have me to worry about.

"I grew up in Hawaii. My dad was an astrophysicist at the university." She sat up. "Oh, and speaking of astrophysics, I have some errands I need to run this afternoon." She started to pull her things together.

Had I scared her off? I shouldn't have made that stupid remark about being retired. But maybe she really did have something she needed to do. I needed more data. "Say, can I buy you dinner? I hear Parry's is good." In truth I'd only seen their ad at the hotel, but it seemed upscale.

"That would be lovely, but not Parry's. There's a nice little place just off the beach, I could meet you there. It has some interesting native food."

"Not jellyfish, I hope?"

She laughed. How could I not fall in love with an intelligent goddess who appreciates my sense of humor? "No, but we can ask about filet of coelacanth," she said, grinning.

* * *

I got there early (anxious, who me?) and waited at the bar. I'd just finished explaining to the bartender that when you make a Nervous Nellie, the *last* ingredient is the liquid nitrogen, when Renee arrived. I felt my breath sucked away again. She was, as always, gorgeous, with her hair swept back and wearing a ballet dress with flowing skirts and a snug bodice patterned with something that sparkled. "Wow" I said. She smiled.

We didn't have filet of coelacanth, or jellyfish, but it was during dinner that I got the bad news.

"Yesterday you said something about organizing an expedition," I said. "What's that about?"

"It's the Eta Carinae expedition." She said it as though I should know what that meant.

"Eta Carinae?" It sounded like a star name.

"A super massive star about 7500 light years away, it already had one false supernova event a few hundred years ago."

"Oh. I'd thought you meant some kind of archaeological expedition. Aren't there ruins here."

"What? Oh, no, I'm an astrophysicist."

"Oh. Following in your father's footsteps? So what's the expedition?"

"We're going to study it. We want to get some warning of when it goes, or went, hypernova."

"But 7500 light years?" I did the math. "That'd take you fifteen years to get there, even assuming you could stay in warp the whole time." Starships are size-limited, the warp bubble can't be made big enough to let them hold more than a couple of dozen light years' worth of fusion fuel.

"We're not going all the way there. For one thing, we can't; it's embedded in a massive gas and dust nebula." When matter encounters a warp bubble, it gets ripped apart by the tide at the warp boundary, and some of the resulting energy release comes through as radiation. Most of interstellar space is empty enough to be harmless, but a thick nebula or dust cloud could be lethal. "But mostly we don't need to. For all we know it's already gone hypernova. If we can, we just want to get close enough to set up a listening post that will give us plenty of warning. Two hundred light years nearer will give us that many years warning, if the wavefront isn't already closer than that. We'll need it."

"Bad?"

"We're talking about a hypernova here. They thought it went supernova back in 1843. It outshone everything in Earth's sky except Sirius, but it's still there. It's flickered a few times since. When it really blows, it will be brighter than the rest of the galaxy combined. The terraformed planets *should* be okay, their magnetospheres and atmospheres will protect them, but anything and anyone in space or on an airless body would be in trouble. If it sends a gamma ray burst our way, well, that's an extinction event." She paused, a somber look on her face. Then she smiled and shook her head. "But T-space is off axis for that...if it isn't precessing."

"I had no idea." I hadn't, my interest in astronomy had been mostly limited to navigating around the forty or so light year bubble of nearer stars known as T-Space.

"The scary thing is it might have already detonated; our astrophysical models and data aren't quite good enough to know. It's unlikely, but the wavefront could be here next week."

I thought about that, of massive waves of gamma and x-rays sleeting through space, killing anyone caught off-planet, destroying satellites, devastating space stations. The impact would be horrendous, or worse. "So you're going out to set up early warning posts."

She nodded and swallowed the bite she'd just taken. "That and general exploration too. We want to see how far in that direction we find terraformed planets, and whatever else is out there."

I felt a knot in my stomach that wasn't from the dinner. Renee had already mentioned a couple of hundred light years. "So, you're not talking about a short trip, are you?"

She smiled a wry smile. "No. At least six months in warp, each way. Plus time to explore, refuel and resupply along the way. We're estimating about two years outbound with exploration stops, perhaps a year on the way back.

"That's a long time to be out of touch."

"We'll be sending back reports every few months by message torpedo."

I raised an eyebrow at this. Of course there's no such thing as faster-than-light radio; the fastest way to send a message is via starship. A message torpedo is a self-contained robot starship, about three meters long and shaped to almost fill the reverse-teardrop warp bubble. It looks like an ice-cream cone or an old nuclear weapon reentry vehicle. The comparison with the latter is apt. To get the best range and speed they squeeze the most power into the smallest space; they're fueled with antimatter. The containment system is supposed to be failsafe, and I'd never heard of an accidental antimatter explosion, but a message torpedo is a potential bomb. "The Space Force let you have antimatter?"

"Just for the message torpedoes. It's a joint civilian-military mission. They'll have oversight." She paused to take another sip of her wine. "Of course, there'll be no way we can receive any messages unless we stay in one place for a long time, but that's not part of the plan. So we won't get news or be back home for three years. We'll head back immediately, of course, if we find out part way that Eta Carinae has already blown."

Part of me hoped it had.

* * *

After dinner I talked Renee into coming back to my ship with me. "We can have dessert and after dinner drinks. I've got one of the best autobars money can buy, and a great collection of music."

"You have your own ship? Okay, I'd like that."

We made our way through the spaceport and out to the field. She caught the name of my ship as we went aboard. She whirled, eyes wide.

"*Starfire*!? My gosh, Jay is short for Jason? You're *that* Jason Curtis? I didn't...." her voice trailed off, confused or embarrassed.

"Um, yeah". The story had gotten around.

"But that's amazing, a close approach to a star like that."

"That was stupid, I only did it because I was desperate". I'd miscalculated a jump, had to refuel, and the only source of hydrogen was the star's atmosphere. Lucky for me it was a cool star, and I'd had shade.

"It's a useful technique, shielding your ship with an asteroid like that. We use it to drop probes into stars." She grinned at me. "But you're the only person I've heard of to do it personally."

"I wouldn't try it on anything hotter than a red dwarf. But I promised you dessert and a drink." I desperately wanted to change the subject. "Do you like Beach Boys music?"

"Who?"

I told the music system to play a random selection while I had the galley find us cheesecake and a couple of Drambuies.

A little while later, we were in each others' arms, the rest of dessert and drinks forgotten, when the melodic "Surfer Girl" came on. I thought it apropos, but Renee tensed.

"Jay, we should stop."

"I won't tell if you won't."

She pushed back. "No, Jay, I'm sorry. We just met. In two days I'm going to disappear for at least three years. I don't want anyone to get hurt." Her or me? Perhaps she didn't know. She paused then, as if weighing what to say next. "And besides—" she started to continue, but I stopped her.

"No, I'm sorry Renee, you're right." It took a lot of willpower to say those words. I wanted to argue, come up with something persuasive to make her stay, but I knew that was the testosterone talking. I gritted mental teeth and got to my feet, and pulled Renee to hers. "We should call it a night while I still can." I grinned, but I was only half joking.

Renee smiled. "Thank you Jason. There are still some gentlemen left after all."

She came closer to give me a quick kiss, but the kiss stretched out, becoming more than just a goodbye peck. Renee seemed to have changed her mind. Knowing that either way I'd hate myself in the morning, I chose the honorable path and pushed away, gasping. "We'd better get you home before... well, just before."

* * *

When I woke up the next morning—well, closer to noon—I found a message from her on my omni.

"Jason," it said, "thank you for last night. Call you later. — Renee." I smiled to myself. There was more. "PS - we really do have to go our separate ways soon, remember what I told you." Told me? Oh, right, falling in. Way too late.

* * *

We went to the beach again the following afternoon. The waves were down and I tried surfing again, but the real attraction was watching Renee surf. She rode the waves like she'd been doing it all her life, which she probably had. I sat out the last few runs and enjoyed the view, until finally she brought the board up and flopped beside me.

"Hey, watch who you're splashing!"

She laughed. "A little water never hurt anyone."

"That," and I pointed out at the ocean, "is *not* 'a little water'."

I tried to sound serious but couldn't keep a straight face. "You're fantastic out there, but I've told you that. How about letting me show you something that I'm good at?"

"Oh? What's that?"

"Flying. A Sapphire isn't exactly an aeroplane but she handles pretty well. Want to go for a spin? And perhaps a couple of loops and rolls?"

She looked at me warily. "You're kidding, right?"

I chuckled. "Yes. I've flown aerobatics but I wouldn't in *Starfire*, not with a passenger and not without good reason. It's more fun with something designed for it. But we can do some sightseeing from the air."

"All right, Jay, that sounds like fun."

* * *

Something was happening back at the spaceport. At first they didn't want to let us onto the field. There was a guard at the door from the port building.

"Sorry sir, the field is closed at the moment," he said. He was armed, which wasn't unusual except that he held an assault rifle at the ready, rather than a holstered pistol. I didn't remember there even being a guard there earlier.

"What, why?"

"I can't say, sir. It's only for a few hours, come back later."

"Look, my ship's out there, the *Starfire*, you can't keep me away from my ship."

At this he looked a little less sure of himself. "Can I see some ID? You too Ma'am, if you're with him."

We showed him our IDs, which he examined. He turned and keyed his headset, muttering something I couldn't quite hear. Finally he nodded and turned back. "Alright Mr. Curtis, Ma'am. You're cleared to go to your ship, but please keep clear of the main field."

"Of course, thank you. What was—"

Renee nudged me. "Come on Jason, I'll fill you in."

As we skirted the field walking toward my ship, I looked across to where the Eta Carinae Expedition ships—two of them, anyway—were parked. Another ship, with Space Force markings, was parked near them.

"Renee? What's going on?"

"Sorry Jay, I should have realized they'd close the field. They're transferring the message torpedoes today, so they've beefed up security."

"Here? Why not do that in orbit, or deep space?"

"I don't know all the details. We've had some schedule slippage on getting our ships ready for space, and it can be easier to work where there's gravity and air. They probably want to just get it done quickly."

"I guess they're the experts." It wasn't like Kakuloa had a very busy spaceport.

We were almost at the *Starfire* when the distant roaring noise I'd been hearing finally caught my attention. That was a ship coming in on thrusters, and the field was supposed to be closed. I turned to look for it just as an alarm klaxon sounded. What happened next went too fast for me to follow all the details.

I saw several bright flashes and streaks of smoke, and an explosion rocked the Space Force ship. Guards and Space Marines ran in different directions across the field, some of them firing weapons. Several other people—I didn't see uniforms—shot back at them. Small explosions ripped the far side of the field and thick clouds of colored smoke drifted across, blocking my view of the spaceport buildings. A ship, no doubt the one I'd heard approach, descended onto the field, long-legged gear down, with a

cargo ramp already lowering from its belly. The field was a ca-
cophony of gunfire, alarm klaxons, and shouting. Three men ran
toward the new ship from out of the billowing smoke, two guiding a cargo pallet, the third shooting back into the smoke. Nes-
tled in support frames on the pallet were a half-dozen long, ta-
pered ice-cream cone shapes; the message torpedoes.

Renee, beside me, shouted. "Jason, they're stealing the antimatter!"

"Get down!" I said, and crouched down myself, pulling her.
We'd both been standing there staring instead of diving for the
dirt at the first shots, but things had happened too fast. As I
watched, one of the two men guiding the pallet staggered and fell.
The third slung his gun over his shoulder and helped the other
push the cart up the ramp. Another explosion hit the Space Force
ship. It wasn't going anywhere.

"Renee, stay low and run for those ships," I said, pointing to
a couple of other ships parked on the same side of the field as
mine. "Stay clear of the *Starfire*."

"Why? What are you doing?"

"Going after them."

"*What?*"

"Somebody has to stop them. They took out the Space Force
ship."

"I'm going with you."

"*No!* I don't want you hurt, and someone has to tell the authorities that I'm one of the good guys. Now go." I pushed her
back towards the spaceport buildings, dim behind the smoke
clouds, and towards the shelter of the other ships.

I ran in a low crouch to the *Starfire*. As I ran I keyed my omni
to open the hatch. I glanced back. Renee was at a safe distance,
still running in a low crouch. Across the field the hijacker's ship
had its cargo door closed and was powering up thrusters, prepar-
ing to lift.

I dashed to the cockpit and hit the emergency start button as
I strapped in. A few long seconds later I too was airborne, and in
pursuit. I just had to figure out a way to stop them.

* * *

I wasn't sure how, but I knew they had to be stopped. Nobody raids a shipment of antimatter message torpedoes because they want to send a letter. As I hauled *Starfire* into the air and turned to follow the hijackers, a plan began to form.

I had flown formation and aerobatics in my flying club. The *Starfire* isn't as agile as the aircraft we flew there, but I didn't have to be that fancy. If I few close enough, the bad guys couldn't engage their warp drive.

Matter—me and the *Starfire* in this case—that touches the warp boundary is ripped apart at the atomic level by the gravity gradient, with a violent energy release. Ship control systems are programmed to avoid that. If I stayed close to them, their warp drive wouldn't engage. There was a remote chance the bad guys could override it, but then we'd all be dead and it wouldn't matter.

I checked my instruments. By now I was halfway to space, closing on the terrorists' ship.

I had to close with them before we got too far out of the atmosphere. A planet's gravity won't prevent the warp field from forming, only skew the direction. But where there's still more than a trace of atmosphere, the ship's safety interlocks will shut out the warp generators.

Their ship's main thrusters flared and they started to pull away. They'd spotted me and boosted harder. It looked like they were pushing three gees. I pushed *Starfire* to four-and-a-half. One thing about the hull of a Sapphire, it's strong. With my aerobatic practice I knew I could take more gees if I had to. But this stern chase was impractical, and I didn't want to fly into their exhaust. I projected their course then pitched my ship up to a higher angle and increased thrust to six gees.

It didn't take long to clear atmosphere. I throttled back, putting Starfire into a slow roll and looking for the other ship. If I'd estimated right...I had, there it was below me, and I was to sunward of it. I dove.

Unless their pilot was far better than his flying had shown so far, the first sign they had of me as I bore down out of the sun— or Alpha Centauri B—was my braking thrust buffeting their ship. I held formation at about two meters away. It was dicey; much further and they might be able to warp away, closer and we risked collision. I'd flown in tighter formations, and in atmosphere where you worry about random vagaries of wind and turbulence, but that was with a cooperating pilot in the other craft. This guy wanted to get away from me.

He tried the obvious, pulling directly back, but I was on him. He tried a couple of sideways jinks, but I watched his control jets and compensated almost before he'd moved. You could tell this guy was just a pushbutton pilot, he'd never done any real flying. He rolled left but I just ignored it; it didn't change the distance between us so he still couldn't warp out.

That's when I realized that I didn't have an exit strategy.

What the hell was I going to do out here? I could stop him from warping away, but I couldn't make him *do* anything without risking my own ship. Crap. If I were really unlucky, when and if the Space Force ultimately showed up, they might assume that I was in cahoots with them and blow both of us apart. I'd better get on the radio.

"Kakuloa Control, this is *Starfire* holding position with the guys who hijacked the antimatter torpedoes. I'm...." Wait, this was an open frequency and the bad guys would be as curious about what I was going to do as I was.

"Starfire, *Kakuloa Control. Say again?*"

"Kakuloa this is *Starfire*. Request secure channel." They'd have my public encryption key on file from my earlier landing. I was already telling my comm system to use theirs.

"*Roger* Starfire, *go to secure on 191.8*" they said, telling me which secondary channel to use. I flipped over and hailed them again.

"Kakuloa, *Starfire*, secure on 191.8. How do you read?"

"*Five by five*, Starfire. *What the hell's going on? Did you say you were holding position with the terrorist?*"

"Affirmative. I'm keeping them out of warp."

"*I hope you're a damn good pilot, but thanks. What are your intentions?*"

"Uh, I was hoping you could tell me. I can stay close but this can't last forever." As if to emphasize that, the terrorist pilot chose that moment to perform a complicated mix of translation and rotation thruster firings to try to get away. I scrambled trying to follow, and came close to banging my starboard vertical stabilizer—my right tail fin—against his hull. That gave me an idea, but I'd check my other options first.

"Kakuloa, how long before the cavalry gets here?"

"*The what? Sorry* Starfire, *no Space Force ships in-system —*"

Oh, crap.

"*— the nearest is off Sawyer's, along with their Space Guard. We've signaled them.*"

Not so bad, then. Sawyer's World orbited Alpha Centauri A, when they'd said "in-system" they'd been talking about the Kakuloa system around Alpha Centauri B. Right now the two were about 23 AU apart, or a bit more than the distance of Uranus from Sol. Still, it would take about three hours for a radio signal to reach there from here. Add to that however long it would take for a Space Force ship to get into position to do the twenty-second jump to this system, plus the time from wherever they came out of warp to where the terrorist and I were dancing around.

"So, three-plus hours then, Kakuloa?"

"*Sorry about that,* Starfire. *Sit tight, we're checking other possibilities.*"

The terrorist ship danced another little jitterbug, then powered up main thrusters to try to get away. I followed, cursing under my breath. Sitting tight was one thing, but I wasn't sure I could stand to play tag with this guy for three hours. At least he couldn't warp out while he was firing thrusters; a warp bubble intersecting an exhaust plume isn't healthy either.

They cut thrusters abruptly and I almost overshot, but quickly maneuvered back to take up station again. How was I going to get out of this? Pissing off a shipload of terrorists who had just hijacked a pallet of antimatter message torpedoes didn't seem like something with a high survival index. At least they couldn't do anything to me that wouldn't kill them too.

Then I saw their airlock door slide open. Oh?

There were two of them, suited up, in the airlock. One braced himself against a grab rail, holding on to the other. The other pointed an assault rifle at the *Starfire*. Oh crap.

I goosed the forward thrusters to drift my ship back relative to theirs, and I saw the rifle's muzzle flash and heard the impact of bullets somewhere on the *Starfire*'s hull. She was a tough ship, and had once taken a hit from a piece of asteroid without much problem, but a hit in the wrong place could still be trouble. The recoil sent the gunner twisting back; he and his buddy hadn't been braced quite right. They scrambled to get back into position. About then *Starfire*'s forward attitude jets came even with the air-lock.

I twitched the control stick.

To the guys in the airlock, it must have looked like somebody had aimed a cannon at them and fired. I mourned the lack of shot in my "cannon", but the exhaust plume was enough to blast them tumbling back into the airlock. With any luck, the exhaust had hazed up their helmets, or even flash-blinded them, but I wasn't going to hang around to find out. I fired my side thrusters to move the *Starfire* around their ship, away from the open hatch.

"Starfire, *this is Kakuloa Control.*"

"Go ahead Kakuloa." I wondered what they'd come up with.

"*Patching* Deep Star Two *into the channel.*" *Deep Star*? That was one of the expedition ships. Another voice, female, came over the comm.

"*Jason? Are you okay?*"

"Renee? What's going on?"

"*We're lifting now, we'll be clear to warp in about five minutes.*" That wasn't a normal trajectory for a ship like *Deep Star*, they must be pouring it on. "*We're going to Alpha-A to contact the Space Force.*" Good, they'd beat the radio signal by almost two hours. "*Hang on, the cavalry should be here in a half-hour.*"

I'd be surprised if that were true, it would depend on where they came out in the Sawyer system, and whether there was a Space Force ship ready to go on just a few minutes' notice. I figured at least an hour, but that beat the two-plus hours now waiting for them to get the radio call.

"Thanks, *Deep Star*. I'll be here. Renee, be careful."

"*You too, Jay.* Deep Star *out.*"

* * *

"*Hey,* Starfire, *come in.*" This was over the public channel. I had wondered when the terrorists might get around to calling me.

"This is *Starfire*. Identify yourself, please."

"*Who do you think? Listen, we got no quarrel with you, why don't you just back off before you get killed?*"

"Right now I'm think I'm in one of the safest places around. You can't do anything to me without hurting yourself."

That drew several minutes of silence from the radio, together with a few more twists, shimmies and turns from their ship which I followed like a skilled dance partner. Then....

"*Back off or we'll drop one of these on Kakuloa City.*"

Now, there was a problem. They'd have to do more than just drop it, we were in some kind of orbit and I was sure that the antimatter containment could withstand normal reentry. But what *could* they do? I flipped back to comm two.

"Kakuloa Control, did you hear that last? What would it take to detonate a message torpedo?"

"*Roger* Starfire, *we heard it. That information is classified, we can't tell you.*"

"Damn it, man, is that a credible threat or not? Is there any way it could be rigged as a bomb? Could you shoot it down?"

Whoever was manning the radio didn't answer right away. I could imagine some hasty discussion in the control room.

"Kakuloa?" I asked.

"*Okay. Someone who knew what they were doing, who had access to the right tools and classified information, could rig that in about an hour. Or they could just stuff the housing with high explosives in about ten minutes.*"

"Damn. And shooting it down?"

"*Not likely. We don't have anything armed, the best we could hope for is somebody ramming it. We'd still get a blast but if it were high enough that wouldn't matter. We've got ships scrambling to take off now.*"

"Starfire," it was the terrorists on comm one again, "*did you hear us? Move away or we drop one.*"

"I heard you. The way I figure it even if I do back off you'll just use them on some other city. If I stick around you'll be caught before you have a chance to do that, and they'll wipe you for mass murder if you hit Kakuloa. Your best bet is to just give yourselves up." Unlikely, but it couldn't hurt to suggest it.

"*We'll kill you first.*"

Yeah, I was afraid of that. "We've all got to go sometime. Maybe they'll erect a statue in my honor." That was pure bluster on my part. I've faced deadly situations before, any pilot has, but I could always see a way out of them. I was really beginning to regret putting myself here, but I was committed. I wasn't going to back down now. I looked at the clock; still at least twenty minutes before help arrived, more likely forty.

"*We're prepping a torpedo. If you don't back off in five minutes we'll launch it.*"

I would have taunted them, but they were too close to the edge. Help wasn't going to arrive in five minutes. I had to consider my other option.

There would be at least three of them aboard: the pilot and the two who'd tried to shoot at me from the airlock. At that thought I looked over their ship carefully, to make sure nobody was trying to sneak around the hull with a weapon in hand. It was clear. There'd been others on the field, although I'd only seen the one who'd been shot near the cargo ramp. What else did I know about their ship? I didn't recognize the make and model, but that was my ignorance rather than anything unusual about it. It was about the size of my *Starfire*, but differently configured.

"Kakuloa, this is *Starfire*. Did you get the make of their ship? I, uh, want to make sure I stay clear of any surprises."

"*Okay,* Starfire, *it looked like a Staravelle class. Small cargo bay, sleeps four, range about three parsecs. Their transponder was rigged so we didn't get full details.*"

"Thanks, Kakuloa. Do you have diagrams?"

"*Uh, generic ones, sure,* Starfire. *Uploading them now. What are you planning?*"

"Just staying alive and trying to keep them from bombing you or anyone else. I'll keep you posted."

The other ship fired full thrusters for a moment just then. They couldn't listen in on my encrypted conversations with Kakuloa, but they could tell I was talking. Perhaps they hoped to catch me off-guard. It didn't work. I caught them easily, and now I knew the pilot was still at the controls.

"*Three minutes,* Starfire."

I brought up the Staravelle deck plans on a side screen. Fuel tankage on the sides. The cargo area was midships with the bay doors underneath. That matched what I'd seen on the field, where they'd loaded the message torpedoes. They'd be in the cargo bay—and the terrorists could pop one out the bay door. If I positioned myself in front of it they could shoot at me from both the cargo bay and the airlock, so that wasn't going to work. If they were making a bomb there'd be at least two of them in the cargo bay, the pilot was still in the cockpit, and there could be one other. More if they doubled up on the sleeping arrangements.

The plans showed that the warp units, fusion plant and life support were all arranged to the sides and aft to balance the center of gravity, with landing gear wells at roughly the four corners of the rounded trapezoidal deck plan. Sleeping quarters were behind the cockpit, which was on the upper or dorsal surface forward of midships. The main load-bearing paths—and the strongest parts of the ship—would be to the landing gear and the thrusters. While the overall shape was aerodynamic it wasn't designed for prolonged atmospheric flight. It wasn't a lifting body like the *Starfire*, and lacked wings or tail fins. The cockpit and dorsal surface would be the weak area.

"*One minute,* Starfire. *Back away* now!"

"You sure you don't want to just give up?" One last chance.

"*Stop fucking around,* Starfire. *Back off or we bomb.*"

"How do I know you'll leave Kakuloa alone if I do?" When I moved, I wanted them to think I was backing off. Their pilot wasn't good enough to counter what I intended, but if he moved the wrong way it would be worse for me.

"*Why would we waste one of these if we don't have to? Now back away.*" The voice held a confident note. Gotcha!

"Standby." I thought to wonder if their pilot was suited up, and realized that *I* wasn't. There'd been no time, and there was none now. I'd have to take my chances without my suit. I hit a switch and the cockpit door sealed behind me. That would have to do.

I nudged my thrusters to move into position. Their pilot would be ready to warp as soon as I was clear; his attention would be split between his panel and watching me. The *Starfire* drifted a bit and rolled, which brought my upper surface to his port side, still close enough to inhibit their drive.

"*Move it,* Starfire." They were getting impatient. I'd move it alright, but not the way they wanted.

"I'm moving." So saying, I rolled *Starfire* as hard as she'd go, bringing her forward. I saw their ship's side swing by overhead and I felt and heard a shuddering *crunch* as my portside fin crashed into and through their cockpit, my fin's spar much stronger than their thin pressure hull at that point. I yawed to port, twisting the fin to enlarge the hole I'd made and inflict more damage on their ship's control circuits. Warning lights lit on my own panel. My fin was ruined, of course. I wouldn't be able to re-enter without repairs, but right now I had too much else to worry about.

Both ships turned and drifted towards each other. Their nose swung down toward my cockpit. If my hull cracked I'd lose my air. And if their cargo bay was still intact they could still bomb Kakuloa. I pitched down, away from them, and tried to translate free. *Starfire* skewed around at an odd angle. Damn, I was tangled. I fired the control jets in different directions but with no luck. Pointing my nose as far away from their ship as the trapped wreckage of my fin would let me, I lit up my aft main thrusters with full force.

Starfire jerked sideways a bit, groaned, and tore free. I shut off the thrusters. There was enough debris floating loose right now that they couldn't go to warp even if their controls still worked, which I doubted. My exhaust had scorched their upper hull and plumes of vapor vented from holes in its surface. The cockpit area was a jumble of torn metal and plastic. I couldn't see the pilot. He *might* have survived if he'd been in a suit. I hadn't wanted to kill him, but there'd been no choice. I couldn't dwell on that now, the cargo bay was still undamaged. If the rest of the crew was alive, they could still target Kakuloa. Or at least blow both of us up.

I moved around to their underside. Sure enough, the cargo bay was opening. It moved slowly, in fits and starts, like somebody was cranking it open manually. The door power must be out. My portside fin was a ruin so I started to line up my starboard fin. This would be tougher, with all the structural beams on this side of their ship, but what else could I do? I saw flashes from the partly open cargo bay and heard impacts on my hull. They were shooting at me again. I heard a loud *bang* then a hissing noise. My hull was pierced.

As long as the hole was small I had a few minutes. It's not like the vids where everything instantly explodes into space; air can only get through a hole so fast, after all. But they were still shooting at me, and I was getting tired of this.

I pushed my nose down and away, making my attitude jets shake their ship and throw their aim off. Would they be getting ready to detonate the bomb to take me with them, or were they still hoping to drive me off? I continued my turn; let them think I was leaving. I heard more impacts on the hull. At minimum my heat shielding was ruined. More warning lights lit on my panel but I couldn't tell if the rear cabin was leaking. I switched on the aft window and saw their cargo bay swing into view. The hatch was open wider, and they were still shooting.

The firing stopped when my big aft thrusters lined up on the cargo bay the way my maneuvering jets had earlier on the airlock. Someone squeezed around the edge of the cargo bay door and pushed off from it sideways. I let him go, he'd be caught in the explosion anyway. Then I fired the main thrusters.

I fully expected that to be the last thing I ever did. My exhaust would cause the torpedoes' containments to fail, or set off the explosives, and all the antimatter would detonate. The view aft went dazzling white, acceleration slammed me back in my seat, and it took me a few seconds to realize that if the antimatter had detonated I wouldn't have had time to experience even that much.

I cut the thrusters a couple of kilometers from what was left of the terrorists' ship. My exhaust would have killed anyone still in the cargo bay, and would have damaged the whole underside of the ship, heatshielding or not. If the backsplash hadn't gotten the terrorist who'd crawled out just before I fired, he'd be drifting away from the ship with no way to get back. The Space Force could pick him up when they got here.

My ears popped, and I heard the hissing again. Of course, I was losing pressure through the bullet hole. I had to suit up before it got serious. I undid my seat straps and turned to leave the cockpit—my suit was back by the airlock—and noticed the big red UNPRESSURIZED warning blinking on the cockpit door. That meant the *other* side was unpressurized, not this side. Not yet. My main cabin had lost all pressure. I was trapped in a leaking cockpit with no way to get to my suit.

I turned back and keyed the comm. "Kakuloa, I have a problem."

* * *

I quickly apprised them of the situation. They were happy to hear that the threat from the antimatter was past. The only immediate suggestion they had was to tear up small bits of fabric from anything handy and set them adrift to find and help plug the leak. I was already doing that. By the end of the discussion the inside of the cockpit looked like one of those snow-globes, well shaken. Slowly the pieces drifted towards different parts of the cockpit; the seams and joints between the walls, control panels and access panels. The leak had to be behind the panels. How would I patch that?

I forced myself to calm down, put the recent combat manoeuvering out of my mind and focus on this as though it had just happened. What was the drill? Right.

The main life support ducts routed through the upper part of Starfire's hull and must have been damaged when I ripped away from the terrorists' ship. Pressure valves in the ducts would have closed to stop loss when they sensed vacuum. I just had to reroute air to the cockpit via the secondaries. I'd still be leaking, but it would give me more time. Meanwhile Kakuloa was working on a way to get a guy with no space suit and no air lock from one ship to another. If I tried to reenter with *Starfire* in the shape she was in, it would be a short, hot, trip.

Or would it?

A hundred and fifty years of aerospace tradition held that when you approach a planet with an atmosphere, you use that atmosphere to aerobrake, scrubbing off your speed on superhot air. Heat shielding was lighter and cheaper than the fuel needed to back down on your exhaust like a Moon lander. But now I couldn't trust my heat shield. What about fuel?

I scanned the warning lights clamoring for my attention on the control console. Damn! I was leaking fuel too. I quickly toggled the isolation valves and got the leak limited to a single tank. I still had enough.

Would I have enough air?

Ground to orbit takes less than ten minutes—at three gees and high speed. Normal reentry takes much longer than that. With the damage to *Starfire*'s heat shielding and aerodynamics, I had to keep the airspeed down. At a hundred kilometers an hour through a hundred kilometers of atmosphere, I'd need an hour to descend. Call it fifty minutes to get to where the air was breathable. That was *after* spending ten minutes at three gees to kill my orbital speed. Crap.

I got back on the radio. "Kakuloa, this is *Starfire*. Please tell me you have something."

"*We're working on a couple of possibilities,* Starfire. *We're prepping a portable airlock now, we can rendezvous in twenty minutes, but. . . .*" the voice trailed off.

"How do I get from the cockpit to the airlock?"

"*That's the 'but'. Depending on the damage to your ship, we can set it up right outside the cockpit door. You just wait for it to pressurize, open the door and you're out.*"

"And if you can't?"

"*Then we attach it to the hull, with someone inside to cut a hole into the cockpit.*"

It sounded risky. "Cutting with what, how do I keep from getting fried?"

"*We have an expert on this, he happened to be groundside from the shipyards. He knows his stuff.*"

"Shipyards?" I'd read something about the Kiahuna Orbital Shipyards now that he mentioned it. "Do they have a drydock?"

"*An airdock, yes. But they're on the other side of the planet from you now, in a different orbital plane. It'd take you hours to get there.*"

Normally, yes it would, using standard orbital mechanics and burning minimal fuel to make changes. "I could warp there, a millisecond jump tangent to the planet, then jump back to the other side." Assuming my drive was intact, but none of the damage so far was anywhere near the warp generators.

It took Kakuloa a few moments to respond, I could imagine them having gone pale at my suggestion. Then: "*You'd still have to match orbits, and you don't know exactly where you'll come out.*"

"You pin-pointing me on radar after the jump will be faster than orbiting the planet."

"*True. You'll have almost twenty kilometers a second of relative velocity to kill.*"

"Ten minutes at three gees, I can do that."

"*Okay, Starfire, it's your call. Wait one.*" While we were talking he'd uploaded the orbital elements to me, and I started to work my course. Then he called with a question.

"Starfire," he came back, "*this is going to sound stupid, and I should have asked sooner, but are you declaring an emergency?*"

I lost it. Air was hissing out of an unseen leak in my cockpit, bits of paper and cloth were blizzarding around the cabin and sticking to nooks and crannies on the walls, my control panel was a constellation of yellow and red caution and warning lights, my aft cabin was airless, I had a fuel leak, my heat shielding was probably damaged and I had no spacesuit. Was I going to declare an emergency? I laughed until tears came.

"Starfire?"

I managed to stop laughing, gasping for breath. "Sorry Kakuloa," *gasp, pant,* "that was the funniest thing I've heard in a long time."

I knew why he'd asked, of course. Regulations. I'd already broken plenty, starting with lifting off without clearance, and my maneuvering around the planet would break more. There'd be forms to fill out and reports to file when this was all over. It would go much, much smoother with the bureaucracy if there was a declaration on record.

"That's affirmative, Kakuloa, *Starfire* is declaring an emergency."

* * *

I finished putting in the course. A one-millisecond warp jump would put me about 150,000 klicks from the planet, not quite half the distance from Earth to its Moon. There I'd fire my thrusters to kill the velocity difference between me and the shipyards, then warp back to the other side of the planet to where I could finish the rendezvous on thrusters.

Diagnostics showed nothing wrong with the warp engine, the board showed green for the drive components. I hit the button. With an annoying beep, the MATTER PROXIMITY WARNING lit up. Between my leaking air and fuel, space around the Starfire was too crowded for the warp to engage. Life is not fair.

Would there be any point in declaring another emergency?

I had less than an hour of air left. There was no way standard orbital moves would get me there soon enough, and I was running out of time to do a powered landing.

"Kakuloa, I can't warp. What's the timing on a rescue?"

"*Almost everything's aboard now, but it'll be at least thirty minutes to rendezvous.*" Between my skewed orbit and Kakuloa's rotation, we'd been moving away from each other. "*If you could move closer....*"

Rendezvous is tricky enough when only one vehicle is doing all the maneuvering. I'd caught the terrorists' ship because I was never far from them in the first place. Trying to meet my rescuers halfway was a lot more complicated. But there was another possibility. "Wait one, Kakuloa."

I plugged the problem into the computer. It took some persuading to get it to optimize the trip for time, it kept wanting to save fuel. Finally I got the trajectory. It would be rougher than I thought. I radioed Kakuloa with my plans. "Tell Kiahuna that I'm on my way."

"*Roger that,* Starfire, *they're standing by. Good luck. We'll keep this channel open for you.*"

"Thanks." I keyed the last of the sequence into the autopilot. It was too complicated to fly by hand, and I'd be near anoxia toward the end. I was going to do a powered orbit, at higher than normal orbital velocity. The catch was that I'd be pushing *down* at five gees for nearly fifteen minutes, simulating the gravity of a much heavier planet to force a fast, tight orbit around to where the shipyard would be. Matching velocity to Kiahuna Shipyards was minor compared to that. I could survive it, but I'd have only minutes of air left—if that—when I reached the airdock. I started the sequence. The *Starfire* rotated into position, then fired main thrusters. I must have been in bad shape; after a couple of minutes at five gees, I passed out.

* * *

I woke up strapped to a stretcher with an oxygen mask on my face, moving along a corridor. A young man in a white jumpsuit was at the foot of the stretcher, guiding it with one hand while propelling himself along the hand-holds with the other. We were in zero gee. He noticed my open eyes.

"Welcome back, Mr. Curtis. You're in Kiahuna Shipyards, we're taking you to the sickbay. You're doing fine."

I had a strong sense of deja vu, and mumbled something about this becoming a habit. He didn't get it. But I was clearly safe, and could relax. I closed my eyes again.

* * *

When I woke up again I was in gravity, and Renee was there.

"Jay, you're awake!"

"I hope so. Where?"

"Still at the Shipyards, the sickbay's in the spin gravity section. It's been a couple of hours. How are you feeling?"

I thought about that. I felt bruised all over, probably from the long stretch at high gee in the powered orbit, and I had a killer headache. I looked up at Renee. "Just great; you're here." I said. If she blushed, her tan hid it, but she lowered her eyes for a moment and smiled.

Just then the medic came in. "Mr. Curtis, good to see you awake."

"Thanks. How am I doing?"

He grinned. "Blood oxygen's up to 98 percent, a few minor contusions, no permanent damage. I'll give you something for the headache."

"How did —"

"You were hypoxic when you came in. If you *didn't* have a headache I'd be very surprised." He peered into my eyes, then looked at the display above my head. "Any nausea? Dizziness?"

I shook my head no, and regretted it. Headache.

"What's the last thing you remember?"

"Before or after I woke up on the stretcher on the way to sickbay?"

"Good enough. No symptoms of brain damage."

"You mean other than launching myself after a terrorist ship carrying a hijacked load of antimatter with no plan and no spacesuit?"

He chuckled. "Well, no *additional* brain damage, anyway."

"Jay," Renee took my hand, squeezed it. "That was incredibly brave. They're calling you a hero."

"Brave? No, I wasn't even thinking about that. Something had to be done and I was the only one around to do it."

The medic gave me a wry smile. "That sounds like a hero to me." He turned to leave, then turned back. "Oh, and whenever you feel up to it, you're free to leave, but there's some law enforcement types who'll need a statement."

"Of course."

* * *

The whole mess delayed the departure of the Eta Carinae expedition by two weeks, by which time the yards had finished repairs to my *Starfire*. They'd made quick work of it, and aside from a few rents in the hull and the damaged portside fin, the damage wasn't extensive. I'd done far worse to the other guy. Sapphires are built tough and there are a lot of them around, so any parts they couldn't fab they'd managed to find within the Alpha Centauri system. I took delivery on-planet the day before Renee's expedition was due to leave. This time they'd be loading the message torpedoes at a rendezvous somewhere in deep space.

I hadn't seen as much of Renee as I'd hoped. Between my statements and interviews with police and Space Force officials, and her involvement with the rescheduling of the Carinae mission, we kept missing each other. I began to wonder if she was avoiding me.

The last night before their departure I stayed aboard *Starfire*. Renee had declined my invitation to join me, even for dinner or dessert, insisting that she had to finish packing, but agreed to meet me there for breakfast. That's when she dropped her bombshell. I was drinking coffee in the *Starfire*'s galley when she showed up.

"Morning, Jason," she said, giving me a friendly kiss on the cheek.

"That's all?" I got up and reached to put my arms around her, but she backed off.

"No, Jason, I'm leaving today, let's not drag it out."

"I've got my ship back, how about I tag along with the expedition?" I just blurted that out, I hadn't considered the implications at all.

"No, Jason, you can't."

"But —"

"It's not the ship, it's not the expedition, it's me."

I had no idea what she was talking about. Oh, part of me knew what was coming, but it wasn't telling the rest of me, so the next came as a surprise.

"Jason, I don't know who you are. You scare me, that's why I've been avoiding you."

"I scare you?" I didn't think I'd come on that strong.

"What you did, the terrorists. That was brave but incredibly impulsive. You're unpredictable."

"But, but I saved the antimatter." And whatever they were planning to use it on.

"You did, and I'm proud of you for that. But you killed three men, and that scares me."

"But that was self-defense, they were bad guys."

"I'm sorry Jason." Her eyes were tearing up. "I know that, intellectually. It still scares the hell out of me."

"But...." I didn't know what to say. I could see it from her point of view: a guy you've only known for a couple of days does something foolhardy if heroic and kills three people. I didn't even feel bad about the last two, they'd been shooting at me. I did feel a little guilty about the pilot, but only a little. And Renee was about to leave on a three year mission, so she didn't need any entanglements. I still felt like I'd been gut-punched.

"I'm sorry, Jason. I shouldn't have said anything. I know it's not rational. And you probably wouldn't anyway, but I don't want you to wait for me."

Was that it? Did she think it would hurt less this way? I'd have preferred the truth. Maybe that was truth, but it wasn't all of it.

"Oh, okay." I put a brave face on, or tried to. "Well, I guess this is goodbye then. It's been fun." The words came out mechanically, I could barely think. "Let me walk you to the door," I said as I got up.

"All right."

We stepped out onto the spaceport field. The morning sky was overcast. Across the field I could see two of the Carinae Expedition ships, the others would be in orbit. I stood there, staring across the field at nothing, Renee still beside me. She turned to me.

"Jason," she said, gently, "I didn't, don't want to hurt you. But...but I did, didn't I? I'm sorry."

"It's not your fault," I said, trying to maintain a brave face while dying inside. "You tried to warn me. I don't blame you."

"I'm sorry, Jason," she repeated, then started to turn away. "I have to go."

"I know." I felt my eyes starting to water, I blinked it away. I tried to make light of it. "I can't even say we'll always have Parry's."

The corner of Renee's mouth turned up, just a bit, and she moved to give me a last hug, but I forced myself to put an arm up to stop her. "No, you need to go, get to your ship and your," the word caught in my throat, "husband."

Her eyes widened and she took a step back, her gaze shifting from my left eye to my right, and back. "How...you knew?"

"Not until just now. I thought it might be a possibility, but I wasn't going to say anything if you didn't. But this morning you're wearing a ring."

"I...You do scare me, Jason, but more for what I might do than for what you might do. I'm sorry. We were taking separate vacations before the expedition." She looked away.

The gray clouds started to spit their first few drops of rain. "I thought it might be something like that," I said. Had I? Yes, I think part of me knew it all along. "Never mind. Go, get to your ship. Maybe we'll run into each other when you get back." Three years. A lot could happen.

"You'll get over me." She sounded unconvinced, but turned away.

"Probably," I lied.

I watched her walk away across the spaceport field to her own ship. The rain was coming down harder now. She turned at the boarding ramp, waved, and then turned again into the arms of another man, and they went into the ship together.

I stood for a moment, watching, the rain pelting me, then I turned. I went back into the *Starfire* and flopped onto my bed, staring at the overhead, my face wet. A thought came to me. A few days ago I'd searched the entertainment database for Renee's name. "Audio system: artist Left Banke," the original was the best. "Title *Walk Away Renee*. Play".

As the haunting violin melody rose, I thought about the Eta Carinae expedition. If, no, *when* the star went hypernova, the impact—even here 7500 light years away—could make a few kilograms of antimatter seem like a damp firecracker. This expedition meant a lot to humanity. I thought Renee had meant a lot to me.

I wished them luck, and hoped we wouldn't be hearing from them soon.

END

Subscribe to my newsletter
at www.alastairmayer.net

Subscribers get publication announcements and occasional bonuses. Email addresses are only used as above and never shared.

See my blog at www.alastairmayer.org, which also links to the T-Space Wiki.

Please consider leaving a review, even just one line. Several Amazon algorithms and other decisions (such as whether to record an audiobook version) depend on the number of reviews a book receives. *Thank you!*

Other books by Alastair Mayer

Mabash Books trade paper editions are available from Amazon or order through your favorite bookseller. Some volumes are also available in hardcover.

The T-Space™ series comprises:

The Alpha Centauri Trilogy: ISBN
- *Alpha Centauri: First Landing*   978-153-913229-5
- *Alpha Centauri: Sawyer's World*   978-154-691328-3
- *Alpha Centauri: The Return*   978-197-403548-9

The Kakuloa Series: ISBN
- *Kakuloa: A Rising Tide*   978-1-948188-074
- *Kakuloa: The Downhill Slide*   978-1-948188-227*
- *Kakuloa: Crash and Burn*   978-1-948188-241*
- *Kakuloa: The Tide Turns*   978-1-948188-265*

                    * forthcoming

The Carson & Roberts Series: ISBN
- *The Chara Talisman*   978-1-948188-098
- *The Reticuli Deception*   978-1-948188-111
- *The Eridani Convergence*   978-1-948188-159
- *The Centauri Surprise*   978-1-948188-180
- *The Pavonis Insurgence*   978-1-948188-203

Ebook editions are also available.